THREE HOURS

A SEVEN SERIES NOVEL

DANNIKA DARK

ALSO BY DANNIKA DARK:

No man had ever offered me his heart.

In three hours, one man offered me his life.

PROLOGUE

WHEELER RUBBED HIS EYES AND sat on a wooden step that led off the main porch of their oversized house. He was drained after pulling an all-nighter and helping Lexi review the company expenses. She owned Sweet Treats and did a damn fine job, but one person couldn't do it all. April managed the first location on the human side of town—the one that sold candy—and Lexi had hired Izzy to manage the bakery in the Breed district. Lexi didn't want to close the candy store, even if it meant having to deal with the IRS.

Breed didn't associate with humans. They established their own banks, bought and leased land, ran their own businesses, and didn't pay one goddamn dime in taxes. There they were, smack-dab in the middle of the city and off the human radar. But since Lexi had chosen to keep the original store, she needed someone to help sort out quarterly payments, licenses, contracts, and handle number crunching to maximize profits. Austin, his Packmaster and brother, had *voluntold* him for the job, so it wasn't like he had a lot of choice in the matter. Wheeler had a professional background in finance and contracts, so there was no getting out of it.

Sweet Treats had become a family business for the Weston pack. Three years ago, Lexi had signed a lease in the Breed district to open up the second location, serving pastries and coffee. The bakery made a hell of a profit—more income than they could have ever imagined for a start-up company. Successful establishments were usually restaurants, bars, or clubs, so they capitalized on the absence of specialty shops. Lexi could bake her ass off and had taken several courses at the human college to combine the school's techniques with her natural abilities. Trevor had even gotten in on the action, playing his acoustic in the back corner whenever it was slow, attracting new customers walking by. His main job, however, was working behind the counter, passing out compliments with the cupcakes. Flirty bastard.

Wheeler tapped his shoe against the porch step, swatting at a dizzy gnat. A gust of wind knocked around an old swing hanging from a branch of the oak tree that was about fifty feet ahead to his left. April's hummingbird feeder in the redbud tree needed a refill. He admired the property spread out before him—over one hundred acres of land with the option to buy more as the Weston pack grew in size. The driveway on his right led to a private road, and there was plenty of room to park their cars. High grass and wildflowers led down to a grove of trees and a shallow creek on his left.

"I'll be back later!" Lexi yelled excitedly as she raced past Wheeler and down the steps.

The only thing he caught sight of was her long hair, long legs, and sneakers without socks.

Austin swaggered out and leaned over the wooden railing, water dripping from the ends of his dark hair and running down his bare back. "Damn, I love that woman when she's fired up like that."

"So we all heard last night," Denver grumbled. He got up from his chair and walked barefoot into the house. April briefly peered over the top of her book before turning the page.

The brothers were spaced apart a good deal in years, except for Denver and Austin, who only had fifteen years between them. You'd never guess by their personalities that Denver was the older of the two, not to mention he didn't look a day over thirty. That's just how Shifters aged.

"Where's your woman off to?" Wheeler asked, resting his forearms on his knees.

Austin scratched his unshaven jaw. "She's heading out to see that friend of hers, Naya. Lexi wants to do something or other with the menu, and Naya knows someone who designs those things. I don't think it's a big mystery to figure out what a bakery sells, but Lexi wants to spend some money on those little paper menus to put in everyone's bag. Now, whose idea was that?" he asked, glaring down at Wheeler.

"Sometimes you have to spend money to make money," Wheeler said indifferently. "That kind of litter sits around a person's house and begs them to buy more cookies. You said you wanted my help, so if you got a problem with it—"

"No, you're good." Austin swept his wet hair back and shook the water from his hands. "But now she's thinking about redoing the menu and *adding* things. Whatever she comes up with, I'll need you to look it over and double-check the cost analysis. She's stressing herself out over ways to make more money."

"I get the impression you're helping her work out that stress."

Austin chuckled, and mischief flashed in his eyes. "I appreciate what you've done to help out with the business. You've pulled your weight in adding money to the pot; just thought you should know that." He shielded his pale blue eyes from the bright sun. "You ever think about getting another job? I know Sweet Treats has a lot going on, but we can manage if you want to branch out. There are plenty of Packmasters who could use professional advice in overseeing their money and building on that. Wouldn't hurt pack relations with them, either."

Damn, Wheeler hated this conversation. Wasn't he already doing enough managing their own finances? He just wasn't at a place where he was ready to put himself out there again. "I'll keep it in mind."

A ladybug flew in Austin's direction and landed on his tatted shoulder. Austin grinned and let it crawl on his finger, watching its wings buzz frantically as it tried to figure out if it wanted to trust a wolf. "Why don't you follow Lexi and see what those two are up to? Make sure Naya doesn't talk her into something stupid, like selling alcohol."

"Thanks, but no thanks," Wheeler said gruffly.

"Look, they've been best friends for years, and I don't see that friendship ending anytime soon. You need to get over whatever issues you've got with Naya. I know you've got a thing about hating cats, but we don't have any proof of what her animal is. She's probably messing with our heads, and someday we'll find out she's really a mare. Even still, that's a shitty excuse to hate a woman." Austin tapped his hand on the wooden ledge and headed back inside.

Everyone surmised Naya's animal was a cat, although Wheeler's twin brother had made a bet on a grizzly bear. On the few occasions when she'd swing by the house or meet them at Howlers, Wheeler would slip the fuck out. He didn't want to risk another confrontation with an unpredictable woman like her.

One who had slapped him in public four years ago. And no, he couldn't let it go. Man, if his brothers had witnessed that scene, they would *never* have let him live it down. Shifter women knew how to keep a man in line, but there was a certain level of respect afforded a wolf in front of his pack. Clearly, Naya wasn't a wolf.

And yet he couldn't forget that molten kiss she'd planted on him not two seconds after striking him. The sharp sting on his cheek combined with her lush lips moving across his mouth had fired up his wolf—the traitorous bastard. Wheeler had never simultaneously felt so much loathing and lust for anyone. Maybe that's why he kept his distance; no woman should have that kind of influence over a man. Naya had given him a verbal declaration of war—her kiss a sample of what he'd never have. That was pretty arrogant on her part to assume he'd care, and yet all these years later, he still thought about that kiss.

"Where do you want to go for your birthday, sweet pea?" April asked Maizy from their gliding chairs next to the front door.

Maizy had her legs drawn up in the chair and was preoccupied with braiding a strand of her blond hair. It was May, and that meant eleven candles on her birthday cake. Time had flown by so fast, and she'd gone from princess movies and pink outfits to riding a bike and reading books. Most Shifters homeschooled their children, so she hadn't been influenced by human culture outside of a little television. Reno thought she'd learn more from the world watching his action movies than some of the other drivel she enjoyed about fairy tales.

Maizy peeled up the corner of the Band-Aid on her knee, exposing a cut she'd gotten while speeding down the driveway on her bike and hitting the brakes too hard. She'd been alone at the time and hadn't asked permission to ride. After Reno had heard what happened, he bought Maizy a helmet, something she'd not had since none of them thought she'd need one out in the country. Lynn had grounded her from riding the bike for a week, but Maizy took her punishments without complaint.

Wheeler scooted to the left and leaned against the banister, watching with amusement as the two humans conversed without looking at each other. April had her nose buried in a novel, and a yellow butterfly briefly caught Maizy's attention as it fluttered by.

"Eleven is a big day," April continued in a singsong voice. "That means we have to have something very special for the birthday girl."

A smile wound up Maizy's face and pressed dimples into her cheeks. She had reached an awkward stage where she was suddenly self-conscious about how she looked. She was taller and leaner now and had quit pulling her hair up into a ponytail with clips. It seemed like she didn't really know how to wear it anymore, so it had grown long and wavy. Her top second incisor was slightly crooked from an accident she had on the swing years ago, and while Lynn had suggested braces, the men had talked Maizy out of it. Shifters didn't have to deal with those kinds of imperfections, but they'd learned a thing or two while living with humans. Maizy was beautiful just the way she was, and they didn't like the idea of metal wires in her mouth that would make her think she was less than perfect.

"I don't really care," Maizy said. "It's no big deal."

Wheeler cracked his knuckles and felt a hot coal sitting in his stomach. Maybe Shifters didn't make a big deal out of birthdays, but some of the men were looking forward to her party. The reason behind Maizy's sulking was that she had no friends her age to invite. Sometimes the Shifters from neighboring packs let their kids play with her, but most didn't mingle with humans because they perceived them as inferior.

Bastards.

"Well?" April pressed. "If you could have *anything* you wanted for dinner on your birthday, what would it be?"

"I don't know," Maizy replied. "Pizza, I guess."

A smile touched April's lips. Maizy's love for pizza was no secret, so that's what they'd been planning. They were going to take her to Pizza Zone and do the whole cake, ice cream, and presents there. Then she could play with some of the other human children.

Denver shouldered the front door open. "Come help me eat this thing," he said to Maizy while carrying a large green watermelon.

He set it behind Wheeler and began slicing wedges with a large butcher knife.

"That's going to attract ants," April said, watching the juice spill onto the porch and drip through the cracks.

"I thought all the ants were in your pants," he said.

Maizy giggled and took the wedge he handed her.

"Hold on, Peanut. Let me show you how to eat a watermelon proper."

"There's a proper way?" Wheeler asked with amusement. "This I need to see."

Denver ran his hand through his wavy blond hair, slicking it back with the sticky juice from his fingers. He stood up and leaned against the railing. "Damn right there's a way you're supposed to eat these. Watch and learn from the master."

Maizy glanced up at Denver with inquisitive blue eyes, waiting to see what he was going to do. Denver mashed his face in the sweet melon and Maizy smiled, setting her piece on top of the ledge before the juice ran all the way up her arm.

When Denver lifted his face, a rivulet of pink juice dribbled down his chin. He chewed a few times and then spit the black seeds across the lawn.

"Holy smokes, Denver! That's disgusting!" April shot out of her chair and went inside.

Wheeler grinned when Maizy tried to imitate Denver, except she spit the entire bite of melon out. Undeterred, she tried again.

"Don't swallow the seeds, whatever you do."

"Why not?" she asked with a mouthful of fruit.

"Because," Denver replied in a deadpan voice, "you'll grow a watermelon in your belly."

Her eyes widened. "Nuh-uh."

Wheeler stood up and went inside the house. He headed upstairs to his bedroom and closed the door, immersing himself in darkness. A few of the rooms were in the center of the house and didn't have windows. He liked it there. Everyone else had chosen the outer halls and it gave him privacy.

After locking the door, Wheeler paced toward his desk and switched on the green lamp. He straightened up a few papers before relaxing in his leather office chair—the one with a small tear in the seat. Sometimes he'd poke his finger at it, even knowing it would get bigger, but he found solace in that small imperfection. His chair didn't feel any less comfortable, and yet most people would have thrown it out and replaced it because of that defect.

Voices drifted up from the lower level, and someone ran down the hall. By the heavy footfalls, it sounded like one of his brothers.

Wheeler pulled open a small drawer in the hutch. He slipped his fingers inside a slim black case and pulled out a pair of reading glasses. They were black with rectangular frames. No one but Ben knew he wore glasses. Shifters didn't have defects such as vision impairment, tooth decay, and diseases that were prevalent among humans. Their bodies healed, and you just didn't see Shifters walking around with glasses on. Many years ago, Wheeler began getting headaches and noticed he had to hold papers farther away to see the print, which seemed to be getting infinitely smaller. He'd attributed it to long work hours, but when it didn't go away, he secretly made an appointment with a human ophthalmologist. His fears of genetic abnormalities were abated when a simple pair of reading glasses rectified his problem. Shifters instinctively hid anything that others would perceive as a weakness. Because he'd always worked from home, it was something he could easily conceal.

Until he moved in with his brothers. Whenever they'd shove papers under his nose to read, Wheeler would become argumentative and storm out of the room so he could review them later in private. He kept his room off-limits and installed a lock on the door. Ben, his identical twin, didn't have the same deficiency. Wheeler could only draw the conclusion that he was genetically inferior to his brother, and wasn't that a laugh?

As a twin, he'd always felt like half of a whole. They weren't treated as individuals, and he loathed when people referred to them as "the twins." As small children, when Ben misbehaved, he'd blame Wheeler. It was an innocent thing that stemmed from a child who sought approval. After a while, Wheeler didn't flinch when their father would reprimand him for something he didn't do. Wasn't that what brothers did? Look out for each other? Several years ago, Ben had crossed a line and betrayed him. That's when solitude had consumed Wheeler and he'd given up caring. After everything he'd given Ben to show his loyalty and love, he realized it had been in vain. And yet he still couldn't turn his back on blood, nor could he reveal to the rest of the family what had happened between them. It hurt to smile because that would mean forgetting. It felt like a liar's mask.

Which isolated him from the pack. The bitch of it was that his wolf craved companionship and family. He often wondered what it would be like to have a woman to confide in—someone who would always stand by his side, even if his brothers didn't. Obviously that wasn't in the cards, but he couldn't shut off the desire to mate. After all, he was around a hundred years old, and the closer he came to his prime, the more those feelings intensified. The instinctual call to bond had become so strong in recent years that it was misdirecting his feelings toward the wrong women.

The wrong *woman*.

Who also happened to be the wrong animal.

CHAPTER 1

———⊸•⊂⟨⟩⊃•⊶———

"CALM DOWN, CHICKYPOO. I THINK what you already have on your menu are divine morsels of heaven," I said to Lexi. We had spent hours designing a take-out menu for the bakery, and now she was second-guessing herself about replacing her macadamia nut cookies with chocolate chunk.

"But chocolate is so popular, Naya," she said, brows drawing together as she tossed her feet up on my coffee table. I disliked shoes on my glass table, but I had to remind myself it was just a piece of furniture. "The macadamias sell good, but chocolate is a winner. Everyone loves chocolate. You could pour it on sardines and it would sell."

"Sounds delish," I purred.

I tugged on her brown hair and slinked around my white sofa to sit in my favorite oversized red chair in the right-hand corner of my living room. It gave me a full view of my humble apartment. The kitchen was tucked behind a wall to the right of the door but had an open bar where I could see into the room. To my right—behind the television—was a quaint dining room in front of the back door. It faced east, so I was able to enjoy the morning light with my coffee. The bathroom and bedroom were just beyond that. Though it was small, I kept my apartment tastefully decorated.

Misha's silver bell jingled, and my Siamese beauty sauntered across the plush white carpet toward the kitchen. She was cream-colored with a dark face and sooty legs, and she had the most remarkable blue eyes, which were slightly crossed. Lexi always complained about how much I spoiled the cat, but the only thing good enough for my little Misha was tuna or raw chicken and vegetables. That dry stuff humans packaged up looked like something you'd feed a cow, not a natural predator.

"No question. Your macadamia cookies are to *die* for, Lexi. If you don't keep those on the menu, I'm going to disown you as my friend. *Of course* everyone loves chocolate, but most women can't turn down a good nut."

Lexi snorted and tapped her feet together, staring at her blue Converse sneakers. She dressed so plainly for such a stunning brunette. Unlike me, she was slim without all the curves, but her high cheekbones combined with those bourbon eyes just made her stand shoulders above other women.

"Why all the fuss? You already know what sells. It's what I do in my line of work," I said with a sly wink. "Find out what they like and keep dishing it to them."

She drummed her fingers on the armrest. "I hear what you're saying, but I keep wondering if I could be doing better. I just don't want to screw this up and have Austin think of me as a failure. There's just so much more to running a business than I ever imagined. When the cost of goods goes up, my profits go down unless I can find another vendor or raise prices." She waved her hand at the mess of papers on the coffee table. "Thanks for helping me with everything; I don't know what I'd do without you. I went over the cost factors with Wheeler last night, and we're in the black. Maybe I don't want to get too comfortable with our income and become afraid to try new things. The tip jar helps, and God knows that Trevor can bring in extra money when he plays, but I want to keep taking it to the next level. This business could keep our family comfortable for years to come, and I'm just trying to come up with ideas to make Sweet Treats *more* profitable."

"Girl, you practically have a sugar empire in the making. Maybe you should advertise your bakery on the human side of town. Have your friend, April, pass out the menus."

Lexi pursed her lips. "I don't discriminate against humans, but I'm afraid it'll drive away the Breed customers, and they're the ones who bring in the big money. I'll keep it in mind, but for now I better focus on building clients in our own district since we're still pretty new."

"Agreed. If it's one thing immortals have, it's deep pockets. Never sell yourself short, and I still think you should make the cinnamon bread two dollars higher." A quiet moment passed between us. "Honey, I miss having you as my neighbor."

Lexi put her feet on the floor and leaned forward, her voice softening. "It's not like I'm totally out of your life. We still hang out."

I crossed my legs, noticing it was time for another pedicure. "Yes, but I miss the heavenly smell of your baking. Now all I smell coming from next door is boiled cabbage."

Lexi wrinkled her nose. "Well, at least the downstairs neighbors moved. No more Pink Floyd music." A nostalgic smile brightened her face. "I miss having you wander over at odd hours to play cards."

After Lexi moved in with Austin, the apartments had become a dull place to live. I'd met her years ago in the Sweet Treats candy store, and we'd connected right away. I'd had an inkling she wasn't human—sometimes you can just sense it up close. Plus, even though she hadn't gone through the change yet, I'd noticed her habits were indicative of a wolf.

Lexi's expression faltered. "Was my moving here a coincidence? That seemed pretty convenient after I broke up with Beckett."

"Confession: I paid off my old neighbor so he'd move out. Then I threw a little money at the office manager to hold the vacancy. Honey, you were in the middle of a breakup with that cheating man, and I didn't want to see you two kiss and make up. The sooner I could get you settled in a new place, the better your chances were of getting over him. No friend of mine will be a doormat for any man's feet."

Her brows arched thoughtfully, but her eyes were downcast. "I can't believe I loved a man like Beckett. I would never have gone back to him, but how did I not see that coming?"

I scraped my fingernail on the fabric of the chair. "Because Beckett was a man obsessed. You know how human men behave differently around Shifter women. After a breakup, some of them can't let go. They obsess over it until those feelings turn into rage.

If I hadn't been so distracted that evening, listening to music and cleaning..."

"It's not your fault he tried to kill me," she said firmly. "Austin blamed himself for years, and even though we've moved past it, I don't think he'll ever forgive himself for not getting up to my apartment sooner. If he hadn't cared enough about me, then he wouldn't have parked outside that night and I wouldn't be sitting here. Sometimes one second is everything."

Female Shifters were dangerously desirable to human men—probably something in our pheromones or energy. Some would go so far as to stalk or even assault one of us, as this was something I'd discovered in my life as an exotic dancer. I'd never liked Beckett, her ex-lover. He'd always had an abrasive personality and used to pick fights with other men. Maybe that's why Lexi had been attracted to him—those traits would have appealed to the wolf in her. But that's a dangerous combination with human men; they often don't know how to control their compulsive behavior. I'd done everything I could to get her away from that psychotic boyfriend of hers, and I sure hadn't batted an eyelash when Austin's wolf tore out his jugular. It was a good thing *my* animal hadn't gotten a hold of him, or there would have been nothing left of him to clean up but a few bones.

Fate had a sense of humor in pairing me up with a wolf as my best friend. Of all animals! I'd always considered them nefarious creatures—at least the men who came into my club to watch me dance. Always posturing, territorial, aggressive. My mother had raised me to live independently of others, so I couldn't relate to their pack mentality. Plus, my fiery personality would eat them alive.

And so would my animal—a black panther.

Jaguar, to be specific. Common sense dictated how each Shifter animal lived. Those who were lions lived in a pride, and some animal species were loners. Wolves lived among a hierarchy and often congregated in the same cities. Regardless of animal, the instinct to mate was strong among all Shifters, and that's why Shifters often sought out cities populous with their animal. Life was just easier when you shared common ground with someone.

I chuckled to myself while Lexi organized a stack of messy

papers. "Don't you worry about a thing, darling. I have a friend who owes me a favor, and she'll make your menus the most beautiful in the city. In fact, we're ordering extras."

Her eyes widened. "Do I need extra?"

"Of course you do! She's a good friend of mine, and for a first-time customer, I know she'll throw in a few hundred at no charge. Denver can pass them out at Howlers, or maybe your brothers have big connections who might be interested. Everyone is going to want a bite of your cookie," I said with a suggestive wink.

"Only one man gets *my* cookie," she said, nibbling her bottom lip. "And Austin's a man with a hearty appetite."

"Now *that's* what I like to hear," I said, rising to my feet. I adored the chemistry between those two. It almost made me wish I had my own man around the house, but no man had ever fit the bill, let alone paid it.

Packs were fortunate because they spread the wealth around. It wasn't so easy for loners like me. A girl has needs, and one of mine was getting out of this life. I'd been able to set aside money working as an exotic dancer, but in order to quit, I needed enough to support me for centuries. Maybe some turned up their noses at my profession, but without skills, dancing was the only option to make real money. I didn't care about people's silly judgments about my lifestyle. I was a phenomenal dancer, and a woman in control of her sexuality is a powerful thing.

"Do you have the website up yet?" I asked.

She leaned against my front door, crossing her arms with a look of frustration. "I have no clue how to build a website. I live in a house full of Internet illiterates, so none of them can help with something like that. I know enough about computers to be dangerous, but most technology is over my head."

I raised my hand. "Consider it taken care of."

Her shoulders sagged. "Really, Naya?"

"It's the least I can do for a friend."

Lexi gave me a tight hug, and I patted her shoulder before stepping away.

"I really owe you big time. I'm glad Austin made me wait a little while before opening the new store. I'm sure I'd be more stressed out if I hadn't planned ahead. If that's even possible." She smiled and leaned against the door again. "Ivy was a godsend and got a few big clubs interested in placing orders, so we had customers right out of the gate. Some of them came into our store to check us out and that helped spread the word. Even after a couple of years, it still feels like a scramble. I've had so much to do that the website has been the last thing on my mind."

"One day at a time. You're off to a great start, and you made a smart choice hiring Izzy to manage the bakery. You were doing way too much on your own. Don't fret. I'll talk to my guy and have him call you to work something out. He's a *genius*. Met him in the club—a real sweetheart. Sent me tulips and candy, so I finally gave in and went on a date."

"How did that go?"

I smiled wolfishly. "He knows a thing or two about putting RAM into a *hard* drive," I said seductively, sliding my hand down my hip.

Lexi rolled her eyes.

In truth, Scott was too much of a softy for my liking, but he did fix my computer and set me up with free Internet.

Misha slinked around my legs, and I reached down to stroke her soft fur.

"You pamper that furball like she's a little diva," Lexi said with disdain.

I peered up at her. "I should have known you were a wolf when you didn't like my pussy."

"I thought Shifters didn't own pets."

I stood upright and shook some of the hairs off my fingertips. "For obvious reasons, most Shifters *don't* own pets. After living in slavery, most see it as comparable and want no part of it. But I rescued her a few years ago from one of those shelters that puts them down, and now she's my little boo. The only slavery going on in my house is all the hairballs I have to clean up and the litter box, but that just goes with the territory."

Lexi put her hands on her hips. "Well, just remember she's an animal. It's not the same as family."

I jutted my hip out and anchored my fist on it. "We're all animals, darling. I hate to be the one to tell you this, but family has nothing to do with people. It's a kinship you share with another soul. She's my baby, so play nice or I'll make you cat-sit again for some bonding time."

"Do you still want to grab something to eat before I go home?" Lexi asked.

Lexi's favorite place was the Pit, a local barbecue joint. But I always ended up with horrendous sauce stains on my clothes and meat between my teeth. I looked down; my white shorts would never make it out alive.

"Well, I could use a little extra cushion on my hips," I said.

She arched a brow. "Seriously?"

"Absolutely," I replied with an enthusiastic nod.

Lexi had grown up among humans, influenced by their perception of beauty coming in only one pretty package. My legs were thick and my hips curvaceous. Most of the human clubs had strippers who looked like waifs. Not Breed clubs. Our men liked *all kinds* of women. Tall, petite, dark, light, slender, shapely. The variety brought them in and catered to their preferences. Chitah males tipped more for the tall girls, while some of the Shifters threw Benjamins at the redheads. My regulars liked the way I rolled my hips and owned the body my mother had blessed me with.

"Let's do Italian," Lexi suggested, lifting her purse off the bar. "I'm in the mood for pasta, and Olive Garden has the best salads!"

"I'll agree to that, even though being in a room full of humans makes me nervous."

They had amazing breadsticks; I could devour them by the truckload, so I was willing to suffer through the energy suck.

"Great! Let's pig out like old times. I'll call Austin and let him know I'll be coming home late."

"Sounds perfect. Let me just feed little Misha before we go."

After we finished our salads, the waiter served the main course. Lexi had ordered the chicken Alfredo and didn't waste a moment digging in. I leaned over my plate and smelled the heavenly aroma of my tilapia, shrimp, and broccoli. Human restaurants had good food, even though the atmosphere was usually colder and less vibrant. People didn't talk to or look at other customers, and sometimes they didn't even talk to the people at their own table if they were preoccupied on their electronic toys. Being around too many humans drained my energy, and I'd often wondered if there was something to that. A Mage had once told me that most of us had higher levels of energy than humans. Maybe that explained why we thrived in the company of our own.

"So how's work going?" Lexi asked conversationally, slurping up a noodle.

I brushed my dark curls behind my shoulders and then savored a generous bite. "It's the same old drama. We have a new girl with all these ideas, and it's ruffling everyone's goosey little feathers. The bickering is so petty, and sometimes the women act like a group of hungry jackals protecting a pile of bones. I say there are enough bones to go around."

"Don't you mean boners?" Lexi said with a half smile. "No offense, but you work with some crazy women."

"It's much worse now," I added, tasting my wine. "One of our girls went missing, so everyone is clamoring to get the attention of her regulars—especially the men who request private lap dances."

"No one knows where she is?"

I shrugged and swallowed another bite. "It could be nothing. Maybe she just took off and decided she'd had enough of this life. I hate to bring down dinner with such a morose topic."

"Naya, you're always upbeat, which is great, but I want to hear what *else* is going on in your life. Don't keep secrets from me just because it's not polite dinner conversation. Did anyone call the authorities? What Breed was she?"

I poked at my meal, annoyed with the Italian music blaring from the speakers. "Most of the girls are Shifters, and I think her animal was a cougar. Well, that was the rumor anyhow. Lacy didn't have any family, and I doubt our boss called the Council to investigate. Most clubs don't want to attract negative attention for fear it might drive away the customers." I set my fork down and wiped my mouth with the cloth napkin.

"What's wrong?"

Within the past year, work had been so different after the place switched hands. The rumor floating around was that the new owner was a human, but I'd never personally met him. Humans weren't allowed to own Breed businesses, so no one believed it. On the few occasions I'd caught a glimpse of him, he would walk briskly to his office in the back and close the door. The only person allowed in there was Dean, our manager. Dean had recently put his foot down and stopped letting things like tardiness slide. We liked Dean, but lately he looked more like a man who was afraid of losing his job.

"Nothing to worry yourself over," I said, waving my hand. "All the drama that goes with work should stay at work. I'm sure you don't want me to bore you with the details."

Her fork clicked against the plate. "*Bore* me. I'm all ears. I'll tell you some personal stuff if you tell me."

My brow quirked. "*Do* tell, because that's a juicy bone you're waving in front of my curious nose."

She nibbled on her lip and leaned forward. "I want to have a baby."

My eyes widened and I quietly squealed. "*When?*"

Her lips made a funny sound as she blew out a breath. "Jesus, don't get your panties in a riot. I'm not pregnant."

"What's this about then?"

"You know how humans have a biological clock that ticks near menopause? Well, mine ticks every time I go into heat. Not to mention Izzy found out last week that she's pregnant again. All of a sudden, my wolf wants babies. *That bitch.* Here I am about to start up a bakery, and I can't stop thinking about having babies with Austin."

"I bet lots of women think about having babies with Austin."

She grinned in agreement. "He said we should wait. He said it's too soon, and he wants to make sure the pack will stay together and strengthen before we bring kids into the equation. I didn't think kids were a math problem. The last time I was in heat, I was all over him and he nearly buckled. After that, he built that damn heat house out back. So the next time I hit my cycle, I have to stay locked up in there. Do you know how embarrassing that is? It would be one thing if I were single, but I feel like I'm in the doghouse with my own mate."

I circled my finger around the rim of my glass. "So *this* is what goes on in packs."

"Austin is the best lover I've *ever* had, and I really want to feel that with him while I'm in heat. Izzy said it's intense—like *nothing* I've ever felt before. I'm getting the tingles just sitting here thinking about it."

"Me too," I said with a wicked laugh.

We resumed eating and I poked at my salad.

"Anyhow," Lexi continued, "it's been on my mind. Jericho is an amazing dad. When he found out she was pregnant, he came home that night with a stuffed guitar to put in the crib. It plays a little lullaby when you wind the key in the back; it's so sweet," she said wistfully.

Jericho was also doing well with his music from what Lexi had told me. His band, Heat, had gained such a following from Internet downloads that the demand for them to perform had grown exponentially.

My tilapia was so good that it took me a minute to respond. "Enjoy *their* baby until you're ready for your own. You have hundreds of years ahead of you to start a family. The bakery is your time to shine, and you don't get chances like these too often, especially if you're taking care of a bunch of kids. Enjoy Izzy's baby, enjoy selling your cookies, and *then* think about a family. This is one instance where I agree with your wolfman."

"You're probably right. Sometimes I forget I'm going to live for centuries; it's still hard to get used to the fact I'm a Shifter. Austin said it's just my instincts kicking in, but I'm serious… I really want children with him. It has nothing to do with hormones or anyone's expectations—I just want something in this world that's *ours*. To look at a little baby and see Austin's beautiful eyes and my mouth."

"Your big mouth?"

She snorted. "That too. I'm sure he or she would inherit my laugh and Austin's deranged sense of humor. Poor thing."

"Well, as often as Austin runs around shirtless, let's pray for a boy."

Lexi smirked and turned her plate in a circle. "He can't help it. He's hot-blooded."

"You can say *that* again."

"More wine?" the handsome waiter asked, tilting the bottle toward my glass.

I smiled fiendishly and sat back, watching his gaze shift direction when I crossed my legs. He poured the wine so slowly that I thought it might turn back into grapes. I had to admit, I loved putting a rosy blush on a man's cheek. That was in *my* nature. My instincts ran a different course than Lexi's, and I didn't try to fight them.

"Thank you, darling."

He blushed. "My pleasure."

Damn, those humans were so sweet I could just eat them up.

He walked off with a skip in his step, and Lexi shook her head with a private smile. "I still don't get why you're single. You could have any man you set your sights on, including one with money. Is it because of your animal?"

Sly. Lexi was always trying to get me to slip up and reveal my animal in conversation. I didn't as a means to protect myself.

"Maybe it's because of *their* animal. Ever think of that?"

Shifters weren't all united. Quite a few would stand in line to cut my throat if they discovered I was a panther. Centuries ago, even though other Breeds treated us as slaves and outcasts, Shifters had a hierarchy. They would use panthers for entertainment, like the untamed lions in the Roman arenas who would savagely feast upon the soldiers. When a Shifter displeased his owner or committed a crime against another Breed, they were thrown in a pit with a starving panther. Some shifted and fought for their lives. Others tried to escape.

None survived.

I loved Lexi to bits, but she had an intimate bond with Austin that complicated matters. She would eventually disclose my secret if I told her, and then the pack would find out. Denver worked at Howlers and might say something to a customer. In life, you have to look out for yourself because no one else will.

I simply didn't trust a man not to open his big yapper.

"I don't know why you keep it a secret," Lexi said, twirling noodles on her fork. "You should be proud of your animal. I feel a little insulted you're keeping things from me when I tell you everything. I thought we were friends."

Whenever she insinuated it had something to do with me not valuing our friendship, it made me stir in my seat. "You know how much I adore you, but Shifters are private creatures. You didn't grow up in our world, and you haven't experienced some of the hardships we have. What happened a few years back with that crazy second-in-command going after Ivy was just a small taste of some of the dangers in our world. People turn up missing all the time, and show me where the Breed version of the FBI is? Austin doesn't reveal what his animal is, even though anyone with a brain cell can sense an alpha wolf up close. This isn't a safe world like the one you grew up in."

"The human world isn't so safe either," she said, averting her eyes.

I reached across the table and touched her hand, sympathizing with her tumultuous past. "I just want you to get a little seasoned before we go to the next level."

Lexi nodded and lifted her glass of wine. "Are you still coming to Maizy's birthday party? It's tomorrow at noon."

"Wouldn't miss it," I said, sitting back in my seat. "I put my foot down this time and told Dean I had something important going on and needed the full day off. I've only been to *your* birthday parties, and we all know how much fun those were."

Lexi laughed and her cheeks flushed. "There will be no alcoholic beverages at this one, Naya. We don't celebrate children's birthdays quite the same way. And I only passed out once." She held up one finger, which should have been three.

"I have the *perfect* present for the baby."

She tilted her head to the side. "A dress?"

I buttoned my lips. In the past, I had lavished Maizy with princess outfits and costume jewelry. But time marches on, and soon Lexi's little sister would outgrow her love of fairy tales and realize no such thing existed in the real world. The days of dressing up in pretty gowns were ending, but I still loved indulging that sweet girl.

"It's a secret. You'll find out when everyone else does," I sang.

"That worries me."

I nibbled on my breadstick carefully so as not to smudge my red lipstick. "Worry when she's twenty and comes to Auntie Naya for her first sexy outfit. Run for the hills, because her auntie will deliver."

"Over my mother's dead body. That's another thing I haven't mentioned," she said solemnly, setting down her fork and leaning back. "My mom is sending Maizy away."

"What?" I gasped.

"Not now—she's much too young. I think the attack on our home a few years ago really made my mom think twice about the influence we were having on Maizy. She wants to send her off to a boarding school when she's a teen so she can also be around other kids her age. Affluent people do this all the time, and Austin has the money. It's an opportunity for her to get a better education than she is with the homeschooling, and Mom wants to prepare her to live in the human world, not ours. I suggested we just send her to public school, but Maizy's so smart, and Austin thinks it'll do more harm than good. I'm not sure how I'm going to feel about it when the time comes, but I know how I feel about it now. It's not right. She should stay with us until—"

"Until *when?* She's not a wolf, Lexi. She's not going to grow up, mate with a wolf, and move in with his pack. What if she wants to be a doctor or a lawyer? What kind of education can you give her at home that's going to prepare her for that dream? At some point, you're going to have to let her go. She needs to be with her own kind and go to college, get married, have children, and move away. That's what humans do, and no matter how much you want her to live in this world, this isn't where she belongs. You almost gave me a heart attack. I thought you meant she was leaving any day now."

"It might as well be," Lexi grumbled, picking at her breadstick. "Mom is afraid if Maizy stays with us too long, we'll make an impression that can never be undone."

"Lynn is making plenty of money for herself freelancing as an interior designer. Why doesn't she just move out with the little one and buy a nice house in the suburbs?"

That seemed like the logical thing to do, but by the look in Lexi's eyes, I could see she wanted her family close. Pack instinct.

"Mom had no idea what she was getting into with a pack of wolves—especially the men. It's gotten easier with Izzy and April around, and we're a growing family. Mom loves it, and I think part of it is she doesn't feel alone anymore like she did when she lived at home with Maizy. She knew someday Maizy would move away and she'd end up the little old lady living in my father's house by herself. We love having her; she keeps the boat afloat. But my mom's afraid that Maizy will get too comfortable with our way of life. She wants her to fall in love with a regular guy and have a normal life. She accepts me for who I am and realizes this is where I need to be, but I guess I can see her point of view."

I finished my meal and lifted a piece of ice from my water glass, sucking on it while getting lost in my thoughts. "How are you going to handle watching her grow old? And your mama…"

She tapped her fingernails on the edge of her plate. "I try not to think about it, but it's always in the back of my mind. Every time Maizy reads that Peter Pan book, certain scenes just make me cry thinking about how they're going to grow old one day and leave me. I once asked Reno how he feels being with April since she's a human, and he told me that life doesn't make promises. Just because he's biologically *supposed* to outlive her doesn't mean he will. He has a dangerous job, and there's always a chance he might not come home." Lexi glanced at an elderly couple at a nearby table. "I've never taken him for a poet, but he once called her his shooting star. He said you'll never enjoy the moments unless you learn to let go of the fears. I can't argue with that logic because it applies for humans too. You never know when it'll be your time, and maybe that's why I worry. It's not so much watching her grow old, but what if something were to happen and I didn't get all those years with Maizy promised to me? Life just isn't fair."

No, it isn't, I thought to myself. "I'll be at the little one's party tomorrow with bells on."

"Knowing you, you'll literally *have* bells on."

"Just on my lady parts."

Lexi broke out in her silly laugh that Austin dubbed "the Beaker." After she wrapped it up with a snort and a blush on her cheeks, we decided to order dessert.

"Naya, do me a favor?"

"Anything."

"No drama. I mean with Wheeler. He always bails whenever you show up. I don't know why you two hate each other so much, but I don't want anything to spoil Maizy's party. It's not every day she turns eleven, and I feel like we're losing that little girl."

"You have nothing to worry your pretty little head about. This is her special day, and I wouldn't dream of spoiling it. I'm going to bring balloons, presents, and her favorite treat."

Lexi arched her brow. "What's that?"

"Auntie Naya's famous bag of pretzels. I'll leave it to her big sister to bake the most fantastic birthday cake in the entire world. Now how about we order another bottle of red and do a little gossiping before I go to work? I want to hear all about this heat house."

CHAPTER 2

"I SHOULD HAVE NEVER HAD THE fourth glass of wine," I said regretfully on a long sigh. After finishing my first shift, I'd retreated to the dressing room to cool down and change clothes. Club Sin had more action on the floor than I'd seen in weeks.

"Serves you right," Daphne said with a cackle, flipping her bright red hair back. Although calling it red would be stretching the truth since it resembled the color of a sweet potato.

"I made five hundred dollars on one dance alone from the men at the tip rail. They really like it when I wear these panties," I said, shaking my hips and creating a ripple of movement from the beads strung along them.

I never got all the way nude onstage, and I earned higher tips when I wore a semisheer top or bra instead of going topless, which I never did anymore. For me, it was more about the performance than the act of nudity. Let the other girls get down and dirty, but I left the men wanting more. A few years ago, I bought a full latex suit that didn't show any skin outside of my face, hands, and feet. The men could barely stay seated and paid extra to touch the material. You learn things as you go—that sometimes you don't have to give all of yourself away to get what you need in life.

I dabbed my face with a towel and sat down in front of the mirror to count out my money. "Whoever let the Chitahs in tonight should be fired."

"They're usually our best customers," Daphne said, her voice raucous. She put out her cigarette in a black ashtray. "They have more respect for women than most of those nimrods."

I waved a dollar bill. "One guy tipped me a Washington and told me to get another job."

"Oh, *baby*. I'm *so* glad you said something. I've got zero tolerance for cheapskates." Daphne blotted her lips with more Extreme Red and fluffed her short hair.

The dancers were a mix of different Breeds, but the majority were Shifters like me. In the Breed world, our only talent was shifting into an animal, which couldn't earn us money in any practical way. Relics were born with innate knowledge, which meant job security from birth as a healer, advisor, or researcher. They earned an exceptional income and often worked for the same immortals as their parents had, establishing clientele that were passed down through each generation. Sensors were like a vending machine of sorts where a person paid them for an emotional experience. Some customers wanted to relive emotions from a time in their life, while others lived vicariously through the experiences of others. Most Chitahs worked as investigators because of their keen sense of smell, and they had the good sense not to allow their sisters to sling beer or strip on a pole. The Chitah strippers I'd known never got high tips from Chitah males, and in some cases their routines would start a fight in the club. Chitahs didn't like to see their women degrading themselves, as they put it.

I called it paying the bills.

No one had forced me into this lifestyle, and to be honest, I was good at it. Most dance clubs had high standards and expected the girls to be exceptional dancers, performers, and actresses. I didn't want to do it forever, but I had serpentine moves that men had been ogling for years. Why not charge them to look? High-paying jobs weren't easy to come by for Shifters, and sometimes a girl has to make tough choices. I lived a respectable life otherwise—probably one of the most celibate girls in the club. I was very selective of my men; that's one piece of me I didn't give away to just anyone.

"Ugh! Fawn is bleeding their wallets dry," a bright voice exclaimed from the doorway.

Skye still had on her street clothes and slung her purse in a metal locker.

"What's going on?" Daphne asked, her voice edged with concern. "I'm next, and you're freaking me the hell out, girl."

"She's pulling out all the stops with an old Pussycat Dolls song. I think she stole Naya's lollipop theme that was so popular two years ago. Remember that, Naya?"

Boy, did I! The men had eaten it up.

Literally.

"Well, good for her," I said, sorting my tips.

"Easy for you to say. You've already been up." Daphne wrinkled her nose. "Hellfire! Now I have to come up with something good."

I tucked my money away in my silver clutch. "The nurse act is getting a little old, Daph. These men don't want to be taken care of like an invalid. You should stop visiting the human clubs for ideas."

I knew what turned Breed men on. They all had a touch of hero syndrome due to their natural instinct to protect women. Strictly speaking of certain Breeds, of course. A Mage couldn't care less, and the same went for most Vampires. But Shifters and Chitahs? Those men responded to a damsel in distress and ate up any routine that ventured into hero territory. On my next theatrical dance, I planned to bring in chains and play captive.

Daphne slipped on a shiny red skirt that matched her lipstick. "What about a schoolteacher? I could get one of those long rulers..."

Skye sounded like a chimpanzee when she laughed. "Are you kidding me? Most of those men have never been inside a school. And I can guarantee you that they have no desire to be spanked with a ruler."

"On the contrary," I muttered with a surreptitious smile.

"*Do* tell." Skye gasped, scooting beside me on the bench. Her brown hair swished above her fanny, and eyes as blue as the Texas sky beamed at me.

"Some of these tough men are turned on by an assertive female in the bedroom—even the baddest of the bad. It's the one place they're allowed to give up power."

"Why would they want to do that?"

I shrugged. "Submission is a curious thing I know little about. Maybe they're tired of being in control all the time, but I have a feeling that some of these men are broken and feel like they deserve to be punished. From my personal experience, when Shifters see a woman in a position of authority, they become putty in her hands. That's the kind of dancer you want to be onstage and the kind of woman you want to be off. Then you'll have them eating out of your hand."

Her gaze floated toward the ceiling. "Most of the men I date just want to screw and get it over with."

I put my arm around her shoulder. "Hold out, sweetie. Don't give away your cookies to every hungry man. Make them crave it so badly they chase you for a nibble. By the time you say yes, you'll already have them wrapped around your finger. You're young. You'll figure it out soon enough."

"How old are you?"

Fifty-three, I thought to myself. *With the body of a twenty-five-year-old.* That's how Shifter magic worked. "You mean how young," I corrected with a tap on her button nose. "Better hurry up and get dressed, girly. Why don't you walk the floor for a little bit and warm up the men—get them excited to see your act? Don't worry about what one girl is doing on the stage. Those men aren't going to empty their pockets after two beers. You know that."

"You're right. I shouldn't get so worked up about money," she said on a sigh. "Unlike Daphne, who just wants to save up for a trip to Italy."

"Hey! Don't wipe your feet on my dreams," Daphne barked out. "I'm going to live in Italy for a year and find me a nice Italian man who speaks in one of them dreamy accents and makes love to me every morning before breakfast. I've heard Italian Shifters have stamina, so maybe it'll be lunchtime when we're done." After giving her hair another fluff, she sauntered out the door.

Skye got up and stripped out of her jeans. "I've got a little girl to think about."

I whirled around. "I didn't know you had children. Honey! Where is your man?"

She shrugged. "I was mated, but Keller was killed in a bar fight two years ago. That's why I started working here, even though for the first year, Dean would only let me waitress. Now it's just Lola and me. She's three and the sweetest little thing in the world, but I can't take care of her by myself. She stays with my cousin while I'm at work. I'm not happy about the situation, so I'm trying to make some money and… It just seems so hopeless sometimes."

"Skye, you're a goddess." I stood up and fanned out her silky hair, letting it fall over her shoulders. "Long hair, heart of gold, beautiful eyes—what man wouldn't want to make you his mate? Why not find a pretty dress and go to one of the Shifter bars to find yourself a good man? You need help taking care of that baby so you won't have to work in a place like this forever. We all have dreams to get out. Well, most of us," I said with a wave of my hand. "I can't imagine how tough it must be with a baby."

"This is where the money is, and that's why I decided to start dancing. Soon she'll need to be homeschooled, and that's not free if I have someone else do it. The tips I got waiting tables were nothing compared to what I make onstage. Dancing will give me a head start, and then maybe I can find another job. It's pointless to hold out for a man to take care of me; most Shifters don't want to take on another man's baby. It's up to me to care for my little girl. I want her to have a better life than her mommy."

I felt terrible for Skye. Girls who worked jobs like ours were single; no man in his right mind would let his mate dance for money. Packs gave women financial security, and I had a feeling she wasn't a wolf if she was on her own.

I empathized with her situation because she reminded me of a younger version of my own mother. After my papa died when I was just a little girl, my mother worked three jobs until I was old enough to go out on my own. She never judged me for the life I chose and told me everyone has to walk their own path. She died fifteen years ago in a car accident. It's ludicrous to think how she worked so hard to live a good life, only to have it ripped away because she wasn't wearing a seat belt. Had she been conscious, she could have shifted and healed, but my mama had slipped into a coma for two days before they removed her from life support. I stayed by her side, destroyed that she had to spend her last days in a human hospital and not in the comfort of her own bed.

"Naya?"

I blinked the memories away. "Yes? I'm sorry. My mind has been skipping all over the place today. I shouldn't have had wine with my dinner; it always makes me sleepy. Maybe I need to go home early and take a bubble bath." I rubbed my shoulders and yawned. "Although, I've still got a second shift to finish after Daphne."

"I'll cover for you," Skye quickly said. "With the manager, I mean. If Dean asks, I'll tell him you had an emergency."

I smiled warmly. "You can have my slot. I've already paid for it." I reached in my locker and slipped on a stretchy black dress that stopped above my knees. "You go out there and bleed their wallets dry for your baby."

Her smile quickly waned.

I brushed her soft hair away from her shoulders. Skye had a gorgeous smile, so I hated to see the frown in its place and the way she kept fidgeting with the ends of her blue T-shirt.

"What's wrong, chickypoo? You don't seem like yourself tonight."

"It's nothing. It's—"

"Yes, it's *something*. Tell Naya what's wrong."

She rubbed the side of her nose. "I don't know. I think someone's been following me. Maybe it's my overactive imagination running rampant again. Do you think it's possible one of the guys out there could be stalking me?"

I sighed and let my arms fall to my sides. "It's been known to happen with a few of our more delusional customers. They get fixated on a perception of who they think we are and sometimes cross the line. Are you armed?"

Her thin brows arched high enough that they could have touched her hairline.

"Honey, take this." I reached in my purse and pulled out a small cylindrical container. "It's just pepper spray, but that's enough for you to get your point across. Whatever your animal is, she'll protect you if it's anything more than a lovesick puppy. I've had a few in my time, but most are harmless men who just get a little starstruck.

Trust your instinct. If something doesn't feel right, then don't go out alone. This job comes with risks."

She held the bottle of spray and examined the writing. "What about you?"

"I just keep it for show. You need it more than I do. Knock 'em dead tonight."

I kissed her on the cheek and glanced back as I walked out the door. Skye waved at me with a cautious smile that left me uneasy.

Young girls like her always had admirers, and they were too inexperienced to know how to handle men. In the past year, Dean had gradually been working her in, but she didn't get as much stage time as the rest of us. Skye needed a mentor to help her toughen up so the customers didn't walk all over her. Now that I knew about her baby girl, I wanted to help her even more. Maybe the mother-hen syndrome happens to women like me who've been working in clubs for decades, but I'd never met anyone as naïve as Skye and so wrong for a place like this. Most dancers didn't have a family, pack, or someone to look out for us. We were nomads in a savage world.

And those who are alone are always the ones who need the most protection.

After leaving Club Sin, I headed back to my apartment on the human side of town. In most big cities, Breeds lived apart from humans and purchased land to secure that division. But sometimes living too close to other Breeds only stirred up trouble, so years ago, I'd rented an apartment around humans. They came with their own set of drama, but it didn't compare to waking up in the middle of the night to a Chitah fight. It's not as if we could just call the police, so those kinds of outbursts had to resolve on their own.

I slowed my car in front of an animal shelter and put my white Trans Am in park. It wasn't one of the muscle-car models, but sporty with a sunroof. I stuffed several large bills into a white envelope and approached the front door, placing it in my usual spot. Once a month, I donated my daily earnings to the shelter—something I'm sure plenty of Shifters would have scoffed at. I didn't like watching images on the news of those poor little creatures caged and sentenced to be euthanized. How could a Shifter in good conscience look away when we ourselves had once been kept under the oppressive thumb of immortals in a similar manner? Caging animals was offensive, and sometimes I'd fantasize about setting them all free.

But no one can save the world. Instead, I supported the no-kill shelters to keep them in business. Maybe my money would make room for one more animal to find a family who would show it unconditional love.

A chill ran up my spine and I whirled around, narrowing my eyes at the shadows on the dark street as I hurried back to the car. My heels clicked on the concrete, echoing in the quietness. Some people foolishly brushed off chills, unaware that on a warm night it could only mean one thing: a Mage was in the area. Sometimes they were flaring their energy, and other times they didn't bother concealing it. I didn't trust those immortals. Many were ancients, and a whole lot of them walking around had once committed unspeakable crimes against my kind—my family—and even kept them as pets, although what that really translated to was slavery.

I hopped in my car and sped off so fast that the tires screeched. A smart woman never brushes off her instincts, and mine were pinging off the charts.

When I reached a red light, I dialed Lexi's number.

"This is the party to whom you are speaking."

"Izzy?"

"Oh, shoot," I heard her say. "I must have grabbed the wrong phone. I'm sorry. Who is this?"

"It's Naya."

"Right," she said with a laugh. "Sorry about that. Hold on just a second."

I looked around, anxiously waiting for the light to turn green. The city was teeming with other Breeds, but it wasn't typical to find them on the human side of town at this hour.

"Naya? It's Lexi. What's going on?"

"Nothing, girl. I just want to keep you on the phone until I get home. I'm almost there." The light turned green and I floored it. "I left work early because the wine at dinner made me too sleepy to dance."

"Sorry about that. Hope you don't get in trouble. Swing by! We're just sitting around playing cards and munching on snacks. Well, actually we're playing Go Fish with Maizy"—her voice became stern—"who should be in bed."

That wasn't a bad idea. I took a sharp turn and headed their way. She lived close, and that would allow me to get out on an open stretch of road to make sure no one was following me.

"Sounds perfect," I said. "I won't stay long; I need to head home and take care of—"

"The hairball."

"Well, *that's* not very polite." Lexi and I often bantered about my little cat, but I never took it personally.

"No, Naya is coming over for a little while," Lexi said to someone else. "Where do you think you're going? We're still in the middle of a game."

"Hello? Lexi?"

"Sorry about that, Naya. I'm listening. Is something wrong? You don't usually drop in so unexpectedly."

"We'll talk when I get there. See you soon, darling."

Ten minutes later, I pulled into their driveway. The Weston pack lived in a grand home that had once been a hotel in its heyday. Someone had recently built a carport to shelter a couple of the cars, but what they really needed was a garage if they wanted to protect them from hail. I carefully weaved around a blue truck and parked beside Austin's black Dodge Challenger.

Darkness blanketed the property, but lights from inside the house shone onto the wooden porch that wrapped around the front and side of the house. I got out of the car and glanced behind me as I ascended the steps. The humid air put a dewy sheen on my face and I dabbed at it, realizing I had forgotten to wipe off my heavy work makeup.

The door swung open before I could pull a tissue out of my purse.

A grin slid up Denver's face, and he leaned on the doorjamb. "I didn't know you delivered."

"Don't be obtuse," I said, moving around him. "Lexi invited me."

When he closed the door, I glanced down at the pile of shoes by the door. I'd never followed that unspoken rule on my visits, but his eyes traveled down to my black heels as if he were expecting me to take them off. Either that or he was admiring my red polish and toe ring.

"Naya! We're in here," Lexi called out from the dining room.

Their house had a cozy appeal, even though it wasn't my style. Lynn had done an impressive job selecting the decor for each room and adding features like crown molding. Lord knows she'd tried to add a feminine touch to the otherwise masculine furniture. The living room had two areas: a stone fireplace straight ahead, and a seating area to the right in front of the television and stereo. In the winter, they moved chairs in front of the fireplace, but in the summer, they kept that area open. Farther to the right was a study and another small room they only used for parties. The hall to the right of the fireplace went straight to the back of the house. The dining room was on the right, and then you passed a hallway on the left before reaching the kitchen. Lexi had mentioned that the rooms in that hall were probably where the hotel staff slept.

To the left of the stairs was a spacious area that could function as a sitting room. But Lynn had just decorated it with a few accent tables and lacy curtains. I liked that she didn't put furniture in every room, because it left plenty of room for social gatherings and events. Smart thinking on her part since Shifters loved peace parties.

Everyone slept upstairs. Well, everyone except William. He had the third-highest rank in the house below Austin and Reno. I liked William, and I suspected it had to do with the fact he'd traveled to different countries and didn't originate from the South. He used to be Lorenzo Church's second-in-command until he'd struck Ivy with his car by accident. Then he changed hands and joined the Weston pack. At first I'd thought Austin was punishing him by making him live in one of the small rooms off the kitchen, but Lexi mentioned

William had requested that room above all others. Something about how he liked to raid the cupboards late at night.

My heels clicked on the floor when I entered the dining room. "Where did everyone go?"

Lexi stretched back in her chair with a bowl of pretzels in front of her. "Denver is getting ready for work, Trevor and William went to a club, Austin's asleep, and I don't know where the twins went. Jericho tucked Melody in and took off for a gig. Lately Maizy's been wanting to stay up later than Melody, but she kept nodding off, so we sent her up to bed a little while ago. So… it's just us girls," Lexi said with an exaggerated smile, waving her hand toward Izzy and April.

Izzy's flaming red hair was wild and gorgeous, and I wondered if her next baby would be blessed with the same genetics.

"Congratulations, mama! I heard the great news." I made my way around the end of the small table and gave her a quick hug.

She flashed a smile. "I had a feeling I was pregnant, but our Relic came out and performed an exam just to confirm."

I chuckled and took a seat to the left of April, patting her back.

"How did your wolfy react?" I asked, referring to her mate, Jericho.

Izzy admired the sparkly diamond on her finger—not a tradition among Shifters, but Jericho wasn't your average guy.

"Hell's bells, he's over the moon," she said. "Melody's a handful, so I honestly didn't think he'd be ready for more kids so soon. When I asked if he wanted a boy or a girl, he said he doesn't care. He's just been—"

"A knight in shining armor," April interrupted, threading her blond hair away from her face. "Rubs her feet every night after supper. I can only *imagine* what he'll be like when she's actually showing. Remember the last time?" she asked Lexi with a soft chuckle.

Izzy twirled her ring. "I'm a little nervous because twins run in my family. It skips every other generation, so there's a chance I could have more than one in here. Then he'll *really* be on his way to getting his own band."

We laughed, and Lexi looked down at her pretzels wistfully. I could see how conflicted she was and wondered if anyone else had noticed. April carried no such look. By choosing to be with Reno, she'd willingly given up the promise of children—if she even wanted babies. Not all women do.

Izzy sure did. I could tell she was going to give that wolf a litter before it was all said and done.

Denver swaggered in and sat at the head of the table on my left. "Well, I for one can't wait."

Lexi set her elbow on the table and tucked her chin in the palm of her hand. "You just want a boy so you'll have someone to play video games with."

"Shut it," he said.

Denver was a handsome man in an obnoxiously charming sort of way. His smiling eyes were the color of the Atlantic Ocean—deep blue and always sparkling on the surface. I didn't care for men with blond hair, but his was a pleasing shade of dark blond cut in a trendy style—messy with a wave, but not quite long enough to cover the scar on his forehead. With that charismatic smile, he undoubtedly made a killing as a bartender. Unfortunately, most Shifter women wouldn't find his youthful and energetic personality an attractive quality.

"So when are you going to have some little kittens?" he asked me, arching a brow.

"Perhaps I'll have some calves," I replied, leaning my elbows on the table.

"That would be udderly adorable." He winked and we all turned around when Maizy wandered in with sleep in her eyes and a tangle of blond hair in her face.

She had on a pair of blue pajama bottoms and a yellow shirt. I missed the days when she wore pink nightgowns with ruffles on the end. We used to have so much fun dressing up, but she was growing into a woman too soon.

"How come no one told me Auntie Naya was coming over?" she asked gruffly.

"I'm just here for a minute, princess."

Denver swiveled to face her. "Come here, birthday girl."

She flashed her blue eyes at him with a growing smile. "It's not my birthday yet."

He glanced at his watch and masked his humor with a serious expression. "You're right. Only birthday girls get to stay up past their bedtime. That means you need to go back to sleep." He reached out his arms. "Come on, Peanut. The express train is going upstairs, so all aboard."

"The express train is going to crash with that heavy cargo," Lexi quipped. "She's getting too big to carry."

Denver hunched over, letting Maizy leap onto his back and wrap her arms around his neck.

"She'll never be too big for me to carry," he choked out, his face turning red from the lack of circulation. When he hopped and shifted her higher, he was able to grab her legs and release the death grip around his neck. "Say good night, Peanut."

"Good night, Peanut," Maizy replied sleepily. She laid her head on his shoulder and closed her eyes.

Denver turned around and glanced at Lexi. "Tomorrow I need a few hours sleep before we head out, so can you tell everyone to keep it down when I get home from work?"

"I'll kick them out of the house," Lexi promised, pulling her hair out of its ponytail. She threaded her fingers through the top until it was disheveled. "We have to be there at noon, so if you get home early enough, you should be able to sleep for about five hours."

"True that. I'm going to take her upstairs and then I'm outta here."

"G'nite, Maze. I love you." Lexi watched Denver carry the sleepyhead down the hall.

"He can be the biggest dickhead, but he's so good with her," Izzy said. "I used to think it had to do with his lack of maturity, but she's getting older and he treats her differently. Still attentive, but in a different way. I would have never imagined a guy like Denver being such a good watchdog."

"I can't lie," Lexi said. "He's the best. He really listens when she has something to say, and that's not easy in a house like ours when we're all talking over one another. Last week I drove out to Wes's grave. She never got to meet her big brother, but I still want her to know about him. I guess his death is sinking in now that she's older, because she was in such a sullen mood when we got home. She wouldn't talk to me about it, but Denver took her out front and they sat down on the steps. He wrapped his arm around her and just listened to everything she had to say—stuff she's never admitted to me, like how sad she is that she never got to meet Wes. She wondered if he'd like her." Lexi's lip quivered and tears glossed up her eyes. "I can't imagine the absence she has to live with of having never known her brother, and on top of that, coming to grips with reality that her own father didn't love her."

"She has all the love she could ask for in this house," I reminded her. "That's all the family she needs."

Lexi wiped her wet cheeks. "I know, but tell that to a ten-year-old who just wants to know *why*. Why couldn't she have met her brother once, and why couldn't she have had a father who took her to the zoo. The first time she met him was when he dragged her through Austin's house and then shot me in front of her. I healed, but that affected her in a way I'll never understand. How do you explain stuff like that to a kid? Mom does a good job, but Maizy will never have those questions answered, and that's a heavy load to carry in life."

"What did Denver say to her?" April asked.

Lexi turned a playing card in a circle on the table. "I couldn't hear everything through the window. He just kissed the top of her head and let her do all the talking. Maybe that's my problem—I talk too much, and Maizy doesn't want me to put a Band-Aid on everything. I'm just glad there's someone she can go to when she needs to get stuff like that off her chest. I tell her stories about Wes all the time, and what our family was like when Wes was alive. But I don't glam it up; I guess I don't want to make it sound so great that she doesn't appreciate how wonderful things are now, you know? We just went through life thinking she'd forget all that, but kids don't forget. It just takes them a few years before all that trauma catches up and they start thinking about it on a different level, trying to figure out what kind of person they are because of it—or what's wrong with them."

"Princess?" a husky voice said.

April peered around me. "Yes?"

"Are you coming up?"

I glanced at Reno. He was an impressive man who resembled Austin in some ways, but tougher, if that was possible. Reno had the hard edges of a man who had experienced a lot of pain in his life.

He was also wearing a pair of silk pajama bottoms with no shirt.

April smiled approvingly as she stood up, and I had a feeling that ensemble was all her doing. "I think I'm in the mood to listen to some blues music in bed. Good night, everyone. I'll see you tomorrow at the party, Naya?"

"You can count on it."

Reno curved his arm around his mate and kissed the top of her head as they walked off. Somewhere down the hall, I heard her squeal followed by the sound of kissing and whispering.

Out of nowhere, a pang of jealousy struck me. *Where on earth did that come from?*

Being here at this intimate hour gave me a glimpse of what it must be like to live in this house. I adored the way they all treated one another. Sometimes in my quiet apartment, I would sit on the balcony and listen to the neighbors below. It was why I liked having parties. Panthers didn't live in groups and rarely had more than one child, but I still longed for companionship. I missed Lexi; we used to play gin rummy and go shopping on a whim.

"So why are you really here?" Lexi asked, dipping her pretzel into a can of processed cheese dip. "Hiding from another boyfriend who's sitting on your doorstep with a bouquet of roses?"

Izzy spread the cards out before her, turning them in circles and mixing them up.

I rubbed my finger over a small indentation on the table. "I felt a Mage following me tonight. It happened on the human side of town, and I was alone. It could have been one of the customers from the club, but I didn't want to chance leading anyone to my home."

She laughed. "Oh, so you brought a lunatic here?"

"Girly, I'm sure your big strong men can take care of themselves if someone's brave enough to drive up that creepy dark road full of potholes. I needed to get out on an open stretch of highway to make sure I wasn't just imagining things. I didn't see anyone follow me here, so I decided it wouldn't hurt to swing by and see what goes on in the Cole house at this ungodly hour. It's nothing to worry your head about, but a girl can't be too careful."

"Do you have any alarms in your apartment?" Izzy asked in a serious voice. "When I was a rogue, I had a few crazies follow me home. It helps to have alarms—especially if you live alone. Maybe you should ask Reno to install something. He's good with security systems."

"Not a bad idea," Lexi said. "Something is better than nothing."

I decided I'd give it a little thought. But in the back of my mind, I knew if someone really wanted to get at me, a noisy alarm wasn't going to deter them.

CHAPTER 3

DRIVING IN A CAR FULL of balloons wasn't something I'd ever done before, and I added it to my short list of things I'd never do again. Once I managed to get them out of the car, I made my way inside Pizza Zone, wrinkling my nose at the heavy smell of pepperoni. Since this was a casual event, I'd dressed in a pair of black shorts and a turquoise button-up blouse.

Two little boys hurtled by and almost knocked me down. "Oh!" I clutched the box in my arms and kept moving forward, desperately looking for a familiar face in the sea of humans.

"Aunt Naya's here!" Maizy rushed over from a long table on the left side of the room. The lights were low, drawing all the attention to the colorful machines.

"Oh, my. You look astoundingly beautiful today, Maizy."

She twirled in a sleeveless white dress that made her appear older than eleven. Her hair was in loose waves, and the shimmering lip balm she wore was a pale pink.

"Is that for me?" Her blue eyes widened at the size of the box wrapped in shiny red paper and garnished with a white ribbon.

I glanced around. "Well, I can't imagine who else it would be for. Think you can carry it for me?"

She wrapped her arms around the box and stumbled toward the table. "Can I open it?"

I heard a flurry of chuckles, and my stomach twisted into a knot when I saw the pack. This wasn't a party with outsiders and friends; this was a family gathering. I didn't belong, and the shiny balloons laced around my wrists only called attention to that fact.

"Let me take those," Lynn offered. "I'll tie them on the chairs, and you can put the pretzels in one of the bowls. She's so excited to have everyone here. Even Lorenzo came, and you know how he's always bickering with Austin."

Lynn was in her fifties, although I'd never asked her age. I could tell she dyed her hair blond, because sometimes the roots would show scattered grey hairs. Today she had on a dark blue dress with a nice sheen to the fabric. Lynn had class in a natural and effortless way, and she'd always reminded me of a movie star from the golden age of cinema.

Lynn unwound the balloons from my wrists and circled around the long table, tying each one to the back of a chair. Each time she walked near Maizy, she would kiss her on the cheek like a doting mother. Then Lexi would teasingly pout so her mother would give her a kiss on the head and then point out how silly she was behaving. I didn't think she would sit down for a moment; it seemed like there was always something to put up, set out, adjust, or refill.

I rubbed the red marks on my wrists that the balloon strings had left behind. They were nothing compared to the scars on Izzy's wrists, but I'd never asked what the story was behind those. Something terrible must have happened to her, but I admired the courage it took her not to hide them.

One interesting observation was how the pack had split up with the women on the left side of the table and the men on the right. I wondered if they had chosen their seating arrangement or if Lynn had strategically separated them so there wouldn't be any flirting between couples. Only Trevor sat on the women's side. The birthday girl enjoyed her spot at the head of the table, and it looked like she had gone through half her gifts already.

I gave Lexi a hug when she took my purse and added it to the pile.

Before taking my seat, I stopped behind Trevor and peered over his head. "Look who's a big girl," I said to the little angel sitting on Lorenzo's lap.

Lorenzo gave a close-lipped smile that showed his pride. "She's turning three this summer." In a tender motion, he pulled Hope's long hair back so I could get a good look at her chubby cheeks and beautiful long lashes. Unlike Ivy, who always wore a braid, Hope wore her long hair loose and nicely combed. She had Lorenzo's dark eyes and intense features, but her mother's good nature and lovely smile. Such a uniquely beautiful child, sweetly humming a song as she played with the tassels on a leather bracelet he wore around his wrist.

"Naya, come sit next to me. I saved you a seat," April said from the far end. I passed by Izzy, who was holding hands with Jericho across the table. He brushed his thumb over her knuckle while they watched Maizy excitedly unwrapping her pile of gifts. A pretty dress, a game, a drawing kit, and someone had bought her a tall cylinder of candy. She about died when she peeled the wrapper off, and Lexi's mom scowled at Denver, who merely laced his fingers together as Maizy popped off the lid and immediately ate a piece.

The only person absent from the festivities was…

"Sorry I'm late," Wheeler said, his voice dark and smoky as he took the chair across from me. He glared at me for a nanosecond before turning his attention to Maizy.

Wheeler had rubbed me the wrong way when he disrespected April a few years ago. Maybe *they'd* buried the hatchet, but I still felt infuriated each time he flicked a glance my way. Wheeler was probably a man who berated his women and treated them like submissive dogs.

Yet I found myself secretly peering up at him. Wheeler normally kept the circle beard around his mouth and chin neatly groomed, but it looked like he was growing it out along his jaw. It wasn't thick but trimmed close, like a heavy five-o'clock shadow. His white tank top fit his body like a second skin, and every hard curve on his chest created a ridge in the fabric. Wheeler had an average frame with anything but an average build. Not an ounce of fat showed, just lean muscle. There was something dark and desirous about him I couldn't put my finger on, although perhaps it had to do with him being the opposite of every man I'd ever been attracted to. My gaze skated across his tattoos, and when he flashed his amber eyes up to mine, I leaned against April and pretended to ignore him.

I found it immensely distracting to be sitting across from Wheeler. I'm not sure whose twisted idea it was to place us together, but it kept our end of the table silent. His presence made my panther restless as she circled in the dark shadows within my mind.

After the ceremonial opening of gifts and extinguishing the candles, Maizy walked around and gave everyone a big squeeze. Then she reached under the table and handed Denver a brown box with a round lid.

His brows drew together. "Did you forget to open one?"

"No, silly. That's yours."

Denver looked at her with a bemused expression. "That must be yours, Peanut. It's not my birthday."

She folded her arms. "You won't tell me when your birthday is, so we're going to share a birthday. Don't you want to see what I got you?"

For a moment I thought I saw his lip tremble. He quickly tightened his expression and shook his head. When he removed the lid and pulled away the white tissue paper, he huffed out a laugh. "A *straw* hat? I'm not wearing this silly hat."

Denver must have thought it was a joke, because his look altered when he noticed the visceral disappointment glittering in her eyes.

"I'm just teasing." He quickly settled the cowboy hat on his head. "I love it so much that I'm going to sleep in it. My little Peanut bought me a hat," he said proudly.

She smiled wide and gave him a hug so big that his hat fell on the table. "I love you, Denny."

He looked a little embarrassed. "Go spend some of those tokens. Skedaddle!"

As Maizy ran off toward the arcade games, Denver held the hat between his hands, brows drawn together in a scowl. "Whose idea was this?"

Lexi sliced another piece of white cake and put it on a pink paper plate. "Maizy insisted on buying you a present, and she came up with that idea all by herself. Maybe you should just make her happy and tell her when your birthday is."

He put the hat on his head, pulling it low in the front so it sexily obscured his eyes. "No, then it'll be a big thing with her."

"Do you want a slice?" Lexi asked me as she passed down a plate. Apparently, they were doing cake before pizza, which was fine by me.

"Cut me a large slice. And heavy on the icing. No... bigger!"

April gaped at me.

"A girl has to keep her figure." I took the plate they passed down to me. "Don't you agree?" I asked Wheeler.

It was time that one of us behaved like the adult in this awkward situation, so I played nice.

"I agree," Reno piped in, finishing his cake in almost one bite. "I like a woman with meat on her bones." He winked at April.

I wondered how much difficulty he would have extracting his foot from his mouth.

"Are you saying I'm fat?" April tipped her head to the side and Reno chuckled.

"No, princess. I'm saying I *love* the way your thighs wrap around my neck nice and thick."

The men chuckled and April couldn't mask the blush rising on her cheeks.

"What about you, Wheeler?" I pressed. "Does the wolf like a bone or a juicy steak?"

He drew his index finger into his mouth and sucked off a slather of white icing. His brown eyes rose to meet mine, and a shudder rolled through my body. "I like my women skinny, blond, tall, and *quiet.*"

"I think I saw one of those for sale in a magazine advertisement once. Does she store easily under the bed, or do you have to deflate her?"

Jericho spit out his soda and choked from laughter.

I averted my eyes, hoping that would put an end to his indirect jabs. The last thing I needed was for this party to turn riotous, and I'd already made a promise to Lexi. I engaged in small talk with April, ignoring his reply.

"Where's Ivy?" I asked.

April leaned in close, lowering her voice. "She's not feeling well."

Which translated to: Ivy was in heat. I couldn't fathom how women lived in a house full of virile men in that condition. Lorenzo undoubtedly sated Ivy's every need, but did she mingle with the pack? If so, the men must have scattered, afraid of looking at her the wrong way and suffering Lorenzo's punishment. A Shifter couldn't get near a woman in heat without his divining rod pointing the way.

"How's Ivy's business going?" I asked. "I've always envied girls with her talent."

"Keeping her busy." April grimaced after taking a sip of lemonade from her paper cup. "The last time I spoke to her, some big shot was offering her a lot of money to restore a houseful of antiques. They're in poor condition, but he can't let go of them because of the sentimental value."

I bristled when someone brushed up against my back and sat beside me. Ben casually leaned on his left arm and watched me, mischief twinkling in his pale brown eyes. He kept his dusty-brown hair trimmed and his face shaved as smooth as a baby's bottom. Of all the Weston pack, he dressed the most casually, and I don't mean that in a raggedy-jeans and T-shirt way, but rather a man who preferred cotton shirts with collars, and khaki shorts. He might be what Wheeler would look like if he were a normal citizen.

Ben offered me a lazy smile. "I'm glad you came. You should come more often."

His words hung in the air and collected dust before I answered. "I only come when I want to, not when I'm told."

"Mee-ow," he purred, biting his lower lip.

Wheeler's eyes centered on his plate while he slowly scraped the icing off his dessert.

"Are you off tonight?" Ben continued.

"No, I have to work."

"Dilemma. Maybe I can... get you off."

The more his mouth flapped, the less funny he became. Innuendoes were my guilty pleasure in life, but his were incessant and borderline creepy.

When he touched my arm with his index finger, Wheeler shoved his plate forward. The legs of his chair made a terrible noise as he scooted back. "Why don't you check out the video poker in the back?"

"Busy," Ben replied absently, admiring the dark curls of my hair. Wheeler crossed his ankle over his knee and clenched his jaw.

"Melody!" Izzy blurted out.

I looked over my shoulder and watched William stroll through the front doors with a little girl holding his hand. Izzy and Jericho's little girl, to be exact.

Unlike Hope, Melody looked like a handful. Someone had braided only the ends of her tangled hair, so she had flyaway hairs up top and skinny braids at the end. She hadn't inherited Izzy's red hair but looked the spitting image of Jericho, from his milky-green eyes to his brown locks. Melody had Izzy's lips and outgoing personality. She let go of William's hand and strutted toward the table, just as sassy as any three-and-a-half-year-old could be in her white tights, black moccasin boots, and neon-pink shirt. That girl owned her strut and even did a hair flip.

"That one's going to be a handful," Reno murmured. "I don't envy you, brother."

"That doesn't go together," Jericho grumbled at Izzy. "Why do you let her dress herself? It's one thing around the house…"

Izzy patted her hand on the table. "She's stubborn and takes after her father. At least she washes her hair more often."

A sexy grin curved up his cheek. "Baby, you and I make beautiful children, but that girl does *not* take after me. See that walk and the attitude on her face? That's *all* you, Isabelle. You're either born with a sense of style or not," he said, pinching the tattered concert shirt he was wearing.

Melody tugged on a balloon string. "Can I have some cake?"

"Is your tummy better? Maybe you should just sit here for a while and then we'll see."

She nodded and Izzy scooted back to let her sit on her lap.

William flipped a chair around next to Trevor and took a seat with his arms draped over the back. "Mustn't worry about her having a little cake now. She started feeling better an hour ago and already ate a jelly sandwich."

"Thanks for watching her." Izzy pulled Melody's hair back and kissed her head. "That was a big help. I would have stayed, but I already volunteered to set up the table and decorate."

"Say, can I get some of that cake before it's all gone?" he asked, brushing a large curl of his brown hair away from his eyes.

From what I knew about packs, everyone bonded with the children and helped look after them, so it wasn't uncommon for parents to go out and leave their children in the care of the pack.

Trevor slid his plate in front of William. "You can have mine. It's too sweet."

When William turned to look at Trevor, I couldn't see his face anymore. But I saw Trevor's, and his cheeks bloomed with color before he sat back and started retying the laces on his oxfords.

Just as I felt Ben's finger swipe down my arm, Lexi appeared and handed me my purse. "Your phone keeps ringing."

I opened my white handbag and pulled out my slim phone. "Hello?"

"It's Daphne."

"Tell me this isn't a work emergency. I've already talked to Dean about it and he promised me the day off without any interruptions. Darling, please have someone else fill in."

"Skye is missing."

My breath caught. I turned my back on the group and covered my right ear. "What do you mean?"

Ben got up and wandered off.

"One of the girls was going outside and heard a scream. She said a van sped out of the parking lot, and we haven't seen Skye since."

"What makes you think something's wrong? That could have been anything. Maybe it wasn't her."

"I thought so too, but Tina found Skye's purse, a bottle of pepper spray, and her red shoe in the empty parking spot next to her car. She caught a glimpse of a struggle before they took off. Do you know if Skye was having problems with a boyfriend?"

I swallowed thickly and nausea crept over me. When my heart began to race, I stood up and distanced myself from the group. "She mentioned something about being followed. I gave her my pepper spray before I left last night because I thought it was just another fan. *Oh, no.* Daphne, she has a little girl. Did you know that?"

"No. I didn't really bond with her the way you have with all the girls. Dean is super pissed, and he contacted the Council, but they don't give a hoot about a missing dancer. Then he called the higher authority to send a Regulator out to investigate, but they won't bother."

Regulators of the Security Force worked for the higher authority—leaders of different Breeds that were in charge of the courts. They weren't technically government since each big city had one. The only cases they focused on were high-profile crimes. Regulators were dangerous men with katanas. They served warrants, performed investigations, and got the job done.

"See if Dean called her family, or if he has their number on record. I doubt it, but maybe they know something." I tapped my fingernail on my tooth, pacing in a small circle. I could feel a few eyes on me from the table, mostly from the men. Their ears had perked up when I raised my voice, so I made an effort to remain calm. "Daphne, tell Dean he needs to hire a PI."

My eyes skated over to Reno and an idea sprang to mind.

"I'll try," she said. "But if he has to pay out of his own pocket, I don't know if he will. Dean said the owner doesn't want any part of it and suggested Skye was probably mixed up in something illegal."

"Bullshit!" I yelled. I toned it down when Hope made a stinky face at me. Not that the Weston pack cared about cursing around the kids, but maybe I kind of did.

"Daph, I might have someone who can help. I'll see what I can do. Skye is a sweet girl and this just makes me sick to my stomach. Call me if you hear anything."

"You take care of yourself. First Lacy and now Skye. I just can't believe this is happening in our club. All the girls are on edge, so do me a favor and buy yourself something better than a can of mace."

"Will do, chickypoo."

I hung up the phone and pulled in a sharp breath to calm myself. When I returned to my seat, Reno and Wheeler's eyes were locked on me. Hard.

Lexi had migrated onto Austin's lap where she was preoccupied with nibbling on his earlobe. His eyes hooded and she smiled mischievously.

"Better cut that out, Ladybug," I heard him say.

Melody pulled Jericho's hand so hard that one of his fat rings popped off. He finally capitulated and stood up, towering over her. Izzy followed behind them and Melody led the way toward a glass machine filled with colorful stuffed animals. Meanwhile, Denver and Maizy were behind me, throwing balls at a machine.

"Something wrong?" Reno asked in a low voice. The sounds of ringing bells and squealing children overlapped, making it difficult to hear him.

"I'd like to talk to you later, if that's okay."

He pinched his chin and nodded. "No sweat."

A balloon string unraveled from the back of April's chair, sending the shiny object into the rafters overhead.

"Holy smokes, I didn't mean to do that," she said. "I'm sorry, Naya."

I laughed softly. "There are ten more. She won't miss it."

"That's some gift you got her." April pointed toward the box full of purses, scarves, and beads. They were items I would normally have given to charity, but I'd been saving them over the past year for just this occasion.

"Girls love to play dress-up, and she can always use a few accessories. It was no trouble." What I didn't mention to April was that some of the purses were designer.

Wheeler couldn't take his pale brown eyes off me. "What was the call about?"

"My hairdresser couldn't fit me in at three, so it's a crisis."

He gripped the edge of the table and leaned back, looking his usual snarly self.

I shoved all my anxiety into a mental drawer and closed it tight. There would be plenty of time to think about it later, and worrying would only ruin the party. I squeezed my hands into tight fists beneath the table, then stretched out all the muscles so they'd quit shaking. I'd always had a sweet spot for Skye because of the nice things she'd say about people. She wasn't catty; that came with years of practice in a job like ours.

An hour later, everyone had eaten enough cake and pizza to sedate an elephant. Maizy was the belle of the ball, her face beaming each time she reappeared to look at her gifts and give her mom a hug. She loved physical affection, and maybe that wasn't so common among some children her age—especially humans. Shifters adored family, so it was good to see that rubbing off on her.

While Lynn cleaned off the table, William packed up the gifts and hauled them to the car.

I caught sight of Maizy playing an arcade game near the main doors, so I walked over and sat in a red bucket seat facing her. Pizza Zone was a grand room with numerous tables in the center. One area had plastic tunnels for small children to climb through, and all the games were in multiple rows along the outer walls. I glanced at a bright window to my left and thought about Skye.

Reno dragged a tiny red chair in my direction and parked it to my right. "What's the problem?"

I crossed my legs and my anklet jingled. "A friend of mine is missing. Not just missing, someone saw her taken. A van, but I don't know the details. Reno, you're one of the best private investigators, so I was hoping you could help. The higher authority won't touch it and neither will the club owner. I have money, and I'll pay whatever you charge."

"Is she a close friend?"

I touched a loose curl of my hair and it spiraled around my finger. "She's a sweet girl who doesn't have anyone to look out for her. Let's just say I don't like seeing bad things happen to good people."

"Fair enough, but if no one got the plates or a description, that could be problematic," he said in a low register. Reno eased back in his chair and gave the situation some consideration. "This was at Club Sin?"

"Yes."

"Who witnessed it?"

"A girl named Tina. If you need to question them, you'll have to do it discreetly. Our manager has been a pain in the rear lately."

An icy gust of air from the vent overhead suddenly enveloped me, and a million goose bumps erupted across my skin. I shivered and folded my arms, tightly hugging my body.

"I'm not going to sugarcoat it for you. A kidnapping never ends well—not with dancers. I've seen it a dozen times, and most of those girls end up on the black market. They single out the ones without family, and especially girls who don't have much fight in them. Someone like you? Too much work for a buyer, and you'd be hard to sell. But yeah, the sex-slave trade goes on, and it's a dark, ugly world. I've saved a few girls and put them in a safe home, but way too many slip through the cracks. There's no way to save them all."

My heart almost stopped and I clutched my chest. "Please, no."

"It happens," he said with a shrug. "Dancers are easy prey. Mostly it's Shifters, but the black market has room for everyone, regardless of gender or age. There are malicious bastards who have been around for centuries, and not all of them have wised up. Some of the immortals still want to live a barbaric lifestyle where they have Shifters as pets. Makes them feel superior and shit—like a king or a god."

"You mean *slaves*. Humans volunteer to be pets for Shifters, but no Shifter in their right mind would do the same of their own free will."

He sighed and crossed his black boots at the ankles. "I'll do what I can, Naya, but I can't get in too deep. You're a friend to Lexi, so I won't turn you away. To tell you the truth, Austin might see this as a conflict of interest. In any case, I can't promise it's going to be a happy ending. You might never find out what happened to her. You ready for that?"

"I'm not giving up on her. Everyone deserves to have someone fight for them."

"Okay then. Give me Tina's number, and I'll start with her."

"Thank you." I scribbled her number along with Daphne's on a piece of paper, and he tucked it in his wallet.

We quietly watched Maizy play her game. She briefly turned around to fish more tokens out of a purse I'd given her when a young man in a casual dress shirt appeared and took over the machine.

"*Hey*, I was playing that," she said.

"Sorry, kid. It's mine now."

"You can't cut in front of me. I was getting coins." She held one in front of his face, and he gently pushed her arm away.

I leaned toward Reno until our arms touched. "I bet he's one of those *friends of the family* who doesn't have kids of his own. What kind of man would put his needs before a child?"

"A dirtbag, that's who."

Humans fascinated me and I wanted to see how Maizy would react to his bullying. A girl needs to stand her ground and not let a man run over her.

Which is exactly what she did. I almost burst out laughing when she grabbed the back of his shirt and pulled it so hard that a button popped off the front. He regained his balance and glowered at her.

"You can play when I finish my game," she said matter-of-factly. "It's not nice to disrespect a woman."

I laughed heartily that time. "I see the Cole brothers have been teaching her well."

Reno folded his arms.

"Kid, if you don't scram, I'm going to tell your mom you ruined my shirt. Then you'll really get a spanking."

Maizy retaliated by slamming her hand on one of the buttons, looking up at him defiantly.

"Does this kid belong to someone?" he shouted out to the room.

"That human is two seconds away from getting his ass kicked," Reno muttered, leaning forward, his chair creaking.

Maizy changed her strategy and offered her coins to him. "You can have all my tokens if you let me play one last time before I have to go."

"Thanks, kid."

He took the coins, stuffed them in his pocket, and kept playing. Maizy gripped the stick on the machine and when he seized her wrist, Denver materialized.

"Shit's about to get real," Reno muttered, leaning back in his chair and extending his left arm behind me.

Denver snatched the man by the wrist and severed his grip on

Maizy. He put his straw hat on Maizy's head and, without removing his eyes from the man, said, "Go help your mom. We'll play a game as soon as you're done."

Maizy walked away, and Denver's expression became explosive.

"I think you need to cool off," the young man said, snapping his arm back. "If that's your kid, maybe you should send her to obedience school."

Wrong. Choice. Of. Words.

Denver gripped the man's trachea so firmly that his eyes bulged. "Don't you *ever* put your hands on a child," Denver bit out. "That makes you nothing more than pond scum not fit enough to dirty the bottom of my shoe. Normally I'd knock your face in, but today is a special day, so you lucked out. But if you want to continue arguing, we can take it outside and I'll show you how serious I am. Doubt me for *one* second, and I'll make the beating twice as bad. Your call. Now why don't you get the fuck out of here?"

The guy looked like he'd bitten off more than he could chew, so after Denver shoved him back a step, he reluctantly headed out the main door.

"That's why I love the hell out of that kid," Reno said, rising to his feet. "I'll look into your missing friend and let you know what I find. My questions are rapid-fire, so you might want to warn the girls ahead of time."

I stood up and lowered my voice. "Maybe I should mention something else."

"Yeah, what's that?"

"I don't think Skye was the first. Another girl went missing, although none of us saw it. Do you think it's related?"

He touched a scar on his lip and my eyes roamed down to the bulge beneath his button-up shirt. Leave it to Reno to come to a birthday party armed. "That could be problematic. Someone selling to the black market wouldn't be dumb enough to strike the same place twice. Give me a call if you find out anything else. Got it?"

"Absolutely."

"Maizy, it's time to go!" Lexi called out.

Maizy appeared from the right side of the room and ran toward Denver. "Just one more game!"

She approached the machine and looked at it, but she'd given all her money to the jerk.

Denver stepped up behind her, pumped in a few coins, and planted his hands on either side of the machine, becoming a shield while she played her last game. He turned his head, glancing toward the door where the man had gone. I could tell he was itching to go after him, but a good watchdog didn't leave the woman or child they were guarding to act out a boyish impulse.

While he might have had the maturity of a teenager, Denver was no boy.

CHAPTER 4

T HAT EVENING AT THE CLUB, my panther was scratching to get out. Being a Shifter in the city wasn't easy when your animal required freedom several times a week. Years ago, I lived in northern Canada. Lots of space for my animal to run, privacy, and yet there was no way for me to earn a good living. There had been times when I had no food to eat for months, but as long as my panther could hunt, her meals would provide for the both of us. I'd reached a point where I had to choose a life for either my panther or myself—there was no happy medium. Either I could live in a shack in the woods—isolated from civilization—or I could move to a city with more Breeds and make a solid income to give myself financial comfort in the years to come.

After I made my decision, I realized it came with sacrifice. It became too dangerous for me to shift anywhere outside my residence. Occasionally I would take an excursion to the rural areas of Texas and let her out for a day or two, just to give her a chance to run hard and get it out of her system, but I couldn't do that all the time. My boss didn't give me many consecutive days off, so that left me with shifting in my apartment. A Shifter's animal respects those that the human half loves, so nothing ever happened between my panther and Misha. But an apartment was a tight fit, and there was always a risk of a human hearing her growl and calling the police. On rare occasions, I'd find scratches on the wall or other signs of restless behavior. I'm sure the music didn't help calm her, but I kept it on to drown out any sounds she might make.

Maybe if I lived on the Breed side of town, I wouldn't have to worry about humans, but the possibility of having the wrong person discover my animal was equally terrifying.

Whenever I felt the need to shift, I channeled it into my dance. It made my performances erotic, and tips were plentiful because of the savage look in my eyes and predatory movement of my body.

Club Sin had a long stage with one pole and multicolored spotlights. The smaller stages had poles, but they weren't hugely popular in bars except with Chitahs, who seemed to enjoy the acrobatic stuff. The big attractions were the elaborate dances performed on the big stage. We occasionally choreographed together and made it something fun, but usually the girls were trying too hard to earn tips, so they preferred coming up with their own moves if they had to share the stage.

Customers enjoyed the girls putting on a show that told a story, and the chairs around the main stage rarely stayed empty. The rest of the club had curved swivel chairs surrounding polished tables. Many Breed clubs were laid out the same to give customers a sense of familiarity and comfort, so the bar ran along the left side of the room. The VIP area on the right was for private parties, and that's where the girls banked with private lap dances for high-paying customers. No sex went on in our club, although who knew what happened outside the doors? I'd received a number of tempting offers, but no amount of money was worth selling my body like a prostitute. I had enough sense to separate the business from my personal life.

I changed out of my platforms and into a pair of silver heels before heading toward a table in the back where Daphne was slurping on a martini.

"I want that dress," she said, admiring my tight-fitting black outfit.

"Honey, how are you holding up?"

"Freaking the hell out," she replied, poking at an olive with her fingernail. "I had a little chitchat with your friend, Reno. I've never met a PI, but that's one *scary* fucking man. I can't imagine what kind of woman would go for a guy who looks like he eats nails for breakfast."

I plucked an olive off her napkin and ate it. "He's a doll. Have you heard anything new?"

She shook her head. "The girls are scared, and Dean's afraid they'll start looking for another job. What if this is some maniac stalker? Or maybe someone has a personal grudge against the owner and he's taking it out on us. What do you think happened to Skye?"

Daphne still had on her stage clothes, including a classy black top made with small rhinestones that she'd borrowed from me. Long beads draped in loops from the sides and connected between the breasts in multiple rows.

"I don't want to know what happened to her," she said, not waiting for my answer. "Gives me nightmares just thinking about it. Dean won't let the bouncers walk us to our cars since he's more concerned about maintaining order inside, so we're going to start walking each other out in pairs. When you get ready to leave, just grab one of us. If I could afford a bodyguard, I'd hire one, but it's probably worthless unless someone was specifically coming after *me*."

"Do you think it's random?"

"Those two girls had nothing in common except that they both were Shifters. Different hair colors, body types, ages—it just doesn't make sense. Don't serial killers go after girls who look alike?"

"That's one thing I'm *not* an expert on," I said with a nervous sigh.

She sipped her drink and got a faraway look in her eyes.

I patted her hand when she set down the glass. "Don't worry your pretty little head over anything. My friend will look into it, and if there's anything to be concerned about, you can bet he'll help us. Just be sure you're not withholding any information. He's one of the best."

"Everyone can't stop talking about it."

"The girls need to pull it together or they're going to scare off the customers," I said. "Chitahs can smell fear, so that's not the kind of atmosphere we want to create. Keep them calm and let them know an investigator is looking into it. The last thing we need is a nervous girl getting onstage and shifting into her animal. I'm sure some of the men wouldn't mind knowing what her animal is, but if she begins attacking customers..."

Her hand flew up. "Jesus, I know. We had an emergency meeting this afternoon about it. Tina took off work because she was literally shaking, and girlfriend, I just happen to know she's a grizzly bear," Daphne said with a nervous laugh. "These men would crap their pants if she shifted on stage into that bad motherfucker." Daphne stood up and straightened her clothes. "I have to go on in a little while. Wish me luck."

I returned to the dressing room to grab my things and ran my fingers across Skye's locker. I lifted the latch, and when it opened, the first thing I saw was a picture of her little girl affixed to the inside door. My heart shattered. I'd never noticed the photograph before because most of us kept our eyes on our own business. A single piece of cheap tape held it on, and someone had drawn a red heart in the bottom right-hand corner. Lola was a darling child. She was posed in front of a field of wildflowers, clutching a blue toy pony. She had her mama's beautiful blue eyes and must have inherited her father's hair. It fell to her shoulders in brown spirals and led me to believe she was biracial. That sweet baby was probably wondering where her mommy was. Who was Skye's cousin? She hadn't mentioned if it was a man or woman, or even how old they were. Did they have children of their own? I tugged the picture from the locker and slipped it into my purse. She didn't have anything else in there worth looking through. Just a pair of shoes, a jacket, lipstick, two magazines, and some business cards with telephone numbers written on them.

I lifted the cards and stuffed them in my purse. Dean had already cleaned out the other girl's locker, so we didn't have any evidence to go on.

"Walk me to my car," I said, latching on to Fawn's arm.

She smacked on her gum while we strolled across the parking lot to my Trans Am.

I unlocked the door and tossed my things on the passenger seat. "Make sure you do the same and have someone walk you out."

"You don't have to tell me twice. I'm not going to get myself diced up by some sicko who worships Hannibal Lecter." She spun on her heel and swung her hips like a pendulum as she made her way back inside.

After the long drive home, I parked in front of my apartment and sat in the car for a few minutes looking at Lola's picture. The light from the carport let me stare into her sweet eyes, and I thought about the tears that would fill them each night when she went to bed, waiting to be tucked in and wondering if her mommy would be there in the morning.

I opened my clutch and removed the money I planned to give to Reno. Being a creature of habit, I knew that the moment I stepped inside my apartment I'd toss my purse on the sofa and forget about the money. So I gripped the bills in my hand and decided to spread it out in front of the coffee maker before going to bed. That way, I'd see it first thing in the morning.

I strolled across the grass on the stretch of land that led to my apartment. Our manager was too cheap to build a walkway from my building to the parking lot. Instead, a worn path ran from the stairwell to the mailboxes.

The grass made a soft whisper beneath my shoes, and I slowed my pace when a noise in the darkness grew louder. Heavy footsteps trampled toward me from behind, and before I could look over my shoulder, a body tackled me with such force that it knocked the wind out of me when I hit the ground.

He sat on my back and grabbed a fistful of my hair, yanking it so hard that it forced my head back.

"What are you doing?" I grunted, trying to push myself up. "Get off me, you brute!"

"Hold her still," another man said.

A hand appeared in front of my face, holding a slender metal object that resembled an instrument a human doctor might use. It was black and long with a round bulb at the tip.

"Keep your mouth shut and this'll be over real quick," he said.

A click sounded when he flipped it on and he held it directly in front of my right eye. A fast series of strobe lights began flashing in a chaotic rhythm, and I panicked. The right speed of strobe caused Shifters to change uncontrollably. They were prohibited in clubs unless the owner regulated the flicker rate so it wouldn't cause shifting.

A high intensity of pulsing light blinded my right eye, and

I heard a snapping sound as it continued. Shutting my eyes was useless, and I couldn't loosen his grip on my hair.

A tremor rolled through my body, and my black panther clawed to the surface.

Wheeler awoke before dawn and spent three hours at his desk reading. He didn't have a library of books because he preferred reading the news. It was more or less entertainment, since news among humans had no relevance in their lives for the most part. But then he stumbled across a local article about a suspected kidnapping. A witness driving by Club Sin had spotted a woman struggling with someone in a van. Wheeler read and dissected the article three times. He knew Club Sin. It was located in the Breed district just down the road from the Blue Door. According to the article, the manager had made a statement that all his dancers were accounted for.

Of course he had. If there was one thing they all knew, it was to keep their mouths shut around human law enforcement. Immortals were far too intelligent to reveal themselves to humans who, out of fear, would attempt in vain to exterminate them. Perhaps some immortals loved the comforts humans provided them, like modern technology, food, and entertainment. Most came from a time when men had been scavengers and a day's meal was never guaranteed.

Wheeler took off his glasses and set them on the desk, easing back in his leather chair and rolling an unsharpened pencil between his fingers. He thought about the phone call Naya had received at the birthday party and her sudden change in behavior. She worked at Club Sin.

Naya. He closed his eyes, remembering how she'd bantered with him at the party, dishing back everything he served. That was an attractive quality to Wheeler; he became highly aroused by a confident woman with a dominant personality—more than the average wolf. Sometimes he'd hang out at the strip clubs because that's how those women would portray themselves to be, but in conversation, very few could talk about anything of substance. Naya had a sharp tongue and, uncertain if she'd slap him in front of his pack, he'd eased off. After opening his crude mouth, Wheeler had felt a pang of guilt for the undeserved insults he'd given her, so he'd attempted to smooth things over by complimenting the color of her blouse. But she had turned away, engaged in small talk with April, and his kind words had fallen on deaf ears.

Then he thought about Ben sitting beside Naya and touching her.

Touching.

It incited the most unexpected reaction: jealousy. Wheeler's wolf snapped and snarled within him—at his own brother.

They had always had a rocky past, but this riptide of emotion took him wholly by surprise. Jealousy over *Naya?* Granted, he'd fantasized about their kiss many times and despised himself for doing so, but maybe it was how well she'd delivered it. How soft and pliant her lush lips had been against his, the way she'd smelled like cookies and tasted like dark cherries.

Wheeler had a mouth on him, but he didn't make lewd remarks to women like Ben did. His brother always managed to cross a line that went from flirtatious to perverse. Seeing his brother's finger slide up her arm like a matchstick ready to ignite had almost made Wheeler flip the table over.

And that shouldn't have happened.

Maybe it just boiled down to sexual infatuation. There was no denying Naya had feminine curves that made a man's tongue want to measure the length of her body. She kept herself groomed. She had an exotic face, long lashes, and the most intense brown eyes he'd ever seen. She never wore ponytails or dressed down in sneakers. Naya polished her nails, waxed her legs, kept her hair in silky brown curls, and looked flawless with or without makeup. Even small touches like toe rings and anklets had never escaped his attention. Not the kind of woman he'd ever been with before. Someone so in control, so perfect and clean—untouched by the evils that lurked in their world.

He tossed the pencil on his desk and studied the tattoos on his arms. They weaved a long and silent story of his dark past.

A knock sounded at the door and he tensed.

"Got a minute?" Reno asked from the hall.

"Give me a second." Wheeler fumbled with his glasses and hid them in a drawer. He crossed the room, stretching his back before he opened the door.

Reno gave him a flat look. "Mind if I come in?"

Wheeler returned to his desk chair and swiveled around to face the bed. "Shut the door. 'Preciate ya."

Reno closed the door and took a seat on the edge of the bed. "I've got a case I'm working on and need to pick your brain. Remember when you had me look up a name that was coming up on wire exchanges for Sweet Treats back when the owner was still alive?"

Wheeler recalled the details immediately. Lexi's old boss, Charles Langston, had died and left her the business. Wheeler had sorted through the files and discovered he'd been sending wire transactions to a man named Maddox Cane. Maddox had not only turned out to be a Shifter, but a loan shark as well.

"I remember," Wheeler said.

Reno lowered his voice. "Maddox was one of *two* loan sharks circling April at the time. The other goes by the name Delgado. Sound familiar? Same guy Izzy's ex was dealing drugs for. He's been a problem that I want to solve, if you get my meaning."

"What's one thing have to do with the other?" Wheeler straightened his long legs and crossed them at the ankle.

Reno glanced at the news website pulled up on Wheeler's laptop. "Did you hear about the Shifter who went missing at the strip club?"

"A sock goes missing, Reno. A woman is *taken*."

"Yeah, well… semantics. Turns out Delgado owns that club. This guy seems to appear whenever there's a hurricane. I don't like it. From what I know, he's a human."

Wheeler sniffed out a laugh. "How the hell do you know that?"

Reno brushed his hand across his short hair and it made a bristly sound. "April still keeps in touch with Maddox."

"Ah, the pet owner," Wheeler said with disdain.

Reno gave him an apologetic look. "She feels sorry for him, like one of those damn animals she's always rescuing."

"Yeah, she took *you* in." Wheeler snorted and twirled the pencil around on his desk.

Everyone knew April had a compassionate heart, but no one in the house had been thrilled the time she rescued a wild squirrel with a cut on its nose. It got loose in the house, and they found it two days later nesting in Denver's underwear drawer.

Reno scratched his jaw and leaned forward on his elbows. "Anyhow, I had another talk with him not long ago, and he confirmed Delgado's been getting deeper into our world. He's purchased some clubs and—"

"Breed clubs?"

"Affirmative. The latest rumor is Delgado's running cage fights. I recently had a case that hit a wall, but Delgado's name was mentioned."

Fuck. Wheeler's stomach twisted into a tight knot. Everyone knew it still went on in the dark corners of the underworld, but you rarely heard about it within city limits. Anyone caught operating fighting rings would be skinned alive by the higher authority. Cage fights were usually run in rural areas of the country—outside the reach of the law. Shifters would fight against each other in animal form while rich assholes placed bets. Sometimes it was consensual, sometimes it wasn't. Usually the latter. Most fighting rings acquired their Shifters off the black market; it was cleaner and didn't leave a trail. Sometimes children were purchased as a future investment, and they would be raised to be as ruthless as their animal would allow. These young boys grew up to become savage warriors without a conscience—prize fighters that brought in millions for big fights.

Wheeler flicked the pencil out of reach. "What does this have to do with the stripper?"

Reno stood up and tucked his hands beneath his armpits. "Don't you think it's a coincidence that two strippers have gone missing, both Shifters, and the club happens to be run by Delgado? A man rumored to be involved with cage fights? Do the math, brother."

Wheeler's jaw slackened.

"No one misses a stripper," Reno continued. "He's got inside access to unmated, replaceable women. Look, you have experience working for men with a lot of money, and I wanted to see what you thought of all this. I don't know how much money is involved with cage fights, but would it be worth buying up clubs to get access to disposable fighters?"

Wheeler waved a hand dismissively. "Whatever he paid for those clubs is a drop in the bucket compared to what he could be earning in cage fights, especially if he's the one organizing the fights. If he's just selling fighters, that'll bring in a little money, but it depends on what their animal is and how stupid of a buyer he can find."

"What do you mean?"

"Certain animals are valued higher. Panthers aren't easy to come by, so they're the crème de la crème. Sometimes they'll pluck a rogue alpha off the streets, but not many investors will buy a stripper just because she's a grizzly or a tough predator. You know the old saying about how it's not the size of the dog in the fight, it's the fight in the dog? They have to be selective with who they buy off the black market because of the money they're paying, so maybe the strippers are just part of the warm-up fight before the big show. Something to titillate the big bettors—show off the skills of the middle-grade fighters they're trying to sell off. I've worked for some shady men in my past, but none of them dabbled in anything like this—at least not that I knew about."

Reno narrowed his eyes. "Yeah, but somehow you seem to have more information than the rest of us when it comes to this area of expertise."

Wheeler didn't like the insinuation. His brothers assumed the men he'd worked for were involved in this kind of shit. Maybe they thought him no better than a criminal.

"Austin!" Lexi screamed from downstairs.

Lexi shouted for Austin all the time because she hated going up and down the stairs, but the urgency in her voice had both men running out the door.

Maizy walked toward the stairs in her pajamas. "What's going on?"

"Go back in your room," Denver snapped.

She warily returned to her room and closed the door. Denver

and Reno ran ahead of Wheeler, Denver wearing only a pair of sweatpants and still half-asleep.

"Austin, get in here!" Lexi shouted again.

"What's wrong?" Reno said, stomping his boots on the wood steps until he reached the bottom.

Lexi stood by a bright window with her arms folded. "Naya's here. She needs to talk to Austin, and I don't know where he is."

"And *this* is a crisis?" Denver tipped his neck and made it crack. Wheeler glanced at the empty foyer.

"Is she outside?" Reno pulled the sheer curtain away and peered at the front porch.

"She's in the bathroom. What's going on around here?" Lexi narrowed her eyes at Reno. "You've been acting weird, and she's not telling me what's wrong. Something's going on, because Naya doesn't just show up unexpectedly with dirty feet and grass on her clothes."

Wheeler advanced toward the half bathroom beneath the stairs—his heart pounding against his chest. Before he made it, Lexi knocked him aside and pressed her body against the door.

"Naya, open the door and let me in. It's Lexi."

Austin appeared in the hallway and approached Lexi, wiping his sweaty forehead with a rag. "I was out back digging up the tree stump. What's going on?"

Lexi whispered in his ear and Austin flicked his eyes around the room.

"I need everyone out," Austin commanded.

"I'm staying," Reno insisted, widening his stance.

Austin stepped forward with a loaded glance. "As your Packmaster, I'm respectfully ordering you to wait outside. This is private business."

"Go on," Lexi parroted. "Everyone out."

His eyes slid to hers and danced with amusement. "That means you too, Ladybug."

She planted her feet in place. "Naya is *my* friend, Austin."

"Who came here asking to speak to the Packmaster. Rank trumps friendship."

"I'm the alpha female."

He lightly gripped her arm. "Let's go, smartass," he said, walking them all outside. "When someone wants to meet in confidence with the Packmaster, they're going to get privacy. If it's something you need to be involved in, I'll call you in. Promise."

He kissed her cheek to make it right and she wriggled away. Austin popped her butt playfully. "We'll kiss and make up later," he growled.

Regardless of love or brotherhood, they all had to respect rank in order to keep the pack united.

Austin swept back his damp hair. "Denver, run upstairs and clear everyone out. Or at the very least, just keep them upstairs. I want privacy on the first floor. We'll be in my office."

Austin headed to the back of the house where William slept and hammered his fist against the door. Moments later, William emerged from the hall with heavy-lidded eyes, wearing only a pair of white boxer briefs.

As a good pack did, they obediently stepped outside and gave the Packmaster his due respect.

CHAPTER 5

AUSTIN SET A GLASS OF lemonade on a wooden coaster in front of me. I took a long sip, still thinking about the night before. Most Shifters could only remember a minute or two after their shift, and some remembered nothing at all. Sometimes it simply depended on how in control our animal wanted to be. I had a vague recollection of seeing two men when my panther turned around to attack, and then something electrical had frightened my animal and caused her to run. When I'd come to, I was lying outside my front door. Worried the men might return, I'd run across the lawn to retrieve my keys and clothes.

I hadn't even gone inside to feed Misha. I'd slipped on my dress and driven straight to Lexi's house. Someone had *forced* me to shift, and waking up without any memory of it had left me in a frazzled state.

Austin moved behind his desk and took a seat. A tiny sparrow hopped on the windowsill to my right and excitedly flapped away when he caught sight of me. On the left wall, I recognized a painting from Lexi's old apartment of a boat in the dock. Austin had a cozy little setup with an L-shaped desk and a laptop to his left.

"You asked to speak to me privately," he began, his forehead still red from the manual labor I'd pulled him away from. He switched on a small fan and aimed it at his face. I could smell his musky scent and understood Lexi's attraction. He was a beast of a man—muscles in all the right places and a serious way of settling his eyes on a person. "Anything you disclose will remain between us unless you want to bring in a third party. I'm guessing you realize a private meeting with a Packmaster is not given freely. But you're a close friend of Lexi's, so on those grounds, I'm offering you my time."

That was a big deal. Packmasters didn't get involved in other Shifter's affairs, and they didn't take kindly to frivolous requests.

"Austin, I need a bodyguard."

His jaw slid to the side. "For what reason? No offense, Naya, but can't your animal take care of herself?"

I averted my eyes, uncertain of how much information to disclose. "Please keep this between us," I said. "I don't want anyone else in my business. I'm a single woman, and it's not in my best interest to have my personal affairs become gossip."

He nodded slowly. "I understand where you're coming from. What's this about?"

I took another sip of lemonade and the ice clinked against the glass. After setting it down, I used the condensation on my fingertips to wipe a smudge of dirt off my arm. "Last night, a man knocked me down and pinned me on my stomach. I didn't see him because he had a tight grip on my hair and it was dark. He used a device," I said, holding my finger up to my eye. "A quick strobe light—I've never seen anything like it before. Not that small. Precise enough in rhythm to force my animal out."

Concern blanketed his expression. His frosty blue eyes seemed lighter against his dark hair and pensive eyebrows. "Why would someone force you to shift? Did they know what your animal is?"

I smoothed out the rough edges in my voice. "No, but they do now. They couldn't have been Shifters or else the flickering would have made them shift too. That's all I can tell you, and I'm asking you to respect my privacy. I'm coming to you because you have connections, and I don't trust anyone else—not with this. I think you love Lexi enough that you wouldn't do anything to hurt a friend. We've had a couple of girls go missing and…"

I couldn't mention Reno helping or it could land him in a world of trouble. While he was a PI and selected his own cases, the Packmaster might consider it a conflict of interest to help a friend of the family, not to mention here I was, asking for *another* favor from the Weston pack and depleting his resources.

"What makes you think they'll come back for you?" he asked in a raspy voice.

When a muffled sound came from outside the door, I paused and waited for silence. "They weren't trying to rob me. I woke up and all my money was still on the lawn—a lot of money. I'm a last-resort kind of girl, Austin, and you're my last resort. Money is no object. Just for a few days; I wouldn't ask any more of your time."

He sighed through his nose and leaned back. "I'll have Reno—"

"Not him," I quickly said, then masked it with a smile. "Nothing personal, but he's... with April." I gracefully waved my hand. "I... I would feel terrible if something happened to someone in your pack who was mated. April's a sweet girl, and I wouldn't dream of putting her mate in danger. You don't have to tell me his name or what pack he's from. All I need is a man to watch over me while I look into a few things."

Austin brushed back his messy hair and stood up. "How much can you afford?"

"Two hundred a night is the most I can pay. What's the going rate? Is that too little?"

He walked around the desk to my left, a few pieces of dirt crumbling off his shoes. "Two hundred is fine. I'll keep this between us, and I won't assign anyone who's mated. Now that you mention it, I'd prefer it that way."

I would have felt terrible if anyone in Lexi's pack got hurt. Aside from that, Reno *couldn't* watch me. I'd already asked him to investigate the kidnapping.

"Let's keep this between us. If you have to tell Lexi anything in the throes of passion, just say I'm having issues with my manager and I asked for your advice. She already knows there's some drama going on at work. And I don't care who you hire or where he comes from; just make sure it's someone you trust. I'll pay extra."

"Are you working tonight?"

"No, it's my night off." I cupped my elbows and stood up, sitting on the edge of his desk as he lingered by the door. A silly part of me didn't want to leave. I felt protected in this house and understood the power of a pack, something my kind didn't have. I thought about asking to stay over, but aside from imposing on his kindness, I'd never bring my Misha into a house full of wolves.

Just the idea of them chasing her around made my panther want to scratch someone on the ass.

"Will you be home?" he asked. "I'll put someone on you today, but I need to know where you'll be."

"I have to go back to my apartment and take a shower. I feel like a walking hairball, and I shudder to think about the pedicure I'm going to need after running around without shoes like a hillbilly." I pursed my lips while staring at my feet. "It shouldn't take long. After that, I'm heading back to Club Sin to speak with some of the girls. It's a slow period at the club, so I'll hang around until your man shows up."

Austin raked his fingers through his sweaty hair a few times. "He'll be there no later than noon, and you won't even know he's watching. After twelve, you can go wherever you need to. Maybe you should pack up a few things and stay at a hotel."

"Waste of money, not to mention false security," I said, tugging a leaf stem from my hair. "I'm already paying you, and no one drives me out of my home like a rodent. Hopefully those men were nothing but a bunch of pranksters in the middle of a juvenile initiation or dare." I reached out and clasped Austin's wrist. "I know we're not the same, but thank you for not turning me away."

His eyebrow arched with a curious expression, but I knew nothing about his history with panthers. Prejudices existed among the Breeds and weren't easy to eliminate. It's why I enjoyed working in the club; everyone who entered put those divisions aside.

"I don't turn anyone away based on their animal, even if it's a deer."

I winked playfully and opened the door. "Maybe I'm a chimpanzee."

Austin's boisterous laugh filled the open hall and I matched his slow gait. "I'll see if I can find you a banana on your way out."

"On a side note, I know you and Lexi met with the Packmasters and filled out the paperwork to be official mates, but maybe you should consider having a ceremony. It's not the Shifter way, but Lexi grew up thinking she was going to be wearing a wedding dress with flower girls throwing pink petals at her feet." I clutched his arm. "Plus, it would give me an excuse to dress up in a gown as a bridesmaid. It looks like so much fun from the movies I've seen!"

He chuckled warmly and shook his head. "Unless Lexi tells me that's what she wants, I'm not doing it."

I sighed and rolled my eyes dramatically. "Of *course* she's not going to tell you she wants it. It wouldn't be as special if it was *her* idea."

Austin fished in his pockets and jingled a few coins. "Everyone knows she's my mate and that's all that matters."

I skipped a step ahead of him, talking over my shoulder. "Maybe so, Austin Cole, but every woman wants a party in her honor."

"I suppose that would mean I'd have to buy a ring like Jericho did for Izzy. Then where does it end? Next thing you know, she'll expect me to give her anniversary gifts, and then I'll get in trouble for not remembering—"

"Aha!" I spun on my heel. "So *that's* what this is about. You're afraid of forgetting a special day for the next five hundred years."

He shrugged indifferently. "It's not the Shifter way."

"Maybe a compromise needs to be made. Lexi grew up human, and no matter how much you instill your Shifter ways in her, part of her will always cling to their customs. What do you think her brother, Wes, would have wanted? Maybe having a declaration among the local Packmasters and a signed document isn't enough. Maybe Lexi wants to feel pretty for a day."

He moved forward toward the front door. "Now that's where you're wrong." Austin peered at Lexi through the glass. She was leaning over the railing with her feet in the air, the wind blowing her long hair to one side. "My woman is pretty every damn day, and I make sure she knows it."

<hr />

After heading home and taking a deliciously hot shower, I put on a lovely beige dress with a sexy V-neck and paired it with my favorite black ankle boots. Maybe the shoes were out of season, but I loved high heels and studded cuffs. Before leaving the apartment, I made sure Misha got extra food and kisses.

When I reached Club Sin, Reno had sent a text message asking for my location so he could give me the scoop on what he'd found out so far. I ordered the breakfast plate of hash browns, sausage links, and two pieces of buttered Texas toast, then chose a wooden table in the back—far from the customers.

A pair of aviators landed on the table, and Reno grabbed the small chair next to me and spun it around. He sat down with his thick arms folded over the curved back. I giggled when he glanced at my plate and his stomach growled like an angry bear.

"Have a sausage," I said politely.

"That's like offering an alligator a chicken nugget. So here's the deal. I can't track down your friend based on what I've got. No surveillance cameras mean no record of the kidnapping, no license plate, no indication of what direction they headed. The girl who witnessed it go down couldn't describe the men because it was dark and she only caught a glimpse before they sped off, but she thinks there were two—one driving and the other in the back."

Chills swept over my arms when I thought of the two men from last night. I set my fork down and reached in my lap. "This is for your trouble." I handed him the small envelope of cash.

He swung his eyes briefly toward the stage before looking back at my plate. "I found Skye's address, but no one else lives there."

"What about her daughter? She mentioned that her cousin watches her while she's at work."

His brow sloped down and he touched the small scar on his bottom lip. "A mother wouldn't leave her kid at home alone, so the cousin's probably still watching her. I'll check it out and see if they know anything about Skye. You mind telling me why you showed up at the house this morning like someone who woke up in the woods without a clue of what the hell just happened? Trust me, I know that look."

I decided if Reno was already on the case, he needed to know everything. I gulped down the rest of my milk and pushed the glass aside. "Two men tackled me outside my apartment. They didn't assault me or take the pile of cash I was carrying."

His knuckles turned white when he made tight fists with his hands. "What the fuck did they want?"

I shook my head, a wavy swath of hair falling in front of my face. "They forced me to shift. They used a device to lure my animal out. When I woke up, hours had passed and there was no sign of them. Look, I'm not going to beat around the bush. Something's going on in this club and none of us are safe. I'm not going to sit around putting on mascara while someone is kidnapping these women. The local Packmasters don't want to be involved because, let's face it, they think we're nothing but trash. Maybe all you see on that stage is a pretty girl and a nice pair of tits, but these girls have big dreams, and that's why they work their asses off so they can take care of themselves."

"I'm not here to judge," he said, holding up his hands.

"Neither am I. But you and I need to have an understanding that this is personal. Skye has a baby out there somewhere who's wondering when her mommy is coming home."

Reno scratched his bristly jaw. "Damn," he murmured. "Look, I can't promise anything. I don't have enough to go on that'll tell me where they are, or if they're still alive. Humans could have taken them for all I know. I see that shit on the news all the time." He reached out and neatly lined up the salt and pepper shakers, wiping a few granules off the table.

"Count the money and let me know if that's enough. If the extra work will cost more, then I'll have to dig into my savings."

He peered inside the white envelope. "That's plenty."

"I want to go with you to see her cousin, so give me a call when you plan to make the trip."

"Hold up," he said, sitting back in his chair. "That's not the deal."

I scooted my chair closer to him and softened my voice. "If you don't let me tag along, I'll find out the address myself and go alone. I'd rather you do the questioning since you know the right things to ask. I just want to make sure her baby is okay."

Reno's face relaxed and he gave a reluctant sigh. "Fine. I'm not about to grill a woman, so don't expect me to pull out my gun and demand answers. She might remember Skye talking about strange calls or someone hanging around her too much. Look, are you going to eat that sausage or not?"

I gracefully stood up and patted his shoulder. "I love a man who can't say no to a nice piece of meat," I said suggestively. "Call me when you get the address."

Reno was already polishing off my plate when I left the table. One of the new girls strutted by and I seized her wrist. "Do you see the caveman sitting at the table behind me?"

She peered over my shoulder. "Mmm. Sure do."

"Bring him another plate, and pronto. But don't waste your time hitting on him; he's mated."

Her shoulders sagged. "Coming up."

I adjusted my purse strap and sat at the bar, staring at the blue clock on the right wall. Three more hours until noon.

So I waited.

After Reno ordered two more breakfast plates, he lingered awhile longer. I watched him from my spot at the bar. Wolves fascinated me. Especially how loyal they were to their mates. Not once did he look up at the stage with lust in his eyes. Reno was obviously a sexual man, but April must fulfill all his needs and then some. He only noticed the male customers, and he watched them closely. When Dean waltzed in and barked out a few orders, Reno sat back and clocked every move he made. I realized how exceptional Reno was at his job and why he made a good living as a private investigator. He wasn't just on a case when he felt like it but seized every opportunity to collect information. He talked with a few girls and then the bartender before finally leaving.

Fifteen minutes after twelve, I slipped off the barstool and headed out. If Austin was a man of his word, then I now had a bodyguard keeping a respectful distance.

The bright sunshine pierced my eyes when I pushed open the door. The heat settled on me like a heavy blanket, and I slipped on a pair of designer sunglasses.

What I really needed to do was go shopping. The club didn't pay for costumes or accessories—that came out of our own pockets. But if it helped garner more tips, then it was money well spent.

I located a novelty store, and after snooping around for a half hour, found a long plastic chain and a leather collar. Ideas for my next performance were bubbling, but I hadn't quite figured out how to tie it all together. When I discovered costumes in a back room, I practically threw my money at the store clerk.

Bags in hand, I happily stepped onto the cracked sidewalk and caught a cool breeze that ruffled my hair. As I approached my car, which was parked off the main street, my pace slowed to a stop.

Someone had slashed my tires. I walked to the other side of my car and realized they had slashed all four of them. Annoyed, I looked up and down the street, wondering why no one had seen it and called the police. I pondered calling them myself, just so I could flirt with a man in uniform. We didn't involve humans in our business, but I sure loved any opportunity to interact with the men in blue.

A loud engine roared in my direction and a gunmetal-grey Camaro screeched to a stop. "Get in, kitty cat." Wheeler draped his tatted arm across the car door.

Was this a joke? If Austin had sent Wheeler to act as my bodyguard, then I was just going to have to—

"Whoever sliced up your tires still has a big knife, and now you don't have a ride. I suggest you get in before I change my mind."

I narrowed my eyes and walked toward him like a woman who had just caught her lover cheating with another woman. How was a man like him going to protect me? Wheeler came from Planet Asshole and didn't even *like* women! I pulled open the heavy door, tossed my bags in the back, and got in. Before I had a chance to buckle up, his foot dropped onto the gas pedal like a stone and we took off.

"Is this how you normally pick up women?" I said, struggling to buckle my seatbelt.

"Look, I'm not about cloak and daggers," he began. "Austin told me to watch you like a Peeping Tom, but that ain't how this is going down. I chased the asshole who slashed your tires, but halfway up the street, I realized that might have been a diversion to get me away from you. And then I return to find your dumb ass hanging out in the street by the car, practically saying *Take me! I'm all yours!*" he said in a feminine voice, wiggling his fingers.

I removed a small clock that was adhered to his dash and tossed it out the window.

The car lurched. "What the hell did you do that for?" he snarled.

Cool air swirled through my hair and I leisurely straightened the wrinkles on my dress. "Each time you speak to me in that manner, I'm going to punish you, be it destroying something personal or striking you with my hand. But I won't allow any man to berate me in such a patronizing tone. If Austin chose you, then I trust his judgment. But keep in mind your Packmaster wouldn't approve if he found out you were harassing his mate's best friend."

He slanted his eyes my way. "Is that a threat?"

"It's a promise. Perhaps you should direct all that hostility toward the men who are slashing my tires with a sharp instrument."

I jerked forward when he slammed the brakes at the red light and leaned over, getting right in my face. "And *mayhap* your impassive tone is what's setting me off. So why don't you drop some of that self-righteous attitude you carry around like you're better than everyone else and just sit quiet for the rest of the ride? 'Preciate ya."

His words cut me more than I allowed him to see. I feigned indifference and looked out the window while inside my heart constricted. I felt more devotion toward those I loved than he could ever fathom. Maybe I was too tough for some men to handle, but it was the only way to gain control in a world of dominant men. Wheeler had never proven himself to be anything but a man who held contempt for women, and he must have assumed because I was a dancer that I didn't have a brain cell in my head.

"Where are we going?" I finally asked.

He slid on a pair of black shades. "Your place. I'll have someone fix your tires and drive your car over."

"Don't you need my keys for that?"

He eased down in his seat, widening his legs a little. "Sweetheart, I've got friends with skilled hands."

"That I don't doubt."

"Why is everything an innuendo with you?"

I chuckled softly. "I can't help it. When someone is so uptight about sex, it just opens a door. Yours just happens to have a welcome mat in front of it."

Wheeler's cheeks flamed and I looked away in surprise. He really *was* uptight about sex. Sometimes I just liked to rile men up because they secretly enjoyed it, but now I was beginning to see the truth: Wheeler was sexually *repressed*. How curious coming from a wolf. I let my curiosity slide when we eased up to my apartment building.

"Stay here and keep the doors locked," he said, tossing his sunglasses onto the dash. "Give me your keys, and I'll make sure the slasher isn't up there making himself a bologna sandwich."

"All yours," I said, dangling them in front of his face. One of the key rings caught his eye—a silver figure of a couple in a sexual position. He snatched them from me and stalked toward the apartment.

"Hmm. All that pent-up frustration," I murmured, watching him climb the stairs. "This should be interesting indeed."

CHAPTER 6

————◦◦◦◦◦————

W HEELER SCOPED OUT THE APARTMENT and stepped back when a fluffy cat slinked around his legs. *"Jesus.* Why doesn't that surprise me?"

He glanced inside her bedroom, which was bereft of color. White curtains, white carpet, and a white bedspread. Naya must have thought she was Snow-Fucking-White. The red chair in the living room stood out like a wound, as if someone had tried to stab this room with judgment. Some people you could figure out by taking a glance around their house—seeing how tidy they kept it, the shitty art they hung on their walls, and how many mirrors they owned. Naya designed her apartment as if royal sheiks would be stopping in for coffee and a hookah. Lexi had mentioned the wild parties Naya threw, but he wondered how it was possible she didn't have stains on her furniture. Perhaps she didn't have the kind of parties he was used to.

A deep chuckle rolled out of his chest when he imagined what she'd do to a man who spilled merlot on her sofa. For some reason, the mental image of her putting that man in his place brought him great amusement.

His phone rang and he pulled it out of his back pocket. "Speaking."

"Wheeler? It's Lexi."

Shit.

"*Where* are you?" she asked in a slow, accusatory manner that told him she knew exactly where he was, or at the very least, who he was with.

"In bed with my cock buried deep inside—"

"All right, that's enough. I know you're at Naya's, and if you're with her, then I know for a fact nothing is buried anywhere."

He nudged the furry cat away with his foot. "What makes you say that?"

"Because Naya goes for fat wallets, not fatheads. Look, I overheard Austin talking to you this morning. What's going on?"

"Can't say."

Lexi was known for pressing her ear against doors. Shifters respected pack rules, but she was raised by humans and often let her curious nature run away with her, even if it wasn't in her best interest to do so.

She gave an exasperated sigh. "I'm just going to assume that you're there to help, but if Naya's in trouble, I want to know. She won't tell me, and I can't make her. Just… just take care of her and make sure nothing happens. She mentioned a girl at work went missing, and now I'm worried that has something to do with why you're there."

Wheeler twisted the rod on the blinds and peered down at Naya in the car. She was holding a silver compact in front of her face and touching up her burgundy lips. He wandered to the open doorway and leaned against the doorjamb. "You don't have anything to worry about."

"I'm trusting you. If it's serious, see if you can talk her into staying with us."

"Austin won't go for it." Wheeler tapped the toe of his foot against the frame to block the cat from getting out. "He's not going to open his door for an outsider who might bring trouble to the pack. That's the way things work in our world."

"Well, I'll just have a talk with him if that's the case," she replied in a defiant voice. "Is Naya in the room with you?"

"No."

"Don't keep me in the dark if something happens. Okay? And whatever you do, don't drink her coffee."

He shut the door and ambled down two flights of stairs. "Why's that?"

"Trust me," she said with a haughty laugh. "If she offers, just tell her you don't drink coffee or that you're on a caffeine-restricted diet."

"Gotta run." Wheeler hung up and tucked the phone in his pocket.

Naya's dress blew up when she got out of the car and something shifted inside him when he saw her bronze legs. Naya's body had a feminine curve that would make any Breed male with a heartbeat stop and look.

All the women Wheeler had bedded were skinny with light tresses, so the fact that a woman like Naya made him as hard as granite confused him. Arousal wasn't even the right word, because that implied some level of restraint and control.

Wheeler repressed those thoughts and stopped in the middle of the grassy area. "All clear," he said loudly, tossing the keys in her direction. They arced through the air, and instead of catching them, she put her hands on her hips and watched them slap against the concrete in front of her. With demure grace, she crouched down and lifted them with two fingers. Women in service jobs knew the rules about bending over in front of Shifter wolves. Gestures like that were an invitation, so most had mastered the art of the dip.

But for just a fleeting moment, he wished she had ignored the rules.

I didn't break stride when I breezed past Wheeler. We had similar personalities, and so as long as he didn't insult me directly, I could tolerate his condescending attitude.

Once I reached my apartment at the top of the stairs, I unzipped my boots and held them between my fingers. "Take off your shoes, although I can already see I'm going to need to steam clean again," I said, glaring at a few dirty spots by the door.

I loved an immaculate house. It felt like every filthy thing going on in my life was erased when I walked through the door. Little Maizy was the only one who appreciated my pretty furniture, and I always told her that a woman should treat herself like a princess and not expect anyone else to do it for her. While I hoped to find a good man someday who could give me a better life, I wasn't holding my breath. So I pampered myself with little luxuries. There's something so pure about the color white, and I surrounded myself with it. Anything that wasn't upholstered was made of glass—such as tables—and the chairs surrounding my dining table were all white. The only colors in my apartment were a few jade plants and my red chair.

Lexi called it my throne, but I'd fallen in love the moment I laid eyes on it at a garage sale. Everything in my home had been purchased new except for that chair. Lexi used to love going on weekend excursions to thrift shops and garage sales. Never had I imagined I'd be buying used furniture with imperfections, but something about its antique regality appealed to me—even with all its imperfections. I felt more at home in that chair than anywhere else, as if something inanimate could possibly love me back.

So when Wheeler plopped down in it, my insides roiled.

"I'll put on some coffee," I offered.

"No," he said tersely. "I uh… I don't drink coffee."

"That's because you haven't had *my* coffee."

Only Lexi turned down my coffee, and that's because she was always on a caffeine-restricted diet. I put the pot on and drew up the blinds in the living room to bring in the light.

"Would you like to sit in the dining room?"

"No."

I pressed my lips together and pulled the barstools out. "Here. We'll have coffee at the bar."

"Not feelin' it."

I whirled around and clenched my fists. Suddenly, Wheeler's brooding expression ebbed away, replaced with a look of satisfaction.

I had yet to see Wheeler in anything but sleeveless shirts that showed off his ink. Occasionally he'd put on a tight T-shirt, but I didn't think he owned a single garment with buttons or cuffs. Aside from the tattoos, the one thing that swiftly caught my attention was his sparkling brown eyes. They were the color of caramel or sweet tea—just as pale and beautiful as you could imagine the color brown to be. They seemed out of place against the dark contours of his serious expression. Wheeler's hair was brown, disheveled, and longer on top than on the sides. While he was a genetic copy of his brother, Ben, everything about Wheeler stood out.

Especially sitting in my apartment.

His eyes danced with amusement. "You don't like people sitting in your chair, do you?"

"What makes you say that?"

Wheeler was about six feet tall, and he stretched out his long legs until his feet reached the edge of my coffee table. Then he put one heel on it, crossed his ankles, wiggled his toes beneath his white socks, and watched me for a reaction.

I tried to smother it, I really did. But seeing my glass table teeter under the weight of his legs sent me flying into the room. "Let's be adults about this, shall we? You can either sit in your car for the next twelve hours, listening to repeats of Lady Gaga on the radio, or you can show some civility and I'll let you stay inside and watch television."

His eyes flicked over to the TV and back to mine.

"I'll get your coffee, Wheeler. Please try not to spill it."

"You shouldn't talk to a man like he's a child," he said in a smoky voice.

I peered over the bar while filling our mugs. "And you shouldn't speak to a woman like she's a servant," I muttered under my breath.

"What was that?" he yelled.

I strolled into the living room and knocked his feet off my table with a nudge of my leg. I set the cup on a coaster and then took a seat on the couch.

Wheeler leaned forward on his elbows, glaring at the cup. "So why do you strip for money?"

I wasn't offended by his candor. I preferred a man who spoke his mind. My mama had once told me that a woman should measure a man's worth by how well he could carry a conversation, and the best kind of foreplay was verbal.

"Your packs can pool money together, but I'm a loner. It's not as if I can simply go to college and get a great job at an insurance company; that's the human world. If I were a Vampire, I'd have no problem getting a job as a bodyguard. But as it stands, I'm a Shifter. A *female* Shifter. That means that unlike you, no one is going to hire me as a bounty hunter. Tell me what I'm left with as a single woman to make a substantial income?"

"So mate," he suggested, lifting his cup. "Isn't that what your kind does?"

I sipped my coffee and set it on the table, my eyes fixed on the ink pattern on his bicep of a justice scale and dagger. "Do you think I'm not looking for a good man?"

He blew the steam from his mug and when he took his first sip, he began choking.

I furrowed my brow. "Something wrong with your coffee?"

Wheeler grimaced and wiped his mouth with the back of his hand. "No, it's uh… hot. So with all the Shifters who come into your club, you're that picky?"

Misha slinked around my legs and released a soft purr.

"A woman is allowed to have high standards. I need to make sure he can manage his money."

"Ah," he said, leaning back and crossing one leg over the other. "So it's all about money."

"I'm going to live *hundreds* of years, Wheeler. Do you think I want to be an exotic dancer for the rest of my life? I'm afraid I don't have the talent Lexi has to run a bakery. I deserve a better life, and mating for money will give me the security I need to survive. I'm working my tail off to make sure I have enough set aside in case that doesn't happen because, let's face it, we both know there *is* no Prince Charming." I dropped a cube of sugar in my coffee and stirred it with a thin straw. "You can judge me all you like—that's your prerogative. A mating of convenience is not a mortal sin, and plenty of men mate a beautiful woman with zero intelligence. Not everyone believes in love."

"Who said I believe in love?"

Misha suddenly leapt onto his lap and his arms flew up.

I chuckled and crossed my legs, leaning against the armrest. "You're the first wolf she's ever approached. She doesn't even warm up to Lexi, and that's saying something. Did you eat a tuna sandwich this morning?" I quipped.

He bounced his knees in a futile attempt to make her jump down. Misha merely sniffed his armpit and meowed once.

"Mind collecting your cat?"

"Misha's goal is to win over anyone who dislikes her."

Wheeler locked his hands behind his head, glaring at me. "Sounds like your pussy is a glutton for punishment."

I laughed at his innuendo. "Touché. You catch on quick."

"Well, you two just seem to have a lot in common."

His comment nestled in the pit of my stomach, and the conversation went from playful to something else. "How are we alike?"

He opened and closed his legs, but Misha just stepped up on the armrest, placed her paw on his shoulder, and began grooming the hair behind his ear. "Annoying, persistent, and you're only attracted to men who don't like you."

"If that were true, *I'd* be the one crawling all over your lap with my tongue in your ear, not Misha."

When his lips parted and his eyes hooded, that's when I knew that despite the verbal match between us, Wheeler was physically attracted to me. I'm not sure why that aroused me, but it did. My suggestion of seducing him lingered in my thoughts a few seconds too long, so I quickly got up and put Misha on the floor.

I leaned forward and gripped the top of the chair on either side of his head. "I don't like this situation any more than you do, but I've never had anyone speak to me this way. I don't form unhealthy friendships with people, but this isn't exactly a friendship. I need a bodyguard, and neither of us seems to have any choice in the matter. So let's just play nice, okay?"

His eyes glided down my neck and settled between my breasts. Wheeler's pupils widened and, my God, I needed to get away from him. The closer I got, the more I picked up his heady scent. Wheeler was the opposite of the refined men in my life—powerful men with expensive clothes and imported cologne. Most were shorter or had a leaner frame than his medium build. Something began to culminate between us that I knew he must have felt, because he didn't have a comeback. I wondered how it would feel to have those inked arms wrapped around my body, for the bristles on his face to scratch against my stomach as he laved my breast with his tongue. Would his hands feel as rough as they looked? Was he a gentle lover or animalistic?

The ropes of muscle in his arms were taut from the tight grip he had on the armrests of the chair.

Oh, no. This couldn't be happening.

My cell phone rang and snapped me out of my fantasies. I stood up and put my hands on my hips. "I have a feeling that before this is all over, we're going to end up killing each other."

A sardonic smile tugged at the corners of his mouth. "Now that sounds like fun."

CHAPTER 7

WHEELER'S PRESENCE IN MY APARTMENT that afternoon was insufferable. He watched two vampire movies and then brought in a bag of beef jerky from his car to gnaw on. When he slung his legs over the arm of my chair and took a nap, I retreated to my balcony to soak up a little sun in my Adirondack chair. Lexi called, and I changed the topic each time she tried to squeeze information out of me. I had a great deal of respect for Austin's willingness to help; therefore, it wasn't my place to tell his mate something he hadn't disclosed to her himself. I'd lose the pack's respect for not honoring the confidence of their Packmaster, and I needed to stay in their good graces.

She reminded me about their upcoming costume party. Humans only held parties for special occasions, but we didn't play by the same rules. When I used to live in Canada, a Mage had invited me to a masked ball at his secluded mansion, and I'd been deliriously thrilled to go. He'd supplied carriage rides around the property, and we'd dined like kings and queens—drinking from goblets and sampling fine cuisine. Many immortals had old money, so they lived extravagantly. My parties were big, but not showy. Only those I trusted to behave themselves were allowed inside my apartment—everyone else had to mingle on the stairwell or open grounds. I always extended invitations to my human neighbors so no one would call the police.

Although I certainly didn't mind whenever they did show up. I adored men in uniform. I found the symbolism of their attire in relation to their position of power extremely sexy.

Later that afternoon, Wheeler's friend rang my bell to hand me the keys to my Trans Am. Since he'd replaced my tires, I paid him. I guessed every man had "a guy" he could call on a whim who would perform random requests without question.

Sitting around the apartment with a wolf who loved gothic movies wasn't my idea of a good time, so I decided a wax would be less painful to endure. Wheeler offered to drive, and I couldn't help but smile as we pulled up to the shop and I saw the look of objection on his face when he read the sign.

Suffice it to say, he waited in the car.

For Shifters, a good Brazilian wax requires no special care afterward. A quick shift in the bathroom heals up any skin irritation and we're no worse for wear. Luckily my panther was a cooperative girl, but I still went to my usual Breed shop.

After a detailed wax and sprucing up in the bathroom, I headed out to the car feeling refreshed and smooth. The sun warmed my bare shoulders, and Wheeler was snoozing in his Camaro with the windows down.

"Miss me?" I asked, slamming the door shut.

He had a stick of beef jerky in his mouth, his head reclined and eyes closed. Wheeler had a large Adam's apple, and I had an impulsive temptation to run my finger across it.

"Did you get your lady parts all taken care of?"

"Baby smooth. Wanna touch?"

His head bobbed up and he shifted in his seat, stepping on the clutch and firing up the engine. "Is this the fun I have to look forward to for the next week?"

I set my purse on the floor. "Would you rather I be doing something more dangerous to keep things exciting?"

He bit off the end of his stick and chewed. "Maybe."

An old man with a poodle lollygagged in front of the car, looking around as if searching for someone. I stroked my bottom lip with my finger, contemplating something Reno had mentioned about Delgado orchestrating the kidnappings. The only problem was he didn't have evidence to support his theory.

"Take me back to work," I said.

Wheeler scratched his short beard. "I thought you were off?"

I touched my hair, playing with a dark curl. "I'm going to break into someone's office. How's that for a little danger?"

He threw the car in gear and scared the old man with a rev of his engine. "Say no more."

"I would have never taken you for the kind who looks for trouble." And I wasn't being sarcastic. Lexi had always described Wheeler as the brains in the family—a former financial advisor who used to work for high-and-mighty immortals. But I couldn't figure him out. Intellectual men weren't usually thrill seekers, and vice versa. So who was the real Wheeler?

"I don't look for trouble, kitty cat. I just take her out on a date every so often and show her a good time."

I snatched the beef jerky from his hand and tossed it out the window. "Chewing on meat in public makes you look boorish."

"That so? I'm sorry if I can't be as sophisticated as some of the hoity-toity men you hang out with."

"And I suppose I can't be as submissive as some of the bitches you hang out with."

Wheeler had his right hand on the steering wheel and peered over his shoulder at me. "Touché," he said in a silken voice.

He turned onto another street, and I couldn't take my eyes off his tattoos. I was tempted to trace my fingers across the patterns that blended into a uniform piece of art. Why would someone get so many tattoos and seal them with liquid fire? Alphas did it to be recognized, but most avoided the notion of tattoos. It was something humans did to be different, but we already *were* different.

"You can look at them if you want," he said.

"Do you have them all over your body?"

I wasn't a woman who blushed, but I did feel a subtle warmth rising in my cheeks. Could I have been less tactful? I risked a glance and saw he was focused on the road ahead.

"I have a few more," he replied in words as thick as honey. Wheeler had a low register, but not overly baritone. Just a little smoky and mysterious, and only when he got upset did it sharpen in volume and clarity. There was power behind his words when he wanted there to be.

Why on earth am I sitting here thinking about his voice?

I fumbled with my purse and pulled out a stick of gum. "Would you like a piece?"

He snatched the stick and sniffed out a quiet laugh. "I never turn down a piece."

"I see I'm rubbing off on you."

He opened his mouth as if to say something and then snapped it shut.

I chewed on my cinnamon gum and leaned toward the window— the sunshine felt enormously wonderful. Days like this made me regret my panther couldn't bask in the warmth of a summer's day. A truck pulled up beside us and the guy did a double take. His friend leaned over and smiled wide. Then the driver shaped his fingers like a V and put them under his mouth, flicking his tongue up and down.

"Working the pole tonight?" he asked.

"Not for you, sugar," I said. "Why don't you take that tip money you've been saving up and splurge on a bag of potato chips?"

I turned away and noticed Wheeler's eyes were sharp and fiery as he leaned across the car, checking out who I was talking to.

"They recognize me from work," I said smoothly. "I get that every so often from the cheap customers who like to make me work extra hard for their dollar."

"How 'bout you roll up your window and I won't have to come over there and crush your skull?" Wheeler barked at them.

"Please, just ignore them." I touched his arm, which extended in front of me and gripped the door.

Without thinking, I traced my index finger over a chain inked on his bicep that circled around but didn't close. The final link was broken. Near it was a wolf. Tribal patterns and images created a visual display, and I noticed his right wrist had a thick band around it. My God, these were the sexiest things I'd ever seen.

His skin felt nice beneath my fingertips. Wheeler's eyes slanted my way, and he was only a few inches from my face—so close I could smell him.

"You should tell me about these sometime," I said, still outlining one of the tribal patterns with my finger. "I'd love to know why you chose to hide beneath all this ink."

He suddenly wrenched away. "You think I'm hiding? This is me, inside and out."

"You really want people to believe that, don't you?"

Something flashed in his eyes before he looked down, but I caught it. Wheeler switched on the radio and cranked up the volume. "It doesn't matter what the world believes—it's what I believe."

When we arrived at the club, Wheeler remained quiet, shadowing me as I surreptitiously made my way through the back door using an emergency key. I waved at one of the girls coming out of the restroom and suddenly felt a flurry of nerves causing my heart to speed up. When I approached Delgado's office, I turned the brass knob and found it locked.

"Damn," I whispered. "Why did I think it would be that simple? What was I thinking?"

Wheeler knelt down and pulled out a slim metal stick from his wallet. "Turn around, sweetheart. Use your body to hide me."

I snorted. "My body isn't big enough to hide all of you."

He put the metal pin between his teeth and tucked his wallet in his back pocket. "If your ass were as big as your mouth, I'd have all the privacy a man could afford."

"Well then," I purred. "Since there's not much to look at..." I turned my back on him and leaned my left shoulder against the wall, doing my best to keep him hidden. Of course, that meant my derrière was about two inches from his face. Call it my subtle way of sticking it to a wolf.

He released a ragged breath and I peered over my shoulder, watching him pick the lock with a shaky hand.

"Is this what they teach in wolf business school?" I asked conversationally. "You sure are a jack-of-all-trades."

"You'd be surprised what a man in my position has had to do."

"Hmm," I moaned, shifting my hips. "I'm quite familiar with

that position, and I don't think there's anything you could do that would surprise me."

I squeaked when he poked my bottom with the tip of his sharp object.

"Surprised?" he asked with a low chuckle.

"Hurry up," I hissed. "Someone's going to catch us."

The door swung open and by the time I turned around, Wheeler was already inside. He poked his head out. "Are you waiting for the bus? Get in here."

I rolled my eyes and closed the door behind me.

Wheeler folded his arms and lowered his chin. I studied his profile as he approached the mahogany desk. The lines in his face were sharp beneath his facial hair, giving him such a hardened appearance. It seemed contradictory to his soft lips and the intelligence brimming in his eyes.

"Whose office is this?" he asked, lifting an ivory figurine of an elephant from the desk. "Because he has shit taste."

"Didn't you read the sign on the door? This is Damian Delgado's office—the owner of the club."

Wheeler spun around. Then he took another careful look at the room, tugging at the fabric of his black shirt. "So this is where the big cheese hangs out," he murmured.

"I think he might have something to do with the missing girls. You know the laws on slander; I can't make an accusation without proof."

He walked around the polished desk and sat in the brown leather chair. "What makes you think he's involved?"

I placed my hands on the desk and leaned forward. "Because I've worked in dozens of clubs, and I know a thing or two about owners. They don't like trouble, but if a girl goes missing, that's something they would immediately address with the staff. I've never spoken to this man—he's never *once* walked the floor. What kind of owner is that?"

"The *human* kind."

I straightened up and my heart raced. "What makes you say that?"

Wheeler leaned back in the chair and put his black boots on the desk, crossing his ankles. "That's the word, but I can see by the look on your face that it doesn't come as a surprise. He's been stirring up trouble in our world for years. Our laws protect humans, so we can't take him down. He must have paid through the nose to buy up these joints. They make a helluva lot more than the human clubs; that's just a fact." He turned his arm slowly, looking at one of his tattoos twisting around like a vine.

I slinked around to the right side and bumped his chair so hard that his feet slipped off the edge of the desk. "This isn't a day spa. Either guard the door like a good little wolf or help me."

"Help you what?"

I knelt down and pulled open a lower drawer. "Look for incriminating evidence. Don't you watch crime shows? Anything that looks suspicious."

"A smart man doesn't leave evidence lying around for someone to find."

"Maybe he's not a smart man. Search those drawers and I'll look through these."

Wheeler pulled open a drawer with a theatrical flick of his wrist. "Well, that sounds like a swell idea. What do we have in here? Oh, look. Pornography." He held up an adult magazine at arm's length and flipped open the page. "This position looks awfully incriminating to me."

"Why don't you take it home and study it under a magnifying glass?" I suggested while digging through a stack of papers. I carefully put them back and noticed a small book with leather binding and a narrow strap that clipped shut. When I opened it, the pages were filled with contact numbers and notes.

"It says here that Jenny likes puppies, baking sugar cookies, and—"

"Spreading her legs in a national magazine? Classy."

The magazine slapped on the desk. "That's pretty high-and-mighty coming from a girl who works a pole."

I stood up and sat on the edge of the desk. "Have you ever seen me dance?" I asked in a sultry voice. I made an extra effort to smooth out the sharp edges in my tone since I was upset. "Obviously you haven't, or you wouldn't have made such an insulting remark. Dancing is a form of art, and while I *can* work a pole, I don't spread my legs or show my breasts when I'm on that stage." I leaned across the desk and slowly grabbed the magazine, gently setting it back in the drawer. When I stretched across him, I couldn't help but notice the rapid pace of his heartbeat throbbing in his jugular. It made me wonder where else that blood might be throbbing. "I suppose you'll find out soon enough when you come to my show."

"Won't even notice since I'll be watching the crowd," he said indifferently, rising to his feet. "How about you finish up in here while I wait in the hall? Someone might be on the other side of the door, and I don't like surprises, so hurry up."

After Wheeler slipped into the hallway, I finished searching the room. The contact book seemed to be the only thing of value, but what if I got caught stealing it? My paranoia was quashed by the fact that Delgado barely visited the club. Once a month—tops. He wouldn't miss this little book for a day or two, and Wheeler could get me back inside to return it. I tucked the book in my purse and flipped off the light.

But my breath caught when I heard talking just outside the door.

"*Shit, shit, shit,*" I whispered. "Fawn, get your little tushy back to work."

Her manner of speech was like a sixteen-year-old California rich girl. She played up that role, always smacking on gum and sometimes dressing too young for her age. I didn't like that type of behavior; men shouldn't be conditioned to find adolescents attractive.

Carefully, I cracked open the door and peered out. She was smiling up at Wheeler, fanning her one-inch false lashes and drawing attention to the three pounds of glitter spattered all over her eyelids. The next thing I knew, Wheeler backed her into the wall and pressed his entire body against her.

I'm not sure why, but that made my insides crawl. It made me want to grab that stupid elephant off the desk and knock him in the head with it. But since she was buried beneath six feet of man,

I slipped out the door and slinked in front of the bathroom across the hall.

That's when I got a clear view. He had his face buried in her neck, her hand clawed at his black jeans, the hem of her plaid skirt riding up...

"Ahem!" I said, clearing my throat. "Sugar, I'm done powdering my nose."

When he didn't stop, I slung my purse in the air and whacked him in the back of the head. He tensed and then glared at me over his shoulder.

"Sorry to interrupt," I said unapologetically. "I have to go do that thing."

Fawn flipped her long hair back to make sure her tresses weren't shielding her breasts, which were small, round, and aiming bullets at Wheeler through the sheer fabric posing as a shirt. "Sorry, Naya. Didn't realize you had claim on him."

Wheeler looked between us as if caught in the crossfire.

I straightened the strap of my purse over my shoulder. "Sweetie, any man I have claim over wouldn't need another woman to fool around with. I'm all the woman he'd need," I said in a silken voice.

Wheeler's right eyebrow arched in slow motion.

Fawn stroked his arm with the tips of her fingernails. "Another time, daddy." She strutted off, swinging her hips like a pendulum.

Wheeler pivoted around and we headed toward the back door. "What's with that *daddy* shit?"

"Maybe you should tell me, papa. You're the one with his hands up her skirt."

His arm flew out and pushed open the door to the back of the club. I winced at the bright light, and Wheeler's boots crunched on the gravel as we headed toward his car.

"My hand wasn't up her skirt. And for your information, I did that so you could get out."

"Such self-sacrifice," I said over the hood of the car as he unlocked the door. "Some men throw themselves on grenades, but you chose the nearest half-naked woman."

He cut me a sharp glare and got in the car. The heat swelled inside and I rolled down my window while he turned the engine over.

"I could have attempted an intellectual conversation to distract her, but she didn't look like the girl most likely to talk about the influential works of Jackson Pollock."

"You like his paintings?"

Wheeler slipped on his sunglasses. "He's a fucking genius."

"He splattered paint on canvas. An elephant can do that." I waved at a gnat and adjusted the air as we pulled out of the parking lot.

"Explosive creativity. Not everything can be outlined in pencil beforehand. That's a man who thought outside the conventional box. Sometimes things that make the least sense are the most interesting. People don't give enough credit to abstract artists."

"Perhaps you should have let *him* paint your arms."

A laugh burst out of Wheeler—rich and bold—the first I think I'd ever heard. It sent goose pimples up my arms and made me smile along with him. When he didn't say anything back, I lingered on that infectious laugh a little longer. The warm texture of it, how alive he sounded, and I suddenly got a glimpse of the passion beneath his dark, brooding exterior.

Wheeler adjusted his visor. "Find anything back there, Sherlock?"

"Just the little book of names. We'll see what that unearths. After I'm done with it, I'll need you to sneak me back in to return it."

"I think we need to pull over and eat."

My stomach was growling and I hadn't noticed. How could he hear it over the engine? "I could use a bite, although if there's a beef jerky diner in town, I'm going to have to decline your offer."

"Just for that, you're eating by yourself."

"Excuse me?"

The car lurched into a parking space at a burger joint and he shut off the engine. "I'm hungry, and seeing how I'm the one driving the car, that leaves you with little choice in the matter. You obviously have no respect for me, and I'd rather not share a meal with someone who can't shut off the insults."

"You're one to talk!"

"Well, I guess that solves our problem. Maybe fire and kerosene don't go together for a reason. I'll sit at the bar, you find a table. We'll eat in peace and then I'll drive you home... or to your next shave."

"Maybe I'm not the only one who needs a shave," I said matter-of-factly, getting out of the car.

As he stalked inside, I received a call on my phone. "Hello?"

"It's Reno. I have an address for the cousin. Tonight?"

When I stepped inside the diner, a blast of cold air made me shiver. "Tonight is no good. I have to work, and there's not enough time right now for me to do all that. Don't you *dare* go without me," I said, sitting at a table with my back to the window.

He sighed. "It's your money, but I'm gonna have a real problem if you blow me off tomorrow."

"No, tomorrow is good. The sooner the better. Do you want to pick me up or—"

"Have you ever ridden a bike?"

Sweet Mary, no! I'd seen Reno's bike, and after my mother's car accident years ago, riding a motorcycle would terrify me. Nothing between me and the hard pavement but thin air.

"Why don't you stop by, and I'll drive?"

"And leave my bike on the human side of town?" he almost growled.

A man walked in and looked my way before approaching the counter.

"Do you want me to come pick you up?"

I knew that wouldn't go over well. Having a woman in her sporty little Trans Am pick up the big and strong private investigator? I could almost hear male pride crumbling on the other end of the phone.

"This is problematic," he murmured. "We don't have a free car tomorrow. Your swinging by is no good unless you want to get me in deep tar with my Packmaster. I should have thought this out before accepting your offer."

"So let's do this: we meet up at Sweet Treats Bakery. I'll zip in and say hello, and you show up with bike trouble. I'll offer to give you a ride, and your bike will be right in front of the shop where Lexi can keep an eye on it."

"Damn. You're good. Let's do that. Noon okay?"

"See you there."

After the call ended, I looked up and saw Wheeler at the counter eating what looked like a sloppy joe. He sucked sauce off his finger and shoved a few tater tots into his mouth. I was going to have to give him tomorrow afternoon off. Reno would be all the bodyguard I needed, and I didn't want to risk them finding out about each other. Reno might back out completely if he found out too many resources were being extended to me, and I needed him.

My, this was getting more complicated than I first thought.

"Why do I feel like I've seen you before?"

I glanced up at the man who had walked in a moment ago. A pair of narrow shades with orange lenses sat low on the bridge of his nose, allowing me to see his eyes. His neck and forearms were red in contrast to the skin just beneath his sleeves. He had a small potbelly and hair on his knuckles. I only noticed that because the fingers on his left hand were splayed on my table.

"Maybe I look familiar because you were gawking at me when you walked in?" I suggested. I really wasn't in the mood for this; clearly he had seen me perform. It went with the territory, and while most were gentlemen about it, ten percent of those customers felt like they owned me outside the club.

"Ah," he said, as if reaching an epiphany. "Almost didn't recognize you in a dress. I think you look sexier without it. How come I haven't seen you at Palazio's?"

I hadn't worked at that human club in over five years, and those were desperate times. "Because I'm working in a prestigious law firm."

"Well that's a travesty," he said insincerely. "Are you here alone? I'd love to hear all about your new job. Why don't I buy your lunch?"

Wow. Way too eager.

"I'm not interested, and I prefer to eat alone." I didn't say it in a rude way, but I'd learned a long time ago not to give a man the idea he could pressure me. Firm and to the point. That lets a girl know who the assholes are right away.

"That's not very nice. I remember you being so much nicer," he said, his eyes traveling across my body as if they had a passport. "If you're busy now, why don't I take you somewhere this weekend? There's a nice steakhouse up the road." He reached out and brushed his fingers on my arm. "I'm Dave. Is Gypsy your real name, or was that just a stage thing?"

A teenage girl at a nearby table was watching with interest, and suddenly I felt like I could be her life lesson on how she should allow men to treat her.

"No, Dave. I'm not interested, and I'd like you to leave my table. I don't think we'd be having this conversation if you hadn't recognized me from the club. Be a sweetheart and pay attention when a woman says no."

Irritation flashed in his eyes. "A girl who strips for a living isn't a girl who says no a whole lot."

I stood up from my seat and slapped him in the face so hard that his sunglasses hung askew. "Don't you *dare* insult me like that again."

The girl next to me was suddenly holding up her phone, and I knew this was all going on video.

This show needed to end quickly. When I reached for my purse, everything happened so fast. One minute Dave was standing in front of me with a stunned expression, and the next, when I looked up, Wheeler had spun him around and shoved him against the wall. So hard that a picture of an employee's face fell to the floor and smashed into pieces.

Wheeler threw a series of punches—the third splitting Dave's cheek and bright blood appearing. Someone in the back shouted to call the police, and that's when my adrenaline spiked.

Dave erupted with anger and charged at Wheeler, who suddenly stepped aside like a matador dodging a bull in Spain.

When Dave stumbled forward, the teenager stuck out her leg and sent him flying. A chair fell over when he hit the ground. I smirked and gave her an approving wink before grabbing Wheeler by the arm.

Taut arm. His muscles were so tight that he felt like stone beneath my touch. "We have to get out of here, so I hope you filled up on your meat sandwich."

Did he hear me? I wasn't sure. His eyes were locked on the human, and I'd never seen the features of his face so fierce. Moving him seemed impossible, so I slipped four fingers down the front of his pants so I could get a firm grip on his jeans.

That seemed to snap him out of it. When he lightly gasped and turned to look at me, I gave him a hard tug and pulled him toward the door. "Come on, sugar. We're late for the parent-teacher conference."

Once outside, I realized that Wheeler was compliantly following behind me, allowing me to tug him forward. I glanced over my shoulder and saw why. It almost stole my breath how thick he was— so much so that I snatched my hand back before I felt a surprise. The length and size of him pressed so hard against the fabric of his jeans that it looked painful.

"Come on, Romeo. Before the cops show up and wonder why sloppy joes give you an erection."

CHAPTER 8

WHEELER STRETCHED OUT ON NAYA'S white sofa after she went to take a nap in her bedroom. He couldn't stop replaying the events in his head of what had happened earlier at the diner. While sitting at the counter drinking his milkshake, he'd heard Naya's sultry voice sharpen. When he glanced over his shoulder, a man was facing her with his hand on the table. Because of the distance and the music on the speakers, he couldn't hear the conversation.

He'd wanted to turn around and finish his lunch, but something had compelled him to watch—a spark that coiled in his stomach and burned hotter with each passing second. Should he interfere? He was hired to protect her life, not to meddle with her personal business, and a woman like Naya was certainly used to men approaching her all the time. When he saw the man's fingers slide up her arm, his wolf began to snarl and pace within him.

Naya suddenly sprang to her feet and slapped the man in the face. Wheeler had flashbacks of when she'd done the same to him, and a surge of adrenaline poured through his veins like lava. Maybe seeing that should have made him dislike her for being so callous to men, but a smidge of unexpected jealousy bloomed in Wheeler, as if her punishments belonged only to him.

And wasn't that a crazy fucking thought?

Wheeler didn't even realize he was walking in their direction—it was as if his body and brain had disconnected, replaced by animal instinct. When she turned away and reached for her purse, the man curved his left hand across his right shoulder. Wheeler had seen that gesture before, and it meant the guy was three seconds from backhanding her.

Wheeler caught the man's wrist and spun him around. "Thought you were going to do that, didn't you?" he said through clenched teeth.

He blacked out for just a few seconds. It always happened during the first moments of a violent outburst. It didn't matter if humans were watching. In his world, a man didn't put his hand on a woman.

Wheeler shifted around on Naya's sofa and rubbed his eyes. Just thinking about how that scene had played out made his heart thump so forcefully that he could see the rapid pace through the thin fabric of his sleeveless shirt. Then blood rushed to his cock as he remembered the feel of her slender fingers sliding down the front of his pants. That in combination with the way she had forcefully led him out made him ache in a way he hadn't felt in a long time. Even now the constriction was too much, so he freed the button and unzipped his pants, which only made him harder.

"Dammit," he whispered, wanting so badly to stroke himself. Even worse, doing that while thinking of *her*.

His breaths became heavy and he shut his eyes, trying to force himself to sleep. What was it about that scene that had incited such anger and arousal all at once? Maybe it was the thought of the way that man had touched her—invading her space. Or how goddamn sexy she looked standing up for herself and giving that asshole every bit of what he deserved.

Jesus. Wheeler was stroking himself over the fabric. He thought about how ripe she looked in that outfit, how supple her breasts, and even the fact that she had on nude lipstick that matched her dress. Except it had a shimmer that made her lips look wet... as if she had licked them. He imagined her tongue gliding across her upper lip. The next thing he knew, he had pulled his shorts down enough that he could get a firm hold of his cock. He gripped the shaft, rolling his thumb over the tip. Wheeler's body jerked, and his mind flooded with the memory of how her cheeks flushed the moment she'd caught sight of his erection.

An ache tightened at the base of his spine as he stroked even faster. The intensity flared, and Wheeler arched his back, feeling as if something was about to spring loose from his mind if he didn't stop this aching desire. Her brown skin looked the color of cinnamon and honey, and she had exotic eyes that reeled him in with every glance.

He stroked faster. Then his mind raced, thinking about when she had kissed him. How velvety sweet her tongue was, and the way she'd nibbled on his lip. *Christ.* He could still remember the way her kiss tasted, like dark cherries.

Almost there…

"Misha?"

Holy shit! Wheeler didn't have time for buttons and zippers, so he did the only thing that came to mind—he flipped over.

"Have you seen Misha?" Naya asked with a yawn. "I can't sleep without my baby."

"That what you normally wear during naptime?" he grumbled, trying to restrain his approval when he caught a glimpse of her walking past him in a pair of tight cotton shorts and a white tank top. He could see the cups of her ass below the shorts, tempting him to touch. Wheeler smashed his face into the couch pillow, rubbing it hard and wanting to end this humiliation.

"*Misha,*" she sang, peering behind her red chair.

Wheeler's eye popped open as she bent over, her shorts riding up. Oh Jesus, he wasn't going to survive this. Somehow, it was going to kill him.

"Maybe she got out," he mumbled, realizing he was still hard and aching for release.

Naya turned around and folded her arms. "She's slipped out a few times when I've had visitors, which is why I bought that collar. It just seems like I would have noticed. I guess with you around I was too distracted."

"She'll turn up." But what he really meant to say was, *Get the hell out of here and let me zip up my pants.*

Her bottom lip pushed out. "I have to go to work soon. That's too long for her to be out."

"It's a cat. They've lived outside for millions of years."

Her eyes narrowed. "What did I say about wearing your dirty shoes in my house? Take them off."

Not going to happen, he thought. "Think I'll keep 'em on. My feet are shy."

The next thing he knew, she was undoing the laces and tugging off his boot. Something about feeling her removing any article of clothing from his body made him panic; he might end up drilling a hole to China through her couch.

Wheeler bent his leg, trying to pull it away. "Let me sleep. Promise I won't walk on your couch."

"Hold still."

She moved closer, unraveling the lace from his bent leg. He caught a whiff of her perfume and suppressed a groan. Wheeler had experienced all kinds of torture in his life, and yet nothing compared to this. When the second boot came off, she wrapped her hands around his sock-covered foot and he felt himself twitch.

"You have nice feet." Her fingers pressed into the sole, as if debating on whether or not a massage was in order.

Hell no, a massage was definitely *not* in order. Wheeler straightened his leg. "Can't a man sleep in peace?"

Naya appeared in front of him, squatting on the floor. "Has anyone ever told you that you are an antisocial, introverted asshole? I'm trying to be nice and you're..."

He moved his head more to the side to look at her. "I'm what?"

She craned her neck forward and furrowed her dark eyebrows. "Mr. Grumpy."

"Pleasure to meet you, Miss Diva."

Her tongue swept across her lips and the direction of her gaze altered, looking up at his head. It made him self-conscious, but it wasn't as if he could go anywhere. "I'm going to strip out of these clothes, lather my body with soapy suds, and take a long, hot shower. Why don't you do me a favor and look for my pussycat?"

"Sure thing."

Naya stood up, and he listened to her bare feet tread across the plush carpet out of sight. The door squeaked as it moved, but before it closed, she said, "I just had that couch steam cleaned, so I better not find one stain on it."

When the door shut, Wheeler felt his cheeks heat. Was she making the comment because of his shoes, or did she know?

He glanced over his shoulder and everything looked okay from the back. Damn women—always making elusive remarks that left a man paranoid.

Wheeler flipped over and quickly fixed his pants, feeling like a stupid young wolf before hitting his prime. His phone rang and he pulled it from his back pocket. "Yeah?"

"It's Austin. How's it going?"

"Swell."

"By the sarcasm in your voice, I'm going to assume the opposite. Look, you were the only one available I could trust with this job. I know you don't like her, so just be thankful I didn't ask you to stay by her side. Just sit tight in your car and follow close behind. I know it's boring, but just make sure you let me know if you see anyone acting suspiciously. Especially if you sense a Mage."

"A Mage, huh?" Wheeler washed his hands in the kitchen and then leaned against the counter, drying them with a dish towel. "Want to tell me what all this is about?"

"Did I just hear water running?"

"Car wash," Wheeler quickly said.

"Right. Well, Naya's a friend of the family, and she asked for my help. It's not my business to discuss the details surrounding her request. This is serious, brother. Keep a close eye on anyone around her who looks suspect."

"She works in a strip club. Everyone surrounding her looks suspect."

Austin sighed. "Then pay attention to the men who *don't* have bulges in their pants. This shouldn't be for much longer. She should be okay inside her apartment at night, but just stay on her as much as you can."

Wheeler picked up a potato scrubber shaped like a smiling spud and used it to brush his short beard. "Why couldn't she just hire a regular bodyguard?"

"She has trust issues, like all women," Austin said with a chuckle. "It's not like we need her money, but she's done a lot to help Lexi

over the years. I think it's time we did her a good turn. I'm only
charging her so she doesn't make this into a habit. By the way, Ben
wanted me to let you know he's gone for the night. He said a big
tournament is going on and wanted you to keep your phone on."

Wheeler set the scrubber down and stewed for a minute. That
meant Ben wanted him on standby so he could hit him up for money
if he lost his ass in a game. Why couldn't his pack see what was really
going on? As much of a screwup as Ben was, Wheeler couldn't betray
his brother and tell the pack. He felt responsible for Ben, and unlike
the rest of the brothers who were spaced apart in years, he'd grown
up alongside his twin and they had developed a close bond of loyalty
and secrecy. Maybe because they shared the same genes, turning Ben
away would be like betraying himself. Wheeler's love for his twin was
unconditional, even though Ben was the reason he'd almost lost his
life in the panther pits.

"I'll call you if I see anything out of the norm," Wheeler promised.
He stroked his chin, thinking about her tires getting slashed, their
trip to a body-wax shop, breaking into Delgado's office, a fistfight
with a human at a diner, and then him impaling her sofa cushion
with his penis.

No, nothing out of the norm about today. Nothing at all.

⟡

I sat in my dressing room, chilled by the cool air blowing from the
vents. I enjoyed hot weather, and sometimes I thought I might be
happier living on a tropical island, basking in the sun. Maybe it
had to do with my panther, but it seemed like I was overly sensitive
to air-conditioning. The song before my act was still playing, so I
waited nervously while the girls finished their dance. The stages were
booked except at nine, twelve, and three in the morning. During
those hours, one girl got the floor, and it gave others a chance to
either enjoy a well-deserved break or earn extra money performing
private lap dances.

When I'd left my apartment to head to work, it was with a
heavy heart. Misha hadn't returned, and I worried. Wheeler followed

behind me in a separate car, suddenly deciding he needed to keep his distance. I thought about when I'd crouched beside the sofa and looked into his eyes. There was such need there—a craving buried so deep that it made me wonder about his wolf. I didn't know a man could have naughty eyebrows, but Wheeler had them. Pensive and yet slightly arched, like a man thinking about dismantling my outfit.

"You're up," Daphne said, out of breath. She sat next to me on the bench and used a wet towel to wipe her neck and then armpits. "I swear. Dean needs to turn on a little air out there. It's a full house and the only air circulating in this building is in this room. What's wrong? You look like a chicken about to take a swim in the deep fryer."

"I always get jittery when I try a new act," I said, applying a dusting of body shimmer to my neck and chest.

"Well, that's an interesting outfit you have on." Her orange eyebrows arched as she glanced down at my scantily clad body.

"I found a costume shop and did a little work on it with some scissors. You like?"

"You look like a ragamuffin, but if you think the men will go for that kind of thing, then more power to you."

I smiled and stood up, admiring myself in the mirror. I pulled a lock of hair in front of my face and added extra blush on the contours of my cheeks to look animalistic and hungry. I already had defined cheekbones, so the shadowing drew attention to my face. I'd bought a short dress with jagged edges in brown and black—resembling something a cavewoman would wear. I cut it short, added a giant hole from my navel to my right hip, and ripped one strap away from my shoulder. I looked like a sexy woman in the midst of an escape.

I'd spent the past hour applying my makeup. A little rouge and eye shadow marked my wrist where I planned to cuff myself. The manacle at the end of the chain looked realistic even though it was thick plastic. The large links were dark and rusty looking, and I planned to attach them to the pole. I wore heavy liner to draw attention to my dark brown eyes.

"What exactly are you scheming, missy?" Daphne gave me a

serious once-over as she stood up. "You do realize you look like a dirty slave?"

"Exactly," I purred, swinging the chain. "These men have primal instincts I'm about to tap into. Human men want to be taken care of, but this fantasy plays into the Breed mind." I wrapped the chain around the back of her neck, pulling her close. "And you know how our men love being heroes. The Shifters and Chitahs won't know what hit them when they see a helpless woman in need of their protection."

Her eyes widened. "Girl, you might start a war in there."

"Let's just say I'm taking no prisoners." I winked and let the chain fall free from her neck. "I'm about to prove why you should stop learning all your tricks from those human clubs."

I'd given all my plans to our stagehand earlier, and he'd volunteered to help with the effects behind the curtain at the back of the stage. Manny designed props, adjusted the lighting, cleaned the stage, and helped repair torn costumes. One of the girls had told me he was a Relic born without his parents' knowledge having been passed on to him—a defect. Relics made careers from the knowledge their ancestors genetically passed down, making them experts in certain fields. Without that knowledge, they were nothing but a human with a slight chance of being able to have Relic children who might or might not inherit the wisdom that had skipped their parent.

I walked onstage, shrouded in darkness. Customers were happily getting their drinks refilled by beautiful women. I searched the room, looking for Wheeler. When I caught sight of him in the back, twirling a silver butterfly knife, I actually blew out a breath. He had his eyes on the crowd, watching every man sitting alone or who walked past him.

The music changed over and a steady beat and the sound of drums filled the room. I'd selected a rhythmic song that didn't have the distraction of lyrics, and if sex could be translated to music, this song would have been it.

I clamped the cuff around the pole and crouched down on my

side. It wasn't until the spotlight showered me that the men turned their attention my way.

And *boy*, did they! I peered through my hair and saw the tip rail fill up. It wasn't the kind of routine where I collected the money by hand or in the strap of my thong. Breed bars had their own system, and during the main attraction, the stage bouncers set my boxes at the designated areas on the stage for tipping. After the show, I'd walk around and find out who really enjoyed my performance… and how much.

Visual effects appeared on the thin blue curtain behind me where Manny had adjusted the lights along with props. It looked like ripples of midnight blue bringing to life a silhouette of twisted tree limbs. I rose to my hands and knees, looking around as if something were hunting me.

A couple of men gripped the bar around the stage, leaning forward, eyes wide, enthralled by the action unfolding.

Then I slowly tugged at the chain attached from my wrist to the pole. Unable to free myself, I walked around the pole and leapt up, spinning in an acrobatic move with my arm outstretched.

When the beat dropped, I collapsed to the floor. A man gasped and lurched to his feet, thinking I had fallen by accident. I glanced over my shoulder with a panicked expression, every move calculated and dramatic. As I did this, I stood up and pulled at the chain, spinning under it and combining dance moves with an artistic interpretation of a woman in peril. My unkempt hair caressed my body with each sultry turn.

I climbed the pole in search of escape, turning upside down and locking my long legs. Once I had a good grip with my hands, I slowly spread my legs and then swung around, twirling off the pole. The beat sounded like native drums, and I frantically gathered up the chain as the shadows shifted and changed on the curtain.

A predator moved into sight—the silhouette of a black panther.

I looked upon the men with smoldering eyes, drawing them in. The next thing I knew, men were getting out of their chairs to put money in my boxes but also to inch closer to the stage. The bouncers continued pushing them back to their seats, but the men were riveted.

A Chitah's fangs punched out—top and bottom—and a bouncer forced him away from the stage before he flipped his switch and went primal. Luckily, his eyes were still golden. I paid closer attention to how the crowd was responding since I'd never performed this act before and didn't want to incite a riot.

I fell to my knees and arched my back, letting the chain slip between my legs. The beat intensified and I pulled myself up, swinging hard around the pole. After the music reached a crescendo, it fell quiet. Just long enough that a growl ripped through the air and sent a chill up my spine. It was just sound effects, but maybe the intense reaction from the crowd had me on edge. When I sexily approached them, the lights shut out and the panther snarled.

A dim, lustrous red light enveloped me—a foreboding symbol of blood and death. I slid along the polished floor, turning and struggling against an invisible force.

All I could see were bills flying into my boxes and onto the stage. The men were entranced, and I felt like a woman reborn. I'd finally broken away from my gimmicky acts and struck a chord with the audience in a completely artistic way.

My heart raced when I saw a man in black approaching me from offstage wearing a ski mask that only revealed his eyes and mouth. I furrowed my brows. As the man neared, my heart galloped in my chest when I stared into a set of blue eyes.

Panic set in. The beat intensified, the crowd held their breath, and I fumbled with the chain in a feeble attempt to free my hand. It was only plastic—but hard plastic, and there was a trick to getting the shackle undone.

The men in the audience thought it was part of the act. I wanted to yell for help, but they wouldn't believe me, or even worse, it could start a riot and erupt in a fight. I swallowed hard and backed up toward the pole.

"Wheeler?" I called out, looking toward the back of the room. Surely this man wouldn't do anything stupid in front of all these people. I didn't see Wheeler, and that's when my panic ripened into a dark emotion.

I grabbed the pole with both hands and kicked him in the chest. The men cheered, some of them slapping their hands on the tables. Whether or not this was a joke, I wasn't taking any chances.

The masked man stood up and rushed me. The next thing I knew, he gripped my hair so hard that I screamed. A strobe flickered in front of my eyes from a slender instrument…

And my panther emerged.

CHAPTER 9

I CLENCHED MY TEETH AROUND SOMETHING hard and splintery. As I blinked a few times, I realized I was coming out of a shift. I was also chewing on a wooden leg that belonged to a coffee table. I scooted back and picked a wood chip out of my mouth.

Where am I? The last thing I remembered was dancing… and a man forcing me to shift. Oh my God, the memories were rushing back. When the crowd laid eyes on my panther, it was pandemonium. Thankfully, the shackle around her paw had given the customers enough time to escape. She'd fled the stage, panicked by the movement and shouting. I'd struggled to regain control but had lost the battle.

I wiped my mouth and quickly sat up, my hands trembling. The first thing I noticed was the smell. Fresh varnish mixed with pine. The floors and walls were all wood, and there were no windows. A giant flat-screen television hung on the wall ahead of me, behind me was a brown sofa. Beyond the sofa was a bed in what looked like an extension of the room.

"Hello?"

My legs felt like bags of cement as I struggled to stand. I smacked my lips when a specific food craving suddenly ripped through me, creating a gnawing hunger in the pit of my stomach.

"Clothes would be nice," I murmured, glancing around in search for something to cover up with. I snatched the green chenille throw from the back of the couch and wrapped it around me.

In the left-hand corner of the room were two doors. The right door led to a tiny bathroom with a standing shower, toilet, and a vintage pedestal sink. Someone had locked the other door from the outside.

I gave the room another glance. To the right of the television was a kitchenette. Scenic paintings decorated the room with images of grassy meadows, a winding river that stretched toward a mountain, and two wolves standing in front of white birch trees. The landscapes of nature compensated for the absence of windows. No overhead light or fan, just a couple of brown lamps with dingy shades.

"Someone answer me!" I pounded my fist against the door, dizzy with fear and anger. The latter emotion had won the battle. "Open the motherfucking—"

I gasped when the door suddenly swung inward.

"That's quite a mouth you've got on you," Wheeler said, leaning on the doorjamb.

I didn't know whether to slap or kiss him. Maybe both. "Where am I?"

"The heat house."

"The *what* house?"

Then it clicked. He meant the small house Lexi had mentioned— the one that gave the girls a private place to let their hormones fly, or at the very least, a room separate from the house for the couples to unleash their passion.

"You're staying here the night," he said matter-of-factly.

"But Misha—"

"That's not an offer, Naya. Packmaster's orders."

I jutted my hip out. "Well, he's not my Packmaster. What happened? Did I hurt anyone?"

"Unfortunately, no."

"Did you catch the man who attacked me?"

Wheeler stepped forward. "Someone attacked you?"

"Where were you!" I screamed. Accused. Blamed. My lip quivered, not afraid of what could have happened to me, but what could have happened to others *because* of me.

He gripped my shoulders. "Chill and get some sleep. You're just wired up because of the shift."

I wriggled free of his grasp. Wheeler stroked the bristly hair on his chin, and the way he looked at me was different—not like before. Not the same. My skin crawled as if I'd been exposed to the core and he'd seen every bit of what I'd been hiding from everyone my entire life.

I smoothed out all the rough edges in my voice. "Why can't I go home?"

"Home isn't safe."

"Since when?"

His brows sloped down as he lowered his chin. Wheeler seemed to have mastered the stern face. "Since thirty seconds ago when you said someone attacked you." His gaze flicked behind me and his lip twitched. "I see you found something to snack on."

I whirled around and looked at the coffee table with embarrassment. My panther had not just gnawed on one leg but chewed off another. It's one reason I'd switched my furniture to glass tables instead of wood.

"I'm sorry about that. I'll have it replaced," I said absently.

Something made me turn around and look at Wheeler—a small detail I had initially disregarded, but now it became a niggling question in my head. "What happened to your eye?"

He touched the dark bruise on his left eye. "That all you plan on wearing?"

"I need to speak to someone who will give me answers."

"As you wish, *Diva*."

"Have a good evening, *Grumpy*."

When he closed the door behind him, I sat on the sofa and huffed out a breath. Had he seen my panther? My God, he must have. But how did I get here? Maybe I'd blacked out in human form, and when he put me in here, I'd shifted back to my panther. I wasn't sure what aftereffects the strobe device had, but it left me disoriented.

A rapid series of knocks sounded on the door. Before I could answer, the door opened.

"Naya, are you okay?" Lexi slammed the door behind her and ran toward the sofa where I was sitting. Then she hissed and lifted up her bare foot. "Dammit! I got a splinter."

"Oh, honey…"

"No, I'm fine." She sat to my left and looked me over. "Seriously. What's going on?"

I shook my head. "I don't know. One second I'm onstage during a performance, and the next, a man came up and forced me to shift."

She grimaced. "In front of everyone? You're kidding me. What the hell kind of lunatic would make someone shift in a Breed club without knowing what their animal was?"

"A fool who knew *exactly* what my animal was."

"Come again?"

I sighed and brushed back my unkempt hair. "The reason I came to speak with Austin privately was to ask for protection. I paid for a bodyguard. Remember the girl at the club who went missing? It happened again, and then someone came after *me*. I don't know what's going on, but I'm frightened. This just doesn't feel like my life anymore. I want to go home and sleep in my bed, cuddle with Misha, and not feel this rising sense of dread that others have me figured out."

Lexi swept her hair behind her shoulders and then clasped her hands together. "We saw your panther."

My blood chilled.

She shook her head. "I've never seen anything like it. Wheeler called ahead to tell us he was bringing home a live panther and to move everyone upstairs until he secured the heat house. Austin had a fit. He went out to meet him by the road and they got into a fight." Lexi shook her head and briefly looked up at the ceiling. "This isn't good. I don't know what Wheeler's standing is with the pack anymore—not after this. When I found out it was you, I begged Austin to let you stay for the night. You were still in the back of Wheeler's Camaro, and Austin yelled at me to get in the house. He's never done that before, but I could see the fear in his eyes. I've heard a few stories about Shifter history, but I guess I never knew how deep-seated the fear of panthers was. Not until I saw that look."

"Was I awake in the car?"

She chuckled in disbelief. "We could hear your cat growling all the way inside. Wheeler didn't have the same look of fear in his eyes that Austin did. I had a good view from the upstairs window. He had a chain looped around your neck and walked you up to the porch as if you were his pet or something."

My jaw dropped. "He *what?*"

Impossible! Was this a joke? Lexi must have been nipping at the wine. There was absolutely no way my panther would have been submissive to anyone, let alone a wolf. I couldn't even consider it.

She pulled her foot up and poked at it, looking for the sliver of wood in her heel. "Well, you've been the talk of the house since your arrival. I'm glad you shifted back, because Austin hasn't been able to stop pacing. A hall connects this room to the main house, but he intentionally built it without windows to make sure anyone using it was safe from outsiders getting in. He put a lock on both sides, but he's never used the outside lock until tonight."

"Why would he lock the door from the outside to begin with?"

"I suppose he was afraid one of us girls might get really horny, break down the door, and mount one of them," she said with a roll of her eyes. "The worst part about it was that the heat house was *my* idea. I was joking at the time, but Austin never forgets anything I say."

I placed my hand over my chest, fighting the urge to have a complete meltdown. I didn't like being weak in front of anyone; that's not the kind of woman I was. I'd always been strong—a fighter—but now it seemed like I was fighting shadows.

"Naya?" Lexi asked in a soft voice, brushing a swath of hair away from my face. "Hey, it's me. I don't care if you're a panther or a skunk; I love you regardless. You hear me? Maybe I'm a little terrified of your animal, and I don't expect we'll be best buddies, but that's fine."

A bubble of laughter burst out, and I smiled. "I'm so sorry for all this. I didn't mean to cause a rift in your pack, and I would have never asked Wheeler to bring me here. I still don't understand how…"

She put her foot down and winced. "Good news. You have a few clothes here. Remember the trip we were going to take to Padre Island and then your dickhead boss called you in to work? You were so pissed off that you flew out the door and left your bag behind. You told me to keep it here until our next trip. It's just outside the door and it probably has everything you'll need, including a toothbrush and all that. I'm going to talk Austin into letting you stay here a while longer."

"No, no. Not necessary."

Her head jerked back. "Oh, really? A maniac is after you and I'm supposed to send you home? Not happening. If Austin kicks you out, then you're staying in a hotel, and I'm going with you."

"Lexi, really, I'm fine. It's nothing you need to worry your pretty little head over."

"You're *not* fine!" she shouted.

"Look at the trouble I've caused! I don't want you and Austin to fight because of me, and I definitely don't want to put anyone in harm's way."

She catapulted to her feet. "You're my best friend, and you could never ask for too much. Hell, you never ask for *anything*. I'm offering, you're accepting, end of story."

"Cat fight?" Denver loomed in the doorway, eating pears straight out of the can.

Lexi glared down at his bare feet when he crossed them at the ankle. "Don't come in here," she said. "There are splinters all over the floor."

"Didn't plan on it, honeypie. Just wanted to watch the show. Heard meowing all the way in the kitchen."

"Wipe that smug grin off your face," she said, shoving at his naked chest. "You're only in a good mood because you won the bet."

I leaned forward, tightening the throw around me. "What bet?"

Lexi twisted around, her face carrying a look of disdain. "These idiots had a running bet on your animal."

"A hundred dollars per person is nothing to sneeze at," he said with a mouthful of pears. "I'm the only one who said panther. We had bets on cougar, bobcat, bear—"

I snorted. "Who thought I was a grizzly?"

"Get out of here!" Lexi shoved him backward, and I heard the can drop on the floor.

"The fuck? I'm not cleaning that up," he said.

The next thing I saw was my bag hurling over Lexi's head and hitting the fridge.

Lexi bent over out of sight, and then I heard the metallic clinking of silverware in the distance.

"You missed!" he yelled out.

"Are you craving anything?" she asked politely.

I waved my hand and stood up. "My old life?"

"Anything you need and I'm here for you. There's a phone on the table," she said, pointing to the long table to the left of the door. "Ring me if you need anything, but we're not locking you in anymore. That was temporary until you shifted back—not that your panther would have figured out how to turn the knob, but I didn't have any say in the matter. My house is yours, so feel free to come out anytime and walk around."

I felt like an interloper now more than ever before. A panther in a house full of wolves? No, I didn't feel the welcome mat rolling out from anyone but Lexi. I unzipped my bag and pulled out something to sleep in. Lexi watched me from the door, eyes brimming with questions, but I knew she was anxious to get back to Austin and smooth things over.

"I suppose this will all be aired out in the morning," I said. "No need to fuss over me. You're a darling for letting me stay despite the circumstances."

Her gaze drifted toward the floor. "No matter how mad Austin is, he remembers what you did for me with Beckett. If someone had discovered the body and called the police, it could have been so much worse. No one asked you to help—you just did it. Maybe that's why no matter how bad this seems, you have nothing to worry about. He'll come around, but I get why he's upset. He has a pack to lead, and Wheeler was pretty stupid for walking you in like that. Anything I can do before I go to bed?"

I hesitated at first, but then dared to ask, "Is Wheeler still awake?"

She hopped on her foot and gave me a peculiar look. "It's late, and I don't want him to upset you."

"Please? Just ask if he'll come in here for a minute."

"If you need me, I'm just down the hall... across the house... up the stairs... and down another long hall." She laughed and covered her mouth before it got out of control. "Good night."

I smiled reassuringly as she closed the door. Then I went into the bathroom and changed. The request for Wheeler had surprised even me, but suddenly I needed him. I also needed to know how he'd gotten so close to my panther without losing his head.

Wheeler twirled the saltshaker on the long wooden table in the kitchen, lost in thought. The lights were out except the twinkle ones strung around the windows along the wall behind him. William sat across from him, picking at the knotty wood on the table.

William Rush had entered the pack around the time Ivy had left. He had an easygoing personality that made it easy to confide in him. It was obvious why he was once Lorenzo's second-in-command but now slid in third in the Weston pack. Reno was the second, but William had a subtle way of leading that was more politic than direct.

"Austin still pitching a fit?" Wheeler asked.

William ran his fingers through the curls of his dark hair and sat back. "I think his mate is smoothing things over the way only a woman can. Did you notice the way she had him *carry* her up the stairs, all because of a tiny splinter? Lexi plays a good game with her man's heart, and she knows exactly what makes it tick." He paused for a moment before speaking. "I know you weren't raised in a pack, but Austin's in a position where he has to make decisions that benefit his family for the short- and long-term. You're fortunate to be sitting here. Let's just say had you pulled that stunt in Enzo's house, he would have strung you up in the tree right beside the panther."

"I had it under control."

"Indeed. Walking a two-hundred-pound jaguar into a house full of wolves, humans, and children. Had you lost control, she could have attacked one of us. Austin had a right to be angry, don't you agree?"

Wheeler cut him a sharp glare. William had a sneaky way of injecting guilt into any man with a simple prick of words. "Maybe I also think my brother could have trusted me and given me a chance to explain."

"You two should talk it out first thing in the morning."

"And mayhap I don't want to," Wheeler growled.

Some forgotten, juvenile part of him wanted unwavering loyalty among his brothers, who were not just pack to him, but family. But that's not the way it worked.

"Perhaps he'll listen, or not. But if you don't plead your case, you'll never give him that chance." William stood up and rubbed his eyes sleepily. "That woman must like you something fierce."

Wheeler scoffed at the remark. "That what you think? Naya despises me with the power of a thousand suns."

William pressed his fingertips on the table, his eyes lit with amusement. "I think we both know that's a lie. Unless it's their first change or they're scared, the animal within us always respects the ones we care for. If you're blind to that fact, then maybe it's just as well. If you know it to be true, then you are a black-hearted man if you choose to mistreat her henceforth, as that woman has feelings for you."

"She doesn't have feelings for me. She's... confused."

A smile hooked one corner of William's mouth. "She didn't look very confused when you escorted her panther onto the porch and patted her side as she rubbed against you. You *do* know why cats rub their faces on things, don't you? They're marking territory."

Wheeler unscrewed the lid from the salt and flung a handful at William. "Get the fuck out of here."

William laughed and shook his head. "Good night, brother."

When he left the room, Wheeler wiped up all the granules of salt from the table. His mind drifted back to the club when Naya had begun her performance...

Jesus effing Christ. *Naya was like a symphony of movement as she walked the stage. He'd never seen anything so captivating as the way she had complete ownership of her body, delivering more than a dance, but using it in a way that evoked emotion. He'd visited many a strip joint, but nothing compared to what he had witnessed. In fact, it struck him in a most profound and unexpected way when he saw the chain shackled to her wrist and her struggle for freedom.*

Had it not been for his damn cell phone ringing, he would have watched the whole performance. He might have been able to save her from the man who had brazenly walked onstage, and you can bet your ass that man wouldn't have made it five steps in her direction. Austin had sent him to protect her, and the one time she needed Wheeler, he was dealing with family shit.

Ben called with an emergency, as usual. To Wheeler's surprise, Ben was in one of the private rooms at the back of Club Sin. Nothing went together better than strippers, money, and gambling, so most club owners combined the three. They weren't small potatoes either. If you played in one of those clubs, then you needed serious cash. Ben normally worked the human tournaments or in casinos, but sometimes he got the itch for a bigger pot, and he'd wander into one of these clubs with a big set of balls and a medium-sized billfold.

And every time, Wheeler bailed him out.

Wheeler had angrily tucked his phone in his back pocket and made his way to the private rooms. Naya was fenced in by bouncers in a crowded room, so he'd only have a short time to resolve this crisis before her dance ended. Once he made his way past security, he found Ben surrounded by three men who looked like they'd been using his face as a punching bag. The fear in Ben's eyes vanished when he caught sight of Wheeler.

"Brother! See, what did I tell you?" he said to the men. "I've got the money; it was just a delay in getting it all here." Ben patted one of the tall suits on the shoulder, who immediately knocked his arm away.

Wheeler gave Ben a punishing stare. A table to the left had cards and poker chips spread all over, as if someone had been thrown on top of it and roughed up. Maybe it was the blood spatter on the queen of clubs that gave it away, or the gash on Ben's cheekbone.

While each of the Weston pack contributed to the family account, they all had their own separate funds. Ben's account was as depleted of money as a Vampire's victim was of blood. Without a word, Wheeler sat down and signed a check.

Meanwhile, a man wearing what looked like a communication device over his ear had turned his head away, listening to someone. Then he approached Ben and baited him with another game—a bigger pot.

Wheeler held his check between two fingers and glared at Ben. "Do you want this? Then say no. We're done here."

Ben filled in the numbers of what he owed and walked out with cocky strut and a smug grin on his face.

"These guys are loaded, Wheeler. I can beat 'em."

"The fuck you can. What am I doing here then?"

Ben stopped him in the hall. "Now I know how they play and all their tells. Sometimes you have to lose a little to hustle the next game. I'm serious, man. That pot could set us up for the next five years. Don't you care about your pack?"

Wheeler pointed a finger in his face. "Don't. If I even hear that you came back in this club to eat a fucking sandwich, then Austin's gonna know about it."

"Fuck you," Ben spat. "Austin doesn't give a shit what I do because I'm bringing in a hell of a lot more money than you."

"And how many times have I had to bail your ass out to get you that money? Your contribution to the pack has been at my personal expense. All my savings, Ben."

Ben snorted. "Yeah, well, spare me the guilt trip. Aren't we a team? You help me and I help the family. What the hell is wrong with that? You need to get that chip off your shoulder. What's past is past."

That last sentiment rang in Wheeler's ears as he sat at the kitchen table, listening to the house creak and shift like older homes often do. He poked at the miniature mountain of salt and wondered how the pack would view his situation if they knew about it. Both brothers thought they were in the right, but there could only be one, which meant the other was wrong. Wheeler had always felt he was the one doing the right thing, but what if he wasn't? What if Austin decided Wheeler was the one who had to go? This was the only place Wheeler wanted to be, and his loyalty for the pack ran deep.

Lexi strolled in wearing Austin's flannel bathrobe.

"How come your hair isn't wet?" Wheeler asked, not used to seeing her walking around in a robe.

She pulled a bottle of water from the fridge and took a long gulp. "I had a splinter. Long story, and you really don't want to know. So tell me, what's going on between you and my friend?"

Wheeler felt a flutter in his stomach and he sat up, his shoulders stiffening. "Nothing's going on. Why?"

She put the bottle back in the fridge and shivered. "Well, you two have been at each other's throats for years, and it just seems odd she's asking for you all of a sudden."

Wheeler looked at her, nonplussed, waiting for the punch line that never came.

Lexi leaned against the cabinet and watched him, expecting an answer.

"What?" Wheeler asked. "Austin hired me to watch her, and that's what I did. Nothing's changed. Your friend's still a diva."

"Hmm. Well, that diva wanted you to swing by her room before bedtime. I don't think that's a good idea. I think it's better if everyone goes to sleep and we all talk in the morning. So don't go in there; you'll just upset her and she might try to run out of here. If I wake up in the morning and she's gone, I might reconsider going to bat for you. Just so you know, I agree with Austin that what you did was dangerous and stupid, but Naya's also my friend, and I'd rather she be here than anywhere else. Austin puts his foot down when he needs to, but he also listens to what I have to say. An influential woman is not someone easily ignored," she said with a smirk. "Get some rest. It's been a long night."

When Lexi left the room, Wheeler stood up. As if led by an invisible string, he walked down the hall and took a left.

Naya had a penchant for playing with his head, and she probably just wanted to yell at him some more. William was mistaken about her feelings for Wheeler. Naya had always made it clear that she considered him her enemy, and it was something she'd told him years ago. Maybe he deserved to be vilified for shouting at April in the middle of a mall, but her actions had almost created a rift between the Packmaster and second-in-command. If Reno had left the pack early on, it might have severed the chances of the pack surviving. Jesus. Wheeler needed this pack more than anyone, so it had scared the hell out of him when an outsider stole money from them, even if it was replaced soon after. He'd long since buried the hatchet with April, but Naya didn't forgive nor forget. Looking back, he couldn't blame her for striking him.

Wheeler reached the door and his chest tightened. His presence would only piss her off, and that woman did unpredictable things when she was under the influence of diva hormones. And Wheeler needed to avoid pissing Naya off so he could stay on Lexi's good side, since she had influence over the packmates in the house.

The connecting hallway looked like a corridor at a hotel—devoid of windows. Beneath the dim lighting overhead, Wheeler slid down the wall next to the door and closed his eyes. Maybe he should have just gone back to his room, but Austin hadn't officially taken him off the job yet, so he stood guard by her door for the rest of the night.

CHAPTER 10

I DON'T THINK I GOT A wink of sleep after Lexi went to bed and left me waiting in vain for Wheeler. While the pack would keep me safe, these were new surroundings, and I was on edge after what had happened with my panther.

The items in my travel bag were a disappointment. I'd forgotten what I'd packed for our trip to South Padre, and what I found were shorts, Capri pants, a couple of bikini tops, and button-up shirts that tied at the midriff. I just wasn't in a fun-and-flirty mood after the night before, so I chose the beige Capris and a white top. I craved a sense of normalcy and found it in simple things, like my favorite strappy brown heels and a toe ring. Once I'd brushed my hair and used gel to bring out the curls, I began to feel more like myself.

"Time to face the firing squad," I murmured. When I swung the door open, I took a step forward and tripped.

"Oomph!" I hit the hard surface of the floor and rolled on my left side.

Wheeler was sitting against the wall with his long legs stretched in front of the door. He groggily rubbed his eyes. "What are you doing down there?" he grumbled in a sleepy voice.

I tapped my hard nails on the wood floor. "Admiring the unique grain in your flooring. I couldn't help myself. The varnish is breathtaking."

He rose to his feet and looked down his nose at me. "You ready for this?"

I sat up and straightened my shirt. "I didn't mean to cause such a fuss."

"Women don't mean to do a whole lot, but they sure do it."

"Where does that sexist attitude come from?"

"Living in a house full of women who never mean it, but do it anyhow."

I sighed and stood up gracefully. "You're impossible."

He walked alongside me. "I respect women. But they're complicated creatures. I'll never understand you, but I have respect for your ability to get yourselves out of trouble more easily than I can."

"Is that so?"

"Yeah. We're both in hot water, but something tells me that all will be forgiven with the great Naya James."

"And you?"

He held the doorknob and glanced at me over his shoulder. "Sweetheart, I'd be surprised if I got to stay long enough to watch you eat your eggs."

Wheeler opened the door to the main house and we walked through a modestly decorated room with a few sitting chairs and accent tables. The door on the left let us into a short hall that opened into the living room.

"No!" I heard a stubborn little voice yell.

"Melody, do it for Daddy. Put this on; it's so super cool," I heard Jericho say.

When we walked into the living room, he was squatting down and holding up a purple skirt that matched her top. Instead, she had on a pair of pea-green tights. Melody's hair was the same as I'd seen at the party—divided down the middle with braids beginning halfway down.

She put her hands on her hips and lifted her chin.

"Melody, this goes with your shirt," he said. "Don't you want to look pretty?"

"Let her wear what the fuck she wants," Wheeler spat out.

Jericho glanced up. "We're going to the movies later."

"And? The fashion police are going to arrest her? She's three. That's a little self-righteous coming from a man who wears leather cuffs, ripped jeans, and eyeliner."

Melody's expression transformed from willful to endearing. She wrapped her arms around Jericho's neck and rested her head on his shoulder. "My daddy loves me. Don't be mean to him."

Jericho picked her up and held her in his arms, giving Wheeler a look of defeat. "How the hell can I say no to that? Thanks a lot, Wheeler."

"Anytime, brother," Wheeler said with a dark chuckle.

"Why does he care what she has on?" I asked quietly.

"Some of the older kids made fun of her clothes once. I guess he didn't want his kid singled out. He doesn't have a thing to worry about with that one. She's not a sensitive girl and she'll stand up for herself."

Without another word, he led me down the back hall toward the kitchen. We turned left and entered the room, the smell of breakfast heavy in the air. Straight ahead, Lexi was humming a familiar song and pulling a pan of buttermilk biscuits out of the stainless-steel oven. Denver hovered nearby, holding a spoonful of jelly and greedily eyeing the plate of french toast.

A long wooden table ran along the right side of the room in front of a beautiful row of tall windows. Austin sat at the left end of the table, and most of the pack was already seated. Some of them looked up at me, but no one said a word.

Wheeler left me standing alone and sat next to Ben with his back to the windows. April and Reno were seated across from them, and Reno was absently stroking her lower back with his left hand.

"Sit down, Denver," Lexi said, swatting him with a dish towel. She took the last bowls of food and set them on the table before sitting on Austin's left.

Denver walked by me and winked. "You look like an ice cream cone."

There were a whole lot of empty seats at the table—room for a growing pack. I drifted forward, deciding that sitting opposite the Packmaster might not be appropriate. Did wolves have rules? I knew enough about pack hierarchy to assume they did.

The small table behind me looked as if Maizy had outgrown it—like an Alice in Wonderland picture. Melody dashed into the room and sat in the opposite chair, sitting on her legs and playing with the magnetic dress-up dolls that someone had hung on the wall between the two girls. Lynn set a plate in front of her along with a purple juice cup.

"But I don't want *that* cup," Melody complained, looking at the plastic sippy cup. "That's for babies."

Izzy craned her neck to get a good look. "Honey, I had the tree fairies bring that cup all the way from Neverland. They said it will give you special powers, and you'll need them for the movie we're going to later." Izzy glanced back at Jericho and lowered her voice. "God knows *I'll* need 'em."

"Don't worry," he said. "No nachos this time."

"Well, it was all in her hair," Izzy went on in their private conversation. "Then it dried and was impossible to get out."

Jericho shrugged guiltily but didn't look as upset as Izzy over it. Instead, he smirked and reached for a plate of sausage patties.

"Have a seat," Austin said to me.

I swallowed thickly and sat on the bench next to Denver.

"At the end—so I can see you."

I quietly rose from my seat and took the chair at the end of the table, facing Austin and his entire pack of wolves.

Everyone seemed in a rush to eat before the conversation turned serious. Everyone except William, who sat to my right with his arms folded on the table, his attention on Austin. He was an astute man.

"Wheeler, I'm going to let you tell your side of the story first," Austin said, holding his fist in the palm of his other hand and then cracking a knuckle. "Speak openly. I think it's pretty damn obvious that confidentiality is out the window at this point."

Wheeler set down his bacon and licked his fingers. "What do you want me to say?"

Austin threw down his fork and Lexi gripped his arm. "I want you to tell me why you walked a panther into our house," he said angrily.

Wheeler briefly flicked a glance at Ben, who stuffed a biscuit into his mouth and was eyeing the plate of colorful berries.

"Because when you task me with something, I comply. Did

guard her only mean in human form? Someone forced her to shift; the club was in a panic. By the time I came in—"

"Came in?" Austin interrupted. "Came in from where?"

Wheeler looked at Ben again, and that's when I realized something else was going on. He pushed his plate forward and put his hands in his lap. "I had to take a piss. She was onstage and the last thing I expected was for her to shift in front of an audience."

"Then?"

Wheeler flicked his eyes up to mine briefly. "Then I loaded her into the car."

"How the hell did you manage to do that?" Denver asked in awe. "A panther? We all saw how big she is."

Wheeler slowly lifted his eyes. "Because maybe panthers can sense fear in a man, and that's all they need to know."

"I would have been crapping my pants is all I'm saying," Denver replied.

Austin turned his attention toward me. "What made you shift?"

I held my chin high. "You mean who. Probably the same man as before. He walked right across the stage."

"And everyone *let* him?" Reno growled.

"They thought it was part of my act, I guess. He had on a ski mask and approached me theatrically." I felt myself wringing my hands beneath the table, so I stopped fidgeting. "He used a strobe, and when I shifted, the room exploded with panic. Some people were running out, but a few others looked like they wanted to capture and kill me. Some of the bouncers kept things under control, but my animal was scared and confused with all the movement. By then the man was gone, and then it darkened. I don't remember anything until I woke up here. I would never have asked Wheeler to bring me here—you have to know that. But what he did was... Well, I respect him for it. He took me to the one place he knew I'd be safe. That's all that I asked of you, Austin. Someone who would protect my life. And he risked his life to do it. I can't excuse his behavior, but I'm just as conflicted about it as you must be."

Austin grabbed a piece of bacon off his plate and devoured it.

"I called to warn you I was coming," Wheeler said defensively.

"It's not like I walked her inside without a heads-up. I wouldn't do that to this pack. I wouldn't intentionally put any of you in danger."

Austin dropped the bacon on his plate and dusted the crumbs off his fingers. "One of the kids could have opened the door and run out. Would you feel good about your decision if we were sitting here this morning and, God forbid, something had happened to one of them? They can't shift, Wheeler. We have to protect our children over anything or anyone else."

Wheeler rubbed his face and I could see the battle raging within. His pack would always come first in his life, but in this instance, he had put me first. I didn't know how to feel about that.

"What I have to say won't make you feel better, Austin. It'll just piss you off. But I had her under absolute control. I don't expect you to understand it, but I did. We can argue until we're blue in the face, but that's just the way it is."

"Did you feel safe because of your knife?" I asked.

Wheeler snapped to attention, his eyes burning with ferocity. "Say again?"

"The only way a man feels safe around a panther is when he's carrying a weapon and willing to use it."

Austin rapped his knuckles on the table, looking between us.

I didn't see admission in Wheeler's eyes, only resentment, but he kept silent.

After another moment, the Packmaster scratched his jaw and sat back. "I didn't give that consideration," he said. "Wheeler, I know you would have protected your pack by any means necessary, so we're going to put this issue to rest. But this doesn't clear your record. If you screw up again, then I'll have no choice but to put you out for good. I can't afford to have a weak link in the chain. I need men who will put this pack above everything, whose motives I don't have to sit here and question. You get off this once, but don't do it again." He shook his head, ready to end the conversation.

"I'll just need a ride home," I said.

"No, I'd like you to stay here," Lexi quickly said, her eyes flicking toward Austin. It didn't look like the offer took him by surprise.

I shook my head. "I don't think that's such a good idea."

"It's a great idea," she countered. "You need a place to stay until this thing blows over, and I need someone to help me organize. They're delivering my menus, and I also talked to your friend about the website. He tossed some ideas at me, but I wanted your input on the layout. You seem to know everyone, Naya. I've never met anyone with so many connections. We also have the costume party coming up, and the guy we were dealing with *tripled* the prices on our outfits. Can you believe it? He wants to charge two per person."

"Two hundred?"

"Two thousand," Austin said in an irritated voice.

"Oh, chickypoo. That's too much! He's taking advantage of you. I know someone who helps some of the girls with their outfits, and we usually end up buying them. He has a warehouse, and you can pick out what you want online and he'll deliver them. He also sells props if you need anything for the house. I can get you a quote this afternoon."

She breathed a sigh of relief. "Thank God. I was starting to panic. Some of the packs must have hit the human shops because they're all sold out unless someone here wants to be a Mutant Ninja Turtle."

Denver started to raise his hand.

I shook my head. "Sometimes when the scammers find out they're dealing with a pack or older immortals, they try to milk them for all they can."

"Well, that's settled. You're staying here." She nudged Austin's arm.

"That's fine," Austin agreed.

I had to admit, it sounded like the best plan. "Before settling in, I need to dash home and pack up a few things. I also want to search for Misha. My poor baby slipped out, and she's probably hiding in the bushes. A can of tuna should do the trick, and I promise I'll keep her in my room. She won't be a bother."

"I'll take her," Reno quickly said. Then I remembered our scheduled trip to see Skye's cousin. "I've got an errand to run, so I'll keep an eye on her. I don't think Wheeler's in any shape to drive her around."

"What's that supposed to mean?" Wheeler bit out.

Reno tapped his cheekbone. "Did you see the dark circles under your eyes? Get some sleep. I'll take over from here."

No one questioned Reno, and why would they? He was the second-in-command.

Within minutes, the conversation had changed to spring flowers and repairing transmissions. I adored how quickly they settled matters and how no one had stormed out. They ate together as a family and resolved their problems without holding grudges.

Wheeler looked beat. Not just tired, but something else was going on. I wanted to ask him where he'd really gone off to at the club—why he had left me dancing alone. By the look on his face, it wasn't the men's room.

The Weston pack was a busy household, and since everyone had made plans that morning, the only available cars were Wheeler's Camaro and Reno's bike. No one was allowed to drive Austin's Challenger, even if it wasn't in use. April and Lexi were headed to work, and a group had gone to the movies with the kids. When we left, Wheeler and Austin were in the back office. I wondered if Wheeler would take a stand, but I didn't know his rank in the pack. I couldn't help but notice his defeatist attitude in the kitchen that morning. He was definitely an outcast, but it seemed unfair to single out the black sheep. Then again, I didn't know his past with his brothers and what other things he'd done to deserve that reputation.

"Something going on with you and my baby brother?" Reno asked.

An errant breeze from the open car window ruffled my hair, and I smiled at a group of skinny bicyclists in colorful outfits as they zoomed by.

"He's just doing what Austin hired him to do."

"Hmm."

"Aren't you a little warm?" I pinched his long sleeve and pulled until it snapped back.

"It's breathable fabric."

"It's eighty-seven degrees, and you're dressed for an expedition to the South Pole."

"I like covering up in public," he murmured, adjusting a pair of mirrored shades on the bridge of his nose. "Didn't there used to be a clock there?" he asked, pointing to the spot on Wheeler's dash where only a few sticky pieces of adhesive glue remained.

I brushed a fleck of lint off my tan pants, wondering if I should bother calling Dean after what had happened. I'd grown to love working at Club Sin, but after this fiasco, there wasn't a doubt in my mind I would be served walking papers, regardless that someone else had instigated the shift. Club owners didn't knowingly hire panthers. Shifters had a long history with slavery, and everyone had a rank on the totem pole. Many had been alive to remember, so it was no surprise if a deer had problems with predators. But panthers had a reputation all our own.

I didn't even realize I'd been cursing until Reno pulled down his shades to get a good look at me.

"I'm fine," I said. "I'm just thinking about my job. Customers talk and rumors spread fast."

"You can always dance on the human side of town," he suggested.

"For nickels and dimes. None of the Breed clubs will hire me once they hear about this, and you can bet they're all talking about it—my ears are already burning. I've always had my panther under control. *Always*. Someone forced me, and if I ever find that man—"

"We're here," he said.

My jaw slackened as I scoped the neighborhood. Reno pulled into a parking space in a shady apartment complex, and I don't mean shady because of trees. Three men were sitting on the hood of a beat-up maroon car, smoking weed. Empty beer cartons littered the edge of the building next to a rusty blue bicycle missing a front wheel. This wasn't even a Breed complex.

"Oh, Skye," I whispered.

"She lives in a better neighborhood than this rat hole," Reno said, lifting a gum wrapper from the floor and putting it in his pocket. "Sure you don't want to wait in the car?"

"I just want to make sure her baby is okay. That's all I'm here for."

"She's with family. Of course she's okay." Reno popped open his door and got out.

I followed behind him up the steps and down a corridor until we reached a green door with a knocker. Reno used his fist instead.

"Hold on, hold on," someone yelled from inside.

Reno kicked his boot on the welcome mat to straighten it out. I glanced toward the pool area, where kids were splashing and squealing.

When the door swung open, a young man who looked in his twenties answered. He had on long yellow shorts and no shirt. He didn't look a thing like Skye—red hair and hazel eyes. His cheeks and nose were bright red, and the skin on his sunburned shoulders was peeling. He smelled like chlorine, and the roots of his hair still looked wet.

Reno widened his stance. "Are you Skye's cousin?"

"Yep. You one of her boyfriends?"

"I'm a PI. I need to ask you a few questions."

The man hitched up his shorts in the back. "I don't know jack shit. Her manager called, and I told him what I know. I bet she ran off with one of her johns."

I folded my arms to keep from wringing his neck. "Don't be an imbecile. She's not a prostitute."

"Whatever. Come on in." He led us toward an open kitchen on the right. "Trust me—I want to find her as much as you do. This kidsitting shit is not for me. My name's Jason."

"When's the last time you saw her?" Reno asked, closing the door behind him.

"Earlier that day when she dropped off the kid."

Jason shoved the laundry off the table and onto the floor. I looked around for signs of Lola, but all I saw were some toys.

Reno took a seat in one of the tiny chairs and it made an awful sound. "Did she ever mention not feeling safe? Anyone ever call her or follow her around?"

Jason lit up a cigarette and put his elbows on the table. "Yep.

About a week before she went missing. She was bitching about someone following her around. Then one night, someone made her shift in her car. I don't know how, she didn't say. Just said she woke up in her car and didn't remember anything." He took another long drag and flicked his ashes into a plastic cup. "I hear strippers get a lot of stalkers, so she had it coming. I've been telling her to get a real job or find a Shifter to hook up with, but she wants to do things her own way. Women," he said with a huff.

"Yes, *women*," I parroted. "The very thought of them having their own minds and doing whatever is necessary to take care of themselves and their children. The *nerve*."

He shot me a frosty glare and looked back at Reno. "You know what I'm talking about. Anyhow, that's all I know."

"And no one else has called for her or come around?"

"Look, I don't live with her." Jason spoke with the cigarette in his mouth while he got up and grabbed something off the cabinet. "She left her phone here when she dropped the kid off that night. You can look through it for yourself, but there's nothing weird on there." He tossed the phone through the air and Reno caught it.

"Where's the baby?" I asked.

"You mean the terror?" He snorted and sat back down, fumigating the room with his smoke. "Sleeping, I hope. I gave her some cough syrup before I went swimming, so that should keep her down for another hour."

"Is she sick?"

"No." He laughed and shook his head.

Rage ripped through me. This man was drugging a child for his own benefit, and then I realized no one else lived here and he'd left her alone!

"Give me the phone back when you're done," Jason said. "And when you find Skye, tell her to get her ass over here. She owes me big for this."

"For taking care of your blood? You pig," I spat out. "And how exactly is it that you earn *your* living?"

"Kidsitting," he said proudly. "I also fix cars."

"Something tells me you earn more for watching your own

family than you do earning a real wage. What decent man charges his cousin money to watch her baby? Family takes care of their own."

His pale brows sloped as he flicked the ashes into the cup. "You must be one of her stripper friends. Your kind is always high and mighty. You think because you pull in good tips for shaking your ass that you're somehow better than the rest of us? If my cousin wants to earn money by showing her tits, then I'm charging her money for watching her kid. You can't judge me on that shit, because she's the one in the wrong."

"You are ridiculous!" I launched to my feet and kicked my chair aside.

Reno sat back and looked at the phone. "If you hear anything from her or anyone else, I want you to call me." He laid down his business card and stood up.

"Mommy," a little girl cried, walking into the room.

I clutched my heart. The little baby didn't have on a shirt, only a pair of green shorts. She was even prettier than in the picture, with spirals of curls down to her shoulders and skin the color of caramel. Her blue eyes were sleepy and looked like she'd been crying. She had a few smudges on her face and hands that someone who loved that child would have cleaned off.

Jason's bare feet slid across the floor as he went to get her. "You've got what you need. The front door is thataway."

"Mommy?" Lola began crying. "I had a bad dream."

"Come on, kid. Quit being a crybaby." He held her hand and she yanked it away. "I said come on." Jason roughly grabbed her arm and that's when a chair went flying.

Reno's chair. It knocked over when he charged at Jason and latched his hand around the guy's throat. "Let go of her."

Jason obeyed, his face turning redder than the sunburn. Reno pushed him toward the counter until his head rested against the overhead cabinet.

"I don't like what's going on here. Not one bit. Family or not, you don't ever handle a child like that. I should snap your neck. I'm thinking about it. Thinkin' real hard."

The cigarette had fallen out of Jason's mouth and onto the floor.

Reno finally let go and knelt down in front of Lola. "I'm Uncle Reno. Does this princess have a name?"

"Lola," she sniffed.

"Princess Lola. We're going on an adventure. Do you like pizza?" She nodded.

"Good. Because on our way to the castle, we're going to get some for lunch."

"The fuck you are." Jason pushed Reno's head, and I guess he thought that might be enough to knock the man off-balance.

He thought wrong.

Reno rose to his feet so slowly that I thought I could hear Jason's heartbeat racing like a stampede of wild horses. Reno towered over him a good six inches. When he put his sunglasses on top of his head and centered his eyes on Jason, that was the last complaint we got out of him.

"Naya, go get her clothes and let's get out of here."

I hurried past them to the only bedroom in the apartment. The mattress on the floor didn't have a sheet, and clothes were everywhere. I frantically grabbed whatever looked like Lola's and stuffed it all in a paper sack I found on the floor. I also took the only toy I could find—a blue pony with a pink mane.

When I returned to the living room, Reno had Lola perched on his left arm. He glowered, keeping an eye on Jason, who was sitting in a chair by the television, his legs wide apart. Lola had put on Reno's sunglasses and was resting her head on his shoulder while sucking her thumb.

"You can bet one thing," Reno said. "Your babysitting days are over."

I crossed in front of Jason's chair and bent over. "Skye may dance for a living, but she has dignity. She's a proud mother, and you're nothing but a coward—afraid of being a man and taking care of your own. You're not even worth the slap of my hand."

I turned around, and you better believe I wanted to slap him. But if I started, I might never stop. What had Lola endured that would make her go willingly into the arms of a stranger and leave the only other person she knew as family?

We headed down to the car, and Reno helped her into the back.

"My name is Miss Naya, and I have someone who wants to keep you company." I handed her the toy pony, and she hugged it against her chin.

"Bella!"

After stopping off for a slice of cheese pizza, Reno swung by my apartment. I searched everywhere outside the building for Misha, and my heart sank when I didn't find her. The first thing I planned to do when I got to Austin's was make a few phone calls to the shelters, just in case they'd picked her up. I went inside and packed a large bag, uncertain of how long I'd be staying with the Weston pack. Change was on the horizon. Usually life shifts in new directions with unfortunate events, more so than it does with positive ones.

When I reached my front door to leave, my blood ran cold.

"Oh my God," I whispered, staring at the note pinned on the door.

Reno tapped on the horn outside. My trembling hand reached up and tugged the paper off the door.

Naya,

Now that I know who you are, it's time that you know who I am.

Delgado

At the bottom was a phone number.

But above the letter, nailed to the door, was Misha's pink collar.

CHAPTER 11

BY THE TIME WE MADE it back to Austin's house, everyone had returned from the movie. After Reno briefly explained Lola's situation to the pack, Izzy scooped her up and ran her a bubble bath. Melody was excited to have a friend her age and pulled out all her clothes to find Lola something clean to wear. When I mentioned the living conditions of the apartment we'd found her in and how Jason had given her medicine to keep her sedated, Denver stormed out of the house. He slammed the front door so hard it put a crack in the frame.

"Bet I know where he's going," Jericho murmured with a nod of his head.

Lynn sent Wheeler to Home Depot to figure out how to repair the door. Wheeler silently went, not having said a word since my return. He must be blaming me for all this. If not for me, he wouldn't be on the outs with his Packmaster, and here I was, being given the red carpet.

I skipped lunch and took a nap on the sofa, overcome with emotion. I didn't tell anyone about the note or Misha's collar. Reno had noticed I was visibly distraught but he probably assumed it had to do with Lola. Shifters didn't keep pets, and they simply wouldn't understand how devastated I was. *Of course* Skye and Lola were more important, but that didn't lessen the love I felt for my little princess. After Jericho's band had swung by on their way to a show, the house quieted.

When I woke up, my head was in someone's lap.

"Sleep good?" a familiar voice asked.

I stared at the black television in front of the sofa, nestling my head against his lap. "I had nightmares."

"I have a suggestion for what'll take care of that."

I furrowed my brow. It didn't seem like Wheeler, so I sat up.

It wasn't Wheeler.

"Ben. Do me a favor and never do that again."

He smirked and combed his fingers through his short hair. "Do what? Put your head in my lap or sound like my brother?"

I scooted away from him and noticed the last spray of golden light sifting through the front windows.

Ben crossed one leg over the other, wearing a pair of knee-length shorts and a button-up shirt. "You were pretty reluctant until I started sweet-talking you. Just face the facts: I'm the irresistible brother."

"You're a grown man who shouldn't be competitive with your twin. It shows your insecurity."

Ben snorted. "I'm not insecure. Wheeler's an ass, and everyone knows it. I pull more money into this house—no question about it. There's no competition to be had. What I can't figure out is why Austin chose *him* to be your bodyguard."

"Maybe it's because Wheeler is smarter and tougher," I suggested in a smooth voice. Ben was undoubtedly attractive. Clean-cut, close shave, a charming smile, and just an easy way about him. Even his body language was open and friendly, from the way his left arm stretched over the back of the couch to the way he made eye contact.

Until his eyes slid south.

"That's an impressive animal you've got," he said. "Wolves are overrated. I've only gone out with two myself. Usually I'll pair up with a grizzly or something along those lines. I've never been with a panther."

"Well, good luck with your bucket list, because I won't be filling it."

I stood up and he gently took my hand.

"You're a beautiful woman, Naya. Don't get mixed up with a man like Wheeler."

"Darling, I don't get mixed up with anyone. I'm not a cocktail drink. I choose my men, and right now, I'm not choosing anyone."

He swung my arm a little and smiled. "It's a shame we haven't gotten to know each other better. There's always too much going on when we have the parties or get-togethers to really talk. You should swing by the house more often. I know you're a busy woman, but I hope you find a reason to visit."

Ben gave my hand a light squeeze and stood up, brushing my arm in a friendly way before heading outside.

Deciding I needed privacy, I returned to my room. Lexi had offered me one of the upstairs rooms, but I felt like an intruder and had convinced her I'd be happier in their attached heat house.

After closing the door, I sat down on the sofa and dialed the number from the note left in my apartment.

"I've been expecting your call," a voice replied. The rich timbre of it made me shudder.

"I presume this is Delgado," I said. "Let's talk business, shall we?"

"Let's. I'm sorry to inform you that we are no longer in need of your services at the club. However, I just so happen to have another position that is opening up."

"And?"

"I ran across a valuable piece of information that suggested you might be of the feline persuasion."

"And who would have passed along a rumor such as that? Did he happen to be carrying a strobe light?"

"Watch the insults. If you take me for a fool—"

"No," I quickly said. "You're obviously a resourceful man. But I'm an inquisitive woman and find it intriguing that you didn't approach me yourself and ask. Henchmen seem so... last century."

"Seems a waste of breath to quibble about such an irrelevant topic."

"So tell me about this position."

"Now it is you who intrigues me. Have you ever fought in the panther pits? I'm not talking about the amateur fighting rings that go on in the back woods. I'm referring to the well-organized fights that take place indoors. There are admission fees and steep bets on the table. Victors are generously rewarded."

"It's illegal."

"No one seems to comprehend that we are the ones in control now."

"We? Rumor has it you're a human."

Delgado moaned a little. "What I am matters little when I fill pockets with gold coins. Shifter history is tainted in blood. These fights give strong men and women a chance to reclaim their honor. How long do you wish to hide in the shadows, ashamed of someone finding out you're a panther? I can give you more than just money. You'll walk among warriors, revered in the most prestigious social circles with the roar of the crowd chanting your name."

"I get that on stage every night."

"Maybe so, but does your panther? What I mentioned is what I can offer your animal. What can I offer you? Riches beyond your wildest dreams. To never worry if you'll have money in three or six hundred years, because this will pay more than the meager wages of an exotic dancer."

I leaned forward and drew in a deep breath. "Did you make the same offer to Skye before shoving her into a van?"

"Do you think I would make such an offer to a cougar? They're the opening act for the big show. I could have taken you forcibly if I wanted."

"No, instead you took my cat." Anger fueled my veins, but I kept my voice calm.

"Yes. Precious little thing. Come willingly and fight for me, and I will treat you like a queen. I've seen you dance, Naya. You're quite the specimen."

The way he talked reminded me of the stories I'd heard about the way immortals spoke of their Shifter slaves. And here he was, just a *human*.

"Will you exchange Skye for me?"

"No."

"And why not?"

He sighed. "Don't waste my time with questions."

"Then let me speak with her," I said coolly. "If I can talk to her and know she's all right, then I'll agree and come willingly. I'll fight for you under the terms of your offer. Treat me well, Delgado, for I *am* a queen. A happy panther is a loyal panther."

It sounded as if he were sucking on his teeth. "If you need evidence that your friend is still alive, then I can agree to that. And once you speak with her, you'll come willingly?"

"Yes," I breathed. "She's a good friend who has a little girl to take care of. Perhaps we can work out another arrangement once I'm your guest."

"Then it's a deal. I'm afraid you'll have to wait a few hours. I need to take care of a few things before I'm able to get to her location. Keep this phone on, and I'll call you back this evening."

"Very well."

I hung up in a panic. I had absolutely no intention of going with this man, but if anyone could trace a call, it would be Reno. He had knowledge of modern technology, not to mention connections with some of the savviest men in the Breed world. I called his cell and asked him to hurry down to my room. I didn't want to raise suspicion by looking for him myself.

"What's going on?" he said, cracking the door and poking his head in.

"Come inside and shut the door," I said in a low voice.

His eyes were alert and brimming with concern. Reno locked it behind him and took a few steps in my direction. "Why did you ask me to bring this?" He held up his laptop.

"I need you to trace a call."

———⊸o⧉o⊶———

"If the human police can do it, we can do it better," Reno said before taking Delgado's number and doing his thing.

His primary concern was if Delgado switched phones. He knew how to trace his call history, but we needed him to be with Skye in order to rescue her. Worst-case scenario—I'd go willingly with Delgado. Reno said we'd cross that bridge and set it on fire once we got the call, but it was too early for him to come up with a strategy.

Delgado didn't know who the hell he was dealing with. I could be just as manipulative, only in a more subtle way.

All the babies were engrossed in a movie about unicorns while I helped in the kitchen. Cooking kept my mind focused, and I baked a giant dish of my famous chicken spaghetti. Once everything had come off the stove, Austin called the pack in to eat.

"Smells delicious," Lynn said, setting my dish on the table. "You'll have to give me this recipe."

But I wasn't hungry. I sat at the end of the table and made sure Lola was doing okay. They had found another small chair and put it at the kids' table, facing the wall. Melody showed her how to play music on her tiny keyboard, and no one complained about the volume. Packs seemed to love everything about having children in their house, even the noise.

Ben walked around me and briefly touched my shoulders. "Can I get you something else to drink?"

"I'm fine."

I couldn't help but notice how Wheeler clenched his jaw, and I wondered if those two were in the midst of a family quarrel.

"Just let me know," Ben said in a low voice against my ear before walking off.

"I've missed your spaghetti!" Lexi spooned a generous helping onto her plate. "Seems like forever since I've had any."

Reno received a text message and abruptly left the table. April carried on with Izzy about selling T-shirts for the bakery. They laughed at the idea of women wearing the Sweet Treats logo on their chest, and Ben suggested they have two cookies in strategic locations.

"I've never seen anyone put it away like Will," Ben said, glaring at William, who was already finishing up his first round. "You put Denver to shame."

"Thank God Denver's at work and didn't hear you say that," Lexi commented. "Otherwise, we'd have an eating competition going on and nothing left."

"I thought that was every night?" Ben said with a laugh.

Aside from my dish, they prepared fried chicken, green beans, coleslaw, and hot links. It looked like this pack loved to eat. My kind of men.

"Naya made the spaghetti casserole," Lexi said, noting that only a quarter of the dish was eaten. "You guys don't know what you're missing."

I turned around again and smoothed my hand over Lola's hair. "How are you feeling, baby? Be sure you eat every bite of your dinner."

"I know," she said. "I like chicken." Lola held up a drumstick with one side mostly eaten.

Maizy held a small book in her left hand, reading while eating.

When I turned around, I gasped. The casserole was now half gone, and when I looked around the table, I discovered why.

"You're going to be sick if you eat all that," I said to Wheeler.

"Doesn't sound like you're very confident in your cooking," he challenged, tapping his fork against his nose.

"Oh, I'm confident, darling. No man can resist what I dish out."

"And you really dish it," he murmured.

"Anything you offer, I'll happily put in *my* mouth," Ben said, reaching for the serving spoon.

"Shut up," Wheeler said under his breath.

Ben smirked and scooped up a forkful, cramming it into his mouth as if in a hurry. "Sometimes there are games you can't win, so you need to learn how to fold and take the loss."

"Speaking of loss, don't you have a game tonight?" Wheeler kept shoveling my chicken spaghetti in, and *my*, didn't that inflate my ego just a tiny bit.

"Yep. Don't wait up on me." Ben rose from his chair and wiped his mouth with his napkin. "Except for you," he whispered as he passed by me.

No one else heard his remark, and Ben left the room.

"Naya, you haven't eaten all day," Lexi scolded. "Try some of my mom's coleslaw."

"I think I'm going to go lie down. I didn't get enough rest last night after everything, and the nap earlier wasn't enough. You go on and enjoy that dish. If you peek in the fridge, you'll find a dessert I whipped up for later."

"Oh my God," she said with a mouthful of spaghetti. "Is it that green stuff? That's the *best* dessert. No one better touch it until I have some."

I smiled and waved good night.

As soon as I reached my room, I kicked off my shoes and tried to ignore the sensation of feeling like a caged animal. I needed to get Misha back, but in my heart, I didn't know if it was too late. A man like Delgado taking care of a cat? I couldn't imagine it, but I also didn't want to imagine what he'd done with her. The only way to keep from crying was to focus on Lola. She needed her mother, and I was going to make that happen. This nightmare had to end. The world is filled with unimaginable evils, but the worst act of evil is turning a blind eye.

I turned the dimmers on above the bed and crawled over the blanket. While the main room was shaped like a rectangle, they had extended the wall using the exact dimensions of the bed, so the only way to get in was to climb onto it from the foot. The lamps in the room were off, immersing the room in darkness. I stared up at the ceiling, trying to allow the dim lights to lull me to sleep.

No matter how many times I pounded on my pillow, I couldn't settle my nerves. I propped myself up on my elbows and looked at the built-in shelf on the headboard. Someone had filled it with a large selection of romance novels—some of which had significant wear on the spine. Probably April's collection, which I found amusing since she didn't go through heat. My guess was that she and Reno used this room as a private getaway.

A knock sounded at the door. I shivered when the air-conditioning came on and a cold breath of air skated over my arms. Across the room, I heard the squeaky hinge from a door opening, but I couldn't see anything since the only lights on were the dimmers in my cubbyhole.

"It's a little early for beddy-bye, isn't it?" I heard Wheeler ask.

"I'm surprised you aren't hunched over in agony from a spaghetti overdose," I said with a snort.

"I'm still hungry."

A shiver rolled over me, and when he moved into sight, I flew up and gripped the covers. "I thought you left."

Ben smiled and tucked his hands in his pockets. "I had a little time to kill. So how about that drink? They keep it well stocked in here. Whiskey, vodka, even wine coolers. Maybe fried chicken wasn't what you needed."

"Ben, get out."

"Whoa," he said, holding up his hands. "Let's not get confused as to what's going on here."

I flipped my hair back. "I'm in bed, and you're uninvited. Which part do you think I'm confused about?"

"I'm just offering a drink to take the edge off. Maybe another time. Didn't mean to ruffle your feathers."

The door suddenly opened and my chest constricted. If it was Reno coming with news on the trace, this was about to get awkward.

"And the plot thickens," a voice said with disdain.

Even worse, it was Wheeler.

Ben turned around. "Just on my way out. Did you want to tag-team or something?" When he vanished into the darkness, I heard a struggle. They were throwing punches, and something fell over and broke.

"Get out of here!" I shouted, standing on my feet. It felt as if I had a spotlight on my white baby-doll nightie.

"You're going to regret that," one of them said, but I couldn't tell which.

"Maybe I'll cut you off," the other growled. "It's time you bail your own ass out."

"Go fuck yourself, since no one else will."

The door slammed and then I had some peace.

"Hello?" I said.

A lamp switched on from the right side of the room. Wheeler crouched down and pulled a can of soda from the short fridge. He held it to his face and turned around, maintaining his distance across the room.

I approached him and pulled the can away. "Here, let me see."

Wheeler averted his eyes, and I lightly touched the drop of blood on his cheek. "It's just a small cut." I ran a thin towel under the faucet and then pressed it to his upper cheekbone, right below his left eye. Most Shifters wouldn't shift to heal minor injuries because it angered our animal if they couldn't stay out. "Hold still for a moment. What did you come in here for?"

He turned the can of soda in his hand, looking down at it. "I haven't seen you eat all day. Maybe I don't want your panther getting hungry."

"Oh. For a fleeting moment, I thought maybe you cared." I stepped closer and peeked beneath the cloth. "Just another minute and it'll clot."

"Why don't you drink this while you're waiting?"

"I'm afraid all those bubbles will give me a headache. Caffeine on an empty stomach will keep me up all night."

"It doesn't have caffeine; it's the green can."

"Read the label," I said, realizing how tall Wheeler was when I didn't have my heels on, which put me at eye level with that gorgeous Adam's apple of his. I was standing against him, and yet I could feel the distance between us. "Well, what does it say?"

"You read it."

"I'm busy with the patient. I'll have a sip if you tell me it's caffeine-free."

"Never mind." He set the can behind him on the cabinet.

I peered beneath the towel and the bleeding had stopped. After tossing it in the sink, I took a step back and looked at him. Something occurred to me that hadn't before. "You can't read, can you?"

"I can read. What do you think I am, an idiot?"

"No... but neither am I."

Wheeler reached for the can and held it out. "It says Dew."

"Spin it around and tell me what the tiny letters on the back say."

He cracked open the can and put it in my hand. "It says *drink me.*"

"Hmm," was all I replied, turning back to the bed. I sat on the edge and took a small sip before setting the can on the floor by the wall. "Why don't you get along with your twin?"

"Brother. Twin is incidental."

"Such resentment."

Wheeler sniffed and stalked forward, hands tucked beneath his armpits. "You wouldn't understand."

"Of course I wouldn't. I'm just a stripper."

His eyes flashed up and I caught a glimmer of something in them that looked like regret. "That's not what I meant. No one understands."

"Neither of us seems to have anyone we can confide in. As much as I love Lexi, she's still so human. She will never grasp the reasoning behind why I've kept my animal hidden for so long, and for that reason, I've kept a lot more hidden from her. You seem like you have way more bubbling inside than that can of soda. If it's one thing I'm known for, it's keeping secrets. After all, I've been doing it my entire life, so I understand the importance of privacy. You'd be amazed at some of the things I know about the men in this town."

He smirked, and one of his brows sloped down at an awkward angle. "That I don't doubt. Men seem to lose common sense when their pants are down."

I narrowed my eyes. "Who said their pants were down? I don't sleep with my customers. What a travesty most people believe such a thing. Yes, there are girls who do, but dancing is just a job. When I'm not at work, I'm just an ordinary woman."

"Ordinary isn't the word I would have chosen."

"Okay then. Sexy," I purred with a sly grin.

Wheeler intrigued me, and after the scuffle with Ben, I could no longer resist the urge to learn more about him. Maybe now that he knew about my panther, it made it easier for me to want to open up. But mostly I felt like he had a lot of buried emotions beneath his gruff attitude that no one in the pack seemed to have noticed.

"Tell me," I said.

"Tell you what?"

"Confide in me and I'll give you honest advice. I'm proposing a unique opportunity for two people to be completely open with each other without any judgment or fear of it leaving this room."

He shook his head, staring at the floor as he paced around. "That's not a good idea."

"Tell me your secrets, Wheeler, and I'll tell you some of mine."

My voice softened, and I realized what I'd longed for. A sense of intimacy during the lonely nights at home when I wanted to complain about my job, my dark secrets, or even my tired feet. I just wanted to have someone there to listen. Strangely enough, Wheeler was the only person I'd ever felt an inexplicable desire to tell all my secrets to, and maybe that's because he didn't come across as someone who would feed me a line of bullshit.

"I'm not a guy who sits around and shares his feelings. This isn't a daytime talk show."

I wasn't about to let Wheeler win this battle. "Switch off the lamp and crawl into bed with me."

He licked his bottom lip and watched me from behind heavy brows.

"Fine. Just stand there and grow roots then. And wipe the smug look off your face. I'm not offering anything but conversation."

"In bed."

"If it makes it easier, I'll start and you can see how serious I am. You have a wicked tongue, but I can see you're not the kind of man who spreads gossip. So maybe that's why I trust you a little more than anyone else. I'm asking you to lie with me because I'm sleepy, and..." My voice softened. "I want to know what it feels like to lie in bed with a man and just *talk*."

Wheeler's mouth opened as if to say something.

"That's right. Men who come to my bed aren't there to talk. I choose the men I sleep with carefully, but not one has ever stayed the full night. They always have somewhere important they need to be. Maybe a silly part of me envies Lexi when she talks about how she and Austin sit up at night talking for hours until they doze off in the middle of a conversation."

Wheeler laughed and turned around. "That sounds about right. I bet I can guess who dozes off first."

I patted the bed beside me. "Men look at me as a conversation piece, not someone they can hold a conversation with. Indulge a woman who's feeling a little down."

When he switched off the lamp, I expected him to leave, so I tucked my legs beneath the covers and stared up at the ceiling. The bed sank down when Wheeler sat on the end. I scooted to the right and turned to face the wall on my right, giving him plenty of room. The light above was dim, almost like a nightlight, but brighter.

He kicked off his shoes and then scooted back. When I peered over my shoulder, he had his fingers laced behind his head, looking up at the ceiling pensively. "I've never been in this room until you came," he said absently.

"I'd assumed you built it."

"Thought you said I couldn't do anything laborious with my hands?"

I smiled. It seems he remembered everything I said, even if it was years ago. "That's an impressive memory you have."

"Hard to forget insults. They stick like verbal glue."

I turned on my back and looked at him. "I'm not going to lie, Wheeler. I despised you back then for how you treated April. I'm not a fan of men who degrade women, and the way you were doing it was arrogant and showy. In a public mall, of all places. Imagine how belittled she must have felt."

"Yeah, it was a shitty thing to do," he agreed. "Knowing her now makes it harder to remember, but back then, she was just a human trying to break apart the pack."

"People are more than who they allow you to see."

"Not me. What you see is what you get."

I pulled the sheet up higher. "So you keep saying, but that's not true. You didn't have to risk your life bringing me here. Let me see your arm." Without waiting, I pulled his right arm away from his head, studying his tattoos closely. "Why does the chain have a broken link?"

The silence was so heavy that I could hear the electric buzzing of the fridge.

"You've never told anyone, have you?" I asked. "There's

something about your past you're hiding. You wear ink on your body like armor, but that's not a confession—it's a defense. Showing isn't telling, not when people don't know what they're looking at." I turned on my left side, staring at the marks on his shoulder. Up close, something about them looked off.

"It can *never* leave this room," he stressed in a low voice.

"You have nothing to fear. I give you my word I'll never speak of anything you reveal to me within this room. I'll tell you some of my dark secrets so we'll be even in the blackmail game. But I expect the same courtesy."

He pursed his lips and gave a short nod. "Deal."

That moment changed everything between us. It's a rare opportunity when a person removes all the layers and allows you to see who they are at the core. Sometimes we don't even get that chance with our own family or friends, and maybe it's easier to let someone you don't have any emotional connection with see that side of you. There's no fear of rejection, ridicule, or withholding love. We had nothing to lose.

"So? Do tell."

CHAPTER 12

As WHEELER PREPARED TO TELL me his dark secrets, I felt a flutter of anxiety. What was the price of this kind of trust between two people who had previously disliked each other? I'd begun to see Wheeler in a different light—glimpses of who he was hiding from the world. A girl in my profession learns a lot about the masks men wear—the double lives they lead. The more I got to know Wheeler, the more he fascinated me. What made a man like him tick? Men weren't grumpy just for the hell of it. Men also didn't risk their lives to save a panther, and that selfless act changed everything about the way I saw him.

"Tell me about the chain," I said, circling my finger around the dark curves of ink.

His chest rose and fell, a quiet breath escaping. "I used to be a big shot in certain circles. Legit work. Saying I worked for a few rich immortals is a gross understatement. I managed their money, made them more, and suddenly I had offers being thrown at me from all directions. I had standards. My clients had to be reputable, meaning no dirty dealings that could land me in Breed jail. My conditions were that they paid me a fair rate and allowed me to work from home."

"Why would that be such a big deal?"

Wheeler rubbed at his chest. "Some of the rich boys live in mansions and like their trusted employees nearby. Sometimes they move their staff into the house to either live or work, that way they can keep a close eye on them. When they find someone good, they don't want another immortal to lure them away with a better offer. That's too much control, and I don't do business with men who don't trust me. Anyhow, it wasn't a big deal to the guys I worked for because I learned how to draw up contracts that made everyone happy."

"So what happened?"

"Ben happened." Wheeler tugged at the short hairs of his beard with his left hand. "He makes money playing tournaments, but he's also got a gambling problem. He wins big, but he loses bigger. Ben was never able to make money the way I could, so he learned early on how to get it fast with little work. He's always been competitive with me, and maybe it didn't sit well with him that I'd finally found a career making more money than he did. We're both good with numbers; he just went in a different direction. He was always betting when we were kids. Always getting us in trouble, always daring me to do things I shouldn't have. Back then, our own parents couldn't tell us apart. It didn't make sense for both of us to take the punishment when he wouldn't admit his guilt, so I stepped up and took his place."

"And your other brothers?"

"I'm older than I look, kitty cat. Reno was a grown man back then and the others hadn't been born."

"Ah. I bet you two were a handful for your parents."

He chuckled nostalgically. "Yeah. Things weren't so bad back then. As the years went on, Ben kept getting in trouble, and I kept digging him out. Maybe it's not all his fault. I had it coming because I conditioned him that way."

My finger ran across the broken link again. "You had what coming?"

Another quiet moment passed. "Back then, we were identical. Even now, people can still tell we're twins. The first time it happened, he lost his ass gambling. I ran into a couple of guys who had a serious issue with how I didn't pay them after losing a game. When I told them my name, it didn't stop them from beating me with a crowbar."

"He impersonated you? Oh my God."

"Yeah. Only *what the fuck* were my words. The worst part about it? After Ben found out I took a beating for him, he said *thanks*. Didn't even apologize for the fact I was tortured for an hour."

"When did all this happen?"

"Mmm..." He gave it a little thought. "Austin was in high

school, or just leaving. We weren't living here, so I don't remember. We stuck around long enough to be there for Austin's childhood, then would visit for extended stays. After that, we diverged and did our own thing. Well, everyone except Ben, who followed me around like a shadow."

I swept my hair back and tucked the pillow beneath my head. Wheeler appeared uncomfortable, so he locked his fingers behind his head, which left me staring at his armpit. I wrinkled my nose when he glanced at me.

"Don't like the view?" he asked with humor in his voice. He dropped his arm again and scooted away. "The pack is oblivious to his gambling addiction because he's portrayed it as a career. To them, *I'm* the problem child."

"But why?"

"Look at me, Naya. Do you really have to ask?"

"So that's why you started changing your looks? You were mistaken for Ben, and were afraid he'd keep doing it."

"The damage was done. He'd ruined my reputation with a few clients, and the bitch of it was, I couldn't explain. Telling the truth would mean betraying my brother, and that's not what a loyal wolf does. The tats put an end to his impersonation game."

"And the chain?"

He scraped his bottom lip with his teeth. Wheeler had more definition in his face than Ben. There was a shadow along the contours of his jaw, his brows sloped at a different angle, and his body type seemed tougher. I grinned when I mentally compared them to spaghetti—one raw and stiff, while the other was cooked and soft.

"What's so funny?" he asked.

"Nothing. I was just imagining you as a noodle."

"You're a strange woman."

"So I've been told."

A smile played on his lips and he wiped it away with his hand. "I doubt that."

"Not everyone finds me attractive. Some don't like my playful personality, but this is who I am. *So what* if I'm a little flirtatious? I enjoy life too much to sulk about it."

"Sounds like you've had nothing but good times."

I sat up on my elbow. "Just because I have a positive outlook doesn't mean my life hasn't been seasoned with tragedy. I had to watch my mother die in a human hospital."

"Shit. I didn't know. Sorry."

"How could you?" I eased back down and shivered. "My papa died when I was just a little girl, and it was up to my mama to take care of me. She worked her tail off to support us, and she did it the right way. Three jobs—and none of them involved taking her clothes off. She left behind some money, but not enough. Her plan was to keep working that pace to give me a future. Mama always said I was too much for any one man, so I needed to make enough money to live on my own. It's hard to find another panther. Most of our kind keep it a secret, although I've heard about some places in the country where they've congregated in large numbers."

"No panther online-dating service?"

"Don't be silly," I said, lightly slapping his arm.

He turned his head to face me. "You could call it Purrfect Connection."

"You're getting less funny."

Wheeler pinched his eyebrow and smiled.

"I had to make tough choices," I continued. "Now I'm out of a job, and I'm not sure if I'll be able to dance again. Not in this town."

"Sometimes when one door shuts, another opens."

"Hmm," I said, tickling his armpit with a stroke of my finger. "Are you sure you're Wheeler and not Ben? That's so optimistic of you."

He narrowed his eyes at me in the sexiest manner before looking back up at the ceiling. "You have connections. Take a job as an event coordinator or personal assistant. Lexi should be paying you for helping with the menus and website, not just the people you're connecting her with."

"That's what friends do for each other."

"True. But you could be doing that for a whole lot of other

people who don't have connections. You seem to know everyone and keep good business relations. I've seen men hire professionals who do what you're doing. Chew on that for a while."

"And who is going to take an exotic dancer seriously?"

"Who wouldn't?"

I laughed and snuggled against the pillow. "Are you going to tell me about the chain, or are you going to keep dodging the question? I have an excellent memory, darling."

His face flushed, but it wasn't from embarrassment. Something else was culminating within him—a confession. "Ben wanted to go big time, always looking for a pot of gold. Then he discovered cage fights. There was an unscrupulous ring in east Texas, deep in the backwoods. You don't mess around with that world. Poker is one thing; Shifter fights are something else."

My heart raced at his admission. I'd never known anyone involved in this life, and it's something that haunted my dreams because of the stories my mother had told me about my father's past.

Wheeler flattened his hands on his chest, rubbing at his shirt as if he were feeling physical discomfort. "Ben lost a fight and took off like he always does. I don't know how he got away with not paying in full up front, but he's always been a smooth talker. That left me to clean up the mess. We lived together at the time, and they tracked down our house. There was a knock at the door, and Ben looked out the peephole and panicked—actually slid underneath the bed to hide. These guys were going to collect their money or cut his throat. What the hell could I do? I had no choice."

"You paid them off."

"Didn't have that kind of money. I made good money back then, but what Ben owed... Forget it. I bargained for his life, but they wouldn't agree. No payment plans, nothing. So I did the only thing I could—the only alternative they offered. I paid off his debt by going into the pits."

"You did what!" I shrieked, sitting up and looking down at him in horror. "Tell me you're kidding."

"The band on my wrist," he continued, holding up his right arm. "That's where they shackled me. A year of my life. A fucking *year*. I was in survival mode; there was no way out even if I came up with the money."

"You fought?"

He rose up on his elbows and looked at me with tortured eyes. "I survived."

"But no one walks out of the pits alive. I've never heard of such a thing!"

"You're right, and it would have been a matter of time before my luck ran out. That's why the chain on my arm is broken. One of the guards got a little too drunk, stood a little too close to the bars, and that's all she wrote. I opened all the cages, but some of them didn't go. Can you believe that? They were gone—mentally," he said, tapping his head.

I hadn't realized I was covering my mouth with my hand. "How did you live?"

"What I did to survive I'll never wash off my conscience. The tats? They started as a way to separate myself from Ben for good. But some of them are hiding scars. Sometimes they'd throw us into the pit in human form against an animal to toughen us up. Sometimes they whipped us. After I escaped, I went back to get my revenge, but they'd already packed up and moved. I never got my due justice."

"You're kidding me. Please tell me this is a joke." Tears welled in my eyes. My God, what this man must have gone through, and all for his *brother*!

"Nope," he said, easing onto his back. "So maybe you get a little tense around people because you think they'll find out what you are and see you as a threat, but I'm the real deal. I'm the Shifter that gives people waking nightmares. I killed to eat, breathe, and live another day. There's no glory in that, even if it was survival. I was undefeated, and they pitted me against some of the baddest fighters out there."

"Panthers?"

His voice cracked. "Yeah, panthers. Maybe that's why I've never been a cat person. Throw a man into a pit against a panther and it changes his perspective on things. I fought them in human and wolf form. Maybe you see me as a reticent man, but when you've stared into the soul of a panther who is dying in your arms and drawing their last breath, something inside you shuts off." He threw his arm over his eyes and went quiet.

"You have to tell Austin."

"I can't," he whispered.

My eyes sharpened and I pushed his leg. "You *have* to. Ben will weaken the pack, and if he gets out of control again—"

"*I can't!*" he roared, leaning up on his elbows. "He's my twin. He's the other half of me. Betraying him would be like killing myself. No matter what's happened between us, I still love him."

His Adam's apple bobbed when he swallowed thickly, and Wheeler fell onto his back and covered his face with his arm again. Rage and shame—that's what this man had been reduced to.

"I'm sorry. I should have never asked you into my bed. Now I know why you've always hated me."

His laugh was short-lived and quiet. "I don't hate you. That's the problem."

When I touched his leg consolingly, he sucked in a sharp breath. And just like that, without the man even looking at me, I turned him on. My whole life I'd used my body to make a man desire me, but Wheeler hardened from a single touch of compassion. I watched his arousal as it began to tighten his pants—straining against the fabric. His entire body tensed, and he kept his arm shielding his eyes as if it could hide him from the truth.

The truth that he wanted me, despite his loathing for panthers. That explained the inner conflict. I was his enemy; I represented what he had killed to stay alive.

I wanted to reach out and touch him some more, but he was too vulnerable.

"Delgado took my cat," I said absently, pulling my hand away.

Wheeler snatched my wrist and leaned forward. "Say again?"

"When I went back to my apartment to get my things, he'd left a note on my door."

"What did it say?" Wheeler sat up.

I shrugged, hesitant at first about how much I wanted to confide in him. But we had made a promise in this room, and I needed to give back some of that trust that I'd taken. "Delgado wants me to work for him."

"Doing what?" he bit out.

I snatched my wrist away. "Not dancing. He took Misha, and for that, he's going to pay. I want to find Skye and anyone else he's holding."

"And how are you going to do that?" he asked, cocking his head.

"A girl has her resources." I leaned on my left leg and sighed. "My father was a great warrior. He was much older than my mother, and he died of old age. You two have a lot in common. He spent time in the panther pits, starved and tortured. My mama said he carried a tremendous guilt on his shoulders and spent the rest of his life in servitude, helping those in need. He fought other people's battles—even saved a pack from rogues once. He did what was right and protected those who were weaker. Maybe that makes him a superhero in my head, but I've inherited his tenacity. I don't run from my problems, Wheeler. Maybe what you see isn't always what you get."

He scoffed and shook his head.

I grabbed his chin and turned it my way. "Do you think growing a beard and putting ink on your body makes you tougher? Don't underestimate me just because I get a pedicure and Brazilian wax. You don't know a thing about what I'll do for my friends. Lexi has an idea, but that's just scratching the surface," I said, speaking close to his mouth.

"And what do you plan to do?"

"Either hunt him or play his game and turn the tables. I'm a born predator," I said with a purr, stroking the prickly hair on his jaw. "The only thing that frightens me is being caught off guard like when those men were following me. Maybe now that everyone knows I'm a panther, I feel more in control than ever." I traced my finger over his bottom lip and felt his hot breath beat against it. "Delgado is going to pay."

"I want in."

"In what?" I tilted my head and half smiled.

"Whatever you plan on doing. I want in."

Wheeler closed his mouth around my finger and suddenly flipped me onto my back. Ancient heat coursed through my veins, and a dark hunger began to emerge. Wheeler sat back on his legs and lifted my foot, holding it below his chin. His eyes briefly skated between my legs since my nightie covered nothing.

"I like this," he said, flicking the loose chain on my toe ring.

Without warning, he put his mouth around my middle toe, clasping the ring between his teeth and slowly pulling it off. Seeing Wheeler perform that act sent liquid fire through my body, and I moaned in response.

When a fist pounded against the door, Wheeler jumped to his feet and vanished in the darkness. I sat up, my heart thundering against my chest.

I'd never be able to erase that visual from my mind.

"What the hell are you doing in here?" I heard Reno ask.

"Checking up on our guest. She didn't eat, you know. And what exactly are *you* doing here?"

It was interesting to hear all the accusations and suspicion in the inflection of their tone without seeing them.

"Both of you come in," I said, scooting to the end of the bed. "There's no sense in playing games since we're all playing the same one. Turn on the light and let's talk about Delgado."

That evening, we snuck out of the house. The Weston pack was used to the comings and goings of the family, so hearing the Camaro firing up raised no alarms. Everyone assumed I had gone to bed for the night. Instead, Wheeler had crept into the laundry room and found a pair of jeans and a dark T-shirt that would fit me, along with some sneakers.

"You look good dressed down," he said when I climbed into the backseat of his Camaro. I didn't like dressing so boyishly, nor did I like how constricting the jeans were. It felt like a costume, so it was weird to have a man compliment me on clothes that weren't sexy.

The car rocked when Reno sat in the passenger seat with his

laptop. Delgado hadn't called, but Reno said they'd be able to track his number—something about using towers. Thank God for men and their electronic toys; I knew little about such things.

"You sure you want to come?" Reno asked in a gruff voice, twisting his neck around so he could see me out of the corner of his eye.

"You strike me as a man who's done this before, and because of that, I'm absolutely positive. The sooner we move in, the better. Skye is my only concern, but if Delgado is there, then perhaps we can kill two birds with one stone."

"I got a big fucking rock with his name on it," Wheeler murmured.

As soon as my phone rang, Reno perked up. "Same number?"

"Yes, same one." I took a calming breath before answering so my voice wouldn't waver. "Naya speaking."

"I've got someone here who wants to say hello."

The car lurched to a stop and Reno's hand flew up in front of Wheeler, signaling him to stay quiet. The engine cut off.

"Hello?" a shaky voice said.

In that moment, whatever fear I'd been suppressing emerged. "Skye? Please tell me you're okay. Did he hurt you?"

"Naya?" Skye wept, her voice broken. "How's my baby? Can you tell her Mommy loves her so much? Please tell my baby girl I'll always love her and I'm so sorry."

Tears streamed down my cheeks, and I didn't bother to wipe them away.

"Is that sufficient?" Delgado asked. "She's alive, and I assure you she's in good hands. I've met my end of the bargain, and you have what you need. That's all I can give you." It sounded as if he was walking. He was out of breath as he talked.

Oh my God, what if there wasn't enough time for Reno to do his trace? I had to stall.

"Let me speak to her again. I have to tell her that her baby's okay."

"That's not what we agreed on. I'm a reasonable man, Naya. Not a man you can lead around by his dick. I'm not going to lie—I'd love to show you the life I can provide you, and it's not an offer I've made to just anyone."

Wheeler and Reno had turned around completely in their seats to watch. I sat in the center, staying calm and focused.

"You're a man of your word, Delgado. And I'm a woman of mine."

"That's what I like to hear," he said in a voice as smooth as bourbon. "Where should I have my men pick you up?"

"If I'm coming of my own free will, then you should give me your address like a gentleman," I said with a sly chuckle. "This isn't just about good business but also mutual trust. It's a misconception to think forcing submission and mistreatment will make a panther angry enough to fight. Let me tell you a little something about panthers. We're savage predators, but if frightened, wounded, or angry, we don't think clearly. I want to believe this is a good deal for both of us. I'm a woman who looks out for herself, and money is a language I'm fluent in."

"Hmm," he murmured. "This should be an interesting arrangement."

"Ever been with a panther?" I said seductively. "There's nothing like it."

I let the thought linger while giving a dramatic roll of my eyes to temper the volcanic look on Wheeler's face. Delgado needed incentive.

Delgado recited an address, and I committed to being there no later than tomorrow afternoon. He said he had somewhere important to be and that my little diversion was stalling his evening. I graciously apologized and ended the call on a good note. Humans were so gullible. Shrewd businessman or not, every man had a weak spot, and it was usually between his legs. Delgado liked to be in control, but I could also sense he preferred fealty over fear. He was a man who wanted to feel like a king in our world, and having a panther at his side would bring him one step closer to that fantasy.

Wheeler drove around while Reno continued typing on his computer.

"Got it," Reno finally said.

Wheeler stopped at a light and glanced at the bright screen on Reno's laptop.

I leaned forward and tapped Reno on the shoulder. "He was on the move, so it looks like we're on a rescue mission, not seek and destroy."

Reno looked around when Wheeler pulled his car into a parking place in front of a fast-food restaurant. "What are you doing?"

Wheeler unlatched his seat belt. "Five seconds."

"Now? You better get it in check, brother."

Wheeler popped him the middle finger and shoved his door open. When it slammed, I leaned close to Reno, picking up the subtle scent of his cologne. Funny how I hadn't given it much thought before, but now that I was near Reno, I realized how much I preferred Wheeler's natural smell to something out of a bottle.

"So what's the plan?" I asked.

"If Delgado took off, we'll just stick to the original plan of getting the girl out. The location he was calling from isn't where I thought it would be. See that?" He pointed at the screen. "Not the area of town where you would keep Shifters caged. I think he moved her to a different location for your benefit."

"To his house?"

"Could be, or just one of his many homes. Rich bastards like to wipe their feet all over the place. I don't know about this. Usually they keep them caged and lightly guarded. But in the city? He's probably got a handful of men on the property. If this doesn't go down as planned, one of them could make a call and tip him off."

"So? Let them," I said flippantly. "I'd love nothing more than to meet the man himself. The legendary human who walks among us like some kind of untouchable titan. That's a man I want to knock on his ass."

Reno's lips eased into a grin. "My kind of girl."

Wheeler reappeared, and the moment he slammed the door, a heavy scent filled the car. He turned around and handed me a paper bag. I peered in at two hamburgers wrapped in thin paper. Maybe I should have raised a complaint that I wasn't hungry or scolded him for taking a detour for burgers, but a wolf had brought me food. My panther stirred with approval, recognizing a male was providing for her.

"Guns blazing?" Wheeler asked.

"No, but I'm packing." Reno shifted in his seat to look at both of us. "We'll drive around and scope the property first. I'm curious if he has Breed or human guards. I ain't gonna church it up for you: if they're Vampires, we're up shit creek. They'll hear us coming before we even ring the doorbell."

"What makes you think Skye is in there?" I asked. "If you lock a person in a bedroom, they're going to try to escape, even if it means burning the house down."

"They might have her tied up," Wheeler suggested. "Handcuffs, in the basement… Chains can wrap around pipes nice and tight."

Reno shot him a hard glare. "Park at the end of the street. I brought some equipment that'll pick up any shortwave communication devices. You two sit tight in the car while I scope out the property. Once I have the information I need, I'll tell you the plan."

"Then why don't *you* drive?" Wheeler suddenly pivoted around and crawled between the seats.

I scooted all the way to the right and ducked when he pulled his legs into the backseat. Meanwhile, Reno simply got out of the car and walked around. The car only had two doors, so I was stuck in the back.

"Comfy?" I asked.

"Damn," he grunted, situating himself. "I didn't realize how snug it was back here."

"Never tested out the backseat of your own car?"

"That's such a human thing to do," he quickly said, rolling his head to the side to look at me. "Nothing could turn me on in this cramped space."

Reno got in and moved his seat back for more legroom.

"You're an ass," Wheeler barked out, shoving at the seat in protest.

I smiled playfully, wondering why Wheeler had switched seats. "Miss me already?"

"I can't drive and twist my neck around to hear you talking. What did he say?"

I ate the last piece of my burger and sighed. "Delgado wants to take care of me. I'm not sure if he's serious or is saying anything to get my panther in his clutches. He's tempting me with money and a high position."

Wheeler stretched one of his legs over to my side. "That kind of thing goes on, you know. I've seen it. Not everywhere, but some owners treat their prized warriors like champions instead of animals. I've seen men get rich with the right owner."

Reno started messing with the radio and stopped on "You Shook Me All Night Long."

I slowly unwrapped the second burger and offered it to Wheeler. "Have a bite."

Wheeler pinched the whiskers on his chin. "I bought those for you."

I scooted closer until our bodies touched and held it to his lips. "Open your mouth."

His lips parted, and Wheeler took a small bite from the burger.

"Thank you for thinking of me," I said quietly, so Reno couldn't hear. "I'm less jittery when my panther's been fed."

I sank my teeth into the same spot Wheeler had bitten into.

"I didn't know what you like," he said.

That made me laugh. "I'm a predator. I like protein."

"But you're too good for beef jerky?"

"A lady should be more refined than drooling on a dry stick of meat."

A pickle slipped out of the burger and onto the wrapper. Wheeler pinched it between his fingers and placed it on his tongue, chewing slowly. It raised the hair on the back of my neck.

"Why did you want to come and be a part of this?" I asked.

Wheeler turned away and looked straight ahead. "Delgado is a man who needs to be stopped."

I curled my hand around his arm and leaned against him. "Is that all?"

He didn't answer, and I suddenly wished Reno would turn

down the radio. Wheeler's muscles tensed beneath my fingertips. I was certain he could see me breathing faster, but Wheeler made no attempts to put his arm around me. I adored his restraint, quietly laughing to myself at the absurdity of my attraction to a man who showed no interest in me. Maybe he was right; maybe I *was* a glutton for punishment. But with him I found an honesty I'd never experienced with anyone else. None of the men who had showered me with physical affection stuck around. It was only a ploy to get what they wanted, and truthfully, I got what I wanted too. I knew the game they played, and that's one reason I'd grown cynical about love. My mama had once told me that beauty was blinding, and men were incapable of loving a ruby in their pocket. She had bewitched my father and had fallen madly in love with him, but she'd often wondered if he would have given her a second glance had she been older or less attractive.

"You sure you want to do this?" Wheeler asked.

We hit a bump and Reno fumbled with the radio.

"Are you asking me to reconsider because I'm a woman?"

Wheeler's right hand slid over my thigh and he gave it a featherlight squeeze. "Maybe I'm asking because it's dangerous and I don't want anything to happen to you."

"You have to say that; you're my bodyguard."

His chest rumbled with a deep chuckle. "Austin gave me my walking papers on that job."

I gave him a peevish look. "Sometimes I feel like I have to beat an answer out of you."

His eyebrow arched. "We wouldn't want that," he said obliquely.

Reno glanced at us in the rearview mirror as the car slowed. "Heads up, boys and girls. We're here."

Wheeler leaned forward and looked at the mansion in the distance. "And boom goes the dynamite."

CHAPTER 13

"**W**HAT DO YOU THINK HE's doing out there?" I whispered.

Wheeler laced his fingers together across his stomach. "Reconnaissance. Peeking in windows, smearing mud on his face, crawling through the flower garden, petting the dog…"

I smacked him on his knee and chuckled. We had put space between us in the backseat. I was the one who scooted away first because when Reno had glanced at us in the rearview mirror, his right eye twitched. I'm sure an exotic dancer snuggling all over the black sheep of his family was enough to raise an eyebrow, and I didn't want to stir up trouble between the two brothers.

I'd spent years disliking Wheeler because of one incident, and while I still didn't think he had handled himself admirably, I was discovering a secret side that Wheeler kept hidden from his own family. This man wore tattoos to cover battle scars, and despite his past fighting panthers, he had still risked his life for me.

"Do you have siblings?" he asked, breaking the silence.

"No. Panthers don't usually have large families. My God, I don't know how Izzy grew up with siblings close to the same age, and not even the same animal! Brave girl."

"Crazy parents."

"You can say that again." I felt the urge to reach in the front seat and crack the windows; the air was growing sticky and warm. "You should at least tell Austin about your past, even if you don't mention Ben."

"I'd rather not talk about this right now. 'Preciate ya."

"Perhaps we can discuss it in bed later," I purred. "You can't keep secrets forever. Your Packmaster needs a better understanding of where you're coming from. You shouldn't be shamed by something that wasn't your fault."

"It was my choice."

I turned to face him. "It was your choice to save your brother."

His lips peeled back. "At the cost of lives? There's no justifying that."

Wheeler's internal conflict seemed clearer to me now. He had to deal with an ungrateful brother, but he also wrestled the demons of feeling like a murderer. Can a person justify killing another to save the life of someone they love? Cage fights were about survival, but Wheeler had already painted himself a killer.

"Family means a lot to you, doesn't it?"

His voice softened. "It's the only good thing I have—the only thing worth fighting for."

"You did that in the cage, you know. Fought for your brother."

"I murdered people!" His voice reverberated off the windows and ceiling.

I pointed my finger in his face. "You didn't walk up to someone on the street and take their life. You and other victims—yes, *victims*—were put in a situation where you had to survive. I'm sure they were just as eager to live as you were and fought ruthlessly."

Wheeler threw his head back. "Not the first one." Three deep lines pressed into his forehead and he rubbed at them. "They don't put new blood in with an experienced fighter the first time. I was caged with another wolf, and neither of us had shifted. He was just a kid. Looked my age, but I could tell he really *was* that age. He gripped the bars, screaming for them to let him out."

"How did they get you to fight? If you were both unwilling…"

Wheeler's hands dropped to his lap and his voice fell flat. "They threatened to kill someone in our families. They used verbal tactics to turn us against each other. When that didn't work, they flipped on a strobe. I shifted, and they were outside the cage, prodding my wolf with electric pokers to piss him off. I could feel his confusion and anger."

"And the other wolf?"

"He didn't shift. I wasn't sure if it was because he'd covered his eyes or hadn't gone through his first change. Just as I slipped away and let my wolf take over, I remember him huddled on the slab of concrete, gripping the bars and crying."

"*Bastards*," I whispered. "Nothing I say is going to make a difference, but you need to put that guilt to rest. Victims always want to think they had some level of control, but that's a lie."

"What do you know about being a victim?"

"That it's perceptional," I said. "You can either live as a victim or become a survivor. The choice is yours, and it will change your life in ways you can't imagine. Have I ever experienced anything like you have? No. But if I had lived my life as a victim of circumstance, then I might have made poorer choices. My self-confidence would be low, and maybe I'd turn tricks like some of the other girls. But I stand behind my choices and my past, and screw anyone who has a problem with it."

A smile wound up his face, and he stared listlessly out his window.

"It's liberating," I pressed in soft words. "Even if your Packmaster is the only one to know, you shouldn't continue carrying the burden of guilt. You might be surprised by what he has to say."

"He'll toss me out on my ass."

"Look at what you did for Ben; do you think your brothers wouldn't do the same for you?"

He centered his eyes on mine, pain glittering in their depths.

I stroked his cheek and pinched the hair on his chin. "I know you love him, but if Austin turns his back on you, then maybe he doesn't love you as much as you deserve to be loved."

"Maybe I *don't* deserve it. Ever think of that?"

My hand slid down to his arm, and I traced my finger across the shadows of his ink. I liked the way he let me touch him even though he sat stoically, as if he didn't deserve affection. Wheeler reminded me of the Tin Man—all rusty and impenetrable on the outside, devoid of a heart. But who could have guessed that beneath all that armor was a man capable of unwavering devotion and love? I saw it in the way he protected his pack no matter the cost to himself. Could I have done the same for another?

I wondered.

"I've never met anyone as dangerous and intelligent as you, Wheeler. Lexi tells me all about her brothers, and I know the kind of work you've done for them as well as in your past. That's a beautiful mind to waste in that enormous head of yours."

"I've never had a woman compliment me for having a big head."

"Now *that* I doubt," I growled sexily.

Wheeler suddenly leaned forward and gripped the seat in front of him. "Shit."

"What is it?"

"Eleven o'clock. We've got company."

Two men walked swiftly toward us—men in dark clothes with stern looks on their faces as they passed beneath a streetlight.

"What do we do?" I whispered.

Wheeler looked at me wide-eyed and suddenly gripped the back of my neck, pulling me into a crushing kiss. His tongue glided into my mouth in a velvety stroke, and the seat made a terrible sound as he shifted the weight of his body onto mine.

"Wait, not like this," I whispered, pushing him away.

His eyes searched mine, looking like a time bomb ready to blow. The men were nearing the car, and when he turned to look at them, I straddled him and melted my lips against his.

Wheeler groaned, his fingers biting into the back of my jeans, where he held on as if he were riding a roller coaster. I shifted my hips and felt him hardening beneath me. The kiss went deeper, and suddenly I couldn't get close enough to him. His whiskers scratched my chin, and his taste was dark and wonderful. My fingers tangled in his hair—pulling and fisting as I rubbed my body against his chest.

A fist pounded against the glass, but Wheeler ignored them. His mouth slid greedily down to my throat while lifting the hem of my shirt. Suddenly, he pulled my bra aside and sucked on my nipple.

I cried out, scraping my fingernails on the nape of his neck. I rocked my hips again, feeling a swell of desire culminating within me.

In the distance were murmurs and fading footsteps—hardly

noticeable over the sound of my heart pounding against my chest or the sound his lips made as they came away from my breast before he quickly followed with a gentle bite. When I looked down and saw my nipple between his teeth and the carnal lust in his eyes, I wanted more.

His touch was electric, and Wheeler couldn't stop running his hand over the thick curve of my hips.

I pulled back his hair and stole a kiss, whispering against his lips, "*Fuego*."

"Huh?" he said, out of breath, not understanding I wanted him to know his touch was like fire.

The car door was wrenched open and I winked at him before climbing off. Reno got in and turned around two seconds after I'd adjusted my shirt.

His eyes darted back and forth between us. "Do I want to ask?"

Cool as a breeze, Wheeler steadied his voice and nodded toward the window. "Two of his men came up to the car. We had to throw them off."

Reno glanced down at Wheeler's erection. "I'd say it was a success. Look, he doesn't appear to have any Vampires working for him. In fact, they look pretty human to me."

"Not surprising," Wheeler said, raking his fingers through his disheveled hair. "Men get paranoid about Vampires turning on them. Most of the big shots I worked for didn't keep any on the premises. Fear of eavesdropping and all that."

Reno reached into the floor of the passenger seat and pulled out a gun, turning the grip toward us. "The guard in back took a smoke break and fell asleep in a chair before I left. I saw one downstairs, two out front, and they don't keep the back door locked. If it is, then you'll have to search one of the guards for the key. You take the back and I'll handle the two jokers out front. The gun is for inside use only. This is a last resort if all else fails. Naya takes the gun for protection. Think you can handle it?"

I adjusted my hair. "If one of the men in the house spots me, I have a better distraction. With you, they'll know something is afoot," I said, touching the gun. "Maybe you should let me go in first as a decoy. They might think the boss sent them their early Christmas bonus."

"I don't like that idea," Wheeler grumbled.

Reno's eyes swung over to his. "Why not? Sounds like a plan to me."

I pushed Reno's hand away. "I don't need a gun."

"The fuck you don't," Wheeler spat.

These men were too much. "Darling, I've got two secret weapons that will bring any man to his knees. Care to disagree?"

In the backseat of that dark Camaro, Wheeler's cheeks flushed. He seemed aware of it and pinched the bridge of his nose, hiding his face behind his hand. "And if they make a call?"

Reno glanced over his shoulder through the windshield. "By then, we're in. We haul ass and go through every room. When we find her, I need one of you to pull the car up front so we can get the hell out of here. Is your car fast enough?"

Wheeler patted the seat. "She's never let me down yet."

Reno pushed open his door. "Let's go."

By the time I climbed out of the car, Reno had taken off.

Wheeler grabbed my hand and we sprinted through a dense thicket of trees toward the back of the house. Delgado had money, and most wealthy men didn't fence in their backyards. Sometimes they had low walls in the distance around the property, but usually there were acres of private land. That's what he had, and the trees provided enough cover until we neared the side of the house. There was a large fountain making enough noise to conceal our heavy breaths.

The guard moved within sight, armed with at least two weapons I could see.

"Now what?"

"I kick some ass," Wheeler said.

I gripped his arm tightly when he took a step forward. "He'll see you coming. He'll radio for help."

"Well, kitty cat, what's *your* plan?"

I peeled off my shirt, bent down, and tucked a leaf in my hair. "Men just love to play hero."

Before he could argue, I jogged toward the guard, stumbling and out of breath. When he pulled out his gun, I quickly tripped to appear helpless and injured. Then I flipped onto my back, holding my chest. "Please help," I whispered.

He peered down at me, mesmerized by the rise and fall of my ample breasts beneath the lacy fabric of my black bra. Then I heard a thwack, and his knees buckled. Wheeler had crept up behind him and smacked him over the back of the head with the butt of his gun.

I leaped to my feet and grinned victoriously. *Whee! This was fun.*

Wheeler knelt down, disarmed him, and pulled a pair of cuffs from the back of the guard's pocket. "Well, isn't that convenient?" He locked the man's hands behind his back and tightened the cuffs.

"Sure you want to waste those on *him*?" I lifted my nose and sauntered around him, feeling his molten gaze on me for a fraction of a second. Then I heard fabric tearing. Wheeler held a strip of material in his hand and balled up another, shoving it into the man's mouth before tying a gag.

"That's not my shirt, is it?"

He winked. "Sure looks like it."

I put my hands on my hips and feigned annoyance, but without knowing how many guards were inside, maybe a woman in a bra would temporarily stun them before they considered firing on us. It sure seemed to have worked its magic on this poor fellow.

Wheeler dragged him around a large bush by his ankles and then stared at him for a minute. "See anything we could use to tie him to a tree?"

"How about that rope?" I suggested.

His eyes flicked up in surprise.

"That would be convenient, wouldn't it? Just leave him and let's go!" I carefully approached the back door, crawling in front of the bushes to avoid someone spotting me through one of the windows. Delgado must have liked his backyard view, because he had windows that went from floor to ceiling.

When it looked clear, I turned the doorknob and slowly stepped inside. A cool gust of air teased my hair back, and I listened for an alarm. Nothing.

The living room had all white furniture. I stood amid white leather sofas, white marble flooring, and a pristine white rug without a spot on it.

"Just in case you're wondering, you didn't die. This isn't heaven," Wheeler whispered sarcastically against my ear.

Voices murmured in the distance, and I quickly moved toward them. Wheeler's arm flew out in front of me, holding me back so he could peer through a large doorway. He pointed to the left, signaling their location.

Wheeler skulked around the wall, and my anger began to bubble. My mother had always said I had a temper like a volcano—dormant for years until provoked by the wrong person. This wasn't a man's job, so I brazenly walked into the room with my catlike strut and straight toward the voices.

Much to the dismay of Wheeler, who had found a hiding spot behind a nude statue.

"Does anyone here know where I can find Damian Delgado?" I announced, moving as sultrily as a woman could.

Two men reached for their guns and hesitated, looking at me and then each other with stunned expressions. They wore black suits with slim ties.

"Hold it right there," one of them said. "Don't move."

Ignoring him, I summoned a naughty smile and approached that man. "I spoke with the guard outside, and he said it was all right to come in. Are you Delgado?" I asked, running my hand down his chest. "He called my boss—asked for his best girl to show him a good time."

The one on my left with the thick sideburns tucked his gun back in the holster. "You have the wrong house. You're going to have to leave."

"Wrong house? But he gave me this address! Doesn't he live here?"

"Not tonight, he doesn't."

I lowered my eyes, ignoring the chatty man on my left and giving all the attention to the guard in front of me—the one who looked like the man in charge. My fingers slipped between the buttons of his shirt so I could touch his skin. "That's a shame. I'm paid through the night. I got an extra bonus to do whatever he asked of me."

"You'll have to get a refund," the guy with the sideburns said.

"Shut up, Mark," my guy said tersely. "Let's just think about this."

"I think we'll be in deep shit if we…"

I unbuckled the guard's pants and slid them to the floor. I knelt down and gazed at him with provocative eyes. That took care of the gun attached to the belt around his waist. All he had left was the one in his hand.

"Oh, shit," he said, out of breath, grabbing the frame of the door.

I stroked him with the palm of my hand. "Do you think your friend will join us? I want to suck on you while he's behind me."

By that point, Mark—the guy with the sideburns—was sold. He set his weapon on the table and fumbled with the latch on his own belt. Most guards in the Breed world weren't as gullible as this, so that told me they were not only human, but Delgado surrounded himself with idiots.

I stood up, undoing the button on my jeans, looking every bit as anxious to get this threesome on the road. The man in front of me tucked his gun back into the holster beneath his jacket and then began stroking himself. So I turned to Mark and licked my lips seductively. His eyes hooded, and when he bent down to take off his shoes, I kneed him in the nose.

Blood spattered everywhere, and I elbowed the other guy in the ribs before pulling the gun out of his holster and sliding it across the floor. When I stood back up, he wrapped his arms around me like a boa constrictor. I used this to my advantage and pulled my feet off the ground, kicking Mark in the chest. He flew against the wall, gasping for breath.

Wheeler appeared out of nowhere and clamped his hand around the throat of the man holding me. I wriggled free just as Mark leapt to his feet, wiping his bloody nose with the back of his arm.

I lowered my eyes to his crotch and giggled out of control. It made him look, and when his own pride distracted him for two seconds, I scratched him in the face with my nails. Pain exploded in my eye when he swung his arm around and struck me, causing my panther to snarl. I tempered that fury and channeled it into my attack.

I'd never been in a fight like this, and I hadn't known a punch could hurt so much. I grabbed a small statue from a glass table and struck Mark over the head with it. Spatters of blood painted the walls like a Pollock work of art. Before he could rise up, I struck him again.

The other guy was at a disadvantage with his pants wrapped around his ankles, and it took only moments before Wheeler incapacitated him as well.

I gulped down a breath and placed a hand over my racing heart as I looked around the house. It was large enough that no one upstairs would have heard us.

"Where's Reno?" I asked.

He snatched my wrist and we rushed through the room, analyzing the layout of the house. When we hit the kitchen, we backtracked into an open area with a massive crystal chandelier above our heads and a circle of gold rings beneath our feet.

We rushed up a flight of stairs and I hurried my pace when I heard a commotion. A voice shouted, something crashed, and Wheeler climbed two steps at a time until he was out of sight.

"Wait!" I shouted. I reached the top of the stairs, panting and holding on to a stone lion as I focused my attention on the noise coming from a wall straight ahead. The banister looped around in a semicircle to my left with an open lounge. The carpeting up here was chocolate brown, and the furniture white.

Doors didn't line the hall, but rather entranceways. On the right, I glanced into a sitting area with a door. There were two brown chairs and a plant between them that reminded me of a doctor's office. I moved farther down toward the noise until the hall curved left, revealing a row of doors.

My legs propelled me forward at breakneck speed when a woman shrieked. "Skye!" I shouted. "Skye!"

Fists were flying and a mirror crashed to the floor as Reno fought a guard. Inside an open doorway, Wheeler was sitting on a man's chest with his hands wrapped around his throat.

Skye was on the bed with her knees pulled up. I rushed to her side and pulled her into my arms. "Let's go!"

Something held her back, and then I noticed the handcuff attached to a thick slat of wood in the headboard. "Wheeler! I need a key for handcuffs."

He glanced over his shoulder. "I'm a little busy."

"Can you stop choking him for two seconds? I need a key."

"If you wait two more seconds, I'll have that key."

I cursed and hurried around the bed, shoving Wheeler off-balance. The man gasped, struggling to pull in air. I flipped him over and felt in his pockets until I found what I needed.

"Now you can finish," I said with annoyance.

After removing Skye's cuffs, I cupped her face. She looked dreadful. "Honey, are you okay? Did they hurt you?"

"I want to go home. Please take me home." Her arms were shaking and she tried to grip my shoulders. I couldn't tell if she had been hurt since there were no marks, but she appeared weak and exhausted. I helped her up and we moved toward the hall.

By then, Reno had knocked out the guard he'd been fighting.

"Take her," I said.

He hooked his arm around Skye's narrow waist. "I got you."

"I have something I need to do," I said, jingling a set of keys in my hand. "If there's anyone else in here, I'm not leaving them behind."

"That could be problematic if Delgado comes home early. Wheeler, get your ass out here! Pull the car around; we're done!" Then he turned his dark brown eyes to mine. "Let's go. We don't have time."

"I'm right behind you," I lied.

Reno picked Skye up and ran down the hall. *Ran.*

I went through several keys before finding the one that opened the door across from us. Empty.

I tried a second door. "Hello?" Another empty room. When I hit the third room, a voice yelled out from inside.

This room looked nothing like Skye's. It was barren of furniture, and Delgado had shackled and chained a young man to a metal ring in the cement floor. This sweet boy didn't look older than twenty, although in Shifter years he could have been ancient. The youthful glimmer in his eyes tipped me off—the one that showed me a boy scared witless.

I fumbled through the keys until I found an odd-looking one.

"I'm here to help you," I said. "Don't hurt me."

"I won't, I won't," he promised. "Just get me out. Hurry! Hurry! He'll come back. He always comes back."

"Why are you in here?"

"This is where he keeps his personal pets," he said under his breath.

I brushed my hand over the short curls of blond hair. "It's not your fault. Nothing that's happened is your fault, including whatever you've done to survive."

It dawned on me that I was looking at a man who could have easily been Wheeler all those years ago. Maybe if someone had said those words to him just once, it would have made a difference.

The young man sobbed, holding his wrists up and looking at them as if they were marked, which they weren't. He grimaced, and the torment he had endured played across his features like a silent film. That's when I knew Delgado had been using this boy for more than just fighting.

"What's your name?" I asked, wiping away his tears. "I'm Naya."

"Evan."

"Listen to me, Evan. We're getting out of here. So I want you to stand up and follow me as quickly as you can. Your life will never be the same again, but you need to make a new life for yourself. Maybe someday it'll be you helping someone else."

That lit a fire in his eyes—one of hope.

I clasped his hand in mine, and I pulled him up with a hard jerk. After that, we never spoke again. I checked three more rooms before we headed downstairs and ran into Reno.

Evan reached for the door, and Reno pressed the toe of his boot against it.

"Not yet. We're not running into the open like target practice. When Wheeler pulls up the driveway, we haul ass to the car. You two keep an eye on the stairs and back of the house."

Wheeler's engine growled outside. Evan bounced on his heels, anxiously looking around. I hadn't noticed until that moment how gaunt he was, which didn't suit his height. His clothes looked two sizes too big and were nothing more than a long shirt and pants with a drawstring. Delgado was a man going on my panther's naughty list, and that was never a good place to be. I smoothed my hand over Skye's long hair, but she kept quiet and rested her head on Reno's shoulder.

"Hold on. We're almost home."

"Open it," Reno said, backing up a step. "Run! Run! Run!"

I swung the door open and chortled.

Wheeler had pulled his car all the way up to the front door and was leaning across the seats, looking at us through the window. "You *said* pull up front."

Reno grumbled out a few obscenities. I darted ahead of him and opened the passenger door, pushing the seat forward. He set Skye on her feet and she wobbled before I caught her around the waist.

"Crawl in. Everything's fine, chickypoo. You're going home."

Evan went in next and then I sat directly behind Reno.

Smoke billowed behind the car as Wheeler spun the tires and said, "Hang on!"

Our heads snapped back when he hit the gas and we tore out of there, kicking up grass and mud where he skidded off the concrete and onto the lawn. He spun in circles until Reno smacked him in the head.

"We don't have time for this shit," Reno yelled.

"This is my fuck-you to Delgado," Wheeler said, turning the car once more before he finally ran over a bush, clipped the brick mailbox, and then bounced onto the street.

"You just fucked up your front end," Reno said, pulling out his phone.

I glanced at three broken nails and realized Delgado was going to know I had a part in this. I didn't naively think he wouldn't have found out anyway, but it left me unsettled, wondering what his next move would be.

Then I thought about Misha. I hadn't seen her in the house, and suddenly I was overwhelmed with a feeling of regret. Why hadn't I searched all the rooms downstairs? She might have been hiding. I put my head in my hands and tried to contain my tears. I didn't want these men to think I cared more for a cat than I did the two people we had rescued, but it didn't diminish the devastation that burrowed through me, knowing I would have to mourn in silence.

CHAPTER 14

T HE FIRST THING WE DID was drop Evan off with his brother. He had been missing for weeks, and while I didn't know what his animal was, I knew he'd be safe in the custody of his three hundred pounds of muscle big brother, who had tackled him in a bear hug.

I waited in the car with Skye, who hadn't spoken a word since we left Delgado's mansion. She stared listlessly out the window to my left, so I scooted next to her and let her know everything was all right.

As soon as we approached the Weston house, Reno got out ahead of us to speak with Austin.

"If anyone can smooth things over, it's Reno," Wheeler said.

"Is he in trouble?"

Wheeler shut off the engine and rolled up his window. "He's a PI; it's his job to be in trouble. But this involved me, so yeah, he's probably going to hear it from Austin for not having kept him in the loop."

"This wasn't just a personal vendetta," I reminded him. "If Austin wants a good reason why you two snuck out of the house on a mission, then make sure you put that little baby in his arms and let him hold her for a few minutes until he figures it out." I angrily pushed the front seat forward.

Wheeler got out of the car and helped Skye to her feet, hooking his arm around her waist and letting her lean against him for support. She looked so frail it worried me. Had Delgado fed her, or was his plan to starve them into submission?

We approached the front porch at a slow gait, allowing Reno

enough time to fill Austin in on what we'd been up to. I knew in just a matter of moments my presence would no longer be welcome here.

Izzy appeared at the front door in her long Pink Floyd T-shirt, holding Lola in her arms. Lola was asleep on her shoulder, and when Izzy caught sight of Wheeler and Skye, she gave her a gentle shake.

Lola opened her eyes and rubbed them. Izzy whispered something in her ear and pointed at Skye. The moment that baby caught sight of her mother, she kicked her legs wildly to get down.

"*Mommy! Mommy!*"

Skye broke from Wheeler's grasp and rushed up the porch steps with newfound energy. When she reached the top, she fell on her knees and wrapped her arms around that baby so tight I thought she'd never let go.

Lola sobbed, still crying out her name.

"Shhh, baby. *Mommy's got you.*" She kissed her several times on the cheek, and I stood in awe of mother and child reunited.

It could have gone another way. That baby might have never known the fate of her mother, who would have eventually lost her life in a cage fight. I wiped a tear from my cheek, the rest of the pack also misty-eyed. Izzy laced her fingers together in a prayerlike gesture, resting them beneath her chin. Jericho rubbed her shoulders from behind, coaxing her back inside.

Just as soon as they were out of sight, Reno stepped out with a small bag and tossed it down to Wheeler. "Put this in the blue truck."

"For what?" Wheeler cocked his head and tested the weight of the bag.

Reno squatted in front of Skye and softened his voice. "There's a pack up in Colorado—a good pack. They take in Shifters who need protection. I go way back with the Packmaster; he's a good man I'd trust with my life. I've sent several men, women, and children to his homestead. It's well protected."

"Colorado?" she asked with uncertainty.

"It's temporary. You'll stay with him for as long as you need, and then he'll start helping you relocate. If you want, there are packs out there who take in other animals. He'll set you up with a new identity and job in any city you want. The property is secluded and no one knows it exists. It's a safe haven. You up for it?"

"Is this necessary?"

"Delgado is still out there, and I'm guessing you don't have any family to take you in. I'm not going to sugarcoat it and tell you everything is fine. When Delgado finds out what we've done, he'll be on the hunt. You're better off starting over. If you stay here, I can't guarantee your safety. He won't think twice about coming after your daughter to teach you a lesson; that's how men like them think."

She picked up Lola and rose to her feet. "*No one* is going to touch my baby."

Lola had her arms wrapped around Skye's neck and was playing with her long hair from behind. It made me smile to see her flipping it about, making ripples in the straight waves of silk. Her cheeks were still wet, but her eyes were filled with joy.

"We leave tonight, and it has to be with the clothes on your back. We can't risk going to your home to pick up anything. If there's something sentimental you really want, I can search the place at a later time and hold on to it for you. I packed a few things for your little girl. Izzy added a few extra toys and a pink blanket. That okay?"

Skye nodded, tears shining in her eyes as she stepped into him for a hug she couldn't even give because her arms were full.

Reno patted her on the back. "Let's go."

Skye descended the steps and then put Lola down. "I can't thank you enough. I'll never know how you did this—how you found me."

I reached out and held her tight. "This is a chance for the new life you've always wanted. You go out and grab the world by the balls."

Skye laughed. "Still the same old Naya."

"Maybe someday you can call me up, if they allow it. Take care of that baby."

"Thank you," she whispered. "Lola is my world."

I kissed her cheek. "Make sure Reno stops off somewhere and gets you some food. You need some meat on those bones."

She snorted. "You've been telling me that since the day we met."

"Don't worry," Reno interrupted. "I got food covered. Time to go."

I knelt down quickly and stroked the brown curls on Lola's head. "Hey there, pretty girl. You make sure you take good care of your mama, okay?"

She giggled. "You got big boobies!"

Wheeler laughed so hard he let out a snort. I scorched him with my gaze, since it was his fault I was running around in just a bra to begin with.

"That's right, sweetie. And if you keep eating every bite of food on your plate, then someday you will too!"

She giggled and I smiled at Skye. "If I can't put meat on *your* bones, then Lola is taken care of," I said, swinging my hips as I walked up the steps.

I passed Denver and headed toward my room. *Time for Naya to make her great escape before the bomb drops.* Packs could be volatile in the clubs; I could only imagine what they were like at home during an argument.

I flipped on the light to my room and put on a button-up blouse. After packing my bag, I turned to head out.

"Going somewhere?" Austin asked. He leaned against the far door at the opposite end of the hall, asserting every ounce of male dominance he possessed.

Without breaking stride, I walked toward him with my chin up. "I'm a grown woman, Austin Cole. And I'm not one of your pack, so don't even consider reprimanding me," I said in a singsong voice.

He leaned hard on that right arm of his and blocked my exit. "Naya, I'm asking you as sweet as pie to get your ass upstairs and wait for me in the game room."

"And I'm asking with a cherry on top to get out of my way before I do something we'll both regret."

His brows knitted together. "Who gave you a black eye?"

"What exactly did Reno tell you?" I put my hand on my hip and lifted my chin.

"That you all raided Delgado's home, rescued two prisoners, and tore up his yard." Austin reached out and took my bag. "What do you think Wheeler will say?"

Good question. Why argue and make myself look foolish? The only thing Wheeler could confirm was that I almost engaged in a threesome.

Austin stepped aside. "Go on upstairs. I don't think after tonight you're going to feel too safe walking home alone. I have a pissed-off criminal tycoon to deal with now."

"He's only a human."

Austin moved aside and let me walk past him. "Maybe so, but you just opened the lid to a basketful of vipers. Just because one of them is a garden snake doesn't mean I'm letting down my guard. Delgado has connections, not to mention Breed employees who do his bidding. Wheeler!" he shouted. "Come to my office."

Austin took my bag with him, and I exchanged a quiet look with Wheeler when I passed him. I ascended the stairs, careful not to wake the sleeping children. When I walked by an open door, curiosity got the best of me.

Trevor was sitting at a cheap desk with tiny plastic pieces scattered in front of him in organized sections.

"You're up late," I remarked.

"Sometimes I have trouble sleeping," he said without raising his head.

I inched into the room and looked around. Model airplanes hung from the ceiling and decorated wooden shelves on every row.

"Is this a hobby or should we have an intervention?"

Trevor moved aside a magnifying glass that was attached to his desk. It swiveled and he angled it away. After rubbing his eyes, he turned around to face me and stretched his legs out. "It helps me."

I lifted a plane and looked at it. "With what?"

He folded his arms and yawned. "It's therapeutic, I guess. I used to be in the closet with my wolf. Building airplanes started when someone gave me one as a gift, but it helped me with maintaining control over my wolf. Now that I'm in a pack, I shift when I want. But I can't seem to stop building planes," he said with a short laugh. "Fucking crazy."

"Maybe you should give some of these to an orphanage before you become a clutterbug."

His chair squeaked as he moved it left and right, looking about the room. "Never thought of that."

"Mind if I sit?" I asked, motioning toward the wooden chair behind me. Trevor nodded and I took a seat. "Austin is coming up at any moment to beat his chest and display his male dominance."

"That's a nightly occurrence. Welcome to our home."

"You're an outsider without any relation to them. What's it like living in a pack? Do you gather outside, howl at the moon, and dance naked?"

He waggled his eyebrows. "That might be fun. But nah, it's pretty normal around here compared to how I grew up."

"Was it terrible?"

He leaned forward in his chair. "The worst. I don't like talking about it, but I'm sure you can guess how a guy like me fit right in."

Being gay, Trevor had undoubtedly faced cruelty at the hands of older wolves in his pack who were against it. Not because they had moral issues so much as they saw a wolf turning away from having children as a betrayal to their own kind.

"I'm glad I wasn't born a wolf," I said. "I can't imagine the controlling lifestyle of a pack."

He sniffed out a short laugh. "That was just *my* family. We lived in bumfuck nowhere, so they were the kind of pack that made up their own rules. Anyhow, my family cut me off. I assumed that's how all packs were until I gave these guys a shot. I'd convinced myself they were going to go back on their word in the first month and force me out, but no one here has ever made me feel like anything less than a brother. Yeah, they razz on me, but I get them back and it's all friendly shit. Nothing personal, and we always eat together. It's hard to stay mad at someone who has to pass you the rolls."

"What's it like?" I asked, my curiosity piqued. "Living with a pack, that is."

His gazed shifted. "It's like... home. No matter where I go or what shit I'm in, I know I've got my pack by my side. I don't have that feeling of being alone anymore. It's hard to get used to the idea new people will come in, because I don't know how they'll fit in with me or anyone else in the family. It's not just about me; I'd be pissed as hell if someone came in and bullied someone in my pack. I feel protective of them."

A strange feeling overcame me, one I'd felt before in the presence of the Weston pack. Envy. A longing to know what it was like to feel love and loyalty from people who truly cared and didn't just want something from me. Everything in my life had become nothing more than an exchange of needs. Men objectified me, and that's why I'd raised my standards on who was good enough to take me to bed. So many men had wooed me for months in hopes of having something unattainable on their arm—a trophy other men could admire. Maybe that's why I'd bonded with Lexi from the beginning; she loved my company and valued our friendship. Most of the girls at the club were catty—always suspicious you were out to steal their act or regular customers. Lexi's was the first true friendship I'd ever known.

Pack dynamic fascinated me, and at the same time labeled me an outcast. Especially now that my secret was out.

"What's wrong?" Trevor asked. "Something I said?"

"No." I looked down and realized I'd misaligned the buttons on my white blouse, leaving an extra one at the bottom.

A knock sounded at the open door. "Sorry, didn't know you had company," William said.

I liked William. I'd once told Lexi he reminded me of a naughty pirate with those loose curls of short hair that sometimes obscured his eyes.

Trevor's chair squeaked when he sat up straight. "What's up?"

William leaned on his left shoulder, his gaze drifting about the room. "Say, a little bird told me your birthday was last week."

Trevor's eyes narrowed and he folded his arms. "April needs to learn to keep her beak shut. I didn't want to make it a thing. It never was before, so I don't see a point now."

Shifters weren't big on celebrating birthdays. When you live for hundreds of years, what's the point of keeping count?

"Well, you buy April gifts," William pointed out.

"She's my girl. Of course I get her gifts. April's human and she likes her presents, but yeah… no big deal."

"Indeed," William murmured. "Shame."

Trevor played with the string on his sweats. "What's a shame?"

"Well, I got you this gift, and now I'll have to take it back."

The back of Trevor's neck turned a deep shade of red. "You got me a gift? Quit bullshitting." He relaxed a little and spun in his chair.

William's hand appeared, holding a box with shiny green wrapping. "Go on and take it. You can throw it in the trash if it's not something you want. No biggie." He spun on his heel and disappeared out of sight.

Trevor slowly peeled the tape from the edges and peered inside. "What is it?" I asked.

He unfolded the paper and let it fall to the floor. In his hands was a model-airplane kit. This one looked like one of those old bombers from World War II. Most of the ones in his room were either commercial airliners or jets.

Trevor set the box on the table and rushed out the door. "William—"

His voice cut off and he stopped within eyeshot. I realized William hadn't left after all, but had been standing in the hall near the door. Trevor's eyes were downcast, staring at the floor before looking back up. "Thanks, man."

William reached out and patted Trevor's shoulder before he walked off.

Trevor kept his eyes steady for a moment before he swaggered into the room. "So what kind of trouble are you in?" he asked in a blustering voice. He noisily wadded up the wrapper and tossed it into the wastebasket.

I stood up. "I suppose you'll find out soon enough. I've been summoned to your game room, and I'm guessing it's not for drinks and a lap dance," I said with a sullen smile as I left the room.

I hadn't even seen Wheeler walk by, but he was already in the room, sitting at the bar with a shot of liquor in front of him. I sat to his left and tasted a sip.

"A whiskey man," I said softly, licking my lips. "Why didn't you use your weapon back at Delgado's? Seems like a lot of trouble to strangle a man."

His eyes flashed up and he looked at me in the reflection of the mirror. "You once said I didn't enjoy doing laborious things with my hands. I disagree."

"Touché."

I still had my fingers wrapped around the glass when he suddenly reached for it. Wheeler held his hand over mine, lightly stroking my thumb with his pinky finger. My heart spontaneously reacted whenever he touched me, and the slightest connection sent goose pimples all over my body and a flutter of nerves to my belly. And it took a *whole lot* to make a woman like me nervous.

Shuffling feet sounded behind us as the pack entered the room. Wheeler pulled the glass away and knocked it back. He quickly poured a refill, spilling a few drops onto the polished surface of the bar.

"Close the door," Austin said.

Lexi swept her hair back. "Do you want me to wake Mom?"

Denver plopped down in the beanbag chair, and everyone else stood behind Austin near the pool table. I slowly swiveled around on my stool and noticed Denver tapping his bare feet on the floor.

"I have work in two hours," he announced.

"It shouldn't take that long." Austin strolled in front of me and turned to face his pack. "As most of you know, the little girl's mother is safe. What you don't know is that Reno and Wheeler drove over to a man named Delgado's house, took out several guards, broke into the house, and—"

"Saved two lives," Wheeler added, still sitting with his back turned to Austin.

"Reno's taking the mother and child to a safe house, so he won't be back for a day or two. Delgado is a big fucking shark in our world. He owns Breed clubs, deals drugs, and it's been brought to my attention that he's also running cage fights."

"Then we have to turn him in," William said with a tight expression.

Austin nodded. "I agree, but as it stands, we don't have evidence.

Our star witness is running for her life, and she's the only one who can testify what went on in that house—or wherever they originally kept her. The higher authority won't serve a warrant without concrete evidence."

Lexi looked up at Austin with a quizzical brow. "You said there were two."

"The other is a young wolf who's too traumatized at the moment to think straight. But yeah, he's our best bet. I don't know how much he knows about the cage fights—how much he's seen."

"I'll talk to him," Wheeler volunteered, polishing off the rest of his drink.

With two fingers, I pushed Wheeler's shoulder to encourage him to turn around and face Austin. He held a submissive posture, afraid of the Packmaster's judgment.

Wheeler turned just enough to face me, but no more.

Austin stuffed his hands in his pockets and gave him a brisk nod. "I'd appreciate that." Then he gave everyone else his attention. "I spoke with Wheeler briefly in private, and while I don't condone anyone defying my orders or keeping secrets, he's not getting the boot. He's still on probation, but he saved two lives, and a little girl has a mother to tuck her in tonight. I'd say our job is done."

"So why are we here?" April asked. A worry line formed between her eyebrows—the kind a girl gets when her man is on the road and not safe in her arms.

"Things won't be safe for a while," Austin said in a rough voice. He cleared his throat and lowered his chin. "Delgado is a human, and he's become a parasite in our world, hiding in dark corners and leeching off our weaknesses to expand his wealth. If we're going to bring him down, then we're bringing him down *hard*. But not at the expense of our family. One stupid move and the Council could dismantle our pack or throw us in jail. Let's keep cool heads, and from here on out, we leave the house in groups of at least two. I don't want anyone going out alone."

"What about the shops?" Lexi asked.

"Work is fine, but go in pairs and no one stays in the shop alone. That's the deal. See if you can flip the schedule so you don't work late hours. One of the part-timers at April's store shouldn't have any problem earning a little extra money. That means everyone," he said, giving the room a pointed look. "Including you, Denver. When you head out later, I want Ben going with you and staying at the bar for your full shift."

"Ben's not here," Trevor said.

"Where the fuck is he?" Austin glanced at the clock over the bar.

Wheeler laughed richly and threw back his head. "That should be on a fucking T-shirt. Front and back."

"What happened to your eye?" Izzy asked me.

I reached up and touched the sore spot. Then she noticed my broken fingernails, so I quickly lowered my hand.

"You want to tell me why you brought Naya along on your little raid?" Austin asked. "She's not pack. She's someone I offered protection, and you threw her into danger?"

"Throw her?" Wheeler exclaimed. "That what you think of her? You should see how she handled those men." He laughed darkly and I found myself slinking down in my seat. *Here come the jokes.* "She single-handedly disarmed two of Delgado's men and took one of them down while fighting the other."

"Hah!" Lexi blurted out in surprise. "Are you serious?"

Wheeler turned all the way around and leaned back on his elbows. "Your friend is one dangerous woman to mess with. She's cunning and plays on the weaknesses of her foes."

Denver chuckled. "What did she do, strip?"

Wheeler hopped off his chair. "Want to say that again?"

Austin pushed him back with one hand. "That's enough. Both of you. Like I said, on my orders as the Packmaster, no one leaves this house without at least one person with them. And for now, let's keep the kids at home."

"That means you, Denver." Lexi erupted with laughter, and Denver wrinkled his nose in retaliation.

Austin stepped in front of me when I slid off my stool. "Where do you think you're going?"

"Home," I said.

"I don't think so."

I patted his chest. "Normally I like my men big and strong, but I don't tolerate men who order me around. Lexi is my friend, so I'll hold my tongue on what I'd really like to say, but step out of my way. I have no desire to be given a verbal lashing in front of your pack just so you can show you're the dominant wolf."

He chuckled and touched the talisman around his neck. Austin was a tough alpha in every way. The tribal ink on his shoulders and upper arms marked him as a Packmaster—becoming a recognizable symbol for anyone who might not know him by sight or name. He was over six feet tall, and that was mighty tall in my book when I wasn't wearing my heels or platforms.

"You're staying with us," he said.

"Was."

"*Are*. I'm not closing my doors to a family friend."

I smoothed my right hand along the edge of the bar. "I don't belong here, and I've already ruffled a few feathers."

"True, but you're still not leaving. Delgado's out there, and no offense, but your apartment is a piece of shit. I could kick down that door drunk and on roller skates."

"I'd pay to watch that," Denver said with a smirk, rising to his feet.

Jericho barked out a laugh. "We got to see it for free at Maizy's last birthday party when you had to take a piss and couldn't get your skates off."

Denver rolled one of the balls across the pool table in his direction. "Shut it, dickhead."

"Stay, Naya." Austin spoke in a gentler tone. "We want you here."

I gracefully put my hands on my hips and softened my voice. "There's only one place men want me, and it's not in their homes."

When I moved past him, he snatched my arm. "Naya, sometimes I think you put on one hell of a show, but you don't have to pull that shit in my house. That's not what my men are about. You're not just a friend to Lexi, but to all of us. You've helped us when we didn't ask for it, and it's only right to do a good turn for a family friend. You've already got your room set up, and you'll be here anyway for the party this coming weekend. Just stick around for a little while until the dust settles and we find out what's what."

"Oh, crap. The party," Lexi whispered. "Naya, I called the number you gave me, but I still need to pick up the costumes and decorations."

"Don't worry, girly," I said. "He delivers for free if it's local."

"I need a punch bowl or something, and a few things to decorate. You're the only one who knows how to throw a good party."

"Hold up," William said, raising his hand. "You already picked out our costumes... without including us?"

"Of course!" Lexi said with a conniving smile.

"Oh, shit." Trevor shook his head. "I am *not* doing this."

"Yes you are," Austin said. "I approved them."

Denver folded his arms. "*That* makes me feel better. You're a bag of nuts if you think I'm putting on whatever she picked out."

Lexi lifted her chin stubbornly. "We all agreed," she said in a voice that made every man in that room shift uncomfortably. Perhaps they were feeling a tad concerned about all the times they'd been difficult with Lexi, but I thoroughly enjoyed watching them squirm in their boots.

Despite my resistance, my heart swelled with gratitude. "I'll stay for the evening, and then we'll see. How does that sound?"

"Purrrfect," he said with a deep chuckle.

The rest of the pack snickered, and I shook my head as I left the room.

"Wait up," a voice called from behind.

I glanced over my shoulder and Wheeler caught up with me.

"I'll walk you down," he said.

"Mmm, and tuck me in?" I teased.

Wheeler didn't reply, but he suddenly reached out and held my hand.

CHAPTER 15

I CRACKED A SMILE WHEN I entered the room and noticed my bag at the foot of the bed. "I guess Austin had no intention of losing our argument." I reached in the short fridge to get a cool drink while Wheeler closed the door. "Do you want anything?"

When I turned to look over my shoulder, I saw hunger in his eyes. I could almost feel it skate across my skin, warming me like a desert wind. Whatever Wheeler wanted wasn't in that fridge. He kept his back pressed against the door as if he were holding the wall up with brute strength.

I walked leisurely toward him with a can of soda.

"I didn't like seeing you with another man," he said with a throaty growl.

Wheeler hissed when I lifted his shirt and pressed the icy can against his belly. "What did you do that for?" Those sexy brows of his sloped at an angle, and I couldn't help but find him wildly attractive when he was provoked.

"Remember what I said before about your tone? Each time you speak to me in that imperious manner, I'm going to punish you."

He tilted his head to the side. "Is that so? And what about when *you* turn on the diva box? Are you beyond reproach?"

"My words are reactive."

"Ah, so that doesn't count. You can say anything as long as it's on the defense."

A blanket of silence fell between us and was so noticeable that I could hear a faint ringing in my ears.

"I'm afraid to see what your idea of punishment would entail," I replied. "Subjecting me to more vampire movies, or perhaps shoving a stick of dried meat down my throat?"

He pointed at my shirt and stepped forward. "Your buttons aren't lined up."

"So?"

I gasped when he ripped my blouse open. Buttons scattered across the wood floor, clicking against the surface and rolling out of sight. The unopened can of soda slipped from my hand.

Wheeler's eyes were provocative and predatory as he licked his lips, eyes still on mine.

"You ruined my blouse," I said, sweetening my tone.

His eyes glittered with intent. "I don't feel a shred of guilt."

I reached down and lifted the can of soda. When I pulled the tab back, it sprayed him in the face. Foam ran over the edge of the can, overflowing and splattering on the floor. When I raised it to my lips, he knocked the bottom of the can and sent it flying out of my hand. I listened to the hissing sound of bubbles complaining as they spread below our feet.

"I was drinking that."

"And now you're wearing it," he said, nodding at the droplets on my chest. "Turnabout is fair play."

"What did I say about speaking to me in that tone?"

His pupils dilated, but he stood absolutely still.

"Take off your shirt," I said.

"Why?"

My voice sweetened. "You ask a lot of questions."

Wheeler stripped off his shirt and flung it to the side.

I stepped forward, lightly circling my fingers around his nipples. Wheeler had a light dusting of hair on his chest—just the way I liked my men. When I felt the tips of his nipples hardening beneath my touch, I pinched them hard.

He hissed and pushed out his chest, his breath quickening, teeth clenched.

Wheeler was an impressive male. A firm physique, tight ropes of muscles along his arms, powerful hands, and exquisite eyes. I'd never seen such a pale shade of brown, and it made his pupils stand out when they were dilated. I didn't mind the short circle beard

around his mouth and the light dusting of whiskers on his face...
even though some of it had scratched at my skin.

Remembering our kiss in the back of his car filled my veins with
heat. But why wouldn't he touch me?

I pulled away from him and lowered my arms. At the loss of
contact, he stepped closer.

"What?" I asked, looking up at him with arched brows.

He scratched his arm, dodging my gaze. "What do I have to say
to get you to do that again?"

"How about... something *dirty*."

A flush of color touched his face. Wheeler wasn't going to ask for
what he wanted, so I began to undo his belt.

"Tell me about the women you normally sleep with."

"Thin, blond..."

"No, I don't care about what they look like. What kind of lovers
were they?"

He sucked in a sharp breath when I stretched the latch and freed
the metal prong. "Submissive. Predictable."

"But that's not what you like, is it?" I reached around and
loosened the belt from the loops. "I'm a perceptive woman. I pick
up on subtle gestures most people ignore, like when your breath
becomes shallow, or how many times you blink when I say certain
words. I think I know what presses your buttons, but I've never met
a man so afraid to be pushed."

"It's not normal," he bit out through clenched teeth.

I folded the belt, looking up at him thoughtfully. "What's
normal? Predictable? Submissive? Is that more attractive to you than
a dominant woman who wants to do something naughty?"

His lips parted, and I glanced down at his erection.

"I didn't like those men touching you." He reached out and
caressed my cheek with the back of his knuckles. "I got turned on
when you attacked them. Do you think that's strange?"

I licked my lips, drawing in his gaze. "I think that's the sexiest
thing a man has ever said to me."

Wheeler stepped closer until our bodies touched. He cupped my
face with his hand, lightly grazing his thumb over my bruised eye.

"I can't seem to shake you out of my mind. Maybe I'm punishing myself."

"Why? Because I'm a panther or a stripper?"

His proximity clouded my thoughts, and I found myself aroused by the ink on his body and the sensual feel of his rough hand against my skin.

"Neither. It's because you're too good for me."

I laughed unexpectedly. "Why would you say a thing like that about a woman like me?" I'd never once had a man say I was too good for him, and that made my heart clench.

He touched the curls on my head, feeling the silky strands between his fingers. "Because you're like those shiny ornaments on the Christmas tree. Too pretty. Too perfect. Something I'm not allowed to touch."

"Why not?"

"Because I'll break you."

I took his hand and held it in front of my face. "Do you think the blood on your hands is still there? Do you think by touching me, it'll make me dirty? I'm not like those other women you've brought into your bed. Your demons don't scare me." I pulled his finger into my mouth and slowly sucked.

His eyes hooded, and a needful groan sounded deep in his throat. "Tell me what to do," he whispered.

Wheeler wanted to submit. Maybe some women would have cracked the belt and punished him hard, but this man had been punishing himself for more years than anyone deserved. He needed to lose control in low doses, without losing dignity.

"Turn around," I said in a sultry voice. "I want to look at all of you. Do it slowly."

Wheeler swallowed and turned in a circle. I admired the ink designs that he wore on his arms like sleeves—the wolf on his right arm, and below it the chain that circled around. Tribal designs, a row of skulls, and an intricate sketch of two playing cards: a joker and a king.

"You only have one animal. That's unusual," I said, thinking about how most men liked snakes, eagles, or scorpions.

"It's bad luck."

"Says who?"

He shrugged, looking down at me over his shoulder. "Says me. My wolf is the only one who gets billboard space on my body."

But when he turned around, the view stole my breath away. Spread across his back was an enormous dragon with wings. The shading was perfected in such a way that it looked as though it had separated from his skin and was hovering over his back. I traced my fingers over the sharp teeth, down the scaly body, circling them over his serpentine claws. "But this is an animal…"

"It's a dragon, not an animal. They're not real."

I pressed my lips against it. "Maybe they are," I murmured, thinking about cruel men like Delgado who had slain innocents and ruined lives. I wondered if my dragon slayer would ever find peace.

Wheeler kept turning until he faced me once again, but he no longer held the amorous look in his eyes—only one of ruin.

"I needed something big to cover up the scars. There were more on my back; that's where they liked to whip us."

Tears burned hot in my eyes. I didn't like knowing someone had hurt him that way. Just imagining him alone in a cell while someone was whipping him…

"Hey, don't do that," he said, wiping one away. "Jesus, I really fucked this up. You see what I mean? You're too delicate for a man like me."

"Is that all you see when you look at me? Just an ornament?"

I walked away and sat on the couch, kicking over the chewed-up coffee table with a thrust of my leg. "Every man has looked at me that way since I can remember," I bit out angrily. "That is the curse of the panther. I've spent my entire life hiding from everyone—even myself. You have the freedom to run in the woods. But me? I have to drive to desolate, godforsaken places to let my panther run loose."

"Fuck that," Wheeler spat, kicking the table even farther away. He knelt in front of me. "There's no law that says you can't roam free."

"There doesn't have to be a law. Imagine if you saw a panther on your property. A wolf you might keep an eye on, but a panther? I'm willing to bet the arsenal would come out. Just look at the panic in your own pack when you brought me here! I'm not free. Even with all the laws and Councils, I'm not *truly* free. You broke your chains a long time ago, but mine will always be locked. You just can't see them, but they keep me from a life I'm not allowed to live. Just knowing what I am puts a target on my back. I dated two men who were ancients, and despite all the changes we've been through, they couldn't accept me."

I clenched my fists. Wheeler, still kneeling in front of me, placed his hands over them.

"That what you think? Because you're a panther, no one will accept you?"

"How open-minded were you before Austin intervened and forced you to watch me? You've always suspected what I am, and that fueled your prejudice."

"Maybe that ain't about hate. Ever think of that?" He lowered his eyes. "Each time I look at you, I feel guilty because I'm attracted to the one person who should want me dead more than anyone, and I don't know what the hell that says about me."

I lifted his chin with the tips of my fingers. "How did you manage to sedate my panther?"

A solemn smile touched his lips. "Fear. Your kind thrives on fear. I don't know if you can smell it or see it in a subtle twitch of an eye, but if there's even a sliver of apprehension, your animal can sense it. The only time you're trusting is with someone who doesn't fear you. Someone who isn't afraid to walk up and handle you—even pat you on the side and be rough. Something I learned in the fights. After a while, I wanted to die. When I made that choice, all the fear went away. The panthers trusted me, even allowed me to nuzzle my face against theirs."

I leaned forward and cupped his face in my hands. "That's why you carry all that guilt. Getting them to trust you made it easier to kill them and win. It gave you hope that you might get out of there."

Something broke in Wheeler, something so deep and impenetrable that when the fracture happened, it was like a snap of electricity. That was it. I'd penetrated the wall he'd built to hide his dark secrets—the ones that questioned his morals and integrity. Wheeler's eyes filled with hot tears, and he grimaced, trying to turn away.

I didn't let him. I held his face firmly and touched my forehead to his.

"Don't look away from me. It wasn't your fault," I whispered, stroking the lines of his face with my fingers. "Stop blaming yourself."

"But it wasn't right," he said, his voice cracking. "It wasn't about survival—it wasn't an honorable fight. It was *murder*. They wanted a fighter, but I was a *killer*."

I pulled his head to my chest and stroked my fingers through his hair. "*Shhh*. I had no idea. Ben may be the gambler, but you're the one who wears the poker face. All that anger hiding a man in pain. You deserve so much more than you think."

Wheeler would never admit the truth to Austin. There was honor in a man who fought for his life, but Wheeler had become suicidal, and men who lost the fear of death were capable of unconscionable crimes. But that wasn't the case here, not really. No matter how you sliced it, Wheeler was still a victim. Despite how he'd won his battles, the only choices he'd had were to live or die. The animals that trusted him died at his hands, and I wondered if maybe that wasn't the most humane thing to do.

It made me think of the animals in the shelters that were euthanized. I'd donated money to make more room in those cages because I didn't want them to die. But which was the real hell for them: living in a cage or death?

My heart shattered as I held this broken man. Wheeler had fought his entire life for his brother, for his family, and for his life. But not one person had ever fought for him.

"They wanted to die," I whispered, threading my fingers through the tufts of his brown hair.

His glassy eyes rose to mine—detached and filled with disbelief. "What?"

"No one subjected to that level of torture wants to survive. You gave up; what makes you think *they* hadn't already given up? What those men did to you was unforgivable, cruel, and karma will come back and slap them on the ass someday. Don't let them win, Wheeler. Your chains are gone, but now you've become your own tormentor." I brushed his tangled hair back and ran my finger over his thick eyebrow. "You're not a killer. You were their angel of mercy."

"I was their angel of death," he said despondently, sitting back on his legs.

"You've turned trust into a sinister word because someone trusting you meant their death."

He sprang to his feet and headed toward the door. "You're right."

I leapt up and hurried after him. "Don't you *dare* turn your back on me," I hissed.

Wheeler placed both hands on the door and leaned forward, lowering his head out of sight. "The carnage I left behind, the screams in my head, the blood in my mouth, the looks on those faces—those things are etched in my mind forever."

I touched the dragon on his back. "Your wolf's mind, not yours. You had no control over your animal."

Wheeler spun around and shouted, "I killed them in *human* form!" His voice tightened. "Not all, but in the end. It wasn't fair to make my wolf do all the dirty work; I had to carry my share of the blame. I'd finally embraced the monster I'd become."

"Please, don't go." I slipped my hands around his sides and kissed his chest. "I trust you, Wheeler. I *trust* you won't hurt me. Please…"

In a swift motion, he lifted me by my waist and spun me around, placing my back to the door as he laved my breasts. His body hummed with desire, whiskers scratching my neck until his lips met with mine. A low growl settled in his chest, and I held on tightly as he pressed himself against me.

Wheeler unleashed his repressed desires, and our kiss became frenzied. My legs wrapped around his waist.

My God… this man possessed so much passion that he consumed me with it.

CHAPTER 16

I 'D NEVER HAD A MAN crave me the way Wheeler did. Every movement of his body against mine was insatiable and animalistic. I'd only been with men for superficial reasons, and sex was sex. But the emotional connection threading between us amplified everything. Wheeler confiding in me acted like an accelerant that ignited a spark into a roaring inferno. The deeper and darker his secrets, the more connected we became.

My thoughts scattered as I kissed him hurriedly, as if we only had moments to consume each other before the world ended.

A rip sounded between our kisses.

"What was that?" he asked out of breath, kissing my neck.

"April's baggy jeans. I think I've outgrown them. Are you sure you can handle all this?"

To answer my question, he reached behind my jeans, found the hole, and ripped it wide. A rush of tingles surged through me and I kissed him deeply. Wheeler held my waist and walked me toward the bed where he threw me down like a sack of laundry.

I bounced and looked up at his predatory eyes. "Now I know how poor little Red Riding Hood felt when the Big Bad Wolf looked at her. Are you like this with all your prey?"

"No," he said with a throaty growl, devouring me with his eyes.

Wheeler was probably a man who contained his passion in the bedroom, and seeing how combustible he was with me sent a shiver up my spine.

"What?" I asked, noticing his hesitation.

"Just wondering if you're going to punish me for ripping your pants."

I got on my knees and crawled toward him like a panther. When

I reached around his jeans, I felt the butterfly knife in his back pocket. I pulled it out and stroked the cold metal down his stomach. "Show me a trick."

He took the knife, and I lay on my back beneath him with my legs slung over the edge.

"Move out of the way," he said. "I might drop it on you."

I reached out and stroked the hard outline pressing against his jeans. Wheeler sucked in a sharp breath. "I trust you," I whispered. Then I put my arms up and lay beneath him. "Show me your teeth, Mr. Wolf. I'm not afraid of you."

We both knew that I could shift and heal, but still I saw fear glittering in his eyes. He gently swung it in a simple maneuver and then closed it.

"I've seen you use that thing, Wheeler. Show me what you can really do."

When he spun it again, I arched my back. I thought his willpower might break, but it fueled him. He did tricks with that knife that were blindingly fast.

I'd never seen anything more erotic in all my life—watching his hands deftly spinning that blade around and the intense look on his face as he kept his eyes centered on mine. He suddenly locked the case with the knife out and tossed it across the room at the wall, where it stuck.

I gasped. "I didn't know you could throw those."

Wheeler stripped me out of my jeans and panties. "Years of practice." He fell over me, creating a friction with the bristles on his face as he worshipped my body with his mouth.

"This is real pretty," he said in a soft voice, brushing the back of his hand over my sex. "Tell your wax lady she's got my approval." His hands gently spread my thighs apart and I drew up my knees. Wheeler's hot breath made me quiver with anticipation, and when his tongue lapped at my skin with one greedy stroke, I arched my back, moaning with need.

He gripped my round hips, and after another sensual kiss, he began to tremble. Wheeler climbed up my body, desperate to get me completely undressed.

"I need you naked," he breathed, panting as if he'd run a mile, and the race hadn't even begun.

I leaned up, and Wheeler fumbled with the latches of my bra beneath my shirt. I heard them pop when he pulled them apart, and then he stripped me out of my blouse.

"Mmm, I can tell I'm going to need a large wardrobe with a man like you," I purred, slowly tossing the destroyed garment to the floor.

He hovered over me with yearning in his eyes.

"Is this what you want?" I asked, sliding my fingers into his jeans. It didn't take long before I found the source of all his discomfort. With dexterous hands, I unfastened his pants and shoved him onto his side.

His elbow hit the wall and he hissed in pain. "Wait," he said, gripping my wrist and scooting toward the center of the bed as if fleeing from me.

"What?"

He wouldn't say whatever it was that had caused a flash of terror in his eyes. That's when I knew he was hiding another secret. Without taking my eyes from his, I pulled at his jeans and shorts beneath. Wheeler had softened, losing some of his arousal as unwelcome emotions began to take hold. He swallowed hard and then clenched his jaw.

How had other women treated him?

I kissed his mouth, then his neck, and worked my way down his body until I reached his hips and thighs. In the places that his pants concealed, Wheeler had scars that he hadn't inked up with tattoos. Places maybe he thought no one would ever look again, or maybe he turned all his women away from him so they wouldn't notice.

I noticed. I kissed each scar from the length of his thigh all the way to the one above his groin. He buried his hands in my hair, closing his eyes and thrusting his hips with need. I wanted to weep for what I saw—how he had taken such abuse—but I refused to let him think it mattered. My hands slid up and down the smooth skin on his lower abs, across his waist, and to his thighs.

Wheeler clocked my every move, and it made me self-conscious about concealing my reaction when I saw what else he'd been hiding from me.

Wheeler wasn't just endowed—he was *blessed*. That kind of blessing made a woman hesitate.

"Sure you're a wolf and not a stallion?" I teased. "Because you're hung like a—"

Wheeler snatched my wrists and pulled me on top so I was straddling him. "Are you going to show me *your* teeth?"

I flashed a smile, showing him my pearly whites.

Wheeler rubbed my thighs, and no smile touched his lips. "Not those. I want you to shift."

"Don't be absurd. I'll kill you!"

He licked his bottom lip, fingers exploring my backside. "I can't be with you unless you show me your panther."

"Darling, this isn't necessary. You've already seen my panther."

His hands continued stroking me. "Not like this. Not when I'm vulnerable."

"I… I can't."

"Naya… I thought we were going to be open with each other."

I trembled, despite the fact he'd somehow managed to walk my panther into the Weston home. My panther might attack him if frightened, and I didn't know how much I'd be able to control her reaction. "I don't want to hurt you."

He swallowed thickly and put his arms beside his head. "I need to know."

"Know what?" I asked, stroking his stomach with the tips of my fingers.

"If the reason I don't fear you is because I want to die, or because of something else."

There it was. Wheeler's ability to walk my animal into the house had raised a deep-seated fear that maybe after all these years, he still didn't feel worthy enough to live.

"Please," he whispered.

Why did this have to be so difficult? I had to trust my panther not to hurt a man who meant something to me. I also had to trust that this man wouldn't kill my panther if something went wrong.

I moved off him and sat down by his legs. "Okay. But don't make any sudden movements, and don't look her in the eyes."

His Adam's apple undulated as he swallowed hard and watched me. *Am I really doing this? I must be crazy*, I thought to myself.

I felt the ripple move through me, and I shuddered as my body shifted in the blink of an eye. Through my panther's eyes, I gazed at Wheeler. His breath quickened and his eyes were wide. He stayed still as my animal moved closer. When she stretched her neck to smell his face, I watched in surprise as he suddenly clasped his hands around her jowls and rubbed hard.

"You're beautiful," he said with a handsome grin, looking her straight in the eye. "You hear me in there, Naya? You're gorgeous."

My heart soared. Wheeler rocked with laughter, holding his hand in front of her mouth as she licked his palm with her rough tongue. When my panther rubbed her face against his, I quickly took control and shifted back to human form.

His laugh filled me with such a wonderful feeling, and it slowly died down as he looked at me with amorous eyes. I straddled him—nuzzling my face against his.

"You're a crazy old wolf. Did you get the answer you were looking for?" I asked, nibbling his earlobe.

"Yeah, kitty cat," he said softly, running his hands over my back. "I got it."

I kissed him and something in his expression had changed.

"What do you crave after a shift?" he asked.

"*You.*"

Wheeler shuddered when I reached down and wrapped my fingers around his shaft, stroking it across my slick cleft. His eyes closed upon contact, and the deeper I took him, the more I had to pull back in small doses to make sure I could take him completely. My heart thundered against my chest as a connection formed between us that I'd never experienced with another man—something on an emotional level that went beyond the physical. His hands had never left me, and they were exploring my thick legs, my soft stomach, my supple breasts, and every glorious inch of my body. But the most arousing part of it all was that he never stripped his gaze from mine.

"You feel too goddamn good," he said in strained words.

"Keep touching me. I won't break."

His fingers squeezed my thighs tight and I moved my body faster. The ropes of muscle in his arms and neck strained, and my nails bit into his chest.

Wheeler roared, his body tense. Something primal heated in his eyes.

He reached up, twisting my nipples between his fingers until they elongated. Then he groaned, cupping his hands over my breasts and grimacing.

"You need to stop... *stop*," he bit out. "I'm about to—"

I circled my hips. "Not yet. I didn't give you my *permission*."

The next thing I knew, I was sailing through the air and onto my back. My head hung off the foot of the bed and he pounded into me—his mouth on my breasts and his scent in my nose. My God, I'd never felt anything so delicious! All the blood rushing to my head intensified the orgasm that was about to crash into us.

He dragged my body back onto the bed and settled his eyes on mine. His rhythm was relentless—each stroke even harder than the last, as if he were punishing me, and he filled me so completely that I'd never felt so taken. Wheeler maintained direct eye contact, and I could tell he liked the power play between us.

"Even... better... than I imagined," he said between heated breaths. "*Christ*, your body feels so fucking good."

I gripped the back of his neck and cried out—a bolt of pleasure taking siege and holding me hostage. My nails bit into his skin and I held on through the most powerful climax I'd ever experienced.

Wheeler didn't stop. He pounded into me, faster, deeper. The headboard slammed against the wall and a book tumbled off.

"Pull my hair," he said in a rough voice.

I moaned and gripped his hair in a tight fist.

"Harder," he growled. "Punish me."

Wheeler didn't really want me to give him pain; he needed someone to take control of his pleasure. So I threw him off me.

With stunned eyes, he watched me turn onto my hands and knees, peering at him over my shoulder. I shook my derriere and gave him a sultry smile. "I'd rather you punish me. Show me how the big bad wolf likes it."

Like a predator, he rose up on his knees and gripped my hips. Wheeler drove his shaft into me so hard that I cried out.

"You like this, kitty cat?" He reached around and stroked me with his fingers. "Did I mention how I like you waxed? *Fuck...*"

Now I understood the power of a wolf in the bedroom when he was in his domain. My insides heated, and I became so wet that he moaned profanities as he slapped his hips against my behind, creating one of the most erotic sounds.

I gripped the sheets, desire coiling tight. He moved faster, and when his fingers brushed over my sex again, I gasped.

Wheeler flipped me onto my back, never losing momentum. I gripped his taut biceps as if letting go meant falling off the earth. Pleasure quickly turned to agony on his face, and I knew he needed to find his release.

"*Now*," I said, my voice firm before it fell to a soft breath. "Come inside me."

His body quaked and he yelled out. Wheeler fell over me, out of breath. My senses were overwhelmed with his heat, his smell, the weight of his body, and the feel of his strong heart pounding against my chest.

Wheeler lifted his head and looked at me with concern. "You okay?"

"My heart is coming out of my chest," I said between ragged breaths.

He lowered his head and whispered something I couldn't hear.

I brushed a tangle of curls away from my face and looked vacantly off to the side.

Wheeler didn't like that and pinched my chin, turning my head to face him. "Something wrong?"

"Do you want the truth? This is the part where you tell me I'm a swell fuck and put on your pants."

His brows slanted in an angry line. "*What?*"

"Men have sex with me; they don't sleep with me. There's always a meeting, trip, or somewhere else they need to be. So they go. I don't have any high expectations, and I don't want you to feel guilty about putting on your pants and heading out. You don't look like the cuddling type, and what would your family think? There's no reason to give me that look." I stroked the soft bristles on his chin. "I hope someday you can open up to Austin—or with your mate."

"What mate?"

When I wriggled free, he gasped and sat up. I casually sauntered toward the short fridge. "The wolf you'll find someday who makes your little tail wag," I said with a grin.

Wheeler sat on the edge of the bed, wiping back his damp hair. "Maybe I'm not the mating kind."

"Beer or water?"

"Beer."

I pulled a longneck from the shelf and strolled back to the bed, standing in front of him and letting the chilly bottle touch his neck. "Can you open it?"

With a swift motion, he used his molars to bite on the cap, and it rolled to the floor.

"My big strong man," I purred, playfully gripping the tangle of hair on top of his head.

He sucked down two long gulps and released an audible breath. "That hit the spot."

I bent down and kissed the tip of his nose. "You can say that again."

His cold tongue licked my nipple and I squealed.

"Come here." He handed me the beer bottle and turned me around to sit on his lap.

"Hmm, I didn't think Mr. Grumpy was the cuddling kind." I took a baby sip and shivered when the bubbles slid down my throat. "Delish."

Wheeler chuckled and squinted at me. "I like the way you talk."

"I seem to recall our conversations going a completely different way."

"That's what I'm talking about. Right there. You breathe fire like a dragon, but you're a classy lady."

Was he baiting me? That negative Nelly in my head began to

doubt his words rang true. Classy? I rested my head on his shoulder, enjoying the feel of his arms around me.

"What's on your mind?" He yawned as he set the bottle down.

"Misha."

"She wasn't in that house. My wolf can smell a cat within a five-mile radius."

I laughed softly. "Well he must have *loved* our close encounter. Here, let me get up. I must be crushing your legs." I bent forward and Wheeler pulled me back down.

"Stay right where you are."

"You'll lose circulation."

He gave a closed-lip smile, playing with a curl of my hair. "That'd be a shame. Trapped in bed with a beautiful woman."

I stroked his jaw. "You should trim off this stubble. I liked it better when you just had the beard around your mouth."

"Huh."

"What?"

"Jericho used to give me shit for that. Said women don't like it."

"Well," I said, nipping on his earlobe, "this woman adores it."

He leaned back onto the bed and pulled me on top of him. "Remind me to buy a razor."

We fell into a deep kiss and then he shifted me to his right side. This was nice. I'd never been able to enjoy the feel of a man lying naked beside me without foreplay or sex. I liked his natural, musky smell. And my fingers couldn't stop brushing over his soft chest hair—short, sparse, and pale brown. He bent his left knee and casually moved it back and forth, tucking his right arm behind his head.

"Do you smoke?" I asked.

"Nope. But after what we just did, I'd say that justifies a cigarette. You?"

"Does my kiss taste like smoke?"

"You taste like dark cherries."

Well, *that* was one I hadn't heard before. "Did you really like my chicken spaghetti?"

Wheeler chuckled. "Your mind is all over the place. If that's just a sample of what you can do in the kitchen, then I might lock you in here for good. I love a woman who knows how to cook."

"Mmmm, and I love a man with an appetite."

Wheeler touched my eyelashes before stroking his finger over my brow. "How did you get such exotic eyes?"

His hand smoothed down my neck, across my breasts, and then between my legs. I lightly gasped—hot with desire once more. As I rolled onto my back, Wheeler's teeth locked on my neck and lightly bit down. I moaned as his fingertips explored my sex and his heated breath skated against my skin.

A knock sounded at the door, and I stood up in a panic.

"Be chill," Wheeler said coolly. "I locked the door."

"Naya! It's Lexi."

"Not a good time, girly!"

I heard keys jingling. "Naya, I'm coming in!"

I don't even remember Wheeler moving. One minute I heard him say, "Shit," and the next he was running.

Running where? Oh my God!

The key slid into the lock, Wheeler slipped on the spilled soda by the door, and I reached down and whirled a sheet around me when the door opened.

"This can't wait, Naya. I have to sort out the stuff for the party now. Austin's giving me a hard time, and he's stressed out over the food order. He kicked me out of bed and said if he has to work late, then so do I." She held her laptop in one hand and glanced down at the wet floor. "What the hell happened?"

The bathroom door slowly closed behind her but didn't shut all the way.

"And why are you standing on the bed?" Lexi began to look around and I leapt onto the floor.

"Do have a seat on the sofa. I was just settling in for the night."

She glanced at the tipped-over coffee table.

"Sorry," I said apologetically. "I had a little tantrum because we didn't get Delgado. I was hoping he'd be there."

That seemed to convince her. She set her laptop on the sofa and bent over to pick up the coffee table. I walked toward her and my eyes widened like saucers when I saw Wheeler's knife stuck in the wall.

I reached out and pulled it free, opening the drawer beside me and setting it on top of a fashion magazine.

Lexi stood up with a button between her fingers. "What's this?"

I glanced at the door and noticed Wheeler must have snatched up his shirt. *Goodness! Our clothes!*

"It was hot in here. Do you mind grabbing the towel from the sink? I don't want you to slip on the mess I made."

While Lexi went to the sink and pulled open a drawer, I hurried back to the bed and stuffed the clothes and shoes in hiding places. I frantically looked around for any other signs that Wheeler was here, and then I realized his smell was all over me. *Sweet Jesus!* I rummaged through my bag and slipped into my nightie.

"Naya, this rag isn't big enough to clean that mess. Let me grab a towel from the bathroom."

"No! I'll get it. Why don't you make us a bowl of snacks while I clean up? I'm so sorry about the mess, sweetie. I've always been a little dramatic," I said with an artificial smile.

I pushed through the bathroom door and felt Wheeler in front of me holding a stack of towels. A small squirt sounded in the darkness, and the sweet scent of my Chanel perfume sifted across my chest. I curved my hand around to his rear and gave it a tight squeeze before closing the door.

Lexi and I had a lot of work to do, including a few calls I had to make to complete our orders and schedule delivery.

It took three hours.

But sitting on that sofa, knowing I had Wheeler in my control—naked in that dark, tiny room—thrilled my mischievous nature immensely.

CHAPTER 17

WHEELER'S FEELINGS FOR NAYA HADN'T changed—he still felt loathing and lust. Lust for obvious reasons in that she was an intelligent woman who pleasured him in ways that no other woman had. Loathing because he sat in her bathroom for hours listening to them ramble on about fountains and drapery. He had begun to wonder if Naya was holding him hostage, because each time Lexi would wind down the conversation, Naya would insist they look at another page on the Internet. Whenever Lexi agreed, Naya would release a devilish laugh. The kind that made him want to bend Naya over his knee and give her a spanking.

He could have slept in that bathroom had he not been so damn scared of snoring. Jesus, Lexi would have kicked him out of the pack for sure. She would have accused him of using Naya—maybe even by force based on how the room had been left in disarray.

What he'd experienced with Naya went beyond sex. Wheeler's compulsive actions had been out of control. When he'd ripped her blouse, he feared her reaction. He feared the magnitude of his desire for a woman whose animal represented death for him. But she'd taken hold of the reins, and that excited him. Suddenly the women in his past had become inconsequential; none of them had ever given him what he truly craved in bed. Not just sex, but acceptance. Intimacy. He'd spilled his darkest secrets to a woman who didn't turn away. Naya didn't look at him like she would a monster; she looked at him like she would a man.

And a monster is exactly what he saw reflecting back at him in the mirror. During his captivity, they had denied him contact with the outside world. No one had known his whereabouts, and he'd later found out Ben hadn't even told the family he'd gone missing.

Wheeler had given himself over to the underworld of cage fighting to save his brother, knowing he might never see his family again. Most fighters only lasted for so long before they lost to someone more deadly. Death was the inevitable outcome; it was just a matter of time.

Wheeler had not only survived, he'd quickly gained a reputation in the underground world of cage fights. It wasn't long before they had put him in with the panthers. Usually panthers went against one another for the highest-paying fights, but his owner thought Wheeler had potential and had arranged for a low-key match with a weak panther.

Wheeler's wolf had won that battle. By then his animal had become bloodthirsty—never hesitating to lunge for the jugular as soon as Wheeler shifted.

It wasn't long before hopelessness had crept into his heart with the realization he'd never see his family again. Most of the scars on his arms had partially healed, but not enough. He'd thought he'd die in that hellhole. But sometimes guards got too comfortable and made foolish mistakes.

It took a year after his escape before Wheeler got in touch with Ben. By then, Wheeler had found one of the best tattoo artists in the city to cover up his scars, but it was also a way to separate himself from Ben for good. They were *too* identical, so maybe doing this would be a little *fuck you* to him for stealing his identity. Wheeler could have hated him, but it was impossible to hate the other half of himself.

Ben obviously hadn't thought he'd ever see Wheeler again. For a while, Wheeler believed he might actually change his ways. He'd promised, after all.

But the promises never lasted long before the gambling would start back up. Wheeler grew facial hair, kept the top of his hair longer, and dressed differently. There was no hiding the fact they were twins, but no one would ever mistake Wheeler for Ben again. Jesus, maybe he should have just started a new life away from his brother, but Austin would be forming a pack, and Wheeler wanted to be a part of it. Hell, he *needed* it. The wolf in him craved family and a sense of belonging. In order to do that, he had to forgive Ben. No matter how fucked up his brother was in the head, they were still born of the same seed. They shared the same DNA, even the same thoughts as they could finish each other's sentences. Maybe sometimes you just have to love someone for who they'll never be in order to move on with your life. Ben's popularity among their brothers eclipsed his own, and for that reason, Wheeler couldn't betray him.

After the cage fights, the first person he'd shifted around was Ben. His wolf didn't attack his brother like he'd feared, but Wheeler knew he needed to make sure his wolf wasn't aggressive or else he'd never be accepted into the pack. His nerves were on edge when Austin had introduced his wolf to his brothers. Part of the process included Austin staying in human form and asserting his dominance as the alpha. Wheeler thought for sure something would spook his wolf and he'd lunge at Austin, but no such thing had happened. Maybe his wolf sensed they were family, or maybe it had to do with them also being wolves.

Wheeler made a quiet decision that he would never shift around Naya. *Ever.* That could never happen. The panther fights were some of the most vicious he'd endured, and no way in hell would he risk putting her in danger.

After Lexi left the heat house, Naya rapped her knuckles lightly on the door and announced he was free to go. When he got up and opened the bathroom door, she'd already switched out the lights and had gone to bed. The only light in the room emanated from a dim nightlight behind the sink.

He eyed the doorknob, but something compelled him to stay.

"What are you doing?" she asked sleepily.

"Scoot over. We're cuddling."

She giggled in a way that made the hair on the back of his neck stand up. Wheeler pulled the sheet over them and pressed their bodies together. She had put on a baby-doll nightie, and he couldn't stop touching the lacy fabric. Damn, she was such a sexual creature, and he was so uptight about sex. Not the act of it, but sexuality itself.

The tenderness.

The vulnerability.

The intimacy.

Wheeler was no stranger to strip clubs, but the performances were impersonal and didn't have the same effect on him as when Naya jutted her hip out and played with the collar of her blouse.

Let alone curled up next to him in a fucking nightie that had him rock hard in seconds. All he wanted to do was touch the long ribbons in front, smooth his hand over the silky fabric, and play with the lacy ruffles along the hem.

He'd never felt a need to sate a woman as badly as he did with Naya. It was no longer about his needs, but hers. Had any of the men in her life cared about her wants and desires? Obviously not if they took off after sex. And when he gently slid her panties down, he made sure her needs were met. Wheeler laughed when she argued, wanting to satisfy him in return. Nope. He wasn't having it.

After they'd fallen asleep, he awoke to the feel of her beneath the sheets, sucking on him hard.

Naya was unabashed about her sexuality, but the best part of that damn night was falling asleep behind her with his face nestled in all those beautiful curls of hair. The smell of her, the feel, and hearing the small grunts and moans as she slept. The way her cold feet would seek out his legs for warmth, her soft breath skating across his arm. She looked like an angel. He hadn't realized how satisfying it could be just to *hold* someone.

Nor had he realized how much pleasure could be gained from waking up on his back to find her holding *him*. She had snuggled against his left side, her arm draped over his chest, leg between his as if she had claimed him.

In the quiet moments of the previous night when Naya was fast asleep and clutching him tightly, a wholly new and unexpected feeling had emerged. One that kept him up the rest of the night, watching the door. Not because he was afraid of someone discovering them, but because he needed to protect what was *his*.

Suddenly it didn't matter anymore if he deserved her, if she wanted him, if people would cast judgment on them, if it would mean losing his pack, or if the whole goddamn world thought they were crazy. He wanted claim on Naya. Of all the fucking practical jokes for the gods to play, he'd fallen for a panther.

A wicked tongue like hers might have put off most men, but Wheeler felt like he'd finally met his equal. Beneath the layers of beauty was an intellectual woman, and that was the secret she kept from the world. She put on a good show, but maybe it's because that's all that men had wanted to see in her.

Not Wheeler. After spending three hours in the bathroom listening to how her mind worked, he wanted to know everything about Naya. For Christ's sake, the woman knew who Jackson Pollock was. Most of the women he'd slept with didn't even know who Ronald McDonald was. Sure, her coffee tasted like motor oil and she owned a cross-eyed cat, but that's what made her endearing as hell.

He could sense morning even without sunlight and decided it was time to make an appearance in the house. Wheeler yanked on his jeans and raked his fingers through his disheveled hair, which looked like a cat had licked it out of shape. He pulled the sleeveless shirt over his head and put on his socks, but it took him a few minutes to find his boots. Naya, in a panic, had thrown one of them into a vase near the bed. He carried them down the hall and set them near the entrance to the kitchen. He figured it would look suspicious if he had them on so early in the morning, since most of the time they avoided wearing shoes in the house.

Lynn had two skillets of bacon frying on the stove.

"Morning," he grumbled.

The early morning sunlight glittered through the windows and cast a pretty light across the floor.

"I heard about last night," Lynn said, using a fork to flip over a piece of bacon. "I'm glad you found that poor woman. I can't imagine what would have happened to her and that sweet little girl."

They all knew. If they hadn't found Skye, the pack would have taken in the child. No question.

Lynn never wandered around in a robe or nightgown like some of the other women did. She had on brown slacks and a flowery shirt that matched.

"Smells great," he said. "I could eat a horse."

"Afraid there are laws against horse jerky," William said from the table, startling Wheeler. "You look mighty... refreshed." William lifted the white coffee mug to his lips, his eyes twinkling.

"Any coffee left?" Wheeler asked.

Lynn set down her fork. "If you want some, you'll have to make it yourself. William just finished off the pot, and I'm running late. I made an appointment to meet with a new client this morning. Oh!" She pulled open the oven and a giant pan of buttermilk biscuits appeared. Lynn set them on a cooling rack and turned off the burners.

"Here, I got it," Wheeler said.

"The bacon—"

"I got it."

She looked at him as if somehow he could ruin bacon by removing it from the frying pan. Lynn patted him on the back and left the room.

William's cup tapped against the table when he set it down. "Mustn't let the bacon burn. I like 'em crispy, not black."

Wheeler irritably scooped the entire pan up with a spatula and dumped the strips into a bowl. He walked over and slid the greasy pile of meat in front of William. "Breakfast is served, your majesty."

"Indeed. Next time you might let them sit on a paper towel for a minute or two."

"The other pan is all yours." Wheeler walked behind William and handed him the spatula before taking a seat on the bench.

William hustled to the stove and turned off the burners, giving each slice of bacon individual attention as he laid them neatly on a paper towel. "Say, Naya is a pretty good warrior, isn't she? I've heard about panthers, but I always thought it was just their animal that knew how to fight."

"She holds her own," Wheeler replied, separating a few pieces of bacon and setting them on his green plate.

A loud snap sounded. "Christ!" William shouted. He rubbed his bare chest and moved the skillet off the hot burner before emptying out all the bacon onto a plate. "There's always one little piggy that wants revenge."

Most of the men dressed casual in the morning. Wheeler's clothes wouldn't raise any eyebrows, except for the fact he was wearing the same outfit as last night. Austin usually got all the way dressed—or at least in jeans—and it probably had more to do with upholding an image. Plus he always had manual work to do at the crack of dawn. He was probably outside right now, chopping wood or digging a moat.

William set the bacon on the table along with a carton of juice and two large bowls of biscuits. "Naya's attractive. Wouldn't you agree?"

Wheeler flicked his eyes up to William and shoved the rest of his bacon into his mouth. "What are you driving at?"

"Nothing. Just couldn't help but notice how comely she is."

Wheeler sucked the crumbs off his fingers and watched him closely. "Keep away from her."

William quickly buried a smirk. "Naya isn't my type. Just can't help but admire a supremely beautiful woman is all. Don't you think? Or... is she not your type either?"

"Why don't you make some coffee before I shove this fork up your nose?"

"*I'll* make the coffee," a soft, feminine voice announced.

Naya strolled into the kitchen wearing nothing but her white nightie, and Wheeler almost catapulted out of his chair.

I didn't like waking up alone, even though I'd done it a million times before. What I did like was that Wheeler had stayed with me all night. We had some sexy times, but he opened up to me in a way no other man had. Not only that, but somehow he'd managed to break down my own walls. I could be myself with Wheeler without fear of judgment or that I wasn't enough. It was the way he smoothed his hand over my hair when I had startled myself awake with a nightmare about Misha. He listened to me talk about her without any snide remarks. When he held me in his arms, I felt relevant—like my thoughts and feelings mattered to someone.

While my heart sank when I'd found the bed empty, I decided to hold my chin high. I kept reminding myself we had a pact behind closed doors, but on the outside, there were no promises. Wheeler wasn't in love with me, and he wasn't going to hold my hand in front of his pack and put a claim on me. I was just an exotic dancer who had spiced up his sex life.

"Don't be foolish," I whispered to myself, walking down the hall barefoot. "Stop those silly thoughts right now."

Thoughts that I might actually love him. That would be disastrous! A panther and a wolf? I couldn't afford to soften my heart for a man who would be ashamed to admit we'd slept together. He had slipped out before dawn, for God's sake.

As I neared the kitchen, I overheard Wheeler telling someone to make coffee.

"I'll make the coffee," I offered.

Wheeler lurched out of his seat, his fingertips pressed against the table.

I pivoted around and put my hands on my hips. "What?"

"You should cover yourself up," he said, voice tight, muscles flexing beneath his tats.

I glanced down. "I *am* covered. This is more than what I wear to work. My gown will hardly raise any eyebrows in this house."

William walked by me with silent amusement on his face. While he rummaged through the fridge, I put on a pot of coffee and watched Wheeler reluctantly sit back down.

I wasn't sure why I felt the need to be naughty around him, but I made it into a game. Wheeler didn't want me parading around in front of the Weston pack in my sleeping clothes, which I found delightfully amusing since Shifters didn't consider nudity a big deal. So I leisurely strolled down the row of cabinets and opened a drawer in front of him. The dish towel dropped on the floor, and I took my sweet time bending all the way over to pick it up.

When I turned around, Wheeler had reached out and gripped the other end of the table. His taut muscles looked like granite.

In my defense, I *was* wearing a thong.

"Morning, Naya!" April gave me a lively smile and took a seat at the table. She had on a pair of sweatpants and a baggy T-shirt.

"Have you heard from Reno?" I asked, twirling the dish towel.

"He called me this morning and said they'll be there around noon or so. Everything's going great, and he's going to talk to the Packmaster and make sure Skye has everything she needs before he leaves. He's done this sort of thing before. It's great they accept any Shifter animal. It's like a big commune or something, but in an undisclosed place. Sometimes I wonder if it's really in Colorado or if he just tells me that to throw me off. I'm just glad it all worked out."

"Me too. I'm making coffee," I said. "Want some?"

"No, I'm sticking with juice. But thanks. Lexi will probably want some."

Lexi wandered in with her hair in a tangle. "Want some what?"

"Coffee," I said.

She stopped in the middle of the room. "Oh, uh… no thanks. I'm probably going to take a nap later on. We had a late night, so I don't want the caffeine to keep me awake."

"I could brew a pot of decaf."

"We don't have any," she quickly said. "Did my mom already leave?"

"A few minutes ago," Wheeler confirmed. "Is Austin awake? I need to talk to him about Delgado."

"What about him?"

Wheeler stabbed his biscuit with a fork and ate it that way. "Well, for one, he's going to be gunning for your friend. That what you want?"

The rest of the pack made their way into the room, quiet and ready to eat. William had put a bowl of fruit down in addition to a jar of strawberry preserves and a jug of whole milk.

"I like the view this morning," Denver said, giving me a playful wink. He took a seat near the end of the table.

Wheeler merely watched him while he continued eating his biscuit like an ogre.

Denver placed two fingers in his mouth and a sharp whistle pierced the air. "Toss me an orange," he shouted at Lexi.

She hurled an orange across the table and he caught it with one hand.

Denver straddled the bench and peeled the orange with his fingers, rubbing the sticky juice on his Atari shirt. Denver usually wore cargo pants or distressed jeans, but I'd seen him wearing long shorts in the summertime. I guess he wanted the women to see how nice his legs were.

"So, what are we going to do about Delgado?" Jericho asked Wheeler. "I have a family to protect. Did anyone recognize you at his house?"

"Doesn't matter," Wheeler replied with a mouthful of biscuit. "He probably had surveillance cameras set up. He's not an idiot; he'll figure it out. Let him get pissed. Angry men make stupid mistakes."

"And sometimes those mistakes are at the expense of innocent people," Austin said as he entered the room. He took a seat at the left head of the table and poured a glass of milk. "I don't want the Council involved, so I'm leaning on my alliances for advice. I've called Prince, and he'll be coming over later on to discuss strategy."

"We were witnesses," I reminded him. "Even if they can't get Delgado because of the cage fights, he was keeping two Shifters in his house against their will. The young man had been sexually assaulted, and I'd say that's enough to at least get his privileges revoked from owning Breed clubs."

Austin rubbed his temple. "Maybe so. But men like him don't go away easily. Human or not, he's got connections and money, and that's a dangerous weapon for any man to wield. Have you heard from him?" he asked me.

I lifted the pot of coffee and carried it to the table. "No, but I'm sure he'll be ringing me at any moment. I left my phone in the other room so I can enjoy a nice breakfast. Let him throw a tantrum on my voice mail and wait," I said smoothly. "Who wants coffee?"

Austin immediately put his hand over the top of his empty mug.

"No, I'm good," Izzy said. "It'll make the baby kick."

Wheeler lifted his mug. "I'll have some."

Lexi choked on something and began a fit of coughing.

"Are you okay, chickypoo?"

She waved me off and gulped down some orange juice. I filled Wheeler's cup to the brim. After that, I filled my own and then took a seat at the opposite end of the table from Austin.

Minutes passed as we had light conversation over breakfast. Melody was a night owl and often slept in. Izzy said she inherited that from her father, and Jericho barked out a laugh and placed his hand on her belly.

Lexi craned her neck. "About time you joined us, Maze. Breakfast is almost cold."

"I don't feel good," Maizy said in a weak voice.

I glanced over my shoulder and saw Maizy in front of the open doorway. Her cheeks were flushed, eyelids droopy, and yet her body was shaking. She had on an oversized red shirt that reached her knees, and it looked wet around her neck.

"What's going on, Peanut?" Denver asked in a jovial tone, not turning around because he was too busy buttering his fourth biscuit.

Lexi stood up. "Maizy, what's wrong?"

"I don't feel—"

Just as Denver turned to look, Maizy collapsed. I hadn't even put my fork down before Denver swung his leg over the bench and rushed to her side. His plate shattered on the floor, and the rest of his juice tipped over on the table.

He dropped to his knees and cradled her head. Denver touched her cheeks and then looked at Lexi over his shoulder. "Jesus, she's burning up. Get the truck!"

"Maizy?" Lexi ran around the table to her. "What's wrong with her?"

Denver lifted her in his arms and turned around. "Someone start the goddamn truck! She needs to get to a hospital!"

Shifter children were prone to accidents, and we only sought help from Relics. But not all Relics were schooled in human diseases and had access to their treatments.

Denver swiftly moved out the door—still barefoot—with Austin and Lexi right behind him.

"Holy smokes, I hope she's okay," April said in a low voice. "I don't remember her complaining she was sick, but sometimes that stuff just sneaks up on you all of a sudden."

"Maybe we should quit taking her out to human places where she can catch all that shit," Wheeler suggested, his jaw tightening.

"Don't blame this on us." Jericho rose from his chair, his long hair falling in front of his face. "We take the kids to the movies and the park because that's what you do in a family."

"She's *human*," Wheeler reminded him. "Maizy's vulnerable in ways your kids aren't."

"Okay, let's calm down," I said. "There's nothing we can do about it now. The doctors will know the right medicine to give her. This isn't the dark ages. Children don't die anymore from the flu like they used to."

"Yes they do," April said. "Well, I hear about it on the news. Probably just sick kids or the young ones. That's why they get vaccinated. Maybe I should talk to Lynn about that."

Jericho tossed down his napkin. "Getting her out in public is what she *needs*. She has to be exposed to all that shit so she can build up her immunity. We can't shelter her here in the Breed world thinking just because we don't carry diseases or viruses, she'll be safe. Eventually she's going to live in that world. Dig?"

"No, I don't fucking dig," Wheeler enunciated, swinging his leg over the bench and standing up. "I brought a panther into the house, and I'm taking my punishment like a man. But maybe I'm not the only one who should be held accountable for endangering lives."

"Hold on, wait a minute," Izzy said, waving her arms. "You are *not* about to say we intentionally put her in harm's way."

"Wheeler has a valid point," William said calmly, reeling in everyone's attention. "I'm not saying he's right or you're right, but I think we *all* need to share the responsibility of what it means to keep our pack safe on all different levels."

William was a slick one, and I could see his influence on the pack.

"Let's keep a cool head," he continued, peeling an overripe banana. "Wheeler is on the defense because he helped a family friend by doing what he was told, although it inadvertently put our pack in danger. He *did* call in advance to give us notice and prepare. Each of us is guilty of irresponsible decisions, and yet we're not held to the same standard of judgment. How many times have we forgotten to buckle our seatbelts or driven another pack member home after a few drinks at the bar? Sure we can shift and heal, but—"

"No, you can't," I interrupted. I pushed my plate away and met the gazes of everyone sitting at the table. "Shifters aren't immortal. I think sometimes we take for granted that we can heal. Yes, it takes a lot to kill us, but my mama died in a car accident. She hit her head and went into a coma—one she never woke up from. Once the human hospitals took her in, I couldn't get her out. She spent days on their machines." I wiped away a tear, my emotions raw. "When they declared her brain-dead, I had to make the decision to take her off life support." All eyes were downcast. "We're not immortal, and we shouldn't live our lives as if we are. Accidents happen, so maybe we shouldn't take each other for granted."

The room quieted.

"I'm so sorry," April said in a soft voice. "I know how you feel. I lost my father in a car accident."

"Honey, I didn't mean to stir up bad memories," I said ruefully. Once again, I'd worn out my welcome, so I stood up from the table. "I'm sure little Maizy will be fine—you all take such good care of her. I'll call Lynn and make sure she knows what's going on. It would be nice if someone changed the sheets on Maizy's bed and fixed up her room for when she gets home. If anyone needs me, I'll be in the heat house."

As I left the room, I glanced over my shoulder and noticed Wheeler pouring his second cup of coffee. He took a sip and grimaced, holding it up to me in silent approval.

CHAPTER 18

ELGADO NEVER CALLED. I KEPT my phone charged, but the more minutes that ticked by without contact, the more nervous I became. Austin was wrong about which weapons make a man dangerous. We're all armed in some form or fashion, but pride is the worst weapon of all.

Even if I left the Weston pack, they were already involved in a way that couldn't be undone. The only honorable thing for me to do would be to see this thing through until the end.

When nervous, I had a tendency to clean. I spent the rest of the morning polishing every corner of my room, including inside the cabinets. When I found myself cleaning each leaf of a fake plant, I decided it was time to mingle with the household. I changed into a pair of red shorts and another white shirt that tied at the bottom. Since I was now a guest under their roof, I went barefoot, respecting their rules.

Austin remained home, waiting for Prince. I helped him move some of the cars out front. Lexi had called us with periodic updates on Maizy. By midafternoon, she confirmed they were still in the waiting room. April invited me to sit with her by the stereo, and she turned on some blues music at a low volume. We talked for a little while, but eventually the chatter died down and she began to read. April was a friendly girl—more shy around men than women—but I adored her sensitive nature.

When someone knocked at the front door, April glanced over her shoulder. "That must be Prince. Austin!" she yelled.

"Why don't *you* answer the door?" I asked with a soft giggle. "The poor man is standing outside and listening to your shouts."

"Normally I would, but I don't always know the rules when

another Packmaster is invited over. They get all funny about stuff like this. A member of the Council came over once and I answered the door in my slippers. That didn't go over well with Austin, especially when I slipped and fell on my butt."

"This is silly. I'll get it."

"Wait, I wouldn't do that. Austin!" she yelled again.

I brushed off a chill and headed toward the door. The house was alight with sunshine that filtered through the sheer curtain and cast a luminous gleam across the wood floor.

I swung the door open and jutted my hip to the side. "You must be the alpha everyone is fussing over," I said in a friendly voice.

Prince was pleasingly tall and dressed in a casual pair of slacks and a grey button-up shirt. I could sense he had a lot of money. Perhaps it was the sparkly gold watch on his wrist, or maybe it was the expensive cologne I'd become familiar with. Packmasters were usually men with brawn, but he seemed gracefully older and sophisticated. His dark hair was pulled into a tight ponytail, and when he removed his mirrored sunglasses, I stared into his eyes for a little longer than was necessary. One was brown and the other a deep blue.

He tucked his glasses in his shirt pocket and inclined his head. "I'm here by invitation. My name is Prince."

"Naya James. Pleasure to meet you."

"The pleasure is all mine, Miss James." He traced his index finger across an eyebrow and assessed me in the way most Packmasters did.

"I'm not a wolf, but feel free to enjoy the view. Come inside." I turned away just as Austin jogged down the stairs to meet him at the door.

"Prince. Thanks for coming on short notice. Have a seat. Do you want anything to drink?"

"Thank you for your hospitality, but no." He swaggered into the living room and sat in a leather chair across from April.

She quickly got up and hurried toward the stairs. "I have to get ready for work."

Prince chuckled as he sat down. "Timid little creature. I find her and Reno to be an anomalous pairing."

Austin rubbed the back of his neck and eased into the leather chair opposite Prince. "Yeah, those two are something else."

Then I realized Austin's behavior had to do with rank. My, the culture of wolves fascinated me. I slinked around the sofa and took a seat in the middle, crossing my legs.

Prince unabashedly appraised me from head to toe, a smile playing on his lips.

"Has something struck you as amusing?" I asked.

His finger and thumb were in the shape of an L, holding up his chin. "Body language intrigues me."

Clearly Prince was an observant man who interpreted every gesture into a meaning.

"Careful not to read into me too much, you might be dyslexic. Had I crossed my legs toward Austin—a mated alpha—it might have given you the wrong message about the nature of my relationship with him."

Austin cleared his throat as a warning not to engage in this topic with Prince.

"No, no," Prince said to Austin. "I don't meet many women who understand the subtle nuances behind posture and the messages behind body language." He regarded me with his gaze. "Then why not put both feet flat on the floor?"

"Because that's not how a lady sits, and I would appear closed off since I'm not facing anyone. This conversation involves me, so it's important I show I'm honest with nothing to hide. Crossing my legs in your direction is not about me showing interest; it's about giving you my attention and trust."

He silently studied me with a closed-lip smile. Austin appeared hesitant to interrupt, so I saved him the agony of watching his friend flirt with me.

"A human purchased the club I work at, and many others. He's behind a series of kidnappings, and it turns out he's using these girls for cage fights."

Prince's smile withered, replaced by a frightening expression.

Austin crossed one foot over his knee, then set both feet on the ground and widened his legs. "Last night we broke into Delgado's house and rescued two Shifters."

"You broke in," Prince said flatly. "Without a warrant?"

"We had enough evidence. He'd made Naya an offer to work for him as a cage fighter."

Prince slanted his eyes toward me. "Is that so?"

I picked at my nail, deciding a manicure was in order. "Someone like me is valuable to a man like him."

"We expected him to call back, but he's gone silent. That makes me nervous," Austin admitted. "I don't expect he'll come busting through my door, but a man with that much money could buy off someone in a position of authority to take me down. By force or false charges. Either way, the unknown kept me up all night."

"How many of his men did you kill?"

"Two confirmed. The others were left tied up or unconscious. We moved the girl to a safe, undisclosed location, so that leaves us with the young Shifter. From what they told me, he's not in good condition. He might have skipped town by now. That's what any sane person who's not in a pack would do."

Prince turned his head and stared at the black television. "How did a human purchase our clubs to begin with?"

"It's been going on for years. Somehow he got his foot in the door long enough to make some good money—enough to pay someone off. Maybe selling drugs to humans is one way he got started, but he's our problem now. We can't touch him because the Breed laws prevent us from going after humans. That's his shield."

Prince laced his fingers together and stretched out his legs. "An egg has a shield to protect it, one that's easily broken. No one is untouchable. And if what you say about the cage fights is true, then you have my full support in taking him down. To be honest, if this was nothing more than his owning a few Breed clubs, I would have walked away. A nuisance? Yes. But by no means a reason to start a war."

"Is that what we have here? A war?" Austin asked.

Prince leaned forward and steadied his gaze on Austin. "I've lived a long time and come from a genetic line so pure that I'll probably

never find a suitable mate who will carry strong children for me—
ones that will live as long as I will. Most of the purity has been bred
out over the years. I've spilled blood on the battlefield and negotiated
treaties. This repugnant human won't rob me of sleep, nor should he
you. But once you let in the roaches, they infect. They spread their
disease until you're surrounded by nothing but vermin. Delgado's
power isn't his personal rise to success—it's the tricks he's learning
about the favor trading in our world. There's money in cage fights,
but if he's keeping personal slaves, then I'd guess his fascination with
us goes beyond money. He wants to dominate us—turn us against
each other like savage animals, just as he does in the cage fights."

"Why Shifters?"

"Maybe it's not just us. Maybe he owns Mage bars, but I doubt
it. Those immortals have insurmountable wealth and are not easily
manipulated. We're weaker because our struggles for independence
are only in the early stages. So many Shifters crave power and money
and are easily bought."

"I can testify to that," I said. "I've worked with all kinds, but
since Shifters have it the hardest, they're likely to do more for the
money. It's a pity."

"And that is our struggle," Prince agreed, leaning back in his
chair. "We went from slaves living on the brink of society to free
men. Yet no wealth to build upon, no home, no land, no skills.
And still many continued to shut us out, even though by law they
could no longer own us. I remember a time when we were turned
away from jobs and no one would accept our business. Packs quickly
formed to gain unity and strength, but it was an arduous battle for
land. Even now we still fight amongst each other because we know
it will take years to catch up to the monetary success the immortals
luxuriate in." Prince's leg bounced a few times, causing his heel to
tap on the wood floor.

"So what are you suggesting?" Austin asked warily.

"Snuff him out."

A flurry of footsteps tromped down the stairs. "I'm off to work,"
April called out.

"Who's going with you?" Austin looked over his left shoulder and watched April drop her purse on the floor.

Trevor appeared at the bottom of the stairs with his guitar case slung over his shoulder. "Don't sweat it. I'm going to see how the human girls like my act."

"This should be interesting," April said. "We serve children."

"Hey, you've got plenty of cougars in there."

"They're probably married!" April slipped on her shoes at the door.

Trevor already had on a clean pair of dress shoes. "Babe, there's no guilt in window-shopping."

They went out the door like a hurricane, and I smothered a laugh.

Wheeler trudged down the stairs and looked like he'd gotten less sleep than I had. He'd showered and shaved, and by shaved I mean he'd taken a razor to his face and trimmed up his beard just the way I'd suggested. Clean on the sides with a circle of whiskers around his mouth and chin that made me think of how bikers sometimes wore theirs.

If my feet had been hidden in a pair of shoes, I would have curled my toes at the sight of him.

I tried to avert my eyes as he entered the room, but it felt like my chin was glued to my right shoulder. He didn't just walk into the living room—he swaggered in a sexy, masculine way. My God, had I ever paid attention to how sinfully delicious Wheeler was to look at? He'd dressed in a long-sleeved black shirt that fit him tight enough to show his lean muscle. I guessed for appearance's sake, he'd covered his tattoos so as not to offend Prince. I also liked the way his jeans fit him—slightly loose in the crotch and…

I looked away and turned my motor off before it began to purr.

When he sat on the sofa next to me, a heavy scent blanketed the air—one of soap, aftershave, and the dark spices of a real man.

I cleared my dry throat, feeling my silly heart begin to beat faster.

Wheeler stretched his arm across the back of the sofa, and I felt a slight tug on my hair. I set both feet on the ground and straightened up.

Prince squinted at me and then his eyes drifted to Wheeler. Hand to God, I felt a heat rising across my chest. Against my white blouse, that would be no good!

"What's the plan?" Wheeler interrupted.

"Wheeler and Reno were the ones who broke into the house," Austin explained to Prince.

"And Naya," Wheeler added.

Prince looked at me, nonplussed. "So you're not a wolf, but you participated in a dangerous mission with a wolf pack?"

"I had a personal investment. I would have gone in without them."

A single eyebrow arched and he turned his attention to Austin. "Let's wait for him to contact you or make a move, and then we'll decide. There's little you can do at the moment without knowing his whereabouts."

"I have his number; we can call him," I said.

"I'm afraid that wouldn't get you far. A man like him doesn't want you to know his next move. He won't accept your terms or conditions at this point."

"He might. I'm a panther."

Prince's jaw slackened.

"He values me at a high price."

Prince curled his lips in and began rubbing his hand across his mouth. I didn't have a doubt in my mind why he looked uncomfortable. Ancients like him had seen the darker side of our past—had lived it. Prince gave Austin a judgmental stare, but Austin merely sat up straight and centered his eyes on him.

"If I take out Delgado, will I have your full support?" Austin asked. "Your protection?"

"My absolute protection—as much of it as I can offer. The laws are in place to create order, but sometimes we have to take the law into our own hands. Discreetly, of course. It's important you don't make any mistakes, because you might only have one chance. Too many failed attempts will draw suspicion to your court—too many eyes you can't afford to have on you. When things like this happen, you want to keep that knowledge to a limited few, such as those sitting in this room right now. Your pack will remain unified, regardless if you conceal information from them. You're their leader, and Packmasters have no obligation to disclose the details behind our orders. We protect our packs, and that's why it's better to only have a handful that could be held accountable if something goes wrong. Your goal is to protect as many of your packmates as possible."

"I'm all for keeping this limited to our private little party," Wheeler said.

Austin lowered his voice. "This isn't the first time Delgado has tangled with our pack, but I'll make damn sure it's the last. To hell with the laws if they protect a man like him."

The slander laws were frustrating. Within the Breed world, an accusation without evidence was a punishable offense. The dynamic in the Breed world was so different than for humans because social chatter built reputations. Our population wasn't as massive, and because of our extended lifespan, slander could financially damage someone in a way that couldn't be undone. It's the kind of thing that could follow a man for seven hundred years, preventing him from forming alliances or offering his services. So our laws decreed that warrants couldn't be issued without substantial written or physical evidence. Jail space was limited; therefore, only serious crimes resulted in a sentencing. The higher authorities had no desire to be held accountable for a botched arrest. We had to be careful not to draw attention to ourselves, and concealing a prison was a tremendous task. Vampires worked for the higher authority to make sure any suspicious humans had their memories scrubbed. We also had spies working in the human world, and hackers erased documented evidence of Breed business.

"Keep me abreast of your actions, Cole. Now that I'm involved, consider me an investor."

"I have my pack leaving in groups of two. I'm not about to shut us in here because of that bastard."

"And you shouldn't," Prince agreed. "Keep your pack moving and split up. When you have an enemy upon you, the worst thing you can do is huddle together as a single target."

"Someone's here," Wheeler murmured, glancing at the front door.

When it swung open, Lexi looked frazzled, still wearing her sweatpants and tank top from this morning. A strand of hair settled in front of her weary face and she tucked it behind her ear.

"How is she?" Austin asked.

Denver walked in carrying Maizy. At eleven years of age, she was already growing out of the little-girl stage I remembered. But she was still dwarfed in Denver's arms.

"It's just an infection," Lexi said, hanging her keys on a nail.

Austin's brow furrowed. "What kind?"

"That's medical jargon for bullshit," Denver bit out. "Six hours in the waiting room before they'd even see her. Those humans are a bunch of dickwads."

"Someone's in a good mood," I said. "How's our baby girl feeling?"

Prince rose from his chair and approached them.

"Fine," Maizy murmured weakly.

Lexi rubbed her face. "They gave her some meds and a shot to lower the fever."

"Which we had to wait another hour for," Denver added.

"The little one is growing so fast," Prince said, closing in on Denver. "May I?"

"May you *what?*" he snapped.

Prince laid his hand upon her forehead. "Human children are often stricken with fevers of unknown origin." He lifted her eyelids and bent down, looking closely at her eyes. "I still see mischief. As long as there's mischief sparkling like diamonds in those blue eyes, then you have no reason for concern." Prince stroked her cheek and Maizy smiled up at him. "Tell me, child, do you remember who I am?"

When Maizy nodded, Denver stepped back and gave Prince a heated stare.

"Why don't you put her to bed," Austin suggested. "It looks like you've had a long day. Are you hungry, Maze?"

"Kinda. Maybe just some soup."

Lexi approached Denver. "I'll take her upstairs. You can shower and get some sleep. I know you have to work tonight."

He angled away from her slightly. "Time for me to dip into some of that vacation. We're going to her room, and I'm hooking up some video games to her TV."

"I don't have a TV," Maizy said.

"You will in about ten minutes." Denver hiked up the stairs and disappeared out of sight.

Lexi leaned over the back of Austin's chair and wrapped her arms around his shoulders. "Mom said she's on her way home to take over."

He kissed the back of her neck and sniffed audibly. "Maybe you should run upstairs and take a shower. We'll be done here in a minute."

"I thought you liked me stinky," she said, her voice sweetening.

"Mmm, then wait for me in bed. Why don't you shift and let your wolf out for a while? I'll bring up some chocolate pudding."

Lexi nibbled on his ear. "I want two cups."

Austin's eyes hooded and he murmured something in her ear. I just loved the heat between those two.

She stood up and stretched her back. "The next time anyone needs to go to the doctor, leave Denver at home. When they handed him the clipboard to fill out information, he whirled it through the open window and they almost called security on him. Needless to say, he didn't like the waiting-room situation. Especially when a drunk stumbled in, not wearing pants, and sang three patriotic songs."

Wheeler chuckled. "Sad I missed that."

Lexi put her hands on her hips. "Well, that's nothing compared to when we were in the room and they gave her the shot. The nurse asked Denver to leave, and you can imagine his response to that. When he pulled out the needle, I should have known things weren't going to end well. You know how they give the shot in the rear? Well, as soon as the male nurse began lifting her shirt, Denver threw him across the room."

"Jesus," Austin breathed, rubbing his face.

"After that, they *did* call security. I thought he was going to shift in that room, so I forced him to leave and wait outside before he got himself arrested. I hope someday I can laugh about it, but right now I just need a nap." She waved a hand and walked up each step as if she were scaling a mountain.

Prince returned to his chair. "That's quite a woman."

Austin nodded proudly in agreement. "I'm a fortunate man. They don't make 'em like her."

I shivered when my hair tickled the back of my neck.

Wheeler scooted down and widened his legs. "Maybe we need to think of a plan B in case Delgado doesn't come after us right away."

Prince chuckled and rubbed his brown eye. "He's human. He'll do something soon. Like milk, humans have a short expiration date, so they don't waste time plotting their revenge. They are impulsive creatures."

Wheeler's phone rang and he lifted his hips, pulling it out. After a quick glance, he abruptly stood up and excused himself from the room.

"Do you know where he might be holding the others?" I asked Prince.

"Not in the city," he said. "It's much too risky, and if they escaped, they'd have a better chance of getting away. These men prefer to keep their fighters in a rural area, miles from any large population. I presume if he owns a place in the country, it's not listed under his name. Do we know whether he owns these Shifters, or is he simply selling them to a third party for profit?"

I shook my head. "Does it matter? Savage men like him should be punished—and quickly."

"Agreed."

Austin steepled his fingers in front of his face, resting his elbows on his knees. "He's going to replace those two, you know. Maybe you should call some of your friends at work and give them a heads-up."

I lowered my eyes. "I doubt they'll want to speak to me after the show I put on. People don't trust panthers."

Wheeler rushed into the room, out of breath. "I need to head out," he said to Austin.

"You know the rules," Austin reminded him. "Take someone with you."

"I'll join you," I offered.

"No, you stay." His eyes flashed up to Austin. "Ben took off before you laid down the rules. He's still got something to do, so he asked me to meet up with him and then head back home."

Austin slid his jaw to the side, looking at him pensively. "There and back."

I turned my head toward Wheeler standing behind me. He briefly lifted one of my curls and let it slip through his fingers. It seemed like such a peculiar gesture that I kept watching him as he walked to the door and lifted his keys from a nail positioned above the letter *W*.

"Be careful," Austin said.

As Wheeler opened the door, he glanced at me over his shoulder. I'm not sure why that left my panther unsettled, but she paced feverishly.

CHAPTER 19

WHEN WHEELER RECEIVED A PHONE call from Ben, he knew he'd gone back to Club Sin to play another game with higher stakes. What Wheeler wasn't prepared for was Delgado on the other end of the line.

"When I got wind one of my girls was a panther, I needed proof," Delgado said. "I'm not a man who believes hearsay, so I ordered one of my men to make her shift onstage to get a better look. That would get her fired, and no one would notice if she went missing. I've had my sights on acquiring a panther for a long time."

"What do you want?" Wheeler said tersely from the hall outside the kitchen.

Delgado sucked in long and satisfied breath, adding a hint of amusement to his voice. "Before Naya's dance, I was playing a game of poker with a Shifter. Funny, I sat there staring at your brother and couldn't believe it. The same face of a man I'd watched fight off a panther with his bare hands when I was in my twenties. You see, I'm not a stranger in your world. I've been in it for a long time, working my way up and learning where the fast money is. Sometimes I lied and said I was a Relic; no one could tell. After acquiring a few clubs, I got all the protection I needed. In my early days, I used to bet on the panther pits. That's where the big money was."

Wheeler's stomach turned when he realized where this was going.

"You were legendary," Delgado said with admiration. "The stakes were always higher when you fought in human form, so you can thank yourself for lending a hand in my wealth. I sat there staring at your brother for a long time—I'll never forget that face.

After a little conversation, he mentioned that he had a twin. Your reputation precedes you, Mr. Cole."

"Where's Ben?"

"Let's make this quick and to the point. I'm quite curious if your identical twin would be as savage as you once were in a match, but I'd prefer to have a sure thing. Either way I'll have someone to fill a sudden vacancy for the panther. Make a choice: you or your brother. One of you is going to be my bitch, so who will it be? Ticktock, Mr. Cole. Ticktock."

Wheeler closed his eyes in a moment of déjà vu. "Where?"

Maybe after all he'd been through, he should have cut his losses with Ben. But saving Ben was the last thread of humanity he had left in him. How could his brothers ever trust him if they found out he had left Ben to rot? How could he live with himself? So Wheeler scribbled down the address and willingly gave up his freedom for his brother's life.

During the drive, he thought about the floral smell of Naya's perfume when she was sitting beside him on the sofa. She hadn't noticed he'd been stroking the soft curls of her hair with his outstretched arm. Wheeler had contemplated putting his claim on her openly, although he wasn't sure what repercussions that would bring. Would his pack accept a panther? They'd brought humans into the house, but this was different. Claiming Naya was a bigger gamble than any of Ben's poker games, because Wheeler was gambling with his heart.

After walking out the front door, he realized that he'd never see Naya again. He wondered if they'd search for him—wondered what Ben would tell them. Would rumors leak about what he was involved in? Would Delgado place his lifeless body on Austin's doorstep?

Jesus. He'd never be able to escape his past.

When Wheeler arrived at the location, Delgado stayed true to his word and released Ben. It surprised Wheeler that Delgado wasn't considering pitting the two brothers against each other in a cage, but then again, maybe his satisfaction would be gained in sending Ben to break the news to the pack.

Ben didn't even make eye contact, but Wheeler could see the

shame on his face. They had beaten him, but not severely. He kept his eyes low to the ground and walked with a steady gait to Wheeler's Camaro and drove away.

Not a thanks, a hug, a sorry, or even a good-bye.

Wheeler had never felt more gutted.

Did he even have it in him anymore to kill for the sake of survival? What the hell was worth living for?

Naya. He laughed to himself. She had forgiven his past, but she'd never accept him for repeating history. Then again, maybe her attraction to him was only physical. If so, she might end up looking to Ben for comfort.

Hell, the bastard would probably offer her consoling words before sticking his tongue down her throat.

Wheeler stared at the shackle on his right arm covering the tattoo wrapped around his wrist. They'd stripped him out of his shirt and had taken his belt and shoes, leaving him in just a pair of jeans. Wheeler thought about how easily he could use his jeans to strangle a guard who got too close. He spent a lot of time working out that plan in his head.

Delgado had mentioned he used his partner's property to house the fighters. Delgado made his money by organizing the events as well as putting in his own fighters. Wheeler knew right away that he was dealing with a novice. Delgado focused on the animal more than the person, whereas most ringleaders didn't kidnap strippers. Rogues were the preferred choice because they had the right kind of temperament for fighting.

Wheeler had no clue where the hell he was because they had blindfolded him during the drive. His room looked like a prison cell, minus the sink and bed. The only luxury provided was a toilet, which was a step up from the bucket his previous owner had made him use all those years ago. That guy used to keep the guards in line by placing them on "bucket duty" as punishment. That left an attractive vulnerability. Whenever guards entered a cell, there were all kinds of opportunities for escape. Unfortunately, his new cell had modern plumbing, so they'd probably only enter when taking him to a fight.

Bastards.

"Is someone thirsty?" A guard taunted him in a cockney accent. He looked like a filthy bum—the blackest stubble on his face that Wheeler had ever seen, and a pudgy nose. "Here you are. This one's on me." He reached in and swung his arm, holding a metal cup, sending a stream of water onto Wheeler's pants.

Wheeler remained seated with his back against the wall and his knees bent. The worst thing to do was engage with the guards. Deep down, they knew they were inferior, so it was commonplace for them to rile up the fighters—especially the new ones. Wheeler just sat back and assessed the guard's stupidity.

"Your raw meat is on the way, you disgusting pig."

Most guards weren't predators. They were deer, horses, or even the occasional bovine. Cows weren't as common, because in the dark ages of their history, they'd been milked and eaten by the poorer Breeds.

Owners only fed the animals—not the humans. So unless you liked chewing on raw meat, you had to shift. They did it as a means to get the animal used to being caged and shackled. Wheeler respected his wolf too much to let him feel like a worthless piece of shit, so he'd learned to eat raw meat in those times.

Wheeler could hear the others stirring in their cells, but he kept to himself. In the end, it just made it harder to kill someone you were on friendly terms with.

A concrete wall stretched along the hall, and he sat there for a long time staring at a crack that ran from the floor right to the center.

Wheeler had a lot in common with that wall.

<hr />

Shortly after Austin walked Prince out to his car, I tiptoed upstairs to check on the baby. I'd always called Maizy the baby because that's just how I looked at children of any age. Innocence is fleeting. I set a jelly sandwich on the small white table next to her bed.

"How are you feeling, chickypoo?" I asked in a hushed voice.

"Horrible," she admitted. "Denny wanted to play games, but my head hurts."

"Do you think you can eat some of this?"

She looked at my plate apprehensively. "I had some soup earlier and now my stomach hurts."

I laughed. "Well, if Denver cooked it, then it's no wonder."

She giggled weakly and rolled to her side. "I hate being sick."

I glanced around at her room at all the signs of a young girl outgrowing her childhood staring back at me. Dolls stuffed in a box near the closet, and a mixture of her past and present in the form of jewelry, stuffed animals, nail polish, and a poster of a boy band. Someone had hung up her small wand on a nail by the window, and it glittered in the sunlight like nothing I'd ever seen. In those particles of light, I thought I could hear a little girl's dreams and laughter. I was beginning to see the young woman she would soon become and finally understood Lexi's sorrow of watching someone she loved fade away.

"How's Misha?" she asked. "I haven't seen her in a long time."

I brushed a wisp of hair away from her face. "She's fine, baby. You go back to sleep."

After kissing her cheek, I stepped over Denver, who was sitting on the floor at the foot of the bed in the midst of a nap. I strolled down the hall and glanced in some of the rooms. Lynn hadn't returned home from her client meeting but had called to check on Maizy and see if they wanted her to bring something for dinner. Austin didn't like the idea of Lynn being out alone, so he called her client and asked the woman to keep Lynn there until William showed up to drive her home.

I turned the corner on the left, just past the game room, down another hallway. The rooms on the right must have overlooked the front of the house. Lexi had told me that when they first moved in, she wanted the room with the balcony. But when the mosquitoes had found their way inside, she switched to a room in the other hall.

So many rooms for a growing pack. All doors were closed with the exception of one. When I flipped on the light, I realized it must have been Wheeler's room. His wallet was still on his desk, open and showing his fake human identification.

Something just didn't feel right.

I smoothed my finger over his laptop and then opened one of the drawers. The tips of my fingers touched a cloth case and I recognized the feel of a pair of reading glasses.

"Hey, what are you doing in here?" Lexi asked in a sleepy voice. "I passed by and saw the light on in the hall."

I quickly shut the drawer and gave her a dazzling smile. "The door was open. I was being my nosy self, snooping like you know I love to do."

"Well, Wheeler will kill you if he finds out you were in here. He doesn't like anyone in his space."

I assessed his meager living quarters. So humble and dreary. A black chair and dark wood flooring just made the room appear drab and depressing. "What could he possibly have to hide in here?" I asked. "Sex toys?"

"No, that's Reno's room," she said with a chuckle. "You have a dirty mind. Let's go downstairs and make some lunch. I'm more mentally exhausted than anything, so there's no way I can lie in bed and stare at the ceiling for two hours. I'll feel better if I move around the house and do something productive."

"What about the bakery?" I asked, stepping into the hall as she closed the door.

"The great part about being the boss is I have staff. The only thing I need to do is come up with the recipes and prep the day before. But Izzy caught on quickly, so between her and Trevor, they always have a handle on things."

"So Izzy's at the store today?"

"Her and two other girls. Jericho's going to stay up there all day to give a hand. God help us all."

"I'm sure he's good with his hands," I purred.

"Izzy's a hard worker, and that's why I made her the manager. She really keeps things moving and the staff on point."

"Hot tamale. You crack that whip, girl! Did they take their baby with them?"

"No, she's in the bedroom."

My brows arched. "Is she okay in there by herself?"

"Melody loves her alone time and spends hours playing with dolls and dressing up. Since Maizy's sick, I'm going to give her another hour and then bring her downstairs. She likes to entertain herself, and that's not always a good thing. One time she found a bottle of Izzy's nail polish and decided to give Jericho's guitar a makeover." Lexi rocked on her heels, her brown hair swishing in front of her face. "So what's going on with you and Wheeler?"

"What makes you think anything is going on?"

She lowered her chin a fraction. "Let's just say that something at the breakfast table this morning tipped me off."

"Let me fill you in on a little secret, girly. Have you ever been to a mechanic?"

"Yeah."

"Most of those men are covered in grease and sweat. Would you want to hug one of them in your finest clothes?"

"Uh, that's a negative."

"Beneath all that grime is a man, and yet all you care about is getting dirty. Sometimes we're more concerned with some of that grime rubbing off on us and how that would make us look to others than doing what's right."

"Naya, I love you, but you make the worst analogies. What does a greasy mechanic have to do with Wheeler?"

"You probably think less of him because he's covered in tattoos."

Her brows arched. "Have you seen that massive dragon on his back? Who does that? Obviously a man with issues, and Wheeler has a file drawer full of them. It's not that I dislike Wheeler; he's grown on me, but it's taken a while. Ben is just easier to get along with."

"So is Denver, but why do you keep comparing Wheeler to Ben?"

"Because…"

My point seeped in. Ben and Wheeler were twins, but they weren't the same man. Yet everyone kept holding Wheeler to Ben's standards.

I tapped her nose and walked by. "Some men have clean skin and are dirty on the inside. Don't judge a book by its cover."

Her voice called out from a distance. "You don't even read!"

I almost ran into Ben as he was hurrying up the stairs.

"Watch it," he growled, brushing past me and stalking down the hall.

I spun on my heel, having noticed the fresh bruises and cuts on his face. I marched after him.

"Naya, where are you going?" Lexi asked.

I reached a door next to Lynn's room and knocked. I jiggled the handle and walked right in.

"Who the hell invited you?" he snarled.

Not Ben's usual charming self, and maybe that's what sent alarm up my spine. "Where's Wheeler?"

"How the hell should I know?" He peeled off his shirt and began to loosen his shorts. "You want to watch? Is that what you're into?" Ben approached me and grabbed the back of my neck, pulling me close.

"Let go of me," I snapped. I backed up a step and shoved his arm away.

"Naya, what's gotten into you?" Lexi asked from the doorway. "Ben? Who the hell did that to your face?"

He lightly pushed me toward the door. "Get out so I can shift. Both of you."

The door slammed and Lexi huffed. "Asshole."

"Wheeler left to get Ben. They were supposed to come home together."

"He's probably downstairs."

After we searched the lower level of the house, I overheard Lexi in the back office with Austin.

"Where the hell is he?" Austin said in a raised voice. "Goddammit."

"I don't know!"

"Did you ask Ben?"

Austin suddenly burst into sight and cut through the living room. "Ben, get your ass down here!" he shouted.

We heard a wolf barking upstairs.

"I'll get him," Lexi said reluctantly.

A minute later, Lexi came downstairs, gripping a brown wolf by the scruff of his neck. The wolf wagged his tail and dropped to the floor in front of Austin, showing him his belly.

"Please don't make him shift," Lexi urged. "I don't want to see all *that*." She waved her hand in disgust at the wolf's belly.

Austin leaned forward and let his alpha power saturate his voice. "Shift."

Like liquid magic, the wolf transformed into human flesh. Ben was on his back naked, and Lexi whirled around and gaped at me. "No matter how many times that happens, I'm sorry, I can't get used to it. Nudity is no big deal, they say. Well, maybe I just have a tiny problem when I have to see a man's penis other than my mate's in my living room!"

I chuckled and patted her shoulder. "Don't feel bad. I think it's mostly a wolf thing. Packs grow up in tight quarters, so they get used to all the shifting. I'm indifferent either way."

"You work in a strip club; of course you don't care about nudity."

"Ladies…" Austin gave us a cold stare.

Ben got off the floor and folded his arms. "Can't a wolf rest in peace?"

"Where's Wheeler? And don't dick around with me. He told me you called and he went to bring you home." Austin stepped forward and looked at him steadily. "Careful what you conceal from me, Ben. I'm your Packmaster."

Ben had paler skin coloring than Wheeler—almost pasty from staying indoors. Wheeler, on the other hand, had an attractive tan from spending time outside. So I couldn't help but notice when the skin on Ben's neck and chest turned blotchy red.

After a moment, Ben lowered his eyes. "Delgado."

"What happened?"

"I don't know. I was playing a game and the next thing I know, a scuffle broke out. When Wheeler showed up, Delgado came out of nowhere and they took him."

Austin's brow twitched. "Why him and not you?"

Ben shook his head. "I don't know."

"Go upstairs and shift. I don't have time for this bullshit."

After Ben eagerly left, Lexi sat on the back of the sofa. "I don't get it. Why would they take Wheeler?"

Austin looked as if he were reading text on the floor. "If you were running a cage fight, which of those two would you think was the toughest dog? He probably sent Ben back to make sure we got the message. *Goddammit!*" he shouted, his complexion turning ruddy.

Tiny goose pimples rose up on my arms.

Denver shuffled downstairs. "What the train wreck is going on down here?"

Lexi spoke without taking her eyes off Austin. "Delgado has Wheeler."

Denver rubbed the small scar on his forehead and closed the distance between us. "So what are we going to do about it?"

Austin looked like he was trying to hold in an explosive reaction. "We're not going to sit around and wait."

"What about…" I gave him a look regarding Prince.

He turned his eyes toward mine. "The game just changed. We need to find every building, house, and park bench Delgado's name is attached to. Delgado just fucked with the wrong pack."

"But Reno's out of town, and he's the only one with connections to do that kind of work," Lexi said. "I can call him, but he didn't take his laptop."

"Give him a call," Austin said. "Tell him put lead on the gas. No one takes one of my packmates."

Something flashed in my mind and I quickly raced out of the room, running full speed down the hall and toward the heat house. I grabbed my purse off the sink and dumped it upside down.

A small leather book flipped onto the floor, settling against my right foot.

"What are you doing?" Austin asked from the doorway, out of breath.

I bent down and held the book between my fingers. "Delgado's personal address book."

CHAPTER 20

E ARLY THAT EVENING, RENO MADE it home from dropping Skye off in Colorado. Austin summoned the pack to the house. After Wheeler's capture, he didn't want to take any chances. He called Prince, who offered support in the form of an alibi if needed, but he couldn't offer us any men from his pack since the conflict had turned personal. William gave his former Packmaster a call and asked Lorenzo for his support. While he and Austin had never been allies, they shared common ground as Ivy had once been a part of the Weston pack, and Lexi was Lorenzo's cousin.

There weren't enough chairs to seat everyone in the dining room, especially with Lorenzo present for the meeting, but Austin had chosen the quaint room to strategize. Izzy's responsibility was to keep the children together, and Lynn had volunteered to secure all the windows and doors—doing regular checks. Denver went outside and moved the vehicles, turning them all toward the main road and spacing them apart so we could get out fast if needed. Jericho had shifted so his wolf could guard the property and alert the pack of any intruders.

William stood behind my chair and gripped the back.

"I can offer six of my men," Lorenzo said. "Keep them along the road and property lines. I'll assign one to sit by the main road and take note of expensive cars passing through."

"That'll work," Austin said in a low voice. "I appreciate your generosity."

A strand of long hair swept in front of Lorenzo's eye when he sat back in his chair. "A human—or *any* Breed—using Shifters for cage fighting must be brought down. What is to stop him from taking one of our women? One of our *children*?" he growled.

"I don't think he has time to raise a child for sport," Reno said.

Lorenzo leaned forward and narrowed his eyes. "Who said it would be for sport? You mentioned the young man had been locked away to satisfy Delgado's perverse needs. Consider that."

A few of the men stirred in their chairs.

Austin tapped his finger on the small leather book. "Naya confiscated this from his office. It's a book with names, numbers, and some notes. Reno looked through it, and we have a few possible leads we're going to check out." He let his gaze slide around the room. "That means splitting up. We have to hit him hard and hit him fast before he has time to move."

Reno suppressed a burp and pushed away his bottle of imported beer. "Skye's phone and business cards were a dead end," he said to me. "Anytime he moved her, she was blindfolded. A few contacts in his book own a lot of land. Not unusual for Breed, but I'm focusing on anyone with property isolated enough to stash some prisoners, although I'm not excluding large homes in the city. We're not going to find the cage fighters there, but maybe he has a few more pets we can rescue. Chances are Delgado is using someone else to store his goods. Probably profit sharing. That way, if anything goes down, his hands are clean."

Austin interrupted. "Delgado knows he's protected in our world, but no human I've known about has *ever* been this brazen and broken so many Breed laws. He's covering his tracks. There are always exceptions to the rules, so I doubt he wants to put that much faith in our laws protecting him."

Lexi spun a deck of cards in a circle. "So who's going? All the men, right?"

He cut her a hard glare. "As it happens, no."

She sat to attention. Shifters weren't especially sexist. The men protected women and children because they cherished them, but a skilled Shifter was treated as an equal hunter, regardless of gender.

"You and I are heading south to a secluded location. Reno and Denver will check out the second location. The rest of the men stay home until I give further notice, but will have the vehicles on standby."

"We're too far out to move fast," Jericho said. "Maybe one of us should head to a centralized area so we can get there quicker."

Reno rubbed his smooth jaw. "Not a bad idea."

"Good. Then it's you," Austin said. "Izzy's pregnant, so she's out."

"Hell's bells," Izzy said. "Every time something happens, I'm knocked up. Way to go, Jericho."

He gave her a salacious wink and grinned.

"And me?" I asked, lacing my fingers together.

Austin scraped his teeth across his lower lip, causing the small cleft in his chin to stand out.

"Send her with one of my men," Lorenzo suggested. "But keep in mind that if your panther does anything to him, I expect compensation."

I shifted in my chair. "I'm not a savage."

"No, but rumors circulate fast, and your lack of control at the club has refueled a lot of concerns about panthers."

"If a wolf went with your man, he could be every bit as dangerous since they're not in the same pack."

"Yes, but the fight would be fair."

I cocked my head and laughed. "So this is all about a fair fight?"

"Let's calm down," Austin said. "Naya will go with one of your men. And no, Church, if something happens, I will *not* compensate you for the loss. Shit happens, and we all know the risk when pairing two Shifters from different packs. He could just as easily shoot her in the head."

Lexi slapped him on the shoulder. "Austin Cole!"

One of the men chuckled.

"We'll keep in communication," he continued. "Whoever finds the target will pass the word immediately. Hang back until we're all there so we can plan our attack. We'll probably need more backup depending on how many guards he's got. Anything else we should consider, Reno?"

He shook his head, and his hand slid onto April's lap, gripping her thigh. "I've busted a few rings this big with a buddy of mine. Expect four to ten guards spread out in the main house, the compound where he keeps the Shifters, and somewhere on the property lines. If they get wind of us, they'll probably call Delgado for backup, assuming he has more guards at his disposal. But that'll take time, so let's just focus on the assholes on the property."

"What Breed are they?" Lorenzo asked.

Reno shrugged. "Usually Shifters. I don't know about Delgado; he seems to have a lot of friends, and that could be problematic."

Austin flattened his hands on the table. "Let's assume they're a mix and prepare for that."

Reno's voice quieted. "I have a stunner."

"Where the fuck did you get that?" Austin said in disbelief.

Stunners were a metal forged with a special magic that could paralyze a Mage if left in his flesh. A Shifter fighting against a Mage was tricky since they could flash and move at high rates of speed and blast us with energy from their hands. Stunners mostly stayed in their possession since their energy didn't work on one other, so their fights were hand-to-hand combat.

Reno smirked. "I've been around the block, boys. Those babies aren't easy to acquire, but I took out a Mage a few decades ago and... well, finders keepers."

Austin nodded. "I think we can prepare a few stakes in case there are Vampires."

Lorenzo's eyebrow arched. "Only certain types of wood will paralyze them."

"I know," Austin replied. "I tangled with a few of them in my last job. The problem is they're too damn strong, so it's almost impossible to get close enough to stake 'em. I learned the hard way that to take down a Vampire without getting your arms crushed, you need to buddy up with them so they're not expecting it."

"Friends close, enemies closer," Reno agreed. "Seeing as we don't have time to make friends, better to be armed than not."

It wasn't long ago that I'd been lying on my sofa, petting Misha and listening to a little salsa music on a lazy afternoon. Now here I was, sitting with wolves and planning an illegal raid.

Had Delgado taken Ben or anyone else in Austin's pack, would I have volunteered as quickly to help? Of all people, why *Wheeler*?

Hadn't he already suffered enough? I couldn't imagine how dejected and enraged he must feel to be right back where he started.

He'd never forgive me. Those intimate moments we shared behind closed doors, the secrets, the physical affection, and the tender words would become nothing but scattered memories of something that was doomed to fail. My heart sank, fearing he might give up this time. What did he have worth fighting for? A pack who was ready to cut him loose? A twin who didn't reciprocate the love and loyalty he did? A good lay from a stripper who was the cause of his predicament?

"Are you okay?" Lexi asked privately while some of the men continued talking.

"No, honey. I'm not okay. I'm far from okay."

"You don't have to do this."

I turned to look her in the eye. "Yes, Lexi, I do. I'm not sure how to explain this without it sounding silly, but I love Wheeler. I adore this man so much that I can't even catch my breath while thinking about him."

Her eyes turned saucer-wide. "What? No... no," she said, shaking her head. "I'm not in the mood for Naya humor."

I leaned in. "Do I look like I'm teasing? Maybe you had your entire life to figure it out with Austin, but I don't need an hourglass to figure out my emotions. I'm the last woman on earth to choose love over money. I've always admired the passion in your family, but I've never felt emotions that deep. Not the kind of passion you feel when someone bares his soul to you, or the kind when a man looks into your eyes because he wants to hear your thoughts. Not until Wheeler. Our connection was like a flame bursting into existence. I regret that I didn't tell him what a remarkable man he is, and I regret that I may never have the chance to tell him how much I love him—for whatever that's worth. I'm not a fool; I know your pack would never invite a panther to live under the same roof. Aside from that, Wheeler has every right to blame me for all this."

"Why? It's not your fault!"

You would never think a slip of a girl like her would have such a big mouth and fire in her attitude, but she did. That's what made her an alpha female.

It's also what made every man at the table look our way and halt their conversations.

"Naya, I have no idea what's going on between you two, so maybe my opinion doesn't matter, but this isn't your fault. We're involved because friends help each other out. I've known you for years, and you've always looked out for me. Not once have you ever asked for a damn thing! You've lavished Maizy with affection, time, and gifts. You've given me advice on business and love, not to mention talking me into buying a few sexy outfits that aren't my thing, but Austin seems to enjoy them."

Denver chuckled and elbowed Austin in the ribs.

"That doesn't make this okay," I said. "I can't help it. I feel responsible in a way that's painful." I placed my hand over my chest, fighting back the tears. *Oh, please don't let me lose control in front of everyone.* My lip quivered. "If anything happens to him, I'll never forgive myself."

Lexi rose from her chair and leaned down to hug me. She smoothed her hands over my back and said softly in my ear, "We'll find him. Who am I to sit here and judge how you feel? I'm so sorry, Naya. Thanks for everything you've done for us. Not just now, but through the years."

She backed away and I glanced across the table. Denver faked a grimace and wrapped his arms around Austin. "*Hold me.*"

Austin shoved him off and Denver chortled.

"I've changed my mind about the pairing," Reno grumbled, shooting Denver a frosty glare.

Denver nodded his head at him. "Shut it. We're Bonnie and Clyde, so deal with it."

"Have you even seen how that movie ends? That's the shit I'm talking about, Austin."

Lexi guided me away. "They mess around with each other all the time, but it's just play. Everyone knows Denver's wolf is vicious, so despite his laid-back attitude, he'll fight when it counts."

"Interesting family. Now that I've seen them in their natural habitat, I understand all your complaints a little better." I wrapped my right arm around her playfully and squeezed.

"I never thought I could live in such a big house with so many people, but I have to admit I love it. We push each other's buttons all the time, but we never cross a line that can't be uncrossed. We might look a little insane to an outsider, but these men have nothing but love for their packmates."

Melody wandered into the living room clutching a baby doll with pink streaks in her hair. "Where's Daddy?"

Lexi beamed. "Come here, sweetie pie, and spin around. We're going to do a flip."

Melody tossed her doll on the floor and turned around, reaching between her legs. Lexi grabbed her hands and pulled her up, causing Melody to flip around until her feet stamped on the floor.

She giggled. "Again!"

After three more times, Lexi was out of breath. "I shouldn't have started doing this. Maizy never liked it, but Mel will probably ask me to do it when she's twelve."

I giggled and patted her cheek. "You'll be a good mama someday."

Her smile waned. "Maybe."

CHAPTER 21

THAT EVENING, WE SPLIT UP and headed to our assigned locations. Trevor and William were on point to guard the front and back of the house, and Jericho's wolf circled the property. Shifters communicated with their animal on a completely different level. During the shift, there's a moment when both spirits inhabit the same space and intentions are understood, so Jericho's wolf knew his job was to guard the territory. Shifters are intuitive creatures, vastly superior to their animal counterparts in the wild.

"What do you do for a living?" Lorenzo's packmate asked in a rich baritone.

"Moreland, I'm an exotic dancer," I said matter-of-factly.

He chuckled. "With a body like yours, it would be a sin if you weren't."

Moreland looked like a strong man. He was three shades darker than me with the appearance of an exotic islander, from his broad nose to his almond-shaped eyes. Most men with long hair kept it free or tied it back. But Moreland had precise rows of braids against his head going back.

"So, how long have you been with Lorenzo's pack?"

Moreland switched on the high beams when we exited the highway. "Since the beginning. Enzo values loyalty, and we've been like brothers since before our change. Except now our brotherhood has grown," he said with a thick chuckle. "He's a better man with a good woman at his side."

"How's Ivy been getting along with her new family?"

"We're glad she chose us—chose him. A Packmaster is only as strong as his mate. She might look like a delicate little flower, but Ivy's fierce. That woman doesn't mess around. Don't get me wrong, she's a compassionate soul and keeps a nice balance in the pack. After they had the baby, pregnancy became contagious in our pack." He laughed and turned the wheel. "It's good to see the mated couples finally having children. Lorenzo made it a house, but Ivy made it a home."

"I guess that makes her a good bitch," I said with a playful smile.

"*Noo*." Moreland wagged his finger. "Don't ever use that word to describe Ivy around Enzo; he'll have your head for it."

"And I thought all this time the wolves defended their use of the word as a term of endearment."

He smiled. "You're funny. Those damn humans always have to dirty up a good word. It seems like most men have a problem with it after they find a good woman."

I looked into the inky woods when he pulled the car off the side of the road. Moreland shut off the engine and the lights blinked out. "You stay behind me. Hear? This is just a reconnaissance mission."

"You men and your war terms," I said with a wave of my hand. "In English, please?"

"We're just window-shopping. How's that for women's terms?"

"Brilliant."

"How did you get involved in wolf business?" he asked. "Just out of curiosity."

"Moreland, I'm going to cut right to the chase because I'm not a woman who censors herself. I'm in love with the man we're looking for."

"Wheeler? Never met him, but I've heard stories about him. The one with the tattoos, right?"

"Yes." I pushed open my door. "The one with the *beautiful* tattoos."

After a fifteen-minute walk through the woods, Moreland slowed his pace. The road was pitch-black without a moon to guide our way. We had kept to the woods, but as we drew closer to the property, I suggested we move onto the road so we wouldn't announce our presence with snapping twigs and rustling leaves. Not to mention the mosquitoes were having a banquet all over my legs.

We'd all agreed upon a set time to call Austin with an update.

Anyone who didn't call, he'd consider captured, which meant that the rest of the group would abandon their location and rush to their aid.

I'd never known how organized wolf packs were until now. I tried to let my predator instincts take over, but the rational side of my brain kept saying I was just a dancer who didn't like dirt on her upholstery and should have stayed home. It had never occurred to me I'd one day be traversing through a forest to rescue a wolf.

Suddenly I sneezed with a loud gasp. Before I knew what happened, Moreland's hand flew over my mouth. I sneezed quietly into his hand a second time—the dirt and pollen from the woods tickling my nose.

"Don't do that again," he murmured against my ear. He waited for a few moments and then we continued.

In the distance, voices overlapped and grew louder. I gripped Moreland's arm when his pace quickened. Pale lights shone through the thicket of trees, and my eyes were wide and alert to our surroundings.

We hurried into the woods and moved far from the road to conceal our approach. A house began to take shape—a large house. The drapes were drawn, and what tremendous windows! They stretched from the first floor to the second on one side of the house, but the inside light created moving silhouettes on the lower level.

"Looks like a party," he whispered, pointing to our right. A row of cars lined the private road.

A sharp prick touched my neck, and I slapped at the pesky mosquito. Instead, my fingers found something long and strange. Moreland turned to look at me and I lost all sensation in my legs. Was I falling? It seemed like he was going to catch me, but then a silver object appeared and pierced his throat. Something that looked like a dart.

———— �∘⋐∘⋒ ————

Wheeler had spent hours examining the chain attached to the cuff on his wrist. He went through every link, hoping these idiots had reused old equipment that might have been damaged by the prisoner before him, scraping it on the floor or pounding it against a hard surface. He couldn't find anything. Wheeler's objective wasn't just to escape; he wanted to find Delgado and bury him in the ground with a spade as his grave marker. The chain spanned five feet and connected to a metal ring secured in the floor near the wall.

Someone a few cells down had been humming and laughing for the past hour or so—a sign of insanity. You take a free man and chain him in a tiny cell, forcing him to kill and rewarding him for it, and some men will crumble beneath the weight of guilt. Wheeler had learned that insanity was contagious to anyone close enough to listen to the ramblings of a man beyond reason.

"Who's in there?" a woman whispered. "Are you a dancer?"

She must have been from one of the clubs.

"Hello? *Please* answer. Lacy's gone now, and she was the only one I had to talk to. Oh God, I just want to go home." Then she began crying. "Please, please... someone talk to me. I'm so scared."

"*Dammit*," Wheeler muttered to himself. "I'm here."

"Who are you? What's your name?" she asked, sniffling away her tears. "No one else here talks to me. Lacy was the only one."

Then the crying started up.

"I'm Wheeler. What's your name?"

"Bo."

"That's an odd name for a woman."

She laughed in surprise. "That's rude. My mom thought I was going to be a boy."

"You work at one of the clubs?"

"How did you know? Yes, I work at Teasers. Are you a Regulator?"

"No." She must have thought he was undercover or something. "Someone I know who works at Club Sin was attacked."

"Lacy?"

"No."

"Oh. Lacy worked there. I just can't believe this! What did I ever do to anyone?"

He listened to her chain angrily slinging around and Bo talking to herself. A woman like her wouldn't last long in a place like this.

What the hell was Delgado thinking? Maybe in the years since Wheeler had left, cage fighting had changed. Maybe they got their kicks from hot strippers going at it.

A door opened at the far end of the hall. From where he sat with his back to the wall, he had a clear view of anyone who passed in front of his cage. Something heavy slid across the floor, and a man spat out a curse.

"Well, *you* fucking carry her and I'll drag him, you big pussy."

The guard passed in front of the bars ahead of him and Wheeler launched to his feet, gripping the door with his free hand. "What are you doing with her?" he shouted.

The guard stopped and shifted Naya in his arms. She was unconscious, and her head lolled to the side. He noticed a sneaker missing, and she had small red bumps on her legs and twigs in her hair.

"Friend of yours?" the guard asked, openly mocking him.

"I want to speak to Delgado!"

A man appeared in front of the cell on the left. "Calm down, Mr. Cole. No need to shout."

The guard holding Naya moved out of sight, and another guard followed behind him, dragging a large, dark-skinned man. After shutting the doors, the guards hurried out.

Wheeler sized up the man in front of his cell. He had deep-set eyes of a pale shade, like hazel or blue. Delgado looked like a slick stockbroker with his brown hair combed back and his outfit of dark slacks and a button-up shirt that molded to his body. He wasn't at all what Wheeler had expected. He'd envisioned Delgado as some sniveling, overweight, greasy human with missing teeth. This man in his forties had all his teeth—sparkling white—and a deep line carved into his right cheek in the shape of a crescent moon. His nose was so straight that it resembled an arrow pointing down. Delgado was agreeable to look at, and maybe that made it easier for people to trust doing business with him. Looks could get a man just as far as they could a woman. His brows weren't sloped in an angry line like Wheeler's sometimes were, and he didn't wear a frown. Nor did he smile. He maintained an impassive demeanor despite the woman sobbing in the cell next door.

"What are you doing with her?" Wheeler asked.

Delgado lifted a cigarette case from his back pocket and opened it, removing a smoke and holding it between his lips. "You see, despite the fact I have one of the most legendary wolf fighters in history, I still want what I want." He flicked the thumbwheel on his slim lighter until a small flame lit up the other end. After a long inhale, he blew a thin haze of smoke into Wheeler's cell. "A panther isn't easy to come by. They used to be more open with their identity until cage fighting became a profitable affair. That's when they started to go into hiding. I used to own a few bars, but then I discovered strip clubs were an infinite source of unattached women in *all kinds* of shapes and forms." He took another slow drag from his cigarette, narrowing his eyes to thin slivers.

Wheeler's lips curled in. "Let her go. We had an agreement. Me for Ben."

"Yes, we did. But I don't like deception."

"What the hell are you talking about?"

Delgado flicked the ashes from the tip of his cigarette and slowly ambled to the right. "Nosy women piss me off. This morning I discovered someone had been in my office. A personal item of mine was missing—a book. Names, numbers, appointments, and just enough details that—"

"You shouldn't have been dumb enough to keep it in an unlocked drawer."

Anger flashed in his eyes and he pulled in another inhale, walking toward the left again. "Had you left the office the way you found it, I might have never known. I rarely go through that book anymore. But someone had turned my elephant in the wrong direction. I'm a superstitious man, and that's not something I'd easily overlook. That's when I knew Miss James had gone behind my back. One of the girls in the club confirmed seeing her there with a man. Was that you?"

Wheeler's grip tightened and he yanked the chain on his right hand in vain.

"Yes, I thought as much. I know how tight packs are, so taking you in was a risk. But I readied my men. After all, I still had another vacancy to fill." A deep chuckle rose in his chest. "My men waited until Naya and the Shifter neared the house before they attacked. I suppose they were too lazy to carry them very far," he said with disdain. "They'll be punished for that. Anyhow, thought you'd enjoy the company. Might be fun to have family here. Brother against brother. Is that man in your pack?"

Wheeler didn't respond.

When the cigarette had burned down, Delgado dropped it on the floor and crushed it with his dress shoe. "I had high hopes that more men would come for you, but maybe you're the sort of wolf a pack is glad to be rid of. Dead weight. Where's the cavalry?"

"Let her go. She's not a fighter. You haven't been in this world long enough to know what I know. Our animals have nothing to do with how dangerous we are. This is bullshit! You have what you wanted—you have me."

Delgado snorted and tucked his hands in his pockets. "I'm not so sure the great savage wolf has much fight left in him. Did you run away all those years ago? Too afraid of dying? As much as I love having you in my possession, I'm not a stupid man. Anyone who is of no use to me I sell on the black market. There are plenty of buyers who think they can turn defects into champions. One man's junk is another man's treasure."

A storm funneled within Wheeler, one so powerful it could have shattered the chain on his wrist. The thought of Naya in a place like this—broken the way he had once been broken—polluted his thoughts.

"I have money," Wheeler offered. "You're a man who talks the language of currency, and I'm a man who knows how to get it. I have a solid reputation in the world of finance. If you're doing this for money, then you'd be a fucking idiot to throw away a lottery ticket."

Delgado's gaze drifted elsewhere as if he was considering it. "That's a tempting offer, but I can't use you for both. I'm guaranteed money if I put you in the cage."

"I can earn you ten times that in other ways."

Delgado's brow arched. "Can you prove that? Can you *promise* that?"

"No, but I can't promise I'll win your next fight either," he subtly threatened.

"I host the fights, so I'll profit regardless of who wins or loses. I run an exclusive club where you pay to play, but some like to keep their hands clean and just watch, so they pay more. You're the kind of starring attraction that would earn me a huge profit. I've made this into an upscale affair from the days in the dungeon. I throw a party; we have drinks, mingle, smoke cigars, and watch a good fight. It's an elite club, and profitable. Some of the men pay extra for time alone with our girls. That's an added perk."

"Let her go!" Wheeler roared, kicking at the bars. "I'll fucking tear off your head if you touch her."

When Delgado chuckled, the line in his cheek deepened. "Oh, I'm not going to touch her, Mr. Cole. I'm leaving the honors to you once she wakes up from the tranquilizer. Save your energy for the cage. See you in"—he glanced at his watch and then winked—"three hours."

CHAPTER 22

F ROM THE TIME I CAME to consciousness, I only had a few
seconds to look around before someone jerked me to my feet.
"Move your ass," he barked. "Your three-hour nap is up."

I followed, still half-asleep, struggling to understand what was
happening. Bars. Rows and rows of bars. A flickering light. I had
been stripped down to my bra and panties. *Maybe I'm dreaming.*
When I closed my eyes and slowed down, I felt a sharp yank on my
neck.

Ow! My fingers clawed at a thick piece of metal beneath my
jaw, and that's the moment I blinked wide-awake. Not only did I
have a heavy manacle around my neck, but a man was leading me
forward by the chain attached to it. I resisted, gripping the links so
he couldn't jerk it again.

But he did, and when he picked up his stride, I stumbled and
tried to keep from falling.

"Better wake her up," a man with a heavy British accent said.
"Here, let me."

A cold splash of water drenched my face, and I choked in a series
of coughs. Some of it had gone up my nose, and I shuddered at the
icy contact with my skin.

"They like it when we wet the girls down before a fight."

"Moreland?" I croaked, looking around for Lorenzo's packmate.

When the guard jerked the chain, my panther snarled at me
to fight back. I kicked the man in the lower back and he buckled,
falling to his knees. When I got some slack on the chain, I pulled
enough of it to wrap around his neck. He was tall, but I tried with
everything I had in me to hang on.

The man who had splashed me with water snaked his arms

around my waist and yanked me off. "Told you we should have shackled her hands," he said. "Delgado said she's a panther."

The other man coughed and unraveled the chain from his neck. "I don't get paid enough for this shit."

"Let me go," I growled. "I'll shift and tear your limbs from your body."

The man I had strangled choked out a laugh. "Just try it, honey. The collar is locked tight for a reason."

I kicked at him while the man holding me started to move forward. He had my arms pinned against my body within his crushing grip. *Oh my God, this was Delgado's psychotic house of horrors.*

"Moreland!" I yelled. And then something else occurred to me. "Wheeler!"

We passed a cell and a young woman with blond curls looked at me with frightened eyes. She backed away from the bars and sat down, holding her knees. Another cage held a pale man with scars all over his body, and the next cell contained what looked like a murderer. His eyes were vacant as he watched us move past. It was as if I'd witnessed the progression of a cage fighter in five seconds.

"I want to speak to Delgado," I demanded. "Tell him Naya James is asking to see him. Tell him—"

"You can tell him yourself," the man ahead of me said.

Bright lights pierced my eyes when we moved into another room. Wet curls of hair stuck to my face, and I fought against my screaming retinas so I could get a look at my surroundings. The room itself was dark except for the bright light straight ahead.

Terror swept over me when soft applause filled the silence of the room. Through my lashes, I saw a raised platform, similar to a boxing ring. Except it was a cage with shiny, narrow bars all around and across the top. Seeing that incited a visceral reaction in me, and I arched my back as far as I could and bit the guard's bristly jaw.

He shouted in pain, and the metallic taste of blood filled my mouth. When his grip loosened, I spun around and punched him in the jaw. He tried to grab my chain, but I ducked and gave him an uppercut right in the groin. He fell to the ground like a bag of concrete, but my victory was short-lived when the chain yanked me onto my back.

Another soft applause erupted from all around, like the sound of gentle waves lapping against a shore. It sent chills up my spine, and that's when I began to pull the world into focus. All around in the dark perimeter of the room were chairs filled with spectators. Men in suits. Men with cigars and glasses of whiskey or cognac. Some looked on with interest while others were making notes in little books.

The chain pulled and the guard led me up a small set of steps to an open door where he pushed me inside and slammed it. Before I could turn around, he pulled the slack on the chain until my back was against the bars.

Oh sweet Mary, no.

Wheeler stood on the opposite side of the cage with his right arm pulled through the bars—a chain shackled to his wrist. They had stripped him out of his shirt and shoes, but he didn't look hurt. I only saw his profile, but I didn't like his despondent demeanor, and his eyes were sullen and downcast.

My heart raced at a wicked beat, and I searched the room for a face. All I saw was darkness and faint silhouettes—ghostly images of men hiding in the shadows and watching with anticipation. Bright lights illuminated the cage, making it seem as if the rest of the world didn't exist.

Footsteps approached from my left. While I didn't recognize the man, I immediately knew who it was when he began speaking, his tone friendly but controlled.

"Gentlemen, I have a treat for you this evening. Please use the devices you've been provided to place your bets. In the left-hand corner, we have a legend among legends. He's been out of the circuit for almost two decades and is a returning champion. Strong. Powerful. Deadly. This Shifter is a wolf, but not just any wolf. He's undefeated against any animal—including panthers. He's fought them in both animal and human form. Those of you who aren't familiar with his face will certainly recognize the name Striker."

The crowd murmured and Delgado let them settle down before continuing.

"In our right-hand corner is something we don't have the privilege of seeing very often in this day and age. Here we have a woman with fight, as most of you just saw," he said with a chuckle. "Stripper by night, and she shares her body with a black panther. Jaguar, to be specific. I've personally seen her animal and it… is… *exquisite*. At least two hundred pounds of solid muscle."

Colored lights blinked in the darkness, presumably from whatever devices Delgado had given them to place their bets with.

"As a reminder of the rules, you may change your bet at any time until the chains are released. Once that happens, your devices will be disabled and there's no going back. Take a moment to consider your wager, and remember the minimum bet requirement. If you can't meet that minimum, then I'll ask you to leave the room. The price for watching without betting is two thousand. And as a generous offer, should the panther be the victor of this match, I will hold an auction. One lucky bidder will have time alone with our lovely lady in private quarters for the entirety of the evening. This is going to be a spectacular show, gentlemen. Place your bets."

My eyes widened as I looked at Wheeler. I wanted to speak, but the cold shackle around my neck was biting into my skin and making me dizzy.

"Ease up on that," Delgado said in a tight voice.

The chain loosened and blood returned to my head.

Delgado approached the cage from behind me and I looked to the left. He smelled like cigarettes.

"My apologies for the unnecessary force on your restraints. Wouldn't want you going in at a disadvantage," he said. "Sorry we haven't formally met, but these things happen for a reason. I'm a strong believer in fate. Are you?"

If I had eaten anything, it would have already been all over the floor.

"Please don't do this," I pleaded. "Let him go."

"*Him?*" he asked with surprise. "Not you?"

"Release him. I'll do what you want. His pack will come after you and cause more trouble; I have no one to claim me."

"Sorry, Miss James. As curious as your request is, that's not good business." He leaned in so his voice wouldn't carry. "Whatever feelings you might have for that man, I'd reconsider in your last moments. He's a ruthless killer; I've seen it myself. There's nothing he wouldn't do to survive, and if you trust him, you're a bigger fool than I took you for. So do me a favor and put on a good show."

When he stepped away, I tugged at my chain. I got four steps into the cell before they yanked me back.

That's when Wheeler swung his eyes up to mine. Those pale brown beauties glowed like embers from a fire, and I didn't recognize the man standing before me.

Slowly the colored lights in the darkness became less frequent until they stopped altogether. The air chilled my arms, which were still damp from when they had thrown the water on me. I wiped my wet hair away from my face and tried to make eye contact with Wheeler. Could I trust him not to kill me?

"Gentlemen, we are releasing the chains."

When Delgado nodded, my shackle clicked and fell away. I stumbled forward just as Wheeler's right arm swung to his side without the chain attached. He stood catatonic, his heavy-lidded eyes transfixed on my legs.

The longer he stared, the more tempted I became to look down. I didn't see anything outside of the mosquito bites, so I reached down and scratched one. Someone in the crowd chuckled.

Now what? No bell sounded. No announcement to begin. Just the sound of ice clinking in glasses, orange glows in the darkness whenever someone pulled smoke from their cigarette, and the sensation of my heart climbing out of my throat.

Wheeler walked along the perimeter of the cage. The fingers on his right hand touched the bars, tapping against each one as he approached me. When he inched near, he gripped the bars on either side of my head and leaned in so close that no one could hear anything but us.

"Shift."

"No," I whispered back, still trembling.

"Shift or else they'll make us both shift."

"My panther will kill you."

His mouth grazed my ear. "That's the point."

My heart leapt to my throat. "I'm not going to do it. *You* shift."

His face appeared in front of mine, hard as a stone. Shadows carved along his cheekbones, and I saw years of torment flickering in the depths of his eyes.

"My wolf will lunge at your throat before you can scream."

"I can't, Wheeler. I'm scared."

"Do you trust me?" He brushed my cheek with the back of his knuckles in a predatory manner. "*Trust me*, Naya."

Had he said that to all his previous victims? Wheeler's eyes were devoid of fear, and his voice never wavered.

"Strobe lights are scheduled to begin in two minutes if the fight is prolonged," Delgado announced.

A nervous flutter tickled my belly.

I cupped Wheeler's face and whispered against his cheek, "I trust you."

Every muscle flexed as my skin erupted, contorted, and I transformed into a black panther. I heard light gasps from the crowd as she circled the cage. She opened her mouth, smelling the spike in their adrenaline. Confused by her surroundings, she growled and paced anxiously. I waited apprehensively for Wheeler to make a move. I wondered how he'd killed panthers with his bare hands. He must have put them in a viselike grip, or maybe gouged their eyes out before gnashing at their throats with his teeth.

Wheeler knelt down in front of my panther and gripped both sides of her face. She trusted him—she lapped his chin with her rough tongue.

Wheeler suddenly raised his hand and slapped her in the face. He did it again, and then punched her in the mouth before sitting back with his arms spread wide and his eyes looking upward, accepting his fate.

Nooo! I mentally screamed.

She growled ferociously, and before I lost consciousness, I forced myself to shift, falling over him. "No, no. Don't you dare do this to me!"

The murmurs in the crowd became loud and argumentative.

"Goddammit, Naya! Shift back!"

"Not if it means this. You can't choose *me* over you!"

He softly touched my hair with his hands. "Who else can I choose? There is *only* you and me, and I will always choose you."

"Turn on the strobe!" someone shouted. "I paid good money for a fight."

"Listen to me, Naya. There's no way out of this. I'm going to make this easy for both of us."

Hot tears streamed down my face. "Don't you dare give up on me," I said angrily.

He laughed. "You want me to fight you? Only my wolf will do it, because I'll never lay a goddamn hand on you."

"You have a family. You can't do this to them."

"Are you saying my life is worth more than yours?" He shook his head. "Are we really fighting over who lives and who dies? Naya, let me do this. It'll be the only noble thing I've ever done in my worthless life."

"Bullshit," I spat. "You and I both know that's a lie."

"We don't have time to argue. Shift before it's too late!"

The lights flickered. I slammed my eyes shut and bent forward with my hands covering my face. My hair created a dark veil, and I heard the crackling of the strobe like snaps of electricity. When it ceased, I slowly raised my head and peered through my hair.

In front of me stood a brown wolf—just like Ben's. His eyes flashed briefly toward the bars around us, and then he pulled in a scent. That's when his lips peeled back, revealing his sharp canines. I sat back on my legs and readied myself for him to lunge at my throat.

I was ready to die for Wheeler, and I didn't feel any fear. The wolf took a step forward, his brow angled in an angry slash as if he had a frown. His eyes were wide and full of fight. I'd never seen anything more terrible and beautiful all at once.

Slobber dripped off one of his fangs, and a low growl rose in his chest until it cut off with a ferocious snarl. Wheeler lunged.

"*I trust you.*"

CHAPTER 23

WHEELER'S MASSIVE WOLF KNOCKED ME onto my back. We were both willing to die for each other, and that's when I knew he loved me back. Maybe I'd never be the woman who found out that kind of devotion by way of candy, roses, or a candlelight dinner, but having a man willing to die for me was the most resounding declaration of love imaginable.

Terrible snarls and growls erupted from Wheeler's wolf as he hovered over me, shaking me by the neck.

But his teeth hadn't punctured my skin. Somehow, Wheeler was still in control. I lay beneath him in disbelief that a wolf could be this tactical. I gripped the sides of his fur, buried beneath the weight of him. My hair tangled everywhere—in my face, around my neck, and even in his mouth.

Shouts erupted from the crowd—no—*cheering*. They would never believe this without seeing blood. All those manicures had finally paid off. I reached up with my sharp nails and dug hard into the flesh of my neck until it drew blood.

Now the wolf had blood in his mouth. I didn't know how this would end, and I honestly didn't care. I just wanted it to be over one way or the other. The wolf thrashed, his teeth touching my neck painfully, but not puncturing the skin. Then he lifted his neck and I saw blood around his jowls—my blood.

More cheers.

"It's over, boys," someone shouted. "I would have never expected that."

"Over in less than five minutes. I get the bonus!" someone else said with a laugh.

They were not only betting on winners, but how long the fight lasted.

I gasped when the wolf lunged again, this time at the back of my neck. I turned facedown and my hair smothered my view. After a few efforts to grab at him, I quit moving.

What was the plan? Oh God, I had no earthly idea what to do next! Did Wheeler have a plan?

Movement sounded from all around us and trickled away as the crowd left the room. Then I heard Wheeler.

"You bastards!" he shouted.

"You're the bastard," the guard with the British accent said. "You're the one who killed her. Don't blame us because you have a dead woman at your feet. Were you like this in all your fights? The most savage warrior, my arse. Nothing but a crybaby."

"She was *innocent*."

The cage door unlocked and another voice sounded. A familiar one I couldn't place. "Stand back so we can collect the body. You'll be rewarded with an exquisite meal tonight. The boss gives the winner a choice between steak and lobster, so think it over."

Wheeler's hand pressed against my back and all the rough edges in his voice smoothed out. "You wouldn't be laughing so hard if she were alive… in panther form."

The last thing I remembered after my shift was Manny, the stagehand from Club Sin. *The bastard!* He'd worked for Delgado this whole time and had been spying on us at the club. It was *his* eyes I saw behind the mask when a stranger walked onstage during my dance and made me shift, and he must have been the one who had attacked me outside my apartment. Those eyes I'd never forget.

By a simple twist of fate, I was the last thing Manny saw.

"And boom goes the dynamite," I heard Wheeler say.

<hr>

Wheeler slanted his eyes at the guard, who was holding a black baton. They wouldn't expect an attack after a match because the fighters were tired and wanted a reward instead of punishment.

Naya had impressed him with not only her cunning actions, but also the fact that despite what he'd told her about his past, she trusted him. Wheeler had thought for sure his wolf would kill her on sight once he shifted uncontrollably, but his wolf tapped into his own emotions about Naya. A Shifter's animal was usually respectful of close bonds, but even so, she was a panther, for Christ's sake! He should have attacked. Wheeler's wolf was calculating and methodical—almost to the point where some had once compared his mind to that of a human.

When he'd lunged at Naya, Wheeler had tried to shift before it was too late, but his wolf refused to give up control of his body. Wheeler had felt his canines latch around her tender throat—her pulse beating furiously against the soft flesh. Yet he'd seen something in her eyes that stilled him.

Trust. Not acquiescence like he'd seen in the eyes of so many he'd killed, but absolute trust that she would somehow survive this. His wolf had put on a ruse so the spectators would think the match was over.

Usually when both fighters were in animal form only one survived, but a match officially ended when one fell unconscious. Wheeler's wolf had thrashed until Naya quit fighting.

In a span of three hours—from the time Naya was placed in her cell until the moment she'd shifted in the cage—everything he'd known about trust had changed. Wheeler feared trust, because it had always led to grave consequences. Naya had tangled herself around his heart and made him feel like a free man—able to talk about the demons that haunted him without fearing judgment. She shared his cynical view on love, and he felt an undeniable chemistry with her. Until the moment he saw the guards carrying her in front of his cell, he hadn't known how deep his devotion ran and how ruthlessly he was willing to fight for her.

When Naya had searched his eyes after he shifted, it was with absolute faith that he'd do the right thing. Christ, it made him want to fight for her even harder. This wasn't infatuation, curiosity, or even about his past. He loved that woman with every breath in him.

Wheeler loved the smoky look in her eyes when she'd flirt,

the tender way she spoke of her family, and the fire that burned on her tongue when anyone threatened her friends. He loved her imperfections—not that she had any on that voluptuous body of hers, but the ones inside her head and heart. The hidden insecurities, her temper, and even the way she loved that damn cat. Wheeler hated cats, and somehow that made this whole situation even more insane.

Of all people, he fell in love with a fucking cat.

As the guard approached Naya to drag her lifeless body from the cage, Wheeler waited to see if she had understood his suggestion for her to shift and attack.

Fucking hell, she was a sight to behold. Her panther sprang at the guard and crushed his throat within her powerful jaws. Wheeler ran after the second man and a fight ensued outside the cage. They threw chairs, punches, and Wheeler found a discarded cigar and burned the guard's face before taking him out.

Naya's panther leapt through the open door, her body moving like black silk. He'd never beheld a panther so agile and muscular. She approached him and rubbed against his side.

Wheeler patted her shoulder. "You ready to take care of business?"

Delgado's voice sounded from the hall beyond the open door. "Dammit, Manny. I told you to bring them back to the…"

Wheeler smiled with all teeth when Delgado appeared in the doorway. "Nice little party you put together," he said condescendingly as he stroked his beard. "You know what I love about men like you? How smart you think you are, but how dumb you *really* are. Did you think a man who escaped all those years ago wouldn't know how to do it again? I know all the flaws and weaknesses of men like you."

"It's impossible. Your wolf—"

"Killed her?"

Wheeler patted Naya's side and her panther growled. The sound was acoustic and deep, rattling the bones of anyone within ten feet.

Delgado backed up a step.

"Wouldn't do that if I were you," Wheeler said. "You know what'll happen if you run from a predator, and don't think your puny little door will hold her back. If you were smart, you'd have steel doors with guards inside and out. But you send in Beavis and Butt-head to clean up your mess?" Wheeler clucked his tongue. "Not the brightest marker in the box, are you?"

"You want your freedom? Fine," Delgado began, trying to smooth out the nerves that were shaking up his voice. "I've made a substantial profit tonight. I offered Naya a chance to work with me, and she was foolish enough to screw me over. I hope you have more intelligence than a stripper. There's enough money to go around if you choose to fight for me. I can set you up with your own room, your own bank account, and we can partner in on this."

Wheeler kept his eyes on Delgado, savoring how easily a man could be broken without a whip or cage. Naya's cat rubbed her head against his side and he stroked her face, feeling the length of her canines when his fingers grazed over her mouth.

Delgado's breathing picked up when he looked down at the panther.

Wheeler cracked a smile. "Don't worry, Delgado. It's not her you need to worry about. I told someone a long time ago that I wanted to put you in the ground, and maybe it didn't mean so much back then, but it sure as hell does now. You put my woman in a cage. *No one* makes my woman a slave," he growled through clenched teeth. Wheeler glanced down at Naya, knowing her animal would only understand his tone. He pressed down on her nose. "Stay."

Wheeler heard the footfalls when Delgado took off, so he ran after him and glanced one last time over his shoulder. "Stay!" he shouted, holding out his hand. The confused panther paced in a circle and growled at him.

He sprinted down the hall, bounded up a short flight of stairs, and flew into an opulent living room. The shocking change of scenery took him off guard for just a moment. The only remnants remaining from the party were empty glasses and ashtrays on the marble tables. The ceiling lifted so high that he could see the second floor, guarded by an ornate iron rail. The house looked more like a hotel with its crystal chandelier and expensive décor.

A shot fired and pain seared through Wheeler's right shoulder. He stumbled, blood trickling down his chest and back.

Delgado stepped into sight on the opposite end of the room, standing in front of a giant window with the drapes closed. "You didn't really think you'd walk out of here, did you?"

Wheeler glanced around. "You only have two guards? That's real interesting."

"You can't trust Breed," Delgado said, taking a confident step forward, his arm still outstretched and aiming the gun. "So long as the guards follow their orders by keeping the cages locked, there's no reason for excess staff. I prefer humans to do my dirty work, but in this new line of business, I needed to bring in a few morons I could trust, just to keep an eye on things when I'm away."

"Fatal mistake numero uno," Wheeler said, strolling forward.

Delgado narrowed his eyes but didn't take another shot.

"You're secluded, so no one will find you. You're discreet, so no one will find out what you're doing. You keep the animals caged so none will escape. But every time you hold one of your little betting parties, that's when you're weak." Blood trickled down Wheeler's arm and splashed onto the white tile. "Any time those cell doors are opened for any reason, including a fight, you're showing your Achilles' heel. If you were seasoned like the men I've known, then you would have had at least ten guards at different checkpoints in the room after the fight ended."

"No one is ever stupid enough to attack," Delgado said, his brows slanting down. "They know it leads to punishment."

Wheeler chuckled darkly and ran his bloody finger across a white chair. "Not everyone is a good doggie."

The gun cracked and this time Delgado missed. Intentionally?

"Shaky hands?" Wheeler asked. "Was this all about money?"

"Immortals don't deserve the wealth they have. Why should I work my ass off for nickels and dimes just because I don't live as long? Now that I've finally made a name for myself in your world, I found someone willing to turn me."

Ridiculous. Men like him always counted on a Mage or Vampire to bring them over, but few ever were. Maybe it's the principle of things, but Wheeler had seen many humans simply disappear after they paid for immortality.

"I don't think you could handle being a Mage," Wheeler said. "You'd fucking electrocute yourself."

"And that's why I chose a Vampire. I don't have to deal with a Creator, and I'll be strong and undetectable. What a waste. I could have made you a rich man at the expense of a few worthless lives."

Wheeler was closing in on Delgado, separated by only ten feet of air.

"So why don't you kill me?" Wheeler asked, holding out his arms. "Here I am."

Delgado gritted his teeth. "Because a buyer offered me five million for you, and that should cover the expense for my Vampire friend."

"So all I am is just a meal ticket into immortality? That might put a damper in your plans if I bleed out from this hole in my chest."

"Then shift."

A smile crept up Wheeler's face. "You sure about that?"

"Not here; in your cell."

Wheeler stepped forward another pace. "And how do you think you're going to get me in that cell? Because your sweet-talking sucks. I know you're not going to shoot five million dollars in the head, so you just proved my point about exposing your vulnerability. You're the one holding the gun, but who the hell is really in control here? That's right. Why don't you put the gun down, sweetheart, and let's settle this like men."

"Do you think I'm a fool? You're a Shifter."

"And you're a pussy. That's what this is really about, isn't it? The only way you can feel less inferior is to cage us like animals and rule us with your money. Fuck your money. I don't have superpowers, so I'm offering you a chance to fight me as a man. I don't need my wolf to win my battles, in case you haven't already noticed. You have the advantage, being that I'm wounded and staining your floor with blood. So here's your chance to really feel like a man and beat the hell out of one of the best. If you knock me out, then you win your money and get immortality. If I win? Well, I just win."

Wheeler was tickling a sensitive nerve all weak men like Delgado had: ego. Beneath all the layers of power, money, and intelligence, was a small boy on a playground who wanted to be the toughest kid. None of his possessions would ever truly make him feel superior the way a man feels when he uses his fists to settle an argument.

"How do I know you won't shift?"

"Jesus Christ," Wheeler grunted. He flipped a coffee table over and broke off one of the legs. "Here, I'll give you another advantage, unless you'd rather use one of those fireplace pokers." He tossed the wooden stick and Delgado caught it.

A second passed before Delgado cautiously set the gun down on a table. He gripped the wooden stake in his hand and twirled it a little to get a feel for it.

Wheeler relaxed and widened his stance. The two men approached each other, and Wheeler instinctively held his left arm in front of him to block any attempts Delgado made to strike. Because Delgado was right-handed, his swings would hit the left side of Wheeler's body. That meant he had to block *and* punch with his left hand since the bullet had gone into his right shoulder, weakening the limb.

Delgado crossed his right arm over his left shoulder and suddenly swung at Wheeler, striking him with the stick on the right arm. When he raised his hand again, Wheeler ducked, taking the blow on his back. Wheeler charged forward and tackled him like a football player.

Wheeler roared, shoving Delgado across the room until he stumbled and fell backward. The two men crashed to the floor and Delgado struck him on his left temple.

"You son of a bitch," Wheeler growled, gripping Delgado's arm and slamming it against the hard marble. The wood clanked against the surface and tumbled out of reach.

Delgado threw his fist and Wheeler couldn't raise his right arm to block, so he head-butted him instead. He heard the crunch of bone before he ever saw the first drop of blood. The second time, Wheeler hit him right between the eyes.

Wheeler lifted his head, dazed for a moment. That's when he saw his butterfly knife displayed on the wall—as if it were a souvenir of a hunt. It had been in his back pocket when they took him. Wheeler liked using that knife for tricks, and when others asked him if he'd ever used it, he always said he was saving it for a special occasion.

It didn't get more special than this.

Wheeler stood up and jerked it from the mount, pulling free the hooks that held it in place. There were other curious items displayed around it, which had become a trophy wall and metaphorical graveyard.

Wheeler straddled Delgado, pressing the blade to his throat. "You will *not* destroy my pack. You will *not* tear apart my family. And you will *never* have my woman!"

Wheeler's wolf remained caged, and the only thing unleashed upon Delgado was retribution and blood.

CHAPTER 24

"WAKE UP, KITTY CAT."
I gazed into Wheeler's eyes and realized he was holding me on his lap. My left cheek was pressed against his shoulder, and we were in the backseat of a car.

Driving.

At night.

The radio playing "Dust in the Wind" by Kansas.

Austin peered over his shoulder from the driver's seat and smiled.

God help me, I wept right on Wheeler's shoulder. He cradled my head and kept smiling down at me. "You knew we were going to make it out of there, right?"

"No," I said with a laugh of disbelief.

"Yeah, well, I did."

"Where's Delgado?"

"I took care of him," he said, allowing his words to settle. "Put him in the ground on that property where no one will find him."

"Bastard got off easy," Austin growled from the front. Lexi's hand appeared, stroking the back of his neck.

I tried to sit up, but Wheeler lightly shook his head. "Just let me hold on to you."

"You couldn't wait to get me in the backseat of a car again, could you?" I teased. "What about the others? We have to go back for them."

"They're free. When you didn't answer your phone, the pack came for you. Austin called the Council and they agreed not to bring in the higher authority. This was Shifter business, and we took care of it."

"But you killed a human."

"Doesn't matter. One of the representatives drove in and witnessed the release of the prisoners. That's all he needed to see. Fifteen in all."

"Two teenagers at Reno and Denver's location," Austin added.

I twisted to sit up and noticed a thin blanket draped over me. Without looking, I could feel that Wheeler had on pants, thank the Lord. I touched his bare chest and noticed a scar I hadn't seen before on his shoulder.

"Did you get hurt? What happened?"

"Shot," he confirmed. "I shifted once, so it's fine."

"You were shot? Austin, pull over. He needs to shift again."

Wheeler smirked. "It's all right. It's not the first time. The other one's beneath my hairline, but this is a scar I'm not going to heal all the way."

I traced my finger over the wound—the skin slightly puckered and pink—and I curled against him. "Now what happens?"

"We go home."

Home. That meant an end to this drama, but it also meant ending my time spent with Wheeler. Maybe that's what made Wheeler holding me in the backseat of Austin's Challenger so bittersweet. I lifted my hand from beneath the blanket and found his, lacing our fingers together. In the darkness, his tattoos were nothing but shadows, occasionally highlighted by fast-moving streetlamps as we traveled. I listened to the hum of the tires against the road and allowed myself to feel swept away, if even for a moment. I enjoyed him with each passing minute—the feel of his strong arms, the heat of his body, and the way his eyes would twinkle when they looked down at me.

Not once in that cage had I feared Wheeler. When his wolf had approached me with a savage look in his eyes, I'd somehow known everything would be all right. Even now in his arms, feeling his chest rise and fall with each breath, seeing his eyes settle on mine whenever I looked up, I still had that feeling.

And it made me tear up again. Naya James was not a crier, and yet here I was, wrapped up in a blanket in a man's arms and weeping like a babe. And how could I have ever imagined a man I'd been so rude to—whom I'd spent years bickering with—could be one of the most compassionate souls I'd ever met?

"We're here," Austin said. "I have to go back and run some errands, Wheeler. Do you want me to drop you off here, or are you coming with me?"

"I'll go with."

My heart sank.

The car slowed to a stop and the engine cut off. Lexi got out and pushed her seat forward so I could climb through the door. When my feet touched the ground, I wrapped the blanket around me and tucked it in like I would a towel.

I glanced up at my apartment, but I didn't see it. All I saw were trees. Disoriented, I turned around and faced the Weston house, lit up inside as if it had been expecting our return.

"Wait a minute. I thought you said you were taking me home?"

Wheeler hopped out of the car and stood next to me, ruffling his tangled hair. "And that's exactly where you are, Naya. Home." He cupped his hands around my neck and looked at me with love shining in his eyes. "I'm not a romantic. I'm scarred, inked, and maybe a little ruined. I regret every shitty thing I've ever said to you, because you didn't deserve it. I'm not a perfect man, but if you'll have me, I'll be *your* man. Whatever that means, I'm yours."

I glanced at Lexi in surprise. "I can't, Wheeler. I feel the same, but I can't live here."

"Why not?"

"I'm a panther. You live in a pack."

Austin patted the hood of his car. "Naya, I'm the Packmaster. What I say goes, and if you want to mate with this bastard, then I'm not going to stand in your way. You've stretched your neck out for us more times than I can count, and you've shown more loyalty than most wolves have with their pack. I don't know how this is all going to work out when I introduce your animal to the wolves in this pack, but we'll figure something out. It's unconventional, but hell," he said with a loud chuckle, "we've already acquired a reputation for being a pack of misfits. Besides, having a panther as an ally is a mighty powerful thing." Austin winked and slid back inside the car.

"Well?" Wheeler asked, his hands resting on my shoulders.

"Are you asking me to be your mate?"

"Naya, I'm begging. I love you too goddamn much to let you go."

I smirked and pinched his chin. "Only an uncouth man such as yourself would propose using foul language. I accept."

"One second, before you go in. I got something for you."

Wheeler tapped on the trunk and it popped open. He reached inside and pulled out a carrier. I heard a frantic meow and my feet propelled me forward.

"Misha?" I bent down and peered inside. "My princess, oh baby! Mama's here," I cried, pushing my finger inside the cage and letting her smell me.

I took the cage and set it by my feet so I could face Wheeler. He was grinning at me with all his teeth—something I didn't see him do very often. So I slapped that grin off his face and then attacked him with a passionate kiss. His fingers clawed at my back and he growled, pressing my body against the car. His tongue went deep and I moaned into his mouth.

"Oh brother," Lexi said, getting inside the car and slamming the door.

Wheeler finally broke the kiss, out of breath. "Why did you do that?"

I bent down and lifted the carrier. "I slapped you for putting my baby in the trunk of the car, and I kissed you for saving her life."

He chuckled. "You're serious about those punishments, aren't you?"

"Just wait until you see what I have planned for you later tonight for slapping my panther."

His eyes hooded and he rubbed his cheek. "I might actually like that."

"Fabulous. Misha is in need of a good brushing."

"Hey, now. Don't you think that's a little extreme? I was only trying to get your panther to kill me."

I chuckled and ran my fingers through my hair. "I have a feeling we're going to be at each other like cats and dogs."

Wheeler made a sexy, deep growl and waggled his eyebrows. I made my way up the driveway toward the porch. Lynn was waiting for me in the doorway, and for the first time in my life, I felt like I belonged somewhere.

Even more, I felt like I belonged with *someone*. And that was even better.

CHAPTER 25

TWO DAYS HAD PASSED SINCE the night of Wheeler's rescue. We'd spent all afternoon preparing the house for the costume party, everyone buzzing around like busy bees. The pack had accepted our arrangement, although we got a few puzzled stares. I decided to remain in the heat house until I figured out how I fit in with the pack. Austin wanted to introduce my panther to the pack, but Wheeler would have to be present since he was the only one she trusted. And I began to trust my animal, realizing that all these years I'd been stereotyping her just as much as everyone else had. Now I knew she wouldn't harm anyone I cared for, and I felt genuine love for most of the pack. Some of them I hadn't gotten to know very well, but I had confidence there wouldn't be problems.

I only had concerns with Ben. He'd been absent, and it hadn't gone unnoticed. Neither he nor Wheeler had discussed what had happened between them, but something was going on. I tried cornering Wheeler in my room to talk about it, but he changed the topic by attacking me with kisses.

He was really good at that, and I loved a man who knew how to start a new topic.

I also loved a man who brushed my cat.

"Naya, you look… I mean, is that costume legal?" Lexi asked.

"Only in three states, but we'll find a way to make do."

I glanced down at my costume, which was more than I'd be wearing if I were still working at the club. A red satin corset with black trim hugged my body, and a black ruffle skirt hung from my hips, short in the front with a slight tail in the back. What really set it off was the garter belt and heels. All our costumes came with masks—mine was a simple black mask over the eyes with feathers on the side.

"Austin still hasn't seen my outfit," she said, holding out her skirt. "What do you think he'll say?"

"Hot tamale! The man is going to pass out cold and need mouth-to-mouth."

Lexi had chosen a classic eighteenth-century ball gown—delicate gold the color of champagne, and a subtle petticoat beneath to give it a lift. An open neckline with a wide ruffle drew attention to her chest, whereas the rest of her body was covered. Her loose sleeves had lace at the wrists, and there was such attention to detail on every delicate texture and fold of the fabric that it was difficult to look away.

Lexi snapped out her fan and flipped her wrist, sending waves of air toward her face. She had pinned up her brown hair and wore only a hint of blush and lipstick.

"If you want to know the truth, darling, all the men will be looking at you. This?" I said, pointing down at my outfit. "They can pay to see it at any hot club. But you are going to make every Packmaster green with envy. You're regal."

She fanned harder. "I feel more like cookies in a hot oven. Can you tell Denver to run downstairs and crank the air lower? When this house fills up with Shifters, it's going to be even hotter. *Dammit!* I have to pee again. This should be a fun evening. I might as well walk around with an easy-access hole in my skirt."

I giggled and approached the door. "Good luck with that. Just don't bend over or you're likely to start a pack war. I'll go take care of the air."

Austin was looming outside the door, anxiously trying to steal a glimpse. He was dressed like a classic gangster in a pinstripe suit, fedora hat, and a black mask. I pushed him back. "Get downstairs and turn on some air. Your mate is about to expire if this house doesn't get any cooler."

"I'm about to expire if I don't see what she's wearing."

"Darling, suspense is the best foreplay. If you think what I'm wearing is arousing, just wait until you see Lexi."

"Why does that worry me," he muttered over his shoulder.

"Perhaps it should if you don't get some cool air going. She's already talking about cutting a hole for easy access."

"Hmm," he growled, jogging down the stairs ahead of me. "I might like that."

Voices overlapped below. The party had been in swing for the past hour, but Lexi wanted to wait until all the important people were there before she made her grand entrance. She knew how important these parties were when it came to pack relations and how other Packmasters perceived Austin. But deep down, Lexi was terrified. She'd never worn anything so elegant and had spent the early part of the evening having second thoughts—afraid she'd make a fool of herself.

"William?"

A gentleman in colonial attire turned to face me. I giggled at his blue breeches and white stockings. The matching blue waistcoat had dark blue trim, and the strange part about it was how well the costume suited him. Well, except for the poufy white scarf tied around his neck.

"What is that thing on your neck?"

He touched the delicate fabric, and a grin tugged the corners of his mouth. "A cravat, m'lady."

"I don't know if I'd be calling me a lady in this outfit, but I'll take it," I purred. "Good thing you weren't wearing one of those white wigs or I wouldn't have recognized you."

He gave a close-lipped smile and adjusted the white mask on his face. "I didn't think I could pull off a wig. Shall we?" William lifted his arm for me to take and escorted me downstairs.

Earlier that day, I'd sat down with Austin for three hours, going over the music selection, stressing that not everyone attending was born in the same century as him. The whole purpose of a masked ball was to evoke a sense of history, so we compiled a playlist. The classical music was a given, but we livened it up with some soft rock, blues, and a few instrumental rock songs.

When we reached the bottom of the stairs, William drifted into the living room and out of sight. I glanced at the punch fountain in the room by the stairs. April had volunteered to refill it as needed, and what a beautiful display! Surrounding the crystal fountain were trays of chocolate-dipped strawberries, vegetables, and caviar with crackers. I'd convinced Lexi to pay for the standing tables we placed around the house, which meant moving some of their furniture into the room that connected to the heat house.

I nibbled on an olive and admired the costumes. Guests wore everything from ball gowns to capes. I adored how the women were dressed—from warriors to maidens. And here I was in a brothel costume sure to embarrass Wheeler.

A man dressed like Batman walked by me and grinned. I smiled politely but inwardly frowned as some of the younger men had chosen costumes more suitable for Halloween. I strolled to the windows and peered through the sheer curtains. Tiki torches lined the property and were affixed to the porch along the railing at a safe height.

"Auntie Naya?" I heard a small giggle behind me.

I turned around and beheld the most adorable creature. Maizy wore a vintage powder-blue dress made from delicate silk, and the front had what looked like a white apron. She clicked her black shoes together and simpered. It wasn't customary for children to be masked at these events.

We walked toward the stairs so guests could help themselves at the snack tables. "You look absolutely darling. How are you feeling, baby?"

"Better. My mom said I could come down for a little while." Maizy sat on the stairstep and looked through the banisters at the guests in the living room. "I think I might just sit here and watch."

"Good idea," I agreed. "The last time Alice in Wonderland went running off, she fell down a rabbit hole. Stay here and I'll make you something to eat."

I filled up a plate with fruit and cheese and handed her a punch glass.

She nibbled on a small cube of watermelon, her gaze traveling around the room. "Where's Denny?"

"Good question," I said. "He's in charge of cleaning up trash and empty bottles."

"Yeah, and having a *blast*," Denver said peevishly from behind. "Thanks for giving me a job where I can parade around in this ridiculous costume."

I turned around slowly and laughed so hard I had to cover my mouth. After Lexi had chosen the Alice costume for Maizy, she suggested keeping the theme and also making Denver as a character from the story. So she ordered the Mad Hatter. He had a tall, lopsided hat atop his orange hair. Rusty blades and spearheads were affixed to the hat along with a ribbon tied at the base. His long black coat and pants might have looked nice had they not been accented with garish scarves and multicolored socks.

"I'm not serving Lexi's cupcakes," he said. "A man's gotta draw the line somewhere."

"Denver, no one is going to make the connection. I doubt anyone here knows who you are."

"The fuck they don't. How come I don't get a mask?"

"Because you get face paint."

He rubbed at his eye, smudging some of the white makeup. "I smell bullshit. Someone didn't want me to get laid."

"Could have been worse. You could be wearing what Lexi picked out for Reno."

He snorted. "True that. I'm outta here." Denver strolled out the front door and into the safety of darkness.

Maizy looked on sullenly. "He always leaves me alone at the parties to talk to those women. I'm his best friend."

I touched her silky hair and gave her a serious look. "He loves you in his own way, but he's also a grown man, and grown-ups like to spend time with people their own age."

She gave it some consideration. "He's closer to my age than he is with some of those women who are three hundred."

I chuckled and lifted her chin. "Someday you'll outgrow Denver. He won't be your watchdog forever, so don't be down in the mouth on a night like tonight. Sit here for as long as you like, and be sure to save a cupcake for me."

Lexi had cleverly placed her cupcakes and other pastries throughout the house with a Sweet Treats display behind them and her new menus off to the side.

Ivy came in through the door, suppressing a laugh with her hand. The layers of fabric on her dress varied in shades of earthy green, and she tilted her body to the side so her gossamer wings wouldn't snag in the doorway. I admired the pretty flowers affixed to her dress, and especially the crown of ivy and tiny white flowers on her head. Her mask looked like butterfly wings and only covered her eyes.

"I see someone's feeling better," I said with a wink.

A blush touched her cheek, and it didn't look like she was comfortable discussing her heat spell.

Lorenzo peered inside, and all I could see of him was a black mask and long hair. "Don't wander far, my fairy. I'll be outside by our tree."

A playful moment passed between them.

"Where's Hope?" I asked, touching one of the flowers on her dress.

"This would be too much excitement for her. She's shy, so all these strangers would frighten her."

"Unlike that one," I said, pointing at Izzy's little girl, who was singing loudly and skipping around in a pink tutu with brown pants.

"I see Melody is becoming quite a handful, and now poor Izzy will have another child to chase after so close in age."

"I thought you liked large families?"

She twirled her wand. "We do, but wolves usually space their children apart by a couple of decades—especially the boys. Having to homeschool is exhausting. The pack helps raise them, but it makes more sense to distance them by years. When they grow up, many will decide to be in the same pack, and those closer in age tend to bicker more and are not as willing to accept their rank."

"Did you happen to see Wheeler outside?"

Her brows arched over her mask. "I heard about you two."

When she moved closer, I could see her light brown skin had a beautiful dusting of sparkles.

Ivy lowered her voice so it wouldn't carry. "Wheeler can appear to be as tempestuous as an angry ocean, but the further you are willing to go, the calmer the waters. I think you two will make a fine pairing. He needs someone to warm those icy waters and give him a chance to shine. Wheeler and Ben are two suns, and how can one outshine the other in the same sky? I've always felt bad for their situation. I've seen Wheeler fight for his pack, and he's a loyal man with a heart. But something keeps him from shining. I hope you're the one to bring that out."

"Always a darling with words of wisdom. I need to mingle before the draft has me shivering."

"I have a date with a few strawberries over there, so maybe I'll see you later."

The gold rugs and eye-catching tapestries I'd talked Lexi into renting lightened up the rooms and added a touch of elegance. I moved into the living room and my breath caught when I noticed a man in police uniform.

Purrr. I loved a man in uniform, and those pale brown eyes watching me through the black facemask made my heart beat faster. He licked his lips and leaned against the wall, running his hand down to the handcuffs swinging from his belt. He had on a long-sleeved shirt, hat, and the shiniest black shoes I'd ever seen.

I feigned indifference and turned away, only to catch sight of Lexi cautiously walking down the stairs. When she neared the bottom, she turned around to run back up, but then Austin caught her arm.

She not only stole his breath but also his words. Austin pulled his mask over his head and gaped at the beautiful woman before him. All he could do was look upon her with reverence. I felt as if I'd been transported back in time, watching a courtship between two lovers amid the glow of a magical evening. He lightly bowed, giving her a mischievous look as he coaxed her down to the bottom of the stairs. I'd never seen a man so proud. His chest must have doubled in size when she took his arm.

I'd honestly expected the man to back her into a wall and yank up her dress. Maybe my idea of what Shifters did at these parties was all wrong. Austin led her around the room as a gentleman would a lady.

I waved at Moreland, who was preoccupied at the snack table. They'd locked him in one of the cells when Delgado's men had captured us, but he hadn't been hurt.

An arm snaked around my waist from behind. "You're under arrest," Wheeler whispered. "Come with me."

Wheeler turned us around with his arm still hooked around my waist, and we slipped into the lounge where April often read. When the door closed, he pinned me to the wall and pressed his entire body against mine. All I could see of him were his eyes and mouth.

I let my hands slide around his belt. "Mmm, are you going to perform a search, officer?"

He growled and then his fingers carefully worked at the laces on the back of my dress. I furrowed my brow when he suddenly unzipped his pants. "Suck on me."

"Kiss me."

He leaned in for a kiss, and that's when I knew. I pushed him away and he moved back against me, trying to kiss on my neck.

"Hurry," he whispered.

"Get off me, Ben." I shoved him again.

"How did you know?"

"Do you really think you're that much alike? You might fool me with your eyes and height, but when I get close enough, the differences are obvious. I know Wheeler's smell, the taste of his kiss, and the way he undresses me. Wheeler would never haul me into a room and demand I get on my knees. Do you know why?" I moved away from the wall. "Because he's not selfish."

Ben reached out and cupped my elbows. "You're not just a little bit curious? No one has to know. We're alone in here. Even if someone finds out, they're not going to blame you. Come on, it's not like it's cheating. Same body, same large cock—"

I slapped him so hard his head turned to the side. Not the same impact as I'd hoped for since he had on the facemask made from a thin material. Ben turned his sharp eyes back to mine and I slapped him again. His police hat fell to the floor and I shoved him back.

"Don't you ever put your hands on me again, and don't compare yourself to Wheeler. You're not even in the same league. I may have to live in this house with you, but there's nothing in the rules that says I have to like you. And while I don't know what happened with Delgado capturing Wheeler, I'm positive you had something to do with it. Wheeler told me *all* about you."

Ben slowly pulled off his mask and tossed it to the ground. "What the hell did he say?"

"That you're a manipulator, a liar, a thief, and selfish. Don't you even care about him? He's done so much for you since you were little boys. Can't you appreciate all that he's sacrificed for you? He's the one with the tarnished reputation—all because he was protecting you. Wheeler *loves* you. Why do you keep using him?"

"Shut your mouth. You don't know a goddamn thing. Nothing but a stage whore, and that's about the best he can do. I'm sick of his guilt trips. You help family; no questions asked. I bring money into this house, and so-fucking-what if he has to lend me some?"

"What about the cage fights!" I shouted.

Ben came at me like a hurricane and covered my mouth. "Shut your mouth before someone hears. I feel like shit about it, but better him than me. He's nothing but wasted talent."

I knocked his hand away. "You ruined him. After the cage fights, how could he go back to his life with a damaged reputation? What sense of normalcy could he possibly feel? Did you even ask him what he suffered through—what he had to endure for your freedom?"

"What's done is done," Ben said ruefully, and I could sense he wasn't an evil man. There was no black sheep in this duo; there were only two brothers struggling to make sense of their identity.

"How many times are you going to keep doing it? When does it end? He's mine now. You can't have him. I won't allow you to use him anymore to save you. What you're doing is out of control, and you need help. It's an addiction, and you don't even recognize it. You keep justifying your actions because it brings money into this house. The next time you're in trouble, you better find a way to save yourself."

"You fucking whore!"

The door swung open as I pushed him away. A stranger looked at us and a few men peered in, murmurs trickling through the crowd.

Ben laughed and bent down to pick up his mask. "We're just role-playing."

Another head peered in, but this man pushed his way inside. He was the antithesis of Ben—dressed in a tight black sweater, gloves, a black cap, a mask over his eyes. He tossed a bag with a money symbol onto the floor.

"What the fuck is this about?" Wheeler couldn't help but notice the smear of burgundy lipstick across Ben's mouth.

Ben glanced at me. "Some mate you picked out, Wheeler. She came on to me."

"That what happened?" Wheeler asked me. He stepped all the way inside and closed the door behind him. Then he turned to face Ben. "You and I both know that's bullshit. Were you hitting on my woman?"

"He tricked me with the mask," I said. "Then we started arguing about you two."

"Shut your fucking mouth!" Ben shouted, pointing his finger at me.

Wheeler slowly grabbed his wrist and moved his arm down. "If you ever point your finger at Naya again, I'll break it off."

The door opened and Austin pushed himself inside. "What's going on in here? I told everyone to go outside and Reno to start the fireworks so they wouldn't have to hear this bullshit. I don't want our pack drama to ruin this party."

"Ben came on to my woman," Wheeler stated flatly, his eyes still on Ben.

Ben looked at Austin apprehensively and held up his hands. "Look, it's a party and we're all drinking. I had on my mask, things got carried away…"

Austin stepped forward and folded his arms. "Carried away? One of the golden rules of this pack is that under no circumstances ever—and I mean *ever*—do any of us go after a claimed woman. Out of respect for her, your brother, and this family. Trust and loyalty aren't just words we toss around; they mean something. If you can't respect that, then we have a serious fucking problem."

"Tell him," I said to Wheeler.

His eyes were downcast, and I knew he was struggling with the truth, fearing what it might mean for his future. Wheeler drew in a deep breath. "A month ago, I would have covered for Ben, but this shit can't go on any longer. I have Naya to think about now, and if the truth means leaving this pack, then at least I won't be alone. Maybe that's what I've been afraid of this whole time—being alone. But I'll be damned if I'm going to do anything from here on out that's going to hurt my mate," he said, glaring at Ben. "Fuck you for dragging me into this. I've hated myself for long enough."

Ben shook his head. "You're making a big mistake. Do you think Austin is going to see it the same way you do? Your ass is out on the street. How can you turn your back on me? I thought we were brothers; I thought we could *trust* each other."

"Trust?" Wheeler snapped. "You're not my only brother in this pack, Ben. But I've bent over backwards my entire life for you, and I owe them the truth."

"What truth?" Austin asked, looking between the two.

Oh God, I knew how much his family meant to Wheeler, and this kind of deception could have terrible repercussions. It broke my heart to see the fractured relationship between two brothers.

Wheeler leaned against the wall and folded his arms. "Years ago, I gave Ben a job as my assistant. Thought I'd get him into finance since he had the smarts and it paid well. But he wouldn't stop gambling, and then I found out he was posing as me so he'd have an extra line of credit. Because we looked alike, he drew my money out of the Breed bank and did other things behind my back while impersonating me."

When Wheeler gave Ben a cursory glance, I understood the meaning. Ben must have seduced Wheeler's women. I couldn't imagine the feelings of inadequacy Ben felt watching his twin succeed where he'd failed.

Ben slumped into a chair, his eyes vacant.

Wheeler continued. "He played against the wrong men and

they wanted him dead. The only way out was to exchange myself for him, and the next thing I knew, I was in a cage. That's right. Your brother fought in cage matches for a year. I gained a reputation as an undefeated champion—a killer. Wolves, black bears, panthers—you name it. These tattoos are the story of my life, but they also cover up my scars."

Austin blanched and dropped his arms to his sides.

"I got all this after I escaped," Wheeler said. "Wanted to make sure we never got mixed up again. Maybe Ben brings in some serious cash, but it comes at a price. You don't know how many times I've had to bail him out when he bet more than he should have. How could I turn my brother away? Some of those dirty bastards wouldn't hesitate to drive him to a river and toss him in with a bag of concrete attached to his ankle."

"Is this true?" Austin asked Ben in a quiet voice, not even looking at him.

Ben didn't reply.

Wheeler kicked his heel against the wall. "So guess what happened the other night when I ended up in the cage again? You got it. That was me saving Ben. Maybe he's right and I'm just a worthless bastard, but you need to know the truth. Ben needs help. I'm not saving him anymore; I've got my woman to think about now."

I touched Austin's shoulder. "Please listen to him. He's not asking you to choose, but this needs to stop."

Austin pulled his mask off his head and ran his fingers through his hair. "It's going to stop, all right. Starting tonight. I want you out of my house. As of this night, you're still my brother, but you're no longer a member of the Weston pack. I'm officially revoking your status as a packmate."

Wheeler hung his head and moved toward the door.

Austin's arm flew out to block him. "Not you. Ben."

CHAPTER 26

"YOU CAN'T DO THIS," BEN argued. "Not without hearing my side!"

"Oh?" Austin said, clenching his jaw. "And what's *your* side of the story?"

Ben stood up and lifted his chin. "We all help each other out in this pack. Every single one of us. Someone's in trouble? I go help."

Austin cocked his head to the side. "I seem to remember ordering you to guard the property a few years back when we had a problem with a rogue pack. You left the house and Ivy was hit by a car."

Ben shrugged. "So? Look how it ended up. She met Lorenzo and now they're happy."

"Are you kidding me?" he shouted. "She could have been killed! Were you gambling?" Austin stepped forward and the room became electric with his alpha power. Even I stepped back. "A wrong doesn't become a right just because it all ends well."

Ben looked down. "Okay. I have a gambling problem. I'll stop and get another job if you want, but you can't throw me out just because I hit on his woman, or even because Wheeler helped me out. It's always been *his* choice. You can't blame me because he was a cage fighter! No one put a gun to his head and made him go."

"Do you think this doesn't hurt me?" Austin asked. "I've always looked up to you as my older brother. I look up to *all* of you. But I'm the Packmaster and have to do what's best for the family as a whole. How do you think I feel, throwing out one of my own brothers? This pack isn't about blood; it's who has your back. It sounds to me like Wheeler has had your back for more years than I can count, and I already know his loyalty lies with the rest of us. Maybe I didn't know this shit was going down, but now that I do, I have an immense amount of respect for him." Then he snapped his gaze at Wheeler. "And no, you're not off the hook for lying to me. You should have come to me. We don't keep secrets in a pack, especially when it's something that makes us weak."

Wheeler lowered his head submissively to his Packmaster.

Austin's voice sounded weary and wrought with pain. "Ben, I will always love you as my brother. You'll still be invited to family functions, and if you want to hang out at the house, then the door's open. We're brothers, and I'll never turn my back on you. But I can't afford to have a weak link in my chain. Your foolishness could have killed Wheeler—twice! And Ivy, for that matter. Who's next? No," he said, shaking his head. "You've had more than enough chances to clean up your act. I hope you get help, and know that whichever pack you choose, I'm going to have a long talk with that Packmaster. You'll get help one way or another. Just not here. You've done enough irreparable damage. Maybe it's harsh, but you got off lucky being my blood brother. In any other pack, you wouldn't have been as fortunate. And just so you know, had I caught you in here with Lexi? Well… I can't promise that I wouldn't have done something regrettable. Pack up and leave tonight."

It was the right thing to do, but my heart broke for Wheeler. He looked discouraged, and his muscles were like granite beneath my touch.

Angry tears sprang to Ben's eyes. "You can't do this, Austin. Not to *family*."

"I'm not cutting you out of our lives, or even our family. But you can't keep putting the pack in danger. That's it. My decision is final."

When Austin stepped aside, Ben walked toward the door. Wheeler reached out to touch his shoulder and Ben knocked his arm away.

"Go to hell. When the rest of the pack finds out what you've done, you think they'll have any love for you?" he said, clearly hurt.

When he left the room, he did it with a dramatic slam of the door.

Austin gripped Wheeler's shoulders and looked him in the eye.

"You okay?" He dropped his forehead against Wheeler's. "Tomorrow we're going to have a long talk, you and I. Maybe now I get where you've been coming from. You're a man I respect, and a good example for the pack. Well... except for the tattoos. That dragon freaks the hell out of people."

Wheeler shook his head. "I never wanted to break up the pack. I wanted him to change but didn't know how to make him. I thought I could keep it under control."

"You've got nothing to be sorry about," Austin said, backing up a step. "Not unless you don't complete your assigned duty by cleaning up the front lawn after the party—then my woman will give you something to be sorry about." He patted Wheeler gently on the cheek. "Join the party. We'll work this out tomorrow."

When Austin left the room, Wheeler slid down to the floor, draping his arms over his legs. He grimaced and shed tears, and I allowed him a moment to grieve for the separation. Maybe now he'd realize that some people are beyond help if they're not willing to help themselves.

I knelt down beside him and pinched at his stretchy shirt. "Thank you."

"For what?"

I averted my eyes. "I've never been with a man who trusts me. I'm not sure how to feel about it, especially since you took my word over your own brother's."

His voice lowered and he wiped his wet cheeks. "I've never trusted him."

I tugged on his black burglar shirt. "You have on the wrong outfit. Lexi chose the police uniform for you. Why did you swap with Ben?"

"Cops piss me off."

"Well, too bad. I have a thing for men in uniform."

"That why you came in here with Ben?"

I lightly pushed his temple. "I thought he was you. I found out soon enough that he wasn't."

"Was he... forceful?" Wheeler jerked his head to the side.

"All I saw was an insecure man desperate to prove he was the better brother. It didn't have anything to do with me. Maybe that little boy inside him still sees you as the better half and that's why he's always tried to take what's yours. But guess what? He was a terrible kisser."

Wheeler's eyes flashed up. "You kissed him?"

"I'd hardly call him mashing his sloppy lips against mine a kiss, but yes. He didn't smell like you, or touch me the way you do. It only took a few seconds for me to know." I stroked the patch of beard on Wheeler's chin. "No one compares to my lover."

"Think we ought to make this official with the papers?"

"Well, I suppose that would be the proper way to go about it, although I'm sure the Council will turn up its nose at our pairing."

Wheeler sniffed out a quiet laugh. "Should we have kids?"

"Mmm," I said, snuggling against him. "You want to make babies with me?"

"Someday. Unless you don't think it's a good idea. I'm not exactly father material."

"I think whether we have a panther or a wolf, we're going to have a beautiful child. With my good looks and your charming personality, how can we lose?"

He wrapped his arm around me and lowered his left leg. "What do I smell like?"

"What do you mean?"

"You said you knew it wasn't me because of his smell. So, what do I smell like?"

I nibbled on his ear. "Smoked meat. You need to stop eating that stuff."

"At least it's not raw meat." He slipped his finger beneath a strap on my garter belt and snapped it against my skin. "This is sexy."

"Do I have a smell?"

Wheeler pulled me so I was straddling him, and he kissed the base of my throat. "When you're not bathed in that perfume, you smell like an oven full of hot sugar cookies." His tongue glided across my skin and I lightly rocked my hips. "Better stop doing that," he said, his voice husky.

"Why?"

The bristly hairs on his beard scratched at my neck as his mouth reached my ear. "Because it would be a damn shame for me to have to rip this costume off you when the party just started."

"Save it for later then. Come on." I stood up and gave him my hand. "Do you think Austin told everyone?"

Wheeler shrugged. "Guess I'll find out when I get the stares or not."

Outside, the sharp snaps and muffled booms of fireworks were sounding off. We stepped onto the front porch and glanced up at the dark sky. Giant sprays of white lights twinkled overhead like pieces of glitter thrown to the heavens. Then another that looked like a green mushroom.

I expected to see the children, but I only saw Melody on Jericho's shoulders at the end of the porch. When I walked down the steps and glanced up, I noticed Maizy standing alone on the upstairs balcony with a melancholy look on her face. She watched the changing colors turn bright and then quickly fade until they were gone.

The front door swung open noisily and I heard footsteps as someone barreled across the porch. I caught sight of Ben just as he threw down his bag and took a swing at Wheeler. The crowd backed away and the fireworks cut off when someone yelled out. Wheeler knelt on the grass and looked up. Without warning, he charged at Ben. Their bodies twirled in the air in a dance of magic as they shifted.

Men standing nearby formed a shield between the two wolves and their women. A few people rolled their eyes as if they were used to seeing someone break the rules of a peace party.

Only in wolf form were the twins identical, and now I could no longer tell them apart.

Lorenzo joined me and pulled his mask on top of his head. "I can always count on the Weston pack to break the rules. This is becoming a tradition."

The voices overlapped, but all I heard were two brothers going at each other's throats. "Do something!" I shouted.

"Only Austin's pack can break up this fight," Lorenzo said. "Half his men are out in the field with the fireworks."

"Where's Reno?"

Lorenzo shook his head. "Probably protecting his human. Anyone who gets involved might involuntarily shift, and the last thing you want to do in this environment is turn packs against each other. They have to finish it out until they tire." Lorenzo lit up a cigarette and chuckled lightly.

Jericho appeared on the porch above them, dressed like a pirate. He swung a bucket and a wave of water splashed onto the two snarling animals. The wolves backed up, startled by the cold dousing of water.

A few bystanders laughed and turned away.

"That should cool them off," Jericho said.

The crowd gasped when one wolf lunged at the other, grabbing hold of his neck. He shook it, and the other wolf yelped, struggling to free himself but not attacking. Blood darkened his fur, and he fell onto his back.

"Holy shit," someone said from behind me. "He went for the jugular! They're going to kill each other for real."

Without thinking, I pushed through the crowd. Someone hooked his arm around my waist and my feet came off the ground.

Austin jogged up, and the closer he got to the scene, the faster he ran. He locked his arms around the aggressor's neck and pried open his jaws. "Let go!" he shouted. "Goddammit, Wheeler. I thought I could trust you."

"No!" I tried to wriggle free and finally elbowed the person holding me. My feet touched the ground and I ran forward and fell to my knees. "Don't hurt him! That's not Wheeler you're holding. That's *Ben*."

"How do you know?" he asked doubtfully, unable to say aloud what we both knew about Wheeler's life in cage fighting.

The wolf continued snarling, his teeth wet with fresh blood.

Austin shook him hard and said in a commanding tone, "Submit."

The wolf reluctantly stilled, but a low growl still rolled from deep in his throat.

I cradled the injured wolf's head below me, stroking his ear. "Because Wheeler would die before hurting Ben."

Austin looked around. "Who shifted first?"

"I saw it," someone said. "The cop swung at the criminal, and then the criminal lunged at the cop. But it was the cop who shifted first."

"Goddammit," Austin cursed under his breath. He looked apologetically at Wheeler. "Is he okay?"

"He's still breathing."

Austin stood up and searched for William. "Escort Ben off the property. He's no longer a member of our pack. Family meeting tomorrow at dawn. Wheeler and Naya don't have to be present; they already know. Everyone, go back to the party, and someone tell Trevor to start up the fireworks again."

"I'll do it," Reno volunteered.

Reno looked relieved to be getting as far away from the crowd as possible in his oversized puppy-dog costume with floppy ears and a tail. Lexi had a sense of humor that not everyone in the pack could appreciate.

"And what about Wheeler?" I asked as everyone wandered away, losing interest.

Austin knelt down and bent over him, stroking his hand over Wheeler's eye. "I'll never doubt you again, brother. *Shift.*"

CHAPTER 27

"WHY CAN'T I OPEN THEM? This is silly."

"Keep them closed," Wheeler said, his words laced with humor.

On the day after the costume party, Wheeler had chosen to avoid his pack and stay in the heat house with me. He didn't want to talk about it, and I didn't force him. He was in pain and the last thing he needed to deal with was judgment. While his position in the pack was secure, he was uncertain how the family would feel about what he'd done. Not just the fight, but the truth.

The whole truth.

Shortly after having a private meeting with Wheeler, Austin had sat down with everyone—except for the children—and detailed everything. Wheeler dodged the family meeting, but I joined and listened to their questions and remarks.

"I knew it," Reno said. "Something was never right with Ben."

It had taken others by complete surprise that his gambling was not just a profession but an addiction. And then there was the history with Wheeler that went back to their childhood. A secret between two brothers. The ultimate sacrifice one had paid to protect the other, and the mistreatment many had thrust upon Wheeler. Maybe he had an abrasive tone and didn't look like the kind of man a person could trust, but he was fiercely loyal and willing to die for his pack.

The revelation of the cage fights had made Denver uneasy. "Can we trust his wolf?"

"Any reason he's shown us not to?" Austin asked, ending the discussion.

After that, an awkward silence had fallen over the house, one

I'd felt whenever I entered a room. It was understandable for a pack to feel disjointed after losing a member, and in a sense, they were in mourning.

So in my usual Naya fashion, I sauntered into the room and gave them my best smile to brighten the mood. I informed them that Wheeler would join us after he finished brushing Misha.

Then Denver chuckled and said, "You sure have him pussy-whipped."

When someone tossed a pillow, the tension melted away.

Wheeler would have to come out of that room eventually, but understandably, he needed time. I could be a pushy woman, but this was one instance when I didn't want to push too hard. Not if it meant losing him.

On the second day after the party, Wheeler left the house for the entire day without telling me his whereabouts. That rubbed my fur the wrong way because we'd promised never to keep secrets from each other.

I never realized until I met Wheeler why they called it falling in love. It hurts. It sometimes takes you by surprise. It scars. But when you find the right person, it doesn't end. You keep falling in low doses each day you're with them. It's in the little things they do, like rubbing your feet without your needing to ask, or waking up to find a pot of coffee brewing and a small heart drawn on the side of the white cup with a black marker.

It gave me something to look forward to—all the days we'd be together and the new things I would discover about the man I chose. Although in many ways, fate had paired us together. The one man who was so wrong for me was the one who fit in my heart so perfectly. Every lock has a key, and all keys have jagged edges and crooked sides. No one is perfect, but we're exactly perfect for the one person who matters.

Poor man. He'd have to suffer through my opinionated nature, my desire to get a second cat, and my headstrong personality.

So as I stood in the upstairs hall with Wheeler's hand covering my eyes, my heart was racing. I never knew what to expect with him.

"Okay," he said. "Open 'em."

I blinked a few times until the blurriness went away.

"You did not!" I gasped, rushing into the bedroom. I squealed and whirled around with excitement.

"I couldn't get it all in here, but if it's too much, I can haul some of it out."

This wasn't Wheeler's bedroom. It was a larger one with a window that overlooked the front yard. A crisp white bedspread covered the mattress, a plush white carpet tickled the bottoms of my feet, and my red chair sat in the right-hand corner of the room. On the left side was Wheeler's desk and leather chair. It had a rip on the side, and I made a mental note that we were going to have a conversation about that later.

I slowly spun around and jutted my hip out. "When did you do all this?"

He shrugged. "Had to sneak it up last night after you went to sleep. Spent all day yesterday hauling it to the truck. Everything else from your apartment is spread throughout the house; you can figure out what you want to do with it. I talked to your leasing office and told them you moved back home."

I smiled and brushed my lips against his, standing on my tiptoes. "You forgot Misha's bed."

"*Nooo*, that's where I draw the line. That cross-eyed cat stays outside."

I chuckled and we moved toward the door. "She sleeps in here with us. You can either bring in her bed, or she can snuggle on mama's neck all night."

Wheeler popped me on the butt. "You're a handful, Miss Diva."

"Mmm, that's what I've been told," I purred.

"But I can still make you blush," he said sexily against my ear.

I smiled up at him. "As I can you."

His eyebrows arched. "That so?"

I cupped my hand against his ear and whispered, "I saw what you were trying to hide on my white sofa. I watched you from my bedroom door."

When I leaned back, his cheeks were aflame.

"Come on, lover." I took his hand and led him down the stairs.

The morning sunshine was past its glory and had faded from a deep orange to pale yellow.

"If you get the cat bed, then I'm putting my license-plate collection on the wall."

My eyes widened and I turned to face him. "Your what? I don't remember that in your last room."

"I keep it in a box."

I took his arm as we made our way to the kitchen. "Darling, you can put your dirty underwear on that wall and I'll still love you. I might punish you for it, but I'll still love you."

"Mmm, punishment," he said between kisses. "Makes me want to be bad."

When I entered the kitchen, my stomach dropped. I recoiled and Wheeler hooked his arm around me.

"The surprise isn't over," he said softly.

Austin was sitting at the head of the table with his fingers laced together and his chin resting on them. He had an enigmatic smile on his face, and it had to do with the two strangers at our table. One was an older man in a short-sleeved flannel shirt. He had a short white beard and piercing blue eyes. The other was a dark-skinned man with freckles, and he had a friendlier expression on his face. Two empty plates sat before them, and the older man wiped his mouth with a napkin and smiled up at me.

"Who are they?" I asked in a low voice.

What made me nervous was that the entire Weston pack was in the kitchen, both standing and sitting around the table.

"The local Council. Feel like getting mated today?"

"What?"

"Feisty girl you got there," the older one said. "Sure you want a wildcat like that?" He chuckled warmly and glanced at Austin. "How are things going with your woman? I still remember the day you signed the papers."

Austin smirked and glanced at Lexi, who was sitting to his left with her chin tucked in the palm of her hand. "Can't complain, Turner."

Wheeler snatched my wrist and led me toward the table. The

white-haired man threw his legs over the bench to straddle it, and I sat down next to him with Wheeler standing beside me.

"A pack witnessing a mating ceremony isn't legal without at least two officials, so there's me and Romeo," Turner said.

I smirked, wondering if he was being facetious or if that was the other man's name.

"Looks like we have a twofer. I have you down for an induction into a pack and a mating ceremony. What's your name?" he asked, pressing the tip of his pen against a small book.

"Naya James."

"Full name."

"That's it. I don't have a middle name."

He sighed quickly and made an audible humming sound with it. "Very well. Sign here to show you're entering this pack of your own free will. At least until you see fit to leave. If any shifter commits a crime against you, then your new pack has full rights to hunt him down on your behalf," he recited as if he'd said the words a million times.

I signed my name and handed the book back to him. He pivoted on his seat and gave the book to Austin.

"By signing your name in that book, you agree to watch over this young Shifter as a member of your pack. You swear to look after her well-being and protect her with your life."

Austin scribbled his name and handed it back.

Turner squinted at the page. "Uh-huh. Looks good. That's official. You're now a member of the Weston pack. Now, on to the second half of our show."

A fever touched my cheeks. I hadn't expected it to happen so soon, but I knew how these things went. A member of the Council stood witness and gathered signatures. We didn't make an elaborate production out of such things, but now I understood what Lexi must have been feeling in wanting to make her mating ceremony more special. It was a beautiful moment I'd never forget. The way the room smelled heavy with bacon and maple syrup, Denver in a faded shirt with a tie printed on the front, Maizy standing with her hands clasped together and watching with wide blue eyes, and the

DANNIKA DARK

feel of Wheeler's hand massaging the back of my neck reassuringly. I'd never forget this moment, because it wasn't just about me finding love, but finding a family. And having everyone here touched me deeply.

I tried not to cry, but when the grizzly old man licked his finger and turned a few pages in the book, I wiped away a tear and leaned against Wheeler, holding the hand he had draped over my right shoulder.

"Here we are," the Councilman said. "One of these days I need to bookmark this section, but my mate got a new fuddy-duddy book she wants me to use with a bunch of tabs on the side. She thinks I can't find things." He leaned in and gave me a funny look.

Izzy giggled from her spot across the table, Jericho standing behind her, his hands on her shoulders.

Suddenly my throat was dry. I kept swallowing and finally took a deep breath to shake away the nervous butterflies.

"You're not going to puke on me, are you?" he asked with a snort. "Okay, maybe I ought to hurry this along before you get cold feet."

I didn't just grip Wheeler's hand—I clung to it as if it were the last life preserver on a sinking ship.

"I stand witness to the mating of Naya James and Wheeler Cole. Wheeler, do you promise to protect this woman, give her your loyalty, hunt for her, and share your bounty?"

"Yeah. I do."

Share his bounty? Maybe somewhere along the lines I had missed the part about words exchanged in a mating ceremony, but I almost wanted to burst out laughing.

"Naya James, do you promise to honor this man and do as you're told?"

"*Excuse* me?" I gasped, ready to stand up.

He chuckled. "That gets 'em every time," he said to Romeo. "Sorry, that's just a little mating-ceremony humor."

"You're getting less funny," I said.

He cleared his throat and took on a serious look. "Naya James, do you promise to honor this man, stand by his side, protect his good name, and always be loyal?"

I frowned. "What about love?"

The Councilman shrugged. "That's always been optional."

"Indeed," William remarked in a judgmental tone.

The man scratched at his white beard. "Not everyone mates for the same reasons. Do you want to negotiate the rules, or shall we proceed?"

"Well, just for the record, I promise to do all those things *and* love him."

"Yeah, me too," Wheeler quickly said.

"Too late," Denver quipped in a low voice. "You flubbed up on that one, bro."

Trevor elbowed him in the side.

The Councilman handed us his little book. "Sign your name, and you are hereby officially mated."

"Isn't that romantic?" Lexi said in a flat voice, her chin still tucked in the palm of her hand.

I winked at her. "Romance comes in all forms, darling. This couldn't be more perfect." I signed my name and handed the book to Wheeler. "Maybe someday you'll get around to having a nice wedding," I suggested.

When Austin's face reddened, I smiled surreptitiously and stood up to kiss my new life mate.

Wheeler pulled his glasses from the pocket in his shirt and put them on. I blinked in surprise, as he hadn't mentioned it to me, but I had suspected as much. They were sexy—a rectangular pair of black frames that made me want to drag him back to the heat house. He read the page in the book carefully and then signed his name. When he looked up, he folded the glasses and set them on the table. "No more secrets. Call me four-eyes and have your fun with it, but I need them for reading, so get over it."

With a snap of his wrist, Wheeler flung the book on the table and snaked his arms around me, scratching my chin with his whiskers as he planted a kiss on my mouth. A little tongue action slipped in and I moaned, squeezing his nipples through the thin fabric of his shirt.

He sucked in a sharp breath. Everyone clapped and made noise, and our two guests slowly stood up to leave.

"Let's save the foreplay for later, kitty cat," he whispered in my ear.

"We'll just be on our merry way," the older gentleman said. "Be good, you two. I don't want to see you in Shifter divorce court." He cackled, and I peered over Wheeler's shoulder to watch them leave.

That's when I saw someone unexpected. Ben stood in the hall outside the kitchen, watching with a rueful expression. Just as Wheeler caught the direction of my gaze and began to turn, Ben walked out of sight.

"What are you looking at?" Wheeler asked.

"Nothing, my love."

I held hope that the two brothers would one day mend the rift between them. God knows they had plenty of centuries to figure it out, and who knows, maybe someday Ben would redeem himself. Perhaps he needed this time away so he could stop depending on others to believe in him and learn to believe in himself.

"Got something else for you," Wheeler said, turning to face me.

"I'm afraid to ask. I'm already on the verge of a fainting spell on your kitchen floor."

He reached down and peeled off his shirt.

"Now?" I asked with a seductive purr in my voice. "Here? If this is part of the mating ceremony for wolves, then I might have an objection."

I watched him smile beneath his scruffy beard, and then I noticed it. My eyes traveled down to his tatted arms and then crossed his chest to the scar from the bullet. I reactively reached out and rubbed my finger on the ink.

"Is this real?"

"Yeah, Naya. This is as real as it gets."

On his right pec near the shoulder, a tattoo of a black panther encircled his scar. Its head was turned with a fierce growl, displaying its sharp teeth. Of all the scars Wheeler had covered, this was one he used his ink to draw attention to.

I looked up into his brown eyes, the color of sweet tea in the morning sun. "I thought you said it was bad luck to get another animal on your body."

He cupped my cheeks in his hands. "Maybe it is when it's something that doesn't matter. You matter."

"Let's eat," Lynn said. "Before everything gets cold. I have three breakfast casseroles in the oven to celebrate."

"Oh, and I made croissants!" Lexi said excitedly, hopping off the bench and scurrying to the kitchen.

"Music to my ears," Denver said, straddling the bench. "Come here, Peanut. Did you think that was fun?"

"It's not like the weddings on TV," she said.

Denver shook his head. "All that stuff doesn't matter."

"Don't tell her that," I scolded. "Maizy, someday you'll find a prince who will sweep you off your feet and give you the dreamiest wedding you've ever imagined. Your mama will be so proud, and you can make your big sister your bridesmaid!"

"I think you can only be one of those when you're single," Lexi pointed out, setting a casserole dish on the table.

I reached over and pinched off a piece of the cheese, taking a nibble. "Rules were always meant to be broken."

"Well, I don't want one of *those*," Maizy declared, nodding her head toward Wheeler's tattoo. She put her knees on the bench and leaned forward on the table, peering at the large bowl of biscuits.

"Yeah, well, what do you want?" Denver asked.

"I want my true love to read to me. And a ring."

"A ring?" he said in an exaggerated voice. "What would you do with a ring?" Denver buttered a biscuit and put it on her plate.

"I don't know."

"Maybe it's because a ring isn't so important. Don't you want a good mate to take care of you?"

Lynn set a jar of strawberry preserves in front of him. "My daughter is going to *marry*, not mate. Isn't that right, honey?"

Maizy smiled and sat down, smelling the biscuit. "Maybe I won't get married. Maybe I'll move to a faraway country and be an explorer."

"There's nothing left to discover, Peanut. It's all been found."

Lexi came up behind Maizy and hugged her tight. "You can be whatever you want to be, Maze. I can't wait to see all the amazing things you're going to do."

This was too emotional! I turned and wrapped my arms around Wheeler's neck, standing on my tiptoes. We held each other for a moment while everyone settled in their places and began talking about the next party.

"Don't ever do that again," Reno said to Austin.

"What?"

"Put Lexi in charge of costumes."

Trevor barked out a laugh. "Reno looked like a neutered stray."

"Say, what if we rotate?" William suggested.

"Then I'm next," Reno quickly said. "How 'bout that?"

Lexi sat down and scooped a helping of casserole onto her plate. "Scrap that idea. I have no desire to see what kind of biker gear Reno would dress me in."

"On the contrary, I might like that idea." Austin winked at her and stole a quick kiss.

"Naya, you're going to help me again for our next party," Lexi said decidedly.

I ran my fingers through the loose, silky curls on my head and grinned. "I think I'm going to retire my dancing shoes and try something new for a change."

Wheeler walked around the table and sat down in his seat. Ben's absence was strangely felt as Wheeler glanced at the empty spot where he normally sat. But it wouldn't be empty for long. I decided my mate would always know someone would be at his side. He quickly turned away and smiled up at me.

"Darling, would you like some coffee?" I offered.

A few people turned their heads and looked between one another.

He pushed his empty cup forward and chuckled, shaking his head. "*Love* some, kitty cat."

Made in United States
Troutdale, OR
11/25/2023

14943828R10195